Chathair Phort L

Something
to
Talk About

Also by Sarah Webb

Three Times a Lady
Always the Bridesmaid

Kids Can Cook
Kids Can Cook 2 – Around the World
Children's Parties
Eason's Guide to Children's Books

Praise for *Always the Bridesmaid*

'A cracking good read . . . a compelling and light-hearted book that you'll curl up with and read from start to finish very quickly' –
Irish Independent

'Lively dialogue and strong female characters' – *The Irish Times*

'It's the perfect holiday read' – *Belfast Telegraph*

'A funny optimistic romance' – *U Magazine*

'An enjoyable read' – *Woman's Way*

Praise for *Three Times a Lady*

'The pacy story and credible characters in this debut should put Sarah Webb's name on the bestseller list' – *U Magazine*

Something to Talk About

SARAH WEBB

POOLBEG

Published 2002
by Poolbeg Press Ltd.
123 Grange Hill, Baldoyle,
Dublin 13, Ireland
Email: poolbeg@poolbeg.com

13 5 7 9 10 8 6 4 2

A catalogue record for this book is available from the British Library.

ISBN 1 84223 071 9

Cover designed by Slatter-Anderson
Typeset by Patricia Hope in Goudy 11.3/15.5
Printed by Mackays of Chatham Ltd.

www.poolbeg.com

About the Author

Sarah Webb has worked in children's bookselling for over ten years, and currently works as a consultant for Eason. She lives in Dublin with her partner and her young son, Sam. She reviews children's books for many Irish newspapers and magazines and has written many of her own, including the popular *Kids Can Cook* series. She also appears regularly on RTE's *The Den*.

Sarah attributes her energy and enthusiasm to having a child in the house and to yoga, which, unfortunately are not always mutually compatible unless you tie your child up (which of course she doesn't!).

Her previous novels, *Three Times a Lady*, and *Always the Bridesmaid*, were bestsellers and she's currently working on her fourth book – *Coming Up Rosie* which will be published by Macmillan in autumn 2003.

Acknowledgements

When it comes to the acknowledgements in a new book I always realise just how lucky I am to have so many people to thank.

As always, first on my list must be my wonderful family – Mum, Dad, Kate, Emma, Peter, Luan, Charlie and Richard for all their love and support. Kate, thanks for the great kite illustrations. And in loving memory of Coco, the best family dog around. We all miss you.

To Ben and Sam for keeping the house together and for keeping me sane. And to Ben for the heady introduction to the world of kites.

To Tanya Delargy, Nicky Cullen and Andrew Algeo for always being there. The best friends a girl could wish for. Thanks for letting me use 'that' discussion – I still think I'm right!

To Jamie Boag, Shirley Robertson, Denise Casey, Niamh Hooper, Jo Peare, Carolyn Thornton, 'Prof' O'Connell, Paul and Di Nolan and the sailing gang – my brilliant bunch of friends – for all the boozy dinners and the support. I hope all your collective families appreciate their Christmas presents!

To Barry Chambers in Wind and Wave, Monkstown for all the kite-surfing info. Great shop, Barry!

To Miriam Brady, my yoga teacher for all the body work.

To all the gang in Poolbeg for yet another interesting book experience, especially my editor, Gaye Shortland. For all the make-up buying trips (oops, sorry, book tours), not to mention umbrellas and new friends for Sam – thanks, Sarah Conroy! Special mention must go to Paula Campbell who makes Poolbeg what it is – a real home for new authors where they can develop and, most importantly, laugh. I loved being involved with the whole publishing process from choosing covers to marketing plans – so thanks, everyone for letting me be a part of it. I hope my next adventure with Macmillan, who are publishing my next book, *Coming Up Rosie*, is just as exciting and rewarding.

To Ali Gunn, my agent, for all her enthusiasm and sound advice.

To Pauline Maher, Treasa Bennett and the girls in St Kevin's in Kilnamanagh, great readers and writers. And to my readers in Loreto Dalkey and secondary schools around the country – keep reading, girls!

To all the Irish booksellers all over the country who have supported my books from the very beginning. To Adrian White, Tom Owens, Alan Johnson, Sally Mimnagh and David O'Callaghan in Eason. To Maria Dickenson, Cathal Elliott, Norman Brunker, James Moore, Turlough O'Brien, Danny Hughes and all the reps. To all the Eason book managers and staff, especially Bert Wright, Caron Butler and Eoin McHugh for all their interest and support.

To Karen Jordan in The Wexford Bookshop for the great sandwiches, and to all the booksellers I met on last year's tour around the country – hope to see you all again soon. Thanks for all the brilliant windows and displays – much appreciated.

To Edel McGovern, my early and very patient reader. I'll print it all out for you today – honestly!

To my old buddy the Epson PC AX (b drive and all!) on which I wrote my first three books and who is now in retirement. They don't make them like they used to! Thanks, Eppie! Gone but not forgotten.

To June Jackson, Pam Grey, Dan O'Regan and Ita Delargy for colouring my life. And to Marty Stanford – I'll never forget you.

To all my writing friends, especially Larry O'Loughlin, Lucinda Jacob, Marita Conlon McKenna and Martina Murphy.

To foster parents throughout the country who give children an invaluable second chance.

And finally to you, the reader, without whom there would be no book. You have enabled me to spend precious daytime hours with my son, and you have empowered me to become the writer I always dreamed of being as a child. I thank you with all my heart.

I hope you enjoy *Something to Talk About*. If you'd like to contact me I'd love to hear from you – write c/o Poolbeg Press, 123 Grange Hill, Baldoyle, Dublin 13 or email c/o *info@poolbeg.com*

To Nicky, the strongest woman I know,
With love and respect.

The miracle is not to fly in the air, or to walk on the water, but to walk on the earth.

CHINESE PROVERB

1

Lucy looked up from her client's ragged cuticles and sighed. Sunlight was beaming in the window, the sky was forget-me-not blue and Making Faces Beauty Salon was the last place on earth she wanted to be. She was dying to get out of the hot, airless cubicle and into the fresh air. She'd arranged to go kite-flying with Max that evening to test his new baby – a huge parafoil kite made of colourful pink and purple nylon. Lucy knew it was pink and purple as she'd chosen the colours herself.

"I'm not making a pink kite," Max had grumbled when she'd suggested the colour scheme a couple of weeks previously. "Blokes won't want to fly a pink kite."

"Don't be ridiculous. As long as it flies it doesn't matter, surely?"

"Don't call me Shirley," he said, "and, OK, if you want pink, then pink it is. But I'll blame you if the only buyers are female."

"Hey, I said pink and purple, not just pink."

"Oh, that's all right then," Max smiled. "That makes such a difference. Pink *and* purple."

Lucy pushed him into a roll of white sailcloth which fell to the ground with a crash.

"Man," Mossy muttered. He'd been asleep on some spinnakers which were waiting to be repaired. "Chill the noise."

"Mossy!" Lucy practically yelled, just to annoy him. "Lovely to see you! How's tricks?"

"Vibing," Mossy smiled lazily, before closing his eyes once more.

"Vibing?" Lucy whispered to Max as they went back to the kite design.

"Don't ask me. You went out with him."

"Thanks for reminding me," she grimaced. "He wasn't even good in bed."

"Really?"

"No," she admitted reluctantly, "I lie. He was good. Vacant, but good."

"Pity. Now pass me that tape measure, there's a good girl."

Lucy sighed as she put the dark-haired woman's left hand into a small bowl of water to soften her cuticles.

"Bad, aren't they?" the woman said. She had short dark hair, a faint American accent and looked remarkably like a young Audrey Hepburn.

"Excuse me?"

"My nails. It's my job. I'm always breaking them."

"Sorry, I was miles away. Your nails aren't that bad." Lucy bit the inside of her lip. She was trying not to frown. The woman's nails were pretty horrific, all ridges and white bumps as if someone had smacked them with a hammer, and she also seemed to have some sort of blue flecks on her hands.

"Paint," the woman explained, as if reading Lucy's mind. "The blue bits."

"Painting the house?" Lucy tried to inflect some interest into her voice.

"No, I'm working with a set-designer. I was painting a sky."

"Right." She wasn't really in the mood for making small talk.

"It's for a production of *Mary Poppins*. In The Olympia."

"That's nice." A memory flitted into Lucy's head of watching the

Disney film of *Mary Poppins* starring Julie Andrews, in the old Forum cinema in Sandycove, sitting on her dad's knee the whole way through. She must have been small – all of four or five at the time, she supposed. She turned her concentration to what her client was saying.

"I'm building a merry-go-round next and then I have to source some kites. It's non-stop –"

"Did you say kites?" Suddenly Lucy began to pay attention.

Max sighed. Another shitty day at the office. The 'office' in question being a shared prefab at the back of Allen's Chandlery and Sails. Mossy also worked there, making and repairing sails for the Allen family when he wasn't off gallivanting at some yacht-racing event or other. Mossy liked to think of himself as a superstar of the Irish sailing world; Max liked to think of him as pondweed. Because Mossy, like pondweed, was the lowest form of life. Unfortunately he had rather a talent for sailcloth.

A six-foot-three blond-haired Adonis, Mossy also had all the charm and subtlety of a sledgehammer, a pneumatic one at that. He had girlfriends strung along the coasts of Ireland and England, and one or two in America. And the worst thing was that, unless you knew Mossy as well as Max did, you'd think he was one of the most charming, delightful, witty and interesting men you'd ever met. Even Lucy had been taken in by his snake-smooth tongue, although she said it was his tan and his highly defined pecs that finally broke her resolve.

At least Max was meeting Lucy that evening. He'd finally finished *The Lucy* as he'd nicknamed his new kite, otherwise known as *Maxfoil Mark 7*. Didn't have quite the same ring as *The Lucy* though.

The loft was baking hot. It was a long, thin wooden building, with two large sewing machines along the left-hand wall and rolls of multi-coloured sail and spinnaker cloth stacked to the right. The cracked windows had stopped opening years ago and were now held together with silver duct tape so ventilation wasn't the best. Max had bought a fan, but Mossy complained that it fluttered his spinnakers when he was trying to sew the seams, so it was rarely turned on.

Three of the walls were covered with posters of sailing events going back many years and photos of Mossy in various states of undress with various equally scantily clad women, and one was scattered with pictures of multicoloured kites flying in azure skies.

But the rent was dirt cheap, and Mossy liked it as he could use Max as a social-secretary-cum-answerphone, to lie to his girlfriends and to pretend to boat-owners that he was busy on their new sails rather than 'catching up on zeds' as he liked to call catnapping. Still, it beat designing bridges and tunnels hands down, Max tried to tell himself as he fielded yet another phone call. Even if he was always broke these days.

"I might have thrown some work your way this afternoon," Lucy told Max as they laid the large kite out on the grass beside Sandymount Strand.

"Really?" Business was brisk but not all that profitable. There was only so much that a customer would pay for a kite, no matter how well made or expertly balanced it was. The Allens sold them in their shop and the remainder were sold on his Web site – *maxkites@skyfree.ie*

"This girl was in earlier – Daria, some sort of set-designer. She needs some kites made quickly. So I gave her your number. She said she'd ring you tomorrow."

"Girl? What age?"

"My age, or a bit younger maybe."

"Girl?" Max snorted.

"Less of that, you," said Lucy, glaring at him. "I'm only twenty-five, after all."

"Again?"

"I hate you sometimes. You know too much."

"Like your real age?"

"Exactly!"

"Was she cute?"

"Typical!" Lucy laughed, putting her hands on her hips. "And I thought you were different!"

"Not at all. Just your average, red-blooded male. So was she?"

"What's that got to do with anything?" She lifted up the kite and the string holders and ran down the steps towards the sand.

"Come back with my kite!" Max yelled, following her.

Lucy turned and faced him, her long, dark, curly hair attacking her pale face in the wind. "She was attractive, I suppose."

Max's face lit up.

"You're sad. You need to get out more. Meet some new people. Get a girlfriend."

Max ran along the sand to catch up with her.

"I don't need a girlfriend," he panted.

"I won't always be around to fly kites with you," she said, handing him the kite strings and walking into the wind with the large pink rectangle. "Jamie will leave Jules soon, you'll see."

Max laughed. "As I keep telling you, Jamie Oliver doesn't even know you exist."

"He will – you wait and see. That's a promise."

"And you call me sad?" Max grinned.

Lucy and Max were sitting at her kitchen table that evening. Her flatmates, Hopper and Alan, were at the Irish Film Centre watching a strange subtitled film with Björk in it. They hadn't fancied it.

"How's Brian?" Max asked, mopping up every last drop of the cream sauce on his plate with a piece of French bread. Brian was Lucy's latest boyfriend and himself and Max didn't exactly get on. In fact, they only just about tolerated each other.

"Liked the chicken, did you?" she laughed, pouring herself another glass of Chardonnay. "More wine?"

"Mmm," he nodded.

"That was a yes, I presume."

"Stop changing the subject. I asked you about Brian." He swallowed the bread and looked at Lucy carefully. She was a master of avoidance.

"I don't really want to talk about it." She sipped her wine and ran her finger along the top of the glass, trying to make it sing. "It's boring."

"It's boring or he's boring?"

Lucy stared at him. "That's a little unfair. He's not boring exactly. He's just —"

"Yes?"

Lucy hesitated for a second before smiling. "OK, so he's a bit boring, only a bit, mind."

"He's an accountant."

"I know lots of interesting accountants," said Lucy, raising her voice.

"So do I. And Brian Lynch isn't one of them."

She dipped her finger into her wine and flicked it at him.

"I wouldn't do that if I were you." He picked up a glass of water. "I'm armed."

"You'd better not," warned Lucy. "If I get wet you don't get any ice cream."

"What flavour?"

"Chocolate chip."

"You win." He put the glass back on the table.

"I always do," she said smugly. She stood up and padded barefoot towards the fridge. The terracotta tiles felt cold beneath her soles. "How much ice cream do you want?"

"Bring the whole tub over. You may as well."

She plonked the tub and two bowls and spoons unceremoniously onto the table.

"I wonder will that girl ring," he said, digging his spoon into the creamy surface and placing huge dollops into the bowl in front of him. "About the kites."

Lucy sat up suddenly. "I'm going to find you a girlfriend. This has been going on too long."

"What?"

"This —" she waved her hands in the air expressively. "Leaving it all to fate. Taking a back seat. Not chatting anyone up. Lack of initiative. Laziness. What would you like me to call it?"

6

"I don't want you to call it anything, thanks," he sniffed, insulted. "I'm quite capable of finding my own girlfriend."

"But you're not! It's been two years since you broke up with Marie. It's time to get back out there."

"I'm happy this way." He could sense trouble. When Lucy got an idea into her head there was no stopping her.

"You're not!" Her eyes lit up. "I've got it – Jenny!"

"Who's Jenny?" He tried not to sound interested.

She ignored him. "I'll ask her over to dinner next weekend. Hopper and Alan can come too." She frowned. "And Brian, I suppose. To even out the numbers."

"But Lucy, who's Jenny?"

"I'll serve ravioli with prosciutto, Jamie has a wonderful recipe for it in one of his first books. I've wanted to try it out for ages. I'm sure Jenny will be free on either Friday or Saturday night – I'll tell you which when I've talked to her. Eight o'clock at my house. And bring wine. Lots of it."

Max sighed. He hadn't the energy to say no.

"She'd better be pretty," he mumbled.

"Sorry?"

"Nothing." He turned his attention back to his now melting ice cream.

2

"Jenny, it's Lucy."

"Lucy, darling. How the hell are you? Haven't seen you for yonks!" Jenny was a model and used to work as a much-in-demand masseuse at the beauty salon.

"Great. Listen, what are you up to next weekend?"

"Um, let me see. Dinner with Floss and some of the modelling crowd on Saturday night, but apart from that I'm free."

"Excellent! You're coming to dinner on Friday night, and I won't take no for an answer."

"Darling," Jenny drawled, "I love your cooking. How could I possibly refuse?"

"Eight o'clock at my place, so."

"Who else will be there?"

"Hopper, Alan, Brian, Paula and Max. You'll like Max. He's lovely. Good-looking too."

"Wonderful!" Jenny said enthusiastically. "I could do with an old romp now that I'm single again."

"I think Max and yourself will get on famously." Lucy crossed her fingers.

"Is the dinner for any special occasion? You're not reaching the non-twenties gang, darling, are you?"

"No!" she exclaimed loudly. Jenny nearly jumped out of her skin. "It's just a nice, intimate dinner for some of my friends, that's all."

"How could I have been so tactless," Jenny purred. "Of course you're not nearly thirty. What was I thinking of? Now, I must run. *Ciao.*"

Lucy put down the phone and wrinkled her nose. It wasn't easy being thirty-one – denial was the only solution. She still felt like a teenager, after all. And most of her friends were younger than her – surely that counted for something? Hopper was twenty-eight and Max was only just thirty.

"What's up?" Hopper asked, plonking herself down on the stairs beside her friend. "Who were you talking to?"

Lucy smiled. Her housemate was unashamedly nosy.

"Jenny. I asked her to dinner on Friday."

"Jenny Kearns?" Hopper asked in amazement. "The model?"

"The very same."

"But why? We won't have anything to say to her."

"Who said you were going to be invited?" Lucy smiled.

Hopper looked insulted.

"I'm only joking." She nudged her in the ribs gently. "Of course you are. Alan and Paula too. And Max."

"Now I'm confused. What's all this in aid of? Where does Jenny fit in?"

"I'm trying to set Max up with her."

Hopper stared at Lucy incredulously. "Max? With Jenny Kearns? Are you mad? She's in another league altogether. Didn't she go out with that Dean guy who's in the Calvin Klein ads?"

"Max *is* good-looking, and he has a lot more to say for himself than a guy like Dean."

"That may be so. But he'll turn up in a T-shirt and jeans. Yellow jeans and a pink T-shirt at that."

"I'll make sure he's properly dressed. She'll love him."

"Right," Hopper murmured doubtfully.

"You don't have to eat with us, you know," Lucy threatened. "I could ask someone else."

"No, don't do that. I'll be there. But do you really have to ask Little Miss Perfect?"

"You know I do. And her name's Paula, Hopper."

Lucy sat in the kitchen, thumbing through *The Return of the Naked Chef,* lingering over the glossy photographs of her favourite pin-up, Jamie Oliver. She just loved his cheeky smile, his twinkling eyes, his chirpy London expressions. Poor old Jamie – he'd just been over-exposed – it wasn't his fault he wasn't flavour of the week any more. She was supposed to be checking the ingredients she'd need to buy for dinner on Friday night, not looking at the glossy pics.

"Oh, Jamie," she sighed over a particularly luscious one, "you're just *pukka*."

She slammed the book shut and gazed out the window distractedly. Brian was calling over this evening and she wasn't sure she wanted to see him. There was no real reason for her disinterest, other than a niggling sense that things between them weren't quite right.

Brian was tall, slim and attractive. He was polite and had nice manners. He had a good job, plenty of money and treated her like a princess. But in her heart of hearts Lucy knew that something was missing. A great big something. She just couldn't put her finger on it.

A robin skipped along the grass, fluttering his wings and chirping merrily. These days everything seemed to remind her of Jamie. It was a killer having a crush on someone so unattainable. Being fixated on Simon Le Bon or John Taylor when you were a teenager was one thing. Being obsessed with a celebrity chef at thirty-one was a little kooky, not to mention a bit sad.

The doorbell rang. Lucy could hear someone answer it.

"Hi, mate," Alan boomed. "Come in. Lucy's in the kitchen."

"Where else?" said Brian. "I'll go on down."

Lucy forced herself to smile as Brian walked in the door. It was

Tuesday evening and he was still wearing a suit, dark blue with a thin pinstripe. He was carrying a black leather document case and a bunch of six perfectly formed red roses, wrapped in expensive-looking black paper and finished with a white silk-ribbon bow.

"Roses for my own sweet rose." He handed the flowers to Lucy.

"Thanks." She held them up to her nose. They had no smell. They might have had at one stage, but now all scent had disappeared. "I'll put them in water." She opened the cupboard under the sink and took out a cut-glass vase. As she filled it with water Brian came up behind her and put his arms around her waist.

"You look lovely," he murmured, kissing her neck.

Lucy was wearing an old pair of jeans and a grey fleece that belonged to Max. Her hair was tied back with an old scrunchie and she didn't have a scrap of make-up on. As Brian always said this, regardless of how she looked, Lucy had no idea whether he meant it or not any more. Today, she doubted it.

"Thanks." She tried not to wince as he nibbled her earlobe.

He turned her around, pressed the length of his body against hers, and began to kiss her deeply. His kisses, as always, were studied, exact and perfectly timed. A few strokes of the tongue, kiss upper lip, kiss lower lip, full kiss on the mouth, and repeat. Lucy wanted him to stop.

"Excuse me," they heard a voice behind them. They jumped apart and Lucy surreptitiously wiped her mouth on the sleeve of Max's fleece.

"Sorry to interrupt," Paula trilled. "I have to fill the kettle. Alan needs a cup of tea."

Paula was still wearing her white and pink Making Faces uniform. On everyone else it looked somewhere between reasonable and ridiculous; on her it looked depressingly great.

Paula owned the beauty salon, bankrolled by her father. She was tiny – all of seven stone, with long, blonde curly hair cascading down her back. She was always immaculately groomed, and no one had ever seen her without her full make-up, plastered on over her sun-bed-tanned skin. Alan, who was one of life's good guys, had been with her for over six months and Lucy and Hopper couldn't understand it.

11

They supposed it was because he was English, hadn't been in the country very long and had been duped into thinking that Paula was fun. That's not saying that she couldn't be fun – give her a few West Coast Coolers or Ritz's and she was a giggling heap – but to say they couldn't stand her was an understatement.

Hopper disliked her the most. Paula was always making fun of Hopper's clothes, her hair, her taste in music. Hopper was Boho Chic and Paula was Top Shop. They were like chalk and cheese.

And the funny thing was that Alan was a lot more like Hopper than Paula. He liked indie music, especially American – Mercury Rev, Elliot Smith, that sort of thing. He wore second-hand clothes, again mainly American, and, like Hopper, he read all the time. In fact he was the best-read man they'd ever met. Paula read magazines and the odd Mills and Boon. It was all topsy-turvy, Lucy thought.

"Thanks for the dinner invite," said Paula. "We'd love to come."

"Dinner?" Brian asked. "Am I invited?"

"Of course," said Lucy. "I just haven't got around to mentioning it to you yet. Is Friday night OK?"

Brian sighed. "I have a work thing that night, Lucy, remember? Mr O'Toole is taking all the partners out to dinner in town."

"That's a pity."

"How about Saturday? You could have it on Saturday. I'm free then."

"We are too," Paula added.

"Sorry," said Lucy. "I've already asked Max and Jenny and –"

"If Friday suits Max, that's all right then," Brian interrupted.

"Don't be like that," Lucy began and then remembered that Paula was still in the room. "The kettle's boiled," she informed her pointedly. Paula was staring at Brian and waiting for the fireworks. The lack of love between Brian and Max was no secret.

"I'll make the tea, I suppose." Paula was disappointed. She loved a good barney. "Anyone else want one?"

"No, thank you," said Lucy.

"I'd love one, thanks," said Brian. "It's not often that a beautiful young woman offers to make me tea."

Lucy glared at him.

"Apart from Lucy, of course."

When Paula had left the room Lucy turned towards Brian.

"I'm sorry about Friday. I'd totally forgotten about your work thing."

"That's OK." He held her hand and stroked it gently. His hands were cool and a little clammy. "What would you like to do this evening?"

"Maybe we could go for a walk? It's a lovely evening."

Brian thought about this for a second. "I'm a bit tired, to be honest. How about we watch some TV and have an early night?"

"You're staying?"

"If that's all right with you."

Lucy couldn't think of any reasonable excuse. "That's fine."

Later that evening Lucy lay awake, listening to Brian's breathing. It was regular and even, just like him. They'd just had spectacularly average sex and he'd fallen asleep straight away. She'd faked it – again – as her body seemed to be turning more and more unco-operative where Brian's 'talents' were concerned. Something would have to be done.

Daria winced as her sister pulled the thin splinter of wood out of her finger.

"Are you OK?" asked Grace. "Did I hurt you?"

Daria rubbed her finger, which was now tender and throbbing. "No, it's fine, thanks."

Grace put the metal tweezers down on the coffee table and smiled. "I don't think you're cut out for model-making. You'll kill yourself with a craft knife one of these days."

"Thanks for the vote of confidence," Daria smiled. "But you're right. I'm in the wrong job. The sooner I get a decent part the better."

"Have you heard back from the interview yet? The one for *Emma?*"

"No. I should hear by tomorrow lunchtime though."

"Give me a ring when you know, will you?"

"Of course. I have to visit a kite place in the afternoon, but I'll call you after that."

"Kites? What for?"

"The *Mary Poppins* set."

"I remember the song," Grace grinned and began to sing 'Let's Go Fly a Kite'.

"Have you ever thought of a job on the stage?"

"Don't be cruel. Besides, the kids don't seem to mind. And that's all that matters." Grace taught Senior Infants in Monkstown National School.

"Do you sing to them?" Daria asked with interest.

"Of course. Songs in French and Irish, and learning rhymes, that sort of thing."

"God love them."

"Shut up, you," Grace squealed, grabbing a cushion from the sofa and hitting her sister over the head with it.

"Mind my finger," Daria protested, before grabbing a cushion herself.

"No mercy."

Daria walked into Allen's Chandlery and looked around. One wall was covered with brightly coloured sailing clothes — waterproof leggings, jackets and fleeces, and the other with all kinds of metal screws and pins, and rope of lots of different thicknesses. She saw some looped metal things which she recognised as shackles. Dawn, the set-designer she worked with, used them all the time.

"Can I help you?" a young man asked.

"Hi, I'm looking for Max."

"He's in the back. I'll bring you through."

Daria followed him towards the rear of the shop where paint and varnish tins were stacked ceiling-high on wooden shelves.

"He's in the loft." He gestured towards a run-down-looking wooden prefab. It had been painted white many moons ago, but was now so

14

covered with stickers and banners that the wood was almost totally covered. *Surf's Up*, Daria read, *The World Loves a Sailor, Kite Flyers Do It With Strings*.

"Go on in."

"Thanks."

She pushed open the door and was hit by a blast of warm air. Although it was only May it was a warm, sunny day. At the far end of the long, narrow room a tall, blond man was cutting a piece of purple material with a large pair of scissors. She watched him for a second. He was wearing a white T-shirt which had seen better days. His blond hair was cut short, almost shaved and he had attractive sallow skin. In fact, Daria thought to herself, he was most attractive all over.

She coughed. He looked up and grinned. He had bright blue and eyes and an open, generous smile. "Hiya," he said, putting down the material and walking towards her. "I'm Max. You must be –" Shit, he thought to himself. I've forgotten her bloody name. Lucy did tell me.

"Daria, Daria Delahunty." She held out her hand formally. "Pleased to meet you."

Max tucked the scissors into the back pocket of his jeans and held out his hand.

"Sorry," he muttered as their fingers stuck together for a split second. "Glue. I was sealing some seams and –"

She laughed. "Don't worry. I'm used to it. I spend my life with glue and paint on my hands. It's not a problem." She wiped her hand on her jeans.

Max noticed that the old denim was covered with flecks of light blue and white paint. He also noticed her long legs and her slim thighs. He tried not to stare.

"So you're looking for kites," he said. "What type exactly?"

"I'm not sure really. It's for a stage set so we'd like them as big as possible and very colourful. They don't actually have to fly; they're just for effect really. What would you suggest?"

Max hesitated for a second. "My kites always fly. They're designed to be in tune with the wind."

15

Daria looked at him carefully. "We could make them fly, I suppose. We could use the wind-generator." She clapped her hands together. "In fact, that would look amazing, kites fluttering in the wind, with long coloured tails. Yes, they'll definitely fly."

"Good." He really wanted to work with this beautiful young woman but he couldn't compromise his art. His kites were not mere ornaments; they were serious aerodynamic flying-machines. "In that case I'd recommend some delta kites and some box kites. And your classic diamond two-sticks, of course."

Daria smiled. "You'll have to explain, I'm afraid. I'm no expert when it comes to kites."

Max pulled out a sheet of paper and began to draw some shapes. "Delta kites look like this – a large, open triangle. Box kites are easy, they're pretty much just that – boxes. And diamond two-sticks are what most children would draw if you asked them to draw a kite – a diamond shape, usually with a long tail."

"And you have some of those here?"

"Yes."

"Great." Daria smiled widely, two dimples forming on either side of her smooth, porcelain cheeks. "And maybe you could visit the set tomorrow? I'll hang them in the morning but I'm going to need some help getting them to fly."

"Tomorrow afternoon should be OK," Max said thoughtfully. He was supposed to be spending the day updating his Web site. But to hell with it.

"I'll give you a ring in the morning to arrange a time."

"Look forward to it. Now why don't we have a look at some of the stock?"

"That girl, Daria, was in today," Max told Lucy that evening on the phone.

"And?" asked Lucy. "Did she order some kites?"

"Loads. Seven in total. She took five ready-made ones and I'm designing two for her specially."

16

"Excellent!"

"Thanks to you. Maybe I should give you some of my cards. You could hand them out to *all* your customers."

"I'd say Paula would have something to say about that. But I could have a go. Though I'm not my clients would be your average customer base."

"You never know. They may be looking for that elusive perfect present for their other half. They might have kids or nephews and nieces or something."

"Maybe. Listen, are you still all right for dinner on Friday night?"

"I'm not sure. Do you really think it's such a good idea?"

"You can't back out now. I've already asked Jenny and she seems very interested in you."

"What did you tell her?"

"That you were very good-looking."

"Lucy! She'll be expecting George Clooney or something."

She was unperturbed. "You'll need to wear something decent – how about your dark blue shirt? Bring it here early and I'll get Paula to iron it for you. She loves showing Alan what a great little housewife she'd make. And your black jeans, the ones I gave you for your birthday."

"Yes, Mum. I'm still not sure –"

"It'll be fine. Trust me, I'm a –"

"I know. I know. You're a doctor." Max, put down the phone. He sat back on the sofa and stared at the blank screen of the television. He had a bad feeling about Friday night. He rubbed his hands which were still sticky – the damn glue was a bitch to get off. He'd have to find the white spirit.

"Well," Grace asked her sister that evening. "Did you get the part?"

"Sorry. I meant to ring, but I got caught up. I'm through to the final three."

Grace threw her arms around her sister. "Well done. That's great news."

Daria smiled. All in all she'd had a very good day indeed.

17

3

"Hi, Max, this is Daria. It's Thursday morning, just after nine. Ring me when you get in, thanks."

Max flicked through the battered dark-red desk diary in front of him and found her mobile number.

"Daria, it's Max . . . um, the kite guy."

"Max, thanks for getting back to me. I was wondering if this afternoon was still OK? About three?"

"Three is fine."

"Perfect! I'll meet you outside the main door of The Olympia."

"I'll have one of the giant Delta kites ready, I hope. I'll bring it with me."

"Excellent." She was impressed. "That was quick. I'm dying to see it."

"See you later then." Max smiled to himself as he put down the phone. The kite he had referred to needed a lot of work. The light carbon fibre spars and spine had to be cut and sanded and he hadn't even begun sewing the small multi-coloured nylon pieces onto the tail yet. He took one final swig of his coffee and set to work.

"Are you busy?" Lucy asked Max midway through the morning. Paula was at a New Age Seminar on healing with crystals and Lucy was making the most of her unsupervised morning.

"Yes, very." He was machine-stitching as he talked to her, the receiver jammed between his head and his left shoulder.

"I thought you were working on your site today," Lucy said suspiciously, hearing the machine humming in the background.

"I have to finish up a special order first, then I'll be desk-bound for the rest of the day." He groaned. "I wish I could afford to pay someone to do the computer-boffin bit. It's so tedious. Listen, I have to go. Joe has just walked in. Talk to you later."

He took his foot off the machine pedal and put the receiver down gently.

"I'm not Joe," Mossy said, staring at Max. Joe Allen was the white-haired owner of Allen's Chandlery.

"I know that." Max put his head down and concentrated on his stitching. Mossy sniffed and walked out again, muttering something about coffee.

Unusual, Max thought to himself as he worked. It was the first time he could remember that he'd intentionally withheld information from Lucy.

Lucy put the phone down and stared into space. There was something up. She could hear it in Max's voice. There was something he wasn't telling her. She hadn't known him for thirty-odd years for nothing.

She felt irritated and irrationally cross. She ran her finger over the phone and considered ringing him back. But Mrs O'Connor would be arriving any minute to have her eyebrows reshaped so she didn't really have the time. She'd ring him after lunch instead.

Daria checked her face in the large, ornately framed gold mirror. She turned on the cold tap, wet her hands and ran them through her short, dark hair. She dotted her lips with plum-red lip gloss and puckered them to spread the colour. She wanted to look nice but, at the same time, she didn't want to overdo it. She was wearing old, paint-stained jeans and a tight black T-shirt, and full make-up would appear incongruous.

She dried her hands on a thick green paper towel and frowned. Her nails were looking worse for wear – the paint, white spirit and varnish were taking their toll. She'd have to pay another visit to Making Faces before her next audition. She smiled to herself. She had a good feeling about *Emma*. The other women in the final three were classically trained, with a rake of theatrical experience between them. They were also a good few years older than she was. But she'd worked with the director, Owen Hughes, in Trinity Players. He was young and progressive and had exciting new ideas about staging the Jane Austen adaptation. She'd seemed to click with him at the last audition and knew she was in with a chance of securing the eponymous role.

Anyway, she said to herself as she rubbed her forefinger over her front teeth to remove faint traces of lip gloss, I'll get a decent part soon. I bloody well deserve it.

Daria had spent the last seven years working in the theatre. 'Working' in the broadest sense of the word. After completing her Arts degree in Trinity College, in English and Drama, her first job had been manning the busy box office at The Gate Theatre on Parnell Square in Dublin. From that illustrious beginning she had progressed to selling programmes, dressing the child actors and finally a real part – a singing Japanese courtier in a production of Gilbert and Sullivan's *The Mikado* in the Olympia. Her strong soprano voice had served her well over the years and she'd sung her way up the ranks in *Cats*, *Grease*, *South Pacific* and various Christmas pantos.

Last year she'd been Cinderella to Twink's Fairy Godmother and Dustin the Turkey's Buttons which had been brilliant fun. And now she was painting scenery for another musical, *Mary Poppins*. She had been offered the lead role, made famous by Julie Andrews in the Disney classic, but she was holding out for something else.

For as long as she could remember she had dreamed of a meaty lead role in her favourite Dublin theatre, the one where she had started – The Gate. And this time things might just go to plan for her. Fingers crossed.

Daria took a deep breath and left the safety of the women's toilet. She made her way down the labyrinth of stairs and corridors towards the main entrance.

"Hi, Max," she smiled as she unlocked and opened the heavy glass and wooden doors. "Have you been here long?"

"A few minutes." His hands were hot and sticky and he could feel a warm blush sneaking up his neck and spreading onto his cheeks. He held onto the long, black nylon kite-bag as if it were a lifebuoy.

"Is that one of the giant kites?" She was dying to see the design. He'd promised something spectacular.

"Yes," he said, still clutching it tightly.

"Follow me," she said, gesturing him inside the warm, red-wallpapered hall. "I'll just lock the door after you," she added, moving behind him.

"I've never been in here during the day," Max said, looking around him. "In fact, I haven't been here for years, except for a couple of concerts and the odd *Midnight at the Olympia* session."

"It's a good venue for concerts." She led him down a corridor, through a red door and up some steep steps. "I saw the Counting Crows here last year – they were great."

"I was at that. The one without Dan 'cause his wife was having a baby." He was starting to feel a little less nervous.

"That's right. Small world." She led him into a room with a high, sloped dingy glass ceiling. "This is the backstage room where we store most of the scenery and props."

Max looked around. The room was littered with a jumble of painted and plain white flats, assorted furniture, an antique large-wheeled black pram, chimney-sweep's brushes, a large round table and old-fashioned high-backed chairs.

"The stage door is over here." She opened the door. Max could see a large grey wind-generator towards the back of the wings on the opposite side. "I've put the kites up," she said, leading Max onto the stage, "but two of them seem to be having problems flying."

Max stared up. The tails of the bright blue, yellow, red and purple square and diamond-shaped kites were fluttering in the draught.

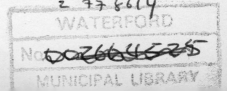

"I'll just flick on the lights and the wind machine and you can have a better look."

A few minutes later the stage was bathed in strong, warming light. Spotlights illuminated the kites which had begun to fly in the gentle artificial breeze.

Daria walked back onto the stage. Max couldn't help but notice that the blue backdrop with fluffy white clouds which had been painted to look like the sky matched her eyes perfectly, the blue bits that was.

"You're right," he said, trying to keep his mind on the job. "The box kite, that's the square 3-D one, and the smaller diamond kite aren't balanced properly for the wind. I'll need to turn the box so it faces the breeze squarely and move the bridle on the diamond."

"The bridle?"

"Sorry," Max smiled. "The piece of line which angles the kite into the wind is called the bridle. You need to adjust the angle for this type of light wind."

"I could turn the wind generator up a bit."

"That would certainly help."

He waited as she fiddled with a knob on the side of the large machine. The diamond kite began to lift, catching the new, stronger breeze.

"Look!" Daria exclaimed. "It's flying!"

He smiled at her excitement. "I'll still need to adjust the box kite."

A little later they stood at the back of the auditorium watching the fruits of their labour.

The giant kite which Max had decorated with a vibrant, multi-coloured clown design was now in place and the rogue box kite was flying steadily.

"They're beautiful," Daria sighed. "Especially the clown."

"Thanks," Max said gratefully. He was pleased with the effect.

"The stage looks so alive, and so childish."

"Childish?"

"I mean childlike," Daria said. Max was still frowning. "You know," she continued, trying to explain. "Happy and fun. Like the world is when you're a child. Safe and trouble-free."

Max turned towards her in the dim light. "Are you saying your life isn't like that now?" he asked gently, immediately regretting the over-intimate question.

Daria paused for a second. Luckily she didn't seem at all offended. "Trouble-free. Sometimes, I guess. But not often. I wish it was."

And at that moment all that Max wanted to do was to hold Daria in his arms and hug the hell out of her.

"Would you like to grab a cup of coffee?" he asked instead.

Daria looked at him and smiled. "Yes. Yes, I would."

"So how did you get into the kite business?" Daria asked as she dipped her spoon into the creamy froth at the top of her cappuccino.

They were sitting on a sofa in Coco's Coffee Shop in Temple Bar. Daria's legs were curled up underneath her, exposing a couple of inches of smooth, tanned leg between the bottom of her jeans and her chunky pink Converse sandals. Although it was a sunny afternoon there was a cool breeze and Max wondered whether her feet were cold. They were both wearing Patagonia fleeces and they'd joked that they looked like twins walking down Crow Street.

"I was working in London as an engineer and one of my English friends had a parafoil," Max began.

Daria raised her eyebrows curiously.

"A parafoil's a power-kite. It's rectangular and I guess it looks a bit like a floating mattress when it's in the air."

Daria smiled.

"I tried flying his one day and I loved it. The next day I bought myself one and I was fascinated with its design. After a while I bought a bigger one but it was bloody expensive so I thought I'd have a go at making one. It took a long time to get the design right, but I finally cracked it. And I ended up making them for friends and friends of friends while I was over there."

"Brilliant. And I suppose your engineering training helped?"

"Yes, it did."

"And then . . ." she encouraged.

"I'd had enough of London – it was too noisy, too dirty, too everything. So I moved back to Dublin, set up Max Kites with the proceeds of my flat and here I am." He sipped his coffee thoughtfully.

"Do you miss London?"

"Not at all. I lived there for three years and it was quite long enough."

"I'm not a fan of big cities either. I grew up in Boston and I'm much happier in Dublin."

"Boston? I thought I detected a faint American twang."

"Damn! I've spent years trying to elocute it out of my system." She smiled.

Max laughed. "You have a lovely accent. Honestly."

"Thanks."

"So when did you move to Dublin?"

"When I was fifteen. My dad's Irish and when he and mum got divorced myself and Grace, my sister, moved here with him. To Wicklow originally and then to Dublin. And we've been here ever since."

"That must have been hard," Max said. "Moving away like that. Leaving all your friends behind."

"It was. But I'd been to Dublin before to visit my gran and my relations, so it wasn't a complete shock to the system."

They talked for a little while longer before she glanced at her watch.

"I have to run in a few minutes. I'm sorry."

Max was disappointed. He'd really enjoyed talking to her and there was so much he wanted to know. "You go on. I'll get this," he said.

"Are you sure?"

"Of course. I'll have the other giant kite ready for you early next week. Maybe we could have coffee again then."

"I'd like that."

"Where were you this afternoon?" Lucy asked Max that evening as they walked into the IMAC cinema in Dun Laoghaire. They had arranged to see the new Brad Pitt film. Max had great respect for the man after his stunning performance in *Snatch*, which, along with *Lock, Stock and Two Smoking Barrels* was one of his favourites. Lucy just thought Brad was delicious eye-candy, plain and simple. She wasn't all that concerned with his acting ability.

"At the post office. I had to send a kite to Donegal urgently."

"I tried a couple of times. Mossy told me you'd been gone most of the afternoon."

"I was trying to avoid working on the Web site, to tell the truth. Do you want popcorn?"

After the film she dropped him back to his apartment in Monkstown. "Now don't forget about dinner tomorrow night," she reminded him as he stepped out of the ancient Audi and into the pouring rain.

"I won't," he said before making a mad dash for the front door. He let himself into the communal hall which always smelt faintly of curry and shook his wet head, splattering a shower of drops into the cool air.

4

"Max has been acting strangely in the last few days," Lucy said to Hopper as she sliced her sharp kitchen knife into a firm red tomato. Hopper was sitting on the kitchen counter, pilfering the raw ingredients of the baby spinach and feta cheese salad. "Would you get your fingers out of there!" Lucy exclaimed, swatting Hopper's hand away. "There'll be nothing left for dinner at this rate."

"No fear," Hopper grinned. "You've enough here to feed a large territorial army! What were you saying about Max?"

"Maybe I'm imagining it, but he's just being a bit – I don't know, evasive, I suppose."

"You two are practically joined at the hip. I'm sure it's nothing. He's probably just got his mind on higher things, like kites."

"Ha, bloody ha. No, that's not it. He wasn't in the loft yesterday afternoon and he made some feeble excuse about being in the post office."

Hooper looked at her friend carefully. "I think you're being a little paranoid. Why would he lie about going to the post office, for heaven's sake?"

"But he was gone for hours, according to Mossy."

"Mossy has no brain cells left. And no sense of time. And why did you need to know exactly where Max was, anyway? You're not even his girlfriend. You're worse than Paula."

"Forget it." She was beginning to feel a little stupid. "Ignore me." She concentrated on the chopping-board.

Hopper took a metal spoonful of a red, tomato-based sauce from the mixing bowl on the counter beside her.

"Hey!" Lucy said, raising her voice. "Leave that alone. It's not finished."

"Tastes finished to me." Hopper licked her lips enthusiastically.

"Listen, you can either give me a hand or join Alan and Paula in the living-room."

"A fate worse than death." She jumped down off the counter and rolled back the sleeves of her green and pink-striped mohair jumper. "I'll help you."

"Good. You can chop the onions."

"Are you crying, Sinead?" Paula asked hopefully as Hopper walked into the living-room. Paula and Alan were sitting on the sofa watching a rerun of *Thunderbirds* on the television. Paula had no interest in it and was filing her nails with a long, pink emery-board.

"Hopper. And no, Lucy had me chopping the onions, that's all."

"Pity."

Alan turned towards his girlfriend. "That's not very nice, Paula. I don't see why you two can't get on. It's getting tiring at this stage."

"She started it."

"Yeah, right." Hopper glared at Paula unpleasantly.

Alan stood up suddenly, sending Paula flying. "I'm going to watch this in my room," he muttered, going out and slamming the door behind him.

"Now look what you've done, *Sinead*."

"One day everyone will find out what an evil little bitch you really are." Hopper walked out of the room, leaving Paula behind her, and marched up the stairs. Paula ran out behind her.

27

"Keep away from my Alan!"

Hopper stared at her in disgust. "If you think I'd go near him after he's been with you you're sorely mistaken. He probably has some sort of disease at this stage. Crabs or something."

"Don't be disgusting! I'm very clean."

Hopper decided against retaliation. It was too much like hard work. Paula gave up and went back into the living-room and began to watch the home shopping channel. Hopper could hear 'never-to-be-repeated' offers drifting up the stairs. She knocked gently on Alan's door.

"Yes. Who is it?"

"It's me," she whispered. "Hopper."

A few seconds later the door opened. Alan stood on the threshold, frowning at her. She pushed past him and sat down on his bed. The room was reasonably tidy, for a boy. There was only one layer of clothes on the floor and the curtains were half-drawn back, letting in some daylight.

"I'm sorry," she began. "She just winds me up. I know it annoys you."

Alan sighed. "Forget it." He sat down on the bed beside her.

"Lady Penelope looks good today," she smiled, trying to lighten the mood.

"Um."

"And String-Ray 2 looks greener than usual. Must be the digital re-mastering."

Alan looked at her. "I didn't know you were a fan."

"There's a lot of things you don't know about me. A whole heap."

His eyes were fixed on her face. He suddenly realised that she had the most amazing eyes – dark chocolate-brown pools that you could get lost in. He felt a magnetic pull dragging him closer and closer towards Hopper and her hypnotic eyes.

"Alan!" Paula's voice cut through the atmosphere. "I want to get changed now. Send that 'thing' away, please." She pointed at Hopper.

"Didn't your mother ever tell you that it's rude to point?" Hopper asked.

28

"Out!" Paula shouted. "Now!"

"Sorry, Hopper," Alan apologised. He got up and followed Hopper towards the door.

"Where do you think you're going?" Paula asked him.

"To watch *Thunderbirds* downstairs," he replied innocently. "I thought you said you wanted to get changed."

"But I'll need help with my basque," Paula purred, putting her arms around his waist. "You know I find the little metal hooks hard with my fingernails." She flicked her tongue over the rim of his ear suggestively and stared at Hopper who was waiting for Alan at the door. "Run along, Hopper. We're busy."

Hopper stomped down the stairs fuming. Little wagon. Paula made her blood boil. She'd bloody well show her. She walked into the kitchen and sat down at the table.

Lucy looked up from the chocolate sauce she was stirring on the hob. "Everything OK?"

"No!"

"What's up?" Lucy dipped her finger into the warm, dense liquid and popped it into her mouth. It was delicious.

"Paula!"

"I know you two don't exactly get on but can you try, just for tonight? Please?"

"I suppose. But tell madam to lay off me, will you?"

"I'll ask Alan to have a word with her."

Hopper sighed. Alan didn't seem to have much control over his girlfriend. She and her Victoria's Secret underwear stash had him wrapped around her little finger.

"What's wrong?" Lucy asked, turning the heat down under the small saucepan and leaving the sauce simmering on the hob. She pulled out a chair and joined Hopper at the table.

"Alan. He's upstairs with Paula. But before she came in I thought we were going to –" She hesitated.

"Go on."

"To kiss. Our heads were really close together and he was leaning over towards me and gazing into my eyes." She sighed again. "I don't know. Maybe I'm imagining it."

Lucy sat silent for a few seconds, thinking. "I think Alan really likes you. And you'd be great together. But what about Paula?"

"What about her? Stupid wench. We'll just have to get rid of her."

"I'll come up with something," Lucy smiled. "A way to get you and Alan alone together." She thought for a minute, tapping the table with her fingernails before clicking her fingers. "I think that might just work, yes. Leave it to me, Hopper."

The doorbell rang. "That's probably Max," Lucy said.

"You can't leave me hanging like that," Hopper spluttered. "What's going through that strange little mind of yours?"

"I'll tell you later," Lucy promised as she opened the kitchen door. The Victorian house was built on a slope and there were four steps between the kitchen door and the long hall.

"Lucy!" Hopper called after her, but Lucy ignored her.

"Hi, Max," said Lucy, opening the front door and kissing him on the cheek. "Come in."

Max handed her a large bunch of daisies.

"Daisies, my favourite. Thanks."

"I've brought a few bottles too, like you asked." Max plonked the plastic Oddbins bag onto the wooden hall floor with a clink and unzipped his jacket.

Lucy looked at his shirt critically. "The jeans are fine but that shirt definitely needs an iron."

"But I ironed it myself before I came out!"

"Did you plug the iron in?"

"Don't be so mean."

"Take it off," Lucy said, walking towards the kitchen. "Bring the bottles down here."

"Yes, Sergeant Major." He was well used to Lucy's bossy streak. In the kitchen he put the plastic bag down on the table, undid the top button of his shirt and pulled it over his head.

"You're such a boy," Hopper laughed. "It wouldn't kill you to undo the buttons."

"It's quicker this way," Max winked. "Comes in handy with the babes."

"You don't do it very often, so," Lucy quipped.

"Thanks a lot. Now who's going to iron my shirt?" He tried to hand it to Lucy. He was feeling a little silly, not to mention self-conscious standing in the kitchen with a bare chest. At least it was warm, he thought to himself.

"My hands are really sticky," Lucy said. "And I have to make the garlic bread. I'll get Paula."

"She's busy," Hopper said ominously. She smelt her hands. "The onion smell has pretty much gone so I'll do it." She took the shirt from Max.

"I didn't know you could iron, Hopper," Lucy said.

"With two younger brothers you learn pretty fast," Hopper smiled. "Just because I don't iron my own clothes doesn't mean I can't do it at all."

"I feel really stupid," Max complained. "I'll do it," he said, "again."

"Max," Lucy sighed, "pour yourself a drink and sit down. There's an open bottle of white in the fridge. And let Hopper do it – you want to impress Jenny, don't you?"

"I suppose. But I don't see how ironing a shirt is going to make much of a difference." He walked towards the fridge and pulled out the bottle of white Fetzer. "Would you like a glass, girls?"

"Please," Hopper smiled. Lucy nodded.

Paula walked in the door in a stunning, black low-cut catsuit. "Me too, please. How nice, served a drink by a near-naked man. Makes a change." She looked Max up and down appraisingly.

"Where's Alan?" Lucy asked.

"In the shower," Paula replied. "He'll be down in a few minutes." She glanced over at Hopper who was unfolding the ironing board. "Can I do that? I'm a whizz at ironing."

"It's fine, thank you," Hopper replied through gritted teeth. She pulled the iron out of a cupboard and plugged it in.

"Oh, but you'll need starch," Paula said.

"Max doesn't like starch on his shirts, do you, Max?" Lucy said quickly, throwing him a look.

"No," Max said in confusion. "It makes me feel starchy."

Paula giggled and batted her eyelashes at Max. "Max," she trilled, "you're so funny."

"We should all move upstairs," Lucy said firmly. "Jenny will be here soon. And I'm almost done here."

"Wait for me," Hopper said. "The iron's only just heating up." She didn't want to miss anything.

They all waited while she ironed the shirt, Lucy keeping Paula occupied by asking her work-related questions. Max was happy just to sit at the kitchen table and flick through an old *RTE Guide* he'd found on the table.

When she was finished, Hopper handed Max his newly ironed shirt and he put it on gingerly as it was still hot.

"Thanks, Hopper. You did a great job," he said. He fastened the buttons quickly. "I'm going upstairs now, OK?" He could hear Alan flicking through the television channels in the front room.

"Fine," Lucy said. "I'm nearly done. I'll be up in two seconds. Would you mind opening the door to people, Max?"

"No problem." He opened the kitchen door and went up the stairs into the hall.

"I think I'll join the boys," Paula said, following him closely, her eyes fixed on his backside as he climbed the stairs. "You look very handsome, Max."

"Thanks," Max replied nervously.

The doorbell rang again.

"That'll be Eugene," Max said. "He's always on time if there's food involved." Eugene was Lucy's younger brother.

Paula tottered past him on her staggeringly high heels. "I'll get it." She pulled back the door and gave the two young men on the doorstep a killer grin. "Boys, do come in," she purred. "Hi, Eugene."

"Hi, Paula, nice to see you again. Please call me Blanco, all me mates do. And this is me best mate, Derek."

Paula giggled girlishly. "Nice to meet you, Derek. I'm Paula." She held his hand firmly and gazed into his eyes.

"And *you* can call me Deco," he smiled.

Superquinn bags full of cans of cider and lager swung by their sides.

"Yo! Sis!" Eugene said to Lucy, spotting the top of her head as she came through the kitchen door.

"Hi, Eugene," Lucy said looking up. She walked up the stairs and stared at him suspiciously. "I didn't know you were bringing Derek," she said coolly. She'd asked her brother instead of Brian, to even up the boy/girl numbers.

"I knew it would be OK, Sis. Come here and give us a smooch."

He bounded over to her, threw his arms around her and kissed her on the cheek. He smelt of drink and tobacco.

"I suppose it's all right. But don't get too drunk, OK?"

"Would we, Lucy?" Derek asked. "You know us."

"Only too well."

They all made their way into the living-room. Eugene flicked through the CDs and put one on. "Semisonic," he said loudly over the music, "*excellento!*"

"Can you turn it down a bit, Eugene?" Lucy asked. Maybe it hadn't been such a good idea to ask her brother along. He was twenty-four going on fifteen, and had all the sense of a three-week-old puppy. In fact, given too many pints he'd probably chew the legs of the furniture. He was still in UCD after a deferred year after the Leaving Cert, a repeated year after failing first year and a year off between second and third year. At times Lucy felt more like a mother to him than a sister. Their own mother, Eileen, found him more than a handful.

"*No problemo*, Sis," he beamed, dancing around the room, practically head-butting the lampshade.

"Has everyone got a drink?" Lucy asked. "Derek, what would you like? Wine?"

Derek smiled. "I'll just crack open one of my tinnies, thanks Lucy. I'll have some wine later."

"I'm fine, Sis. I'll have a beer too," Eugene said.

"I'll bring up some glasses and bottles for everyone else," Max said.

"Thanks," Lucy said gratefully. "That would be great. I'd better check on the food."

"Here, use a tray," Lucy told Max in the kitchen. He was trying to carry glasses like a barman, with his fingers. "It'll be easier."

"Good idea," Max said, taking the tray from her. "Are you OK? You look a little harassed."

"I'm fine," she assured him. "I always get a little nervous before the food is served, that's all." She opened the oven door a crack to check the garlic bread wasn't burning. "And Eugene is practically drunk already. God knows what he's going to be like later."

"He'll be fine," Max said kindly. "He'll just fall asleep like last time."

"You're probably right. My brother, the big party animal. He's like a big kid."

"You love him really."

"I know. I know. He just drives me demented. He's such a waster."

"He's young for his age. He needs time to mature, that's all."

"Mum doesn't help. She mollycoddles him to death, always has."

"It's not easy for her," he said sagely. "She has to be mother and father to him and that's no joke."

"I suppose not." She'd be quite happy sitting in the kitchen all night talking to Max but she was very aware of the guests upstairs. "Jenny better arrive soon, or the garlic bread will be charcoal."

"We can always start without her," he said hopefully. He was starving. Maybe she wouldn't come at all. He'd be very relieved and he could also stuff himself with Lucy's great food.

"She'll be here. She's dying to meet you."

Max's stomach lurched. This whole thing was starting to make him very nervous.

5

"Lucy, darling, sorry I'm late." Jenny smothered Lucy in Chanel No 5 as she kissed her cheek ostentatiously. "This is for you." She handed Lucy a single flower which looked like plastic – one waxy red petal and a phallic pink bit inside. "Fab, isn't it?"

"Thanks," Lucy mumbled, not quite sure what to say. Designer flowers weren't really her thing. She'd preferred Max's friendly bunch of daisies. "Come in and meet the gang." Lucy led the willowy figure into the living-room. Jenny was wearing skin-tight black trousers, a purple lycra top and high-heeled black leather boots. She looked amazing. Lucy wondered what Max would make of her.

"Everyone, this is Jenny. Jenny, the lout sprawled on the floor is Eugene, my brother, also know as 'Blanco'." Eugene beamed up at the stunning woman in front of him. He'd had no idea his sister knew such babes. This one was even better than Paula.

"Beside Eugene is Derek."

Derek jumped up and offered Jenny his hand.

"Howaya," he murmured, staring at her cleavage.

Lucy pushed Jenny towards safer ground. "And this is Alan – he lives here – his girlfriend Paula, and, of course, you've met Hopper before."

"Hi, everyone, hi, Hopper," Jenny said, smiling widely and showing her exquisite set of even, white teeth.

"And last, but not least," Lucy smiled, "this is Max."

"Hi, Max," Jenny purred. "I believe you're single."

Max coughed and blushed. "Yeah, that's right." He glared dangerously at Lucy who was stifling a grin.

"Well then, no point in being coy about it, is there?" Jenny sat down on the arm of Max's chair. "Let's get acquainted, shall we? Tell me all about your job. Lucy told me that you make kites."

Eugene and Derek stared over at Max enviously.

"Lucky bastard," Eugene muttered.

"No kidding," Derek nodded.

"This is 'baby spinach with fresh peas and feta cheese," Lucy explained as they sat down at the dining-room table. They were lucky to have a dining-room, which doubled up as a 'study', a 'spare-room' and 'the drying-clothes-room' depending on what was needed. A long room painted terracotta red with gloriously high ceilings, it was wonderful for entertaining. And entertain Lucy did. Most weekends, even if there was no one special coming round, she set the dining-room table with Hopper's help and served dinner there. Candles, linen napkins – the works.

"This looks wonderful," Jenny enthused. "I still haven't forgotten the wonderful focaccia you gave me for lunch the last time I was round." She touched Max on the arm. "We're great friends, me and Lucy. We have heaps in common."

Max tried not to squirm under her touch. Since first plonking herself down on the arm of his chair, Jenny had touched him, stroked him and picked fluff off his shirt at every opportunity. He was getting a little tired of it. She was a lovely-looking woman – there was no doubt about that, but she was driving him nuts. All she could talk about was clothes, shoes, bags, where one got the best highlights in Dublin, darling, and Max just wasn't interested. After her few perfunctory questions about his job he hadn't got a word in edgeways.

Unfortunately she seemed to have taken a bit of a shine to him – he wasn't sure why.

"Please," Lucy insisted, "tuck in. Eugene, I see you've already started."

"Yeah," Eugene smiled, his mouth full of butter-dripping garlic bread. "Sure have, Sis. Great tucker, as usual."

They all munched away happily for a while, exchanging gossip about the latest Louis Walsh protégées – a young band from Kerry called The Sea Horses.

"Did anyone see the Irish *Blind Date* the other day? It was on RTE 1 before *The Late, Late Show*?" Alan asked, before placing the last crumbly lump of the feta cheese starter into his waiting mouth.

"I saw it," Eugene admitted. "*Strike a Match*, terrible title. Some of the girls were babes, though."

"Remember your one in the red?" Declan asked, nodding his head. "Pure sex on legs."

"What were the men like?" Paula asked with interest.

"Didn't notice," Eugene admitted, soaking up the flavoured olive oil on his plate with a piece of garlic bread.

"Typical!" Hopper laughed.

"They were looking for contestants," Alan mused. "You singletons should give it a go – how about you, Eugene? You'd give them a run for their money."

"The producers or the girls?" Lucy asked, laughing.

"Both," Alan grinned. "You really would be good though, Eugene. Handsome, witty, single, full of one-liners, I think they'd really like you."

"Honestly?" Eugene asked, his chest puffing up like a tropical fish. "I might give it a go, so."

"What about you, Max?" Lucy asked. "Are you game?"

"No, I don't think so."

"Maybe Max won't be single for long," Jenny twittered, beaming at him. She leant over and gently wiped the edge of his mouth with her napkin. "Oil, darling," she said.

37

Max jumped to his feet and began to clear away the plates. "If everyone's finished, I'll start bringing the plates into the kitchen." He picked up some plates and swept out the door.

Lucy followed him down. "What's got into you?" she asked. "You look a little disturbed."

"Disturbed!" Max exclaimed. "I can't believe you thought I'd like Jenny. What was going through your mind?" He put the plates down on the table and folded his arms on his chest. Lucy was standing beside the cooker, having just plunged the ravioli into a large saucepan of boiling water.

"Max, lower your voice. Jenny's lovely. What's wrong?"

"She's so –" Max began, waving his hands in front of him. "I don't know – girlie, I suppose."

"Girlie?"

"You know, girlie – into clothes and make-up and going out. Not real things."

"Like?"

"War," he said, "famine, inflation, the cost of petrol, the euro, books, films –"

"Max! Most people don't want to talk about war or famine over dinner."

"You know what I mean."

"*I* do," Lucy nodded. "You mean she's too flippant and one-dimensional. No one else would though."

"As long as you do, that's all that matters to me."

"Give her a chance. You haven't been talking to her for very long, after all."

"I suppose you're right. Now, what can I do to help?"

Lucy thought for a second. "Fill everyone's glasses up and send Hopper down to me with the rest of the plates. And Max?"

"Yes?"

"Give Jenny a chance."

Max began to sing '*All we are saying, is give Jenny a chance*' over and over to the tune of 'Give Peace a Chance' as he made his way back to the living-room.

38

"Shush, Max, she'll hear you," hissed Lucy.

A few minutes later Hopper came bounding down the stairs with the remainder of the plates.

"Go easy, Hopper," Lucy said. "You'll break my good plates."

"Sorry." She put the plates on the counter top beside the sink. "That was delicious. What's next?"

"You're a human dustbin, Hopper," Lucy laughed. "You should know. You were in the kitchen long enough – ravioli with prosciutto, sun-dried tomatoes, basil and mozzarella. And you can start passing me the plates as the ravioli is just ready."

"Maybe I'd better have a taste, just to make sure."

"Plates!" Lucy said, ignoring her.

Lucy drained the ravioli carefully, curls of steam filling the kitchen. She then spooned the small parcels on to the plates and drizzled each with olive oil. She sprinkled Parmesan shavings and torn basil over the top.

"Will you help me carry these up?"

"At your service," Hopper smiled. She deftly carried three large plates, balancing one on her forearm like a professional. "My early days as a waitress have finally come in handy."

Soon everyone was tucking into their ravioli. Lucy had also prepared a large green salad with honey and mustard-seed dressing which was going down a treat.

"Did you make the ravioli yourself?" Paula asked, cutting one of the delicious parcels in two with the edge of her fork.

"Yes. Max bought me a pasta-making machine last Christmas and there's been no stopping me ever since."

"You clever thing," Jenny said, flicking her long hair back with one perfectly manicured hand. "I wouldn't have the patience, darling."

"Is there any more, Sis?" Eugene asked, running his finger over his dinner plate and licking it.

"There is. Would anyone else like some more before Eugene finishes it all? Alan? Hopper?"

"Please," they replied in unison.

"Jinx, touch wood," Hopper said, tapping the table-top.

"You're so silly, *Sinead*," Paula sniffed at Hopper.

"Sinead?" Jenny asked. "Is that your real name, Hopper?"

"Yes," Hopper admitted, reluctantly. "My friends don't call me that though."

"I think nicknames are childish, myself," Paula said, smiling slyly. "Playground stuff."

"Hold on a minute," Eugene said, gulping back yet another glass of white wine. "Me and me mates all have nicknames."

"I rest my case," Paula said, holding out her empty glass to Alan who was pouring wine like it was going out of fashion. Paula had a habit of getting 'difficult' when she had a mere sniff of alcohol inside her.

"There's nothing childish about me," Derek insisted, in what he hoped was a manly voice.

"Or me," Eugene insisted.

"Your mother has a nickname and there's nothing childish about her either," Hopper said to Paula.

"Really?" Paula asked icily. "What's my mother's nickname?"

"Forget it," Lucy said, trying to smooth over troubled waters.

Hopper wasn't going to let go. "And you have one too, Paula."

The room went silent for a few seconds.

"Who'd like some white chocolate ice cream, with double-chocolate sauce?" Lucy asked, cutting through the silence.

"Go on," Paula insisted, ignoring Lucy. "Tell me, *Sinead*. I'm all ears."

"OK then," Hopper said recklessly. "You're Little Miss Perfect, 'cos you're such a bossy bitch and your mum's Fozzie Bear 'cos she has a facial-hair problem."

Paula gasped. "*How dare you!*" she screamed, jumping to her feet. She ran over to where Hopper was sitting, picked up a glass of red wine and dumped it over Hopper's head. Luckily there were only a few mouthfuls left. Paula raised her arm to slap Hopper.

Alan jumped in just in time. "Paula, outside, now!"

40

"It's that bitch's fault. She should go outside, not me."

"You started it," Hopper spat, wiping the wine off her head and shirt with a napkin.

Alan dragged his protesting girlfriend out by the arm. When the door had closed behind them and Paula's protests could be heard hurtling around the hall, they all looked at each other in amazement.

"I'm sorry," Hopper said to Lucy. "I didn't mean –"

"It's fine," Lucy said, moving the remains of her ravioli around on her plate.

"Is she always that volatile?" Eugene asked.

"Yes," Lucy nodded. "Herself and Hopper don't exactly get along."

"That's the understatement of the year," Hopper grimaced.

"So tell me, Hopper," Jenny said. "I really am very curious. Where did your name come from? Hopper, I mean, not Sinead. If you don't mind me asking?"

"When I was young I used to wear space-hoppers all the time – you know, headbands with wire coming out of them. I had ones with tiny windmills on them and ones with red sparkly love-hearts."

"I remember! My big sister used to have a pair with silver stars on them. They were darling."

"That's where my name came from."

"Mine's from me surname," Eugene interrupted. "You know, White – Blanco."

"And mine's from me name too," Derek said. "Derek – Deco."

"Right," Max grinned. "Thanks for that, lads."

Everyone laughed.

"Do you have a nickname, Jenny?" Lucy asked, pouring a large glass of Merlot for herself.

"My family call me Bambi, because of my big brown eyes." She opened her eyes wide.

"You've lovely eyes," Eugene slurred. "Lovely."

"Why thank you, Blanco," Jenny beamed.

"It's unfortunate that Paula decided to choose this evening to throw a hissy fit," Max said. "But apart from that you must be pleased – everything's going really well. Your brother is in good form." He was watching Lucy scoop ice cream into small glass bowls in the kitchen. He'd offered to help her but there was only one scoop.

"Yes, and he's managed to behave reasonably well so far, thank goodness," she said.

"But the night is still young," Max smiled.

"Thanks, very reassuring. Can you start carrying the bowls up?"

"Ice cream, anyone?" Max asked, walking into the dining room and scanning the table. Paula and Alan were back and Paula still looked livid. Lucy hoped she wouldn't have any more little outbursts.

"Give Paula some," Hopper said. "It might cool her down."

Paula glared at her. Alan put his hand on his girlfriend's arm and whispered something in her ear.

"How about you, Eugene?" Max asked, anxious to take the limelight from Paula and Hopper.

"Have you ever known me to say no, Max?"

"That's a yes, then," Max smiled. "Derek?"

"Please."

Lucy walked in with two more bowls. "Do you want some yourself, Max?"

"Lay it on, girl. You know I love it," Max said in his best Barry White voice. He sat down at the table.

"Max," Jenny giggled, "you're a bad, bad boy."

Max cringed in his seat. He was nervous of Jenny and her roving hands which had wandered onto his thigh on more than one occasion already that evening. He'd have to keep his smart comments to himself.

Lucy served everyone and then sat down.

"I'd like to propose a toast," Hopper said, raising her glass in the air precariously. The red wine sloshed around dangerously in her glass. "To Lucy for the wonderful dinner."

"To Lucy," everyone toasted, raising his or her glass.

"And I'd like to propose a toast myself," Lucy said. "To True Love."

"True what?" Eugene asked.

"Love," Derek hissed in his ear.

"Right," Eugene smiled. His sister was obviously going soft in the head. He joined in the toast. "True Love," he muttered, "and wicked babes."

"Too right, mate," Derek smiled back.

"You have to go ugly early, mate," Eugene told Max, chasing down a handful of peanuts with a long slurp of Bulmer's cider. "That's where you're going wrong."

"He's right, man," Derek nodded sagely. "Chicks like Jenny are out of your league. You need to go for the fat chicks or the ones with glasses."

"Don't listen to them!" Lucy laughed. She was sprawled on the floor beside her brother, her head propped up by his knee. "They don't know what they're talking about."

"Not to mention being sexist little pigs," Hopper said, joining in from the sofa. "That's a terrible thing to say. Besides, Jenny was all over Max earlier, boys – you're just jealous."

"But where is she now?" Eugene asked.

"She had to go home. She has a modelling job in London on Monday and she has an early flight tomorrow," Lucy said.

Before leaving, Jenny had pressed her phone number into Max's hand, kissed him firmly on the lips and whispered, "Ring me, lover boy" in his ear. Max was still recovering.

"I don't think Jenny is really my –" Max began, but no one was really interested in what he was about to say. Eugene and Derek had a well-documented love affair with their own voices.

"I'm telling you, Max," Eugene continued. "You're going for the wrong chicks."

"Would you stop calling us chicks!" Hopper exclaimed. "It's insulting."

"I wasn't calling *you* a chick."

"And what would you call me then, smart-ass?"

"A woman with sensible shoes?"

Hopper hit him over the head with a cushion.

"Hey, that hurt," he protested. "You girls, you're never satisfied."

"What do you mean?" Lucy asked.

"One minute you don't want to be called babes or chicks. And the next minute you're giving out about being called anything else. Make up your minds." He burped loudly.

"Eugene!" Lucy said. "You're disgusting."

"And proud of it. The babes don't seem to mind."

"If you're such a big hit with the babes," Max said, "why are you here tonight and not out on the town, scoring?"

"Now that's an interesting one," Derek smiled lazily. "Basically we need our rest. The babes are tiring us out. This is a lads' night out."

"Right," Max murmured, not believing a word of it. "I see."

"As I was saying, Max," Eugene continued, "there's women out there for the taking. You just have to give them lots of love-vibes." He nodded his head and took a long drag of his cigarette.

"Eugene," Lucy laughed, "where do you get all this? And watch that cigarette ash on the carpet."

They all looked up as Alan came in the door. "Am I missing anything?"

"Where's Lady Muck?" Hopper asked.

"Paula's asleep," Alan said. "She drank enough wine to anaesthetise a large cow."

"Good," she muttered. Lucy glared at her. "Sorry," Hopper mouthed.

"Grab a tinny and join us," Eugene said. "We're just talking about women."

Alan wrinkled his forehead. "And I could probably do with some help."

6

The morning after the dinner party, Lucy rang Max.

"What time is it?" he muttered, cursing her under his breath.

"Nearly one."

Max opened his eyes and looked at the bright red digital numbers flickering on his alarm clock. "It's ten past twelve, Lucy!"

"As I said. Nearly one. So what did you think?"

"About what?" He wasn't in the mood for interrogation, not at this hour of the morning.

"About Jenny."

Max sighed. "I'll ring you back later." He slammed the phone back on the receiver and put his head back on the pillow. The truth was he didn't think much of Jenny at all. But he wasn't in the humour to explain himself. He'd kill Lucy later.

At half past one Max heard loud banging on his door.

"Go away," he yelled from his warm, safe bed. He knew damn well who it was and he wasn't in the mood.

"Come on, Max," Lucy yelled through the door. "I know you're in there. I'll cook you some breakfast. You'll feel better then." She stood on the doorstep for a few minutes, picking at the skin around her nails impatiently. Finally she heard a muffled expletive and a scowling Max opened the door in a white towelling bathrobe.

"Hi, Lucy, how lovely to see you. Do come in." She smiled broadly at Max and pushed past him into the hall.

He rubbed his eyes and glared at her. "I'm going back to bed," he mumbled, turning his back to her.

Lucy grabbed the belt of his robe. "No, you don't. You're coming into the kitchen with me."

Max was too tired to protest. He sighed. "Leave me alone, Lucy. I feel like death." He leant against the wall. "How come you're so chirpy this morning?"

Lucy smiled. "Unlike you, I didn't drink several bottles of wine last night. Not to mention a fair share of Eugene's cider. And a couple of brandies too, if I remember correctly."

Max held his head in his hands. "No wonder I feel so crap. I'll kill Eugene."

"I wouldn't normally say this. But for once it wasn't anything to do with my dear brother. You and Alan stayed up till all hours drinking and talking. I went to bed around three and you were well stuck in – comparing notes on seduction techniques and chat-up lines, if I remember correctly."

"Were we?" Max asked slowly. "How did I get home?"

"Good question. I have no idea. Taxi probably. Now come on." She pointed towards the door at the far end of the hall. "Kitchen, food."

Max's two-bedroom flat, or 'apartment' as he liked to call it, was near the sea-front in Monkstown. On the fourth floor of a modern block, it had commanding views of Dublin Bay if you stood on a chair in the kitchen and looked out over the Victorian rooftops and chimney pots. All the walls were painted off-white, a legacy from the previous tenant, except for the tiny shower-room which was covered from floor to ceiling in garish 70's aubergine-coloured shiny ceramic tiles, with matching shower-pan, sink and toilet.

Max had bought number twenty-seven Monkstown Place on his return from London five years before. And in those five years he had done nothing to the place. The kitchen had come fully equipped with all the 'white things' as Max called them – dishwasher, washer/dryer, cooker. It also had a built-in pine seating unit – two benches which had been salvaged from old church pews and a rectangular matching table.

The white spare room was packed with Max's kiting gear – kites, in and out of their bags, precariously stacked brightly coloured plastic boxes full of rip-stop nylon, glue, whipping cord, duct tape and all kinds of metal loops, screws and pins.

His white bedroom was dominated by the large steel bed which had been custom-made by a friend, 'Spike' O'Driscoll. At each corner of the bed, thin Art Deco posts held the white muslin canopy aloft, which was gathered at the head and held in an attractive steel spiral loop.

Max's books, bank statements, magazines and bills spilled out from tattered cardboard boxes under the bed. His clothes were permanently draped over a chair beside the window and there was always a pile of dirty washing kicked into one of the dusty corners of the room.

The white living-room was small but comfortable with two squashy sofas in midnight blue and an old army chest in front of the gas fire which served as a coffee table. The table was constantly piled high with kiting magazines and in the corner the shelves boasted a shiny black tower of boys' toys – DVD, CD and video players and the associated wires, remote controls and speakers.

Lucy had donated vases, dried flowers, curtains, blinds, cushions and plants over the years in an effort to make the place more homely but it still looked very much the bachelor pad.

Max stumbled into the kitchen, flicked on the lights, winced, decided it was too bright and switched them off again. He climbed clumsily over the wine-rack and sat down on the bench beside the window. He put his arms on the table and rested his head on them slowly and deliberately.

"I'll get you some painkillers," Lucy said, staring at him intently. She went into the bathroom, opened the cabinet over the sink, searched through the ancient hotel toiletries and used disposable razors until she found a box of Solpadeine. In the kitchen she dropped two large white tablets into a glass of water with a plonk and placed it on the table in front of Max. She watched as the effervescent pills bubbled and spat in the liquid.

"There you go," she prodded Max as soon as the tablets had dissolved. "Drink up."

He raised his head, wrinkled his nose and stared at the glass. "I can't," he moaned. "It looks revolting. It'll make me sick. And anyway, you're not supposed to take them on an empty stomach."

"Don't be such a baby. I'll make you some toast. You can drink it after that."

Max thought for a second. "There's some bacon in the fridge, and a packet of sausages."

Lucy laughed. "I thought you were feeling queasy."

Max gave a half-smile. "I'm sure some food would settle my stomach."

After a large cooked breakfast and the painkillers Max was beginning to feel more human. His head had stopped thumping and his hands no longer shook. He ambled off to his bedroom to get dressed, leaving Lucy at the kitchen table flicking through *The Irish Times* which she'd bought on the way over. Her mobile rang in her pocket, belting out the theme tune to *Fraggle Rock* at full volume.

She winced. Must turn down the volume, she thought to herself. She looked at the display screen – Brian, it read.

"Your phone's ringing," Max yelled from his bedroom.

"Thanks," Lucy shouted back. "I hadn't noticed."

"Then answer the bloody thing," Max muttered.

Lucy switched off her phone and stared into space. Brian. She'd have to talk to him, but not now.

"Who was it?" Max walked back into the kitchen dressed in an old pair of jeans and a T-shirt.

"No one really. Would you like some coffee?"

"Brian?" Max raised his eyebrows.

"Yes. I don't really want to talk about it."

"Are you sure?"

"Completely. Let's watch a video. You can choose."

"You got me out of bed to watch a video?"

Lucy shrugged her shoulders. "Sleeping is very antisocial. Dozing on the sofa isn't. I'm doing you a big favour keeping you company."

"You're bats!" Max grinned.

"I know," Lucy smiled. "That's why you love me."

"That has to be one of my top all-time favourite films," Max said, as the end credits of *The Matrix* were rolling.

"Really?" Lucy asked, looking over from the other sofa. They had curled up on one each, covered with fleece blankets, heads bolstered by soft cushions. Lucy, as usual, had the controls. "What are your other favourites, then?" She pulled herself up slightly so that she could see his face. "Give me your top ten."

Max considered for a moment.

"OK, number one would have to be *The Empire Strikes Back*."

"The one with Princess Lea in the gold bikini?"

"Correct. Number two would be *Return of the Jedi*."

"And let me guess, number three is another *Star Wars* film."

"Maybe," Max said thoughtfully. "Although *The Hunt for Red October* is pretty far up there. Along with both the *Toy Story* films, of course."

"With the *Star Wars* films, *Toy Story 1* and *2* and *The Matrix*, that's six," Lucy said. "Four more to go."

"*Men in Black*."

"Seven."

"*The Fifth Element*."

"Eight."

"*The Usual Suspects*."

"Nine."

"And *Lock, Stock and Two Smoking Barrels*. Ten."

"I see," Lucy said. "Interesting."

"What?"

"Nothing," she smiled.

"Come on," he encouraged. "What were you going to say?"

"Just that they're real boy films. That's all."

"Boy films?"

"Yes."

"OK, give me your top ten then, smartass,"

Lucy tapped her lip with her finger. "Let me see. Number one has to be *An Affair to Remember.*"

"Sorry?" Max asked.

"Deborah Kerr and Burt Lancaster. It's the film *Sleepless in Seattle* was based on – it's a classic."

"Right. Sounds scintillating. Any special effects?"

Lucy ignored him. "Number two would be *The African Queen* with Humphrey Bogart and Katherine Hepburn. Another classic."

"You're kidding?"

"No!" Lucy said, insulted. "It's brilliant."

"I suppose you're going to tell me that *The Sound of Music* is number three?"

"No," Lucy smiled, ignoring his sarcasm. "Number four. That reminds me, I have tickets for *Sing-A-Long-A-Sound-of-Music* next week. You're going. It's a charity night in aid of Tallaght Hospital. Mum's selling tickets."

"I am *not* going!"

"You have to go." Lucy smiled. "Mum's expecting you. I've already told her you'll be there. So, tough."

Max groaned. He wasn't in the mood to argue. There was no way on God's earth that he'd allow himself to be dragged along to that. He didn't fancy dressing up as a nun or even a German soldier for that matter and there was no way you'd ever get him singing those ridiculous songs. No way!

"What's number three, so?" he asked, steering the conversation onto safer ground.

"Calamity Jane."

Max looked at her blankly.

"With Doris Day."

Max laughed. "You've got to be joking."

Lucy sniffed. "You know I like musicals."

"I suppose."

"Number four is –"

"Five," Max interrupted. "Four was *The Sound of Music.*"

"Five then. *The Wizard of Oz.*"

"Six?"

"Chitty Chitty Bang Bang."

"Seven?"

"More modern this time, *Steel Magnolias.*"

Max pretended to put his finger down his throat. "Lucy, that's sentimental rubbish!"

"I like it," Lucy said defensively.

"OK, OK. Continue. Number eight."

"When Harry Met Sally."

"Chick flick," Max grinned. "Not the worst though. Nine?"

"Let me see – I know, *Some Like it Hot.*"

"Now that's a good film. Good old Billy Wilder. Excellent choice. And ten?"

"Give me a second." Lucy chewed her lip. "I know! *ET.*"

"You are quite mad, you know that?" His stomach rumbled audibly. "Food time again, I think."

"You can't be serious? You had a huge breakfast."

"I'm a growing boy. Now what are you going to cook for me, slave?"

Lucy threw a cushion at his head.

Lucy pushed closed the heavy blue front door with her shoulder. She could hear the hum of the television coming from the living-room. She walked in. Hopper was curled up on the sofa watching a re-run of *Casualty*, a large, white fleece blanket covering her lower body. She looked up at Lucy.

"Hello, stranger," she smiled, sitting up and moving over so that Lucy could sit down. "Where have you been all day?"

"I was at Max's." Lucy was beginning to feel tired. She rubbed her eyes gently with her knuckles.

"Brian was looking for you. He said your mobile wasn't on." She stared at Lucy. "Is something wrong? You usually spend Saturdays with him."

Lucy sighed deeply. "I couldn't face him today. I wasn't in the mood, to be honest. I just wanted to hang out with Max and do nothing."

"Couldn't you have done that with Brian? What's up? Tell me."

Lucy lay back against the sofa.

Hopper flicked the television off, after having one last lingering look at Patrick, the hunky, troubled doctor. "Can I get you a cup of tea?"

"No, thanks. I'm OK. Can I take a swig of your water, though? I'm a bit dehydrated."

"Sure," Hopper smiled, passing her the bottle of emergency Ballygowan that was lodged between herself and the cushion at her side. "It was digging into me anyway."

Lucy took a long drink and handed it back. It was a bit warm but she was so thirsty she didn't mind. "Thanks."

They sat in silence for a few minutes while Lucy collected her thoughts. Hopper knew better than to rush Lucy. She was tempted to switch *Casualty* back on. She tried not to stare at the blank screen and focused her attention on Lucy instead.

"I don't love Brian any more," Lucy admitted finally. "In fact, at the moment he's really getting on my nerves. It's not his fault really. He's a nice guy – we're not right together, that's all."

Hopper put her arm around Lucy. "I'm sorry. I had no idea."

"How would you?"

"What are you going to do?"

"The only thing I can do. Break up with him. And the sooner the better. Just not today – I don't think I'd be able for it."

"He's calling around later," Hopper warned her. "Or so he said."

Lucy groaned. "If he does, tell him I'm out."

"I can't do that. Where will I say you are?"

"Say there's been a family emergency and that I'll ring him tomorrow. Please?" She looked at Hopper beseechingly. "I'll be your best friend?"

"Oh, all right. But don't make a habit of it. I'm not very good at lying."

"Says who?"

"Thanks a lot."

"Only joking. Now put *Casualty* back on, I know you're dying to."

"Sorry, Brian, she's not in," Hopper faltered.

Brian shifted uncomfortably on the doorstep. "Can I come in and wait for her?"

"There's been some sort of family crisis and I don't know what time she'll be back."

"Is everything OK?" Brian asked with concern.

"Yes, I think so. You know the Whites – Eugene's probably dinged Eileen's car again or something." She attempted a smile. Eugene's escapades in his mother's Ford Fiesta were legendary at this stage. Hopper didn't know how Mrs White put up with him. So far she'd lost the rear-view mirror, the passenger door didn't open as the handle was missing, and both doors had distinct hollows in them from various parking and reversing 'manoeuvres'.

"You're probably right."

"She said she'd ring you in the morning," Hopper said brightly.

"Thanks. See you." He shrugged his shoulders up and pulled his coat around him.

Hopper watched his lone figure walk down the road. She felt sorry for him really. As Lucy said, it wasn't his fault.

"So?" Lucy asked as Hopper came back into the living-room. "What did he say?"

"Nothing much. Ring him in the morning, OK? I feel bad about lying to him."

"I will. I promise. I'm going to bed now. I'm knackered. I never asked. Where's Alan?"

"Out with Paula," Hopper said glumly.

"Don't worry. She won't last much longer."

"You think? You haven't seen her underwear collection."

"And you have?"

"Don't ask."

The following morning Lucy opened her eyes and listened to the wind outside which was gently whistling through the trees. Excellent – kite-flying weather, she thought to herself. I'll give Max a ring. Then she remembered that she had to ring Brian. She lay in bed for a while thinking about what she was going to say to him. The truth would be the obvious choice but Lucy feared that Brian would need a real, concrete reason, not – 'It doesn't feel right'. She sighed. Besides, he kept telling her to 'talk' to him and it was getting annoying. She was better off without him. Boyfriends were just hassle.

The phone rang downstairs. She glanced at the clock on her dressing-table. Eleven o'clock. Early for anyone to ring on a Sunday morning.

"Lucy," Hopper's voice shouted from the hall, "it's your Mum. Lucy, are you awake?"

"Coming!" Lucy got up, pulled on her robe and opened the door. She made her way downstairs and smiled at Hopper. "Thanks," she said as she took the receiver from her.

"Hi, Mum."

"Hi, love. Did I wake you up?"

"No. It's fine, Mum. I was just getting up."

"What are you doing today?" Eileen asked. "Eugene's coming over for lunch. There's something I wanted to tell you both."

"Sounds interesting," Lucy said.

"It involves a little boy called Aran," Eileen said cryptically.

"That's not fair," Lucy complained. "You know I'll have to come over now."

Eileen smiled. She knew her daughter had all the curiosity of a very large moggy.

"See you at around one, Lucy," Eileen laughed.

Hopper was still standing in the hall when Lucy replaced the receiver.

"Ring Brian," she said, glaring at Lucy.

"I'll just have some —"

"Now!" Hopper folded her arms over her chest.

"OK, OK," Lucy muttered, dialling the familiar number. She sat down on the bottom stair and waited for her soon-to-be ex-boyfriend to answer.

7

"Who's Aran?" Lucy asked as soon as she'd stepped in the door of her mum's Dun Laoghaire home. She removed her fleece jacket and threw it on the chair in the hall.

"Hang your jacket up," Eileen insisted.

Lucy smiled. "Yes, Mum." She tried to ignore the fact that Eugene's jacket was draped over the back of the chair or that his bag had been unceremoniously dumped on the floor at the bottom of the stairs. Irish mothers and their sons – she'd had a lifetime of it!

She'd always wondered what Eugene carried in his large, black 'record-bag' as he liked to call it. One day curiosity had got the better of her and she'd opened it while he was eating in her kitchen. She'd found a tinted spot-cover stick, some Lynx deodorant, hair gel, two videos, several CDs, a Discman, a packet of John Player Blue and an old copy of *Hot Press*.

Lucy followed Eileen into the kitchen. Delicious smells were wafting from the oven. Eugene was sitting at the kitchen table, murdering a bacon sandwich.

He mumbled a 'howaya' at her before burying his head in *NME* magazine which was lying open in front of him.

56

"Very sociable." Lucy ruffled her brother's hair.

"Watch the hair, Sis," he said, pieces of bread and rasher clearly visible in his open mouth.

"Eugene! Don't talk with your mouth full."

"Now, Lucy," Eileen chided. "Leave your brother alone."

"What's for lunch?" Lucy asked. "Smells great."

"Roast chicken with lemon and garlic. And roast potatoes."

Lucy sat down at the table, trying to ignore her brother's chomping. "Lovely. Now, tell me about Aran before I burst."

Eileen smiled broadly. "OK, I'll put you out of your misery. Eugene, are you listening?"

"Ug." He took a gulp of tea and swallowed the food. "Of course, Ma." He smiled like butter wouldn't melt in his mouth.

"You know I've been working for the Eastern Health Board?" Eileen said.

Lucy nodded. Eileen was a health nurse, visiting new mothers in the Dun Laoghaire district and helping in the Mother and Baby clinic.

"And you know I applied to be a foster-parent?" Lucy and Eugene nodded. "I was accepted. A boy called Aran and his little sister, Jade, will be staying here from next week on."

"That was quick," Lucy said. It was less than a month since herself and Eugene had met and been 'interviewed' by the social worker.

"Cool!" Eugene said.

"Where will they be sleeping?" Lucy asked.

"In your room and Eugene's room," Eileen said.

Lucy stared at her Mum for a few seconds. "What about my things?"

"What things?" Eileen asked in confusion. She thought Lucy had taken everything to Sandymount when she'd moved out.

"My dolls and my books."

"I thought they could stay in the room," Eileen said gently. "Jade's never had a bedroom to herself and from what I can see she's never had toys or books of her own."

"There's a box of Action Man figures and some Transformers in the attic," Eugene interrupted in excitement. "Do you think Aran would like them? What age is he?"

"He's seven and Jade's five," Eileen said, "and I'm sure he'd love them."

"Deadly," Eugene said. "I'll get them down after lunch."

"Lucy?" Eileen put her arm around her daughter's shoulders. "What's wrong?"

She felt, well, she wasn't sure how she felt exactly. But she was happy for her mum. "It's a lovely thing to do." She pulled her mouth into a smile. "And you'll be a great mum – you already are a great mum. I know we've talked about it and everything – it's just a lot to take in, that's all."

"I know, love. But it'll be fine, I promise."

"Mum?" Eugene asked grinning. "Are you not a bit old for all this?"

"No, I'm not!" Eileen exclaimed. "I'm in my prime. And if I can cope with you, Eugene, I can cope with any seven-year-old."

"Thanks a lot."

"How long will they be here for?" Lucy asked.

"I'm not sure," Eileen admitted. "It's short-term fostering. But I'd say a couple of weeks at least. Their mum has just had another baby. She's young and on her own and she just can't cope with the three of them."

"Poor woman," Lucy said.

"Poor girl, really," Eileen said. "She's only twenty-two."

"Jeeze," Eugene whistled. "Almost my age and three kids already!"

"How does it work?" Lucy asked. "Is she allowed to visit?"

"They'll go to see her every week," Eileen explained, "and the social worker will decide when she's strong enough to look after them again."

"It must be terrible having your kids taken away from you," Eugene said.

Eileen nodded. "Yes, it must. And hard on the children too. They haven't done anything wrong."

"Can we come over and meet Aran and Jade next weekend?" Lucy asked.

"Of course," Eileen said. "I'd love you to."

"How's your mum?" Max asked Lucy that evening. He'd rung Sandymount earlier and Hopper had told him where she was.

"Great," Lucy said. "She's going to be fostering two kids soon and she's very excited about it."

"Kids? At her age?"

Lucy laughed. "That's exactly what Eugene said. But she's a nurse after all, and brilliant with children. I think she'll do a great job."

"I'm sure you're right. I know you mentioned it before, but I didn't realise it would all happen so fast."

"Tell me about it. It's been quite a day. And I broke up with Brian this morning. He called over and we talked."

"I'm sorry, Lucy," Max said kindly. "He was a decent guy, even if he was a bit boring." He thought for a second. "He wasn't very dynamic at all, come to think of it. You need someone with a bit more life. Anyway, how are you about it?"

"Relieved, to tell the truth," Lucy sighed. "I feel bad. But he'll get over it." She decided not to tell Max everything that Brian had said. He didn't need to know. Not really. And besides, Brian was wrong and she didn't want to think about his stupid 'theory' again.

"You did the right thing," Max assured her. "Don't worry about it. I'll take you out next weekend, OK?"

A smile came to Lucy's face. "Do you promise? I'm very upset, after all."

"Sure, anywhere. You can choose."

"Absolutely anywhere."

"Yes."

"Right then," Lucy laughed. "*Sing-A-Long-A-Sound-A-Music* in town on Friday night!"

He groaned. He'd walked right into that one. "I'm not sure –"

"I'm not taking no for an answer, Max. It'll be a laugh. I've persuaded Alan to come and Hopper will be there too. And it'll be full of girls."

His ears pricked up. "Girls?"

"You're like that old one in *Father Ted*," Lucy laughed. "And anyway, what about Jenny?"

"What about her?"

"She gave you her number. Are you not going to ring her?"

"No," Max replied firmly. "No way!"

"I'm sure he'll ring you," Lucy told Jenny later that evening over the phone. "You know what boys are like – they have their stupid unwritten code that they can't ring before Wednesday. I'm sure they talk about it in the toilets. *'No way, man. You can't ring until Thursday. You'll be letting the side down.'*"

Jenny giggled. "I'm sure you're right. I could always call into his office and say hi."

"I'm not sure if –" Lucy stalled.

"That's a great idea. I'll call in to him tomorrow. It's in Monkstown, isn't it? I can say I was in the area."

"I don't know if he'd –"

"What's the address?"

Lucy gave in. "It's 3 Crofton Mews, Monkstown. You need to take the second left after the church and drive down Crofton Road and it's tucked in beside the grassy area."

"Thanks, Lucy. You're a pal."

Lucy put down the phone. Max is going to kill me, she thought to herself.

8

Daria raised her arms above her head and stretched her back. She'd been stooped over all morning painting 'grass' on to a huge sheet of canvas and her neck and shoulders were killing her. She wiped her hands on her denim dungarees and thrust the brush with its green-tinted bristles into a jar of white spirit which was sitting on the old wooden table, along with pots of paint in various shades of green.

She'd worked all weekend and had now almost finished the *Mary Poppins* set. The lighting director was due in that afternoon and Daria was taking the rest of the day off. As soon as the grass had dried, she could add some fake flowers and, once the kites were ready, that was it.

Daria smiled as she thought of Max. Maybe she'd call in and see if he'd finished. It couldn't hurt. She quite fancied a trip on the DART. And maybe they could go for coffee.

She cleaned the paint off her hands in the bathroom and changed into a clean pair of black trousers. She pulled a brush through her hair and grabbed her jacket. Daria was dying to get out of the theatre. She hadn't seen daylight since Friday.

"I'm off now," she called to Trish, the set designer, who was standing on the stage.

"See you tomorrow," Trish smiled. "You've done a great job with the grass. Thanks!"

"No problem. See you tomorrow."

She walked down Dame Street, and thanked her lucky stars that she wasn't sitting in a car. The lights were slow and the vehicles didn't seem to be moving and there were many irate beeps of the horn. She nipped across the traffic and in no time was sitting on the DART and whipping along the rails to Monkstown. It was a lovely, bright, fresh day and looking out the window she decided to take a walk along the beach after her visit.

The train pulled into the station and Daria hopped off and bounded up the metal steps. There was a strong wind blowing and she pulled a white and blue fleece hat out of her small red-leather rucksack and pulled it on. She sauntered up Crofton Road smiling to herself.

"Hi, Max," she said, entering the loft and making her way towards the crouched-over figure.

Max raised his head and smiled. "Hi. This is a surprise. Nice to see you. I'm just finishing off your last kite. Another ten minutes and it'll be ready."

"'It'? Are kites not 'shes', like boats?"

Max stood up. "Na," he grinned. "Definitely 'its'."

Daria laughed. "I was on my way to the beach for a walk, so I thought I'd drop in."

"I'm glad you did," Max interrupted, noticing her slight hesitancy. Was it embarrassment? He'd thought about Daria several times over the weekend and was delighted to see her again. "Did you say the beach?" He cocked his head. He shouldn't but to hell with it.

Daria nodded.

"It just so happens it's perfect kite-flying weather," he said. "I was going to take a couple of hours off this afternoon to test my new baby." He pointed to a large black and purple rectangle which hung over the sewing-machine. "Would you like some company? Maybe you'd like to try flying it too."

"I could give it a go. But haven't flown one since I was a child."

"About time you got back into it then, young lady. You don't know what you've been missing."

He walked over to his desk, wrote 'Back Later' in large black capitals on a piece of cardboard and taped it to the door of the loft. Daria watched as he picked up the kite, rolled it up and put it in a long black bag, along with some long, black sticks, two padded purple and green handles and two plastic rectangles with thin, white string wound around them. He also picked up another, smaller orange bag.

"Can you hold these for a sec?" He handed her both bags which were surprisingly light and pulled a light-grey fleece over his head. "Thanks," he smiled as he took the bags back from her.

"Are you not working this afternoon, yourself?" he asked as they walked down the road.

"No. I was in the theatre all weekend finishing up the set. So I've taken the rest of the day off."

"Good call," Max said. "Can I ask you a personal question?"

Daria hesitated for a second. "I guess so."

"No," Max grinned. "It's nothing bad. I was just wondering where your name came from, that's all. Daria, it's pretty unusual."

"My real name is Doris, Doris Delahunty. But when I was younger *Fame* came out – remember the film and the television series?"

Max nodded.

"Well," she continued, "there was a Doris in that and she was kind of ditzy. The kids in school in Boston used to tease me and call me 'Dopey Doris' so much I got sick of it. So when we moved to Dublin I changed my name from Doris to Daria. It sounded, I don't know, more glamorous, I suppose. And I've been Daria ever since. It's quite a good stage name, too. People tend to remember it."

"Stage name? Are you an actress too?"

"An actor," Daria corrected him. "I'd like to be. If I can get the work. It's not looking all that good at the moment. I've been auditioning for the lead part in *Emma*, but I'm not sure if I'll get it."

"*Emma*. Jane Austen?"

"That's right. They're putting a version of it on in The Gate."

"When will you hear?" he asked. "About the audition, I mean."

"This week sometime."

"Good luck, so," he smiled warmly. "I hope you get it."

"Thanks, so do I."

They crossed over the bridge to the beach. It was low tide and the beach was dry enough to walk on without getting squidgy feet. There were, however, small pools and streams which had to be avoided. Luckily, they both had boots on.

"I'll put the stunt kite together first," Max said. "Once that's flying I'll do the other one." He smiled and plunged his hand into one of the bags. "Would you mind holding these?" He handed her two plastic handles. He then transformed the bright orange cloth from the bag into a stiff triangle with the insertion of two thin struts into material loops at the edges of the kite.

"Now you need to hand me the ends of both lines," he explained. "They're the ones with the metal rings on them."

Daria unwound some of the string carefully and tiny gold loops fell out and dangled towards the ground, spinning in little circles and catching the light. "Here you are," she said, handing him both ends.

She watched as Max expertly attached the lines to the kite with slip-knots. "This is the bridle." He showed Daria the piece of line which was attached the kite. "If you hold a kite by the bridle and it balances, that's how you know it'll fly. See?" He demonstrated. "And where the line meets the bridle is called the towing-point."

Daria nodded and bit her lip. She wasn't sure she understood what he was saying but she watched, taking everything in carefully.

Max noticed her uncertainty and grinned. "Don't worry. You'll pick it up as you go along." He started to walk backwards away from her. "Now hold onto the lines and let them out, OK?"

Daria unwound the lines as instructed. "What are these lines made of?" she shouted to Max. "They seem very strong."

"No kidding! They're Laser Pro Spectra line, pound for pound stronger than steel."

"Right!" She suddenly realised that Max had stopped and that she

64

had the controls. "Max," she shouted anxiously. "Are you coming back to fly this thing?"

"No. I'm launching it. All you have to do is keep your hands level. Don't pull on one side more than the other. Then I'll run back and give you a flying lesson."

"OK," Daria shouted, trying to sound more confident than she felt. "I'll give it a try."

"Good woman! Here we go." He threw the kite up into the air and the wind caught it immediately, making it soar up into the blue sky. Daria concentrated. She could feel the tug on the lines and strove to keep her hands level. The next thing she knew Max was standing behind her. He placed his hands on hers firmly.

"Now if you pull this side, gently, gently, good, see what happens?" The kite swooped to the right in one fast and smooth movement. "Now move it back again, see?" The kite moved back towards the left. "And you can make it do loop-the-loops," he showed her how to make the sharp movements which sent the kite spinning in circles, "and dives."

Daria gasped. "That's amazing. It's so responsive."

Max smiled and removed his hands. "Now you try on your own."

Daria took a deep breath and focused her attention on the kite. She made it spin, dive and swoop for several minutes, before burying its nose with a sudden crunch in the damp sand.

"Damn, I crashed. Will the kite be all right?"

Max laughed. "I didn't want to say it while you were concentrating, but you're pretty good. It's quite normal to crash. But you really had it before that. You just pulled a little hard on the right control, that's all."

"But the kite —" Daria faltered.

"Don't worry." He ran towards the fluttering orange triangle. "It's well used to it. It'll be fine," he yelled, pulling the kite out of the sand and shaking it energetically to get rid of the dark sludgy yellow grains. "Ready?"

"Yes!"

He threw the kite back into the air and it swooped towards the sun once more.

"I'll leave you to it," he said, looking in the other kite-bag which he'd left on the sand beside her. He pulled out the larger kite, placed it gently on the sand, rolled the cover up and shoved it into the pocket at the front of his fleece. He put it together carefully, testing each seam as he went along. This would be the first time MaxPro 9 would be in the air and he wanted to get it right. Especially with an audience, and such a pretty one at that.

Max walked backwards, letting out the kite-lines in either hand. And while he walked, slowly and smoothly, he thought about Daria. Because later, he decided, he was going to ask her out for dinner.

He prayed he hadn't been misreading the signals. Maybe she was just interested in his kites and not in him. But there was something about the way she smiled at him that made him hopeful. And Lucy was right: it was about time he took matters into his own hands. Miss Right wasn't going to drop from the heavens into his lap. Not today anyway.

Max stopped, turned to check on Daria for a moment and once satisfied that she was fine gave an almighty tug on the kite's lines in either hand and launched the MaxPro high into the air. He watched with delight as it took hold of the wind, soaring powerfully along and making strong whooshing noises as it swooped in and out of the air currents.

The pull on his arms was intense but satisfying. Of all kites, Max loved parafoils the best. They exercised your body and your heart, he liked to say. It was a very physical experience, pulling a powerful yet skittish kite from side to side in the wind and he excelled at it. Flying kites, he felt in total control.

Marie, his ex, hadn't much liked kites. In fact she wasn't an outdoors type at all, which had caused a lot of problems in their relationship. Her idea of the best way to spend a fine, dry afternoon was to hit Grafton Street, weaving her way in and out of all her favourite shops – from Brown Thomas and Pia Bang, to Next and

Oasis. Eventually, after nearly two years, they'd gone their separate ways. Max had heard that she'd recently become engaged to a Prada-wearing mobile-phone guru. He was happy for her but a little jealous too. Max didn't want to marry her himself, but he could have been more gracious about it if he was contentedly 'coupled' himself instead of being still single.

"That's amazing, Max," he heard Daria's voice to his right. He looked over and smiled. He could see she was genuinely impressed. She was following his MaxPro with her eyes, transfixed by its manoeuvres.

"Pull the stunt kite in and you can have a go," Max said.

"How do I do that?"

"Pull in the lines, the same amount on both sides, until the kite comes down out of the sky."

"But what if –" Daria began.

"Don't worry if it crashes again."

A few minutes later, after successfully managing to pull her own kite in, only grounding it at the very end, she was standing by his side.

"Stand behind me and put your hands on mine," Max instructed.

Daria wrapped her arms around his firm, fleecy back and her hands made contact with his. She could feel warmth emanating from his hands and moving deliciously into hers. She inhaled his manly, fresh smell distractedly.

"Daria?"

"Sorry. Did you say something? I couldn't hear, the wind –"

"I'm going to adjust my hands now and the kite will move from side to side. It's the same theory as the stunt kite but much more physical."

"No kidding," Daria laughed, as their bodies moved together. She could feel the strain in his hands and arms. "I'm not sure I could do it on my own. I'm not as strong as you."

"Rubbish. You'll be well able. My friend, Lucy can fly two of these stacked together."

Daria was doubtful.

"Slip your hands into these loops and fix them around your wrists,"

Max said. Instead of plastic holders, this kite had padded canvas loops to control the lines with.

Daria fixed them around her wrists. Already she could feel the pull on her arms.

"I'm taking my hands out now, OK?" Max asked.

"I think so." As soon as Max stood away she was pulled forward by the kite's lines. "Shit!" she exclaimed. The kite flew in front of her and she watched it carefully. She was pulled forward another few steps but she managed to keep her balance.

"The MaxPro 12 would literally pull you off your feet," Max yelled from behind her. "It's almost twice the size. I can only fly it in moderate winds."

"I'm glad you didn't bring it then," Daria shouted back. "This one's bad enough."

"You're doing great! Try moving it from side to side."

Daria pulled gently on her right hand. The kite soared right, with a dramatic whooshing sound. "Wow! That's amazing." She levelled her hands before pulling on the left-hand side.

"You're doing really well," Max shouted. He watched her face as she studied the black and purple sky-borne rectangle. Her eyes were dancing in the light and she was frowning with concentration.

Suddenly she fell in a heap on the damp sand with a whack and the kite crashed dramatically to the ground.

"Daria!" Max ran towards her. "Are you all right?"

Daria was doubled up with laughter. "It pulled me off my feet, little devil." She stood up and slapped the sand from her rear with her hands. "I've got a wet bum. But apart from that I'll live."

"A gust must have caught you."

She shrugged her shoulders. "That kite has some pull!" she said. "I'm not really able for it."

Without thinking, he began to rub her shoulders gently through her fleece.

"Mumm, that's lovely," she said, rolling her head.

Max decided to seize the moment. "I was wondering if —"

But just then her mobile phone began to ring and she pulled her rucksack off her back and scrambled for it.

"Sorry," she mouthed to Max, putting her phone to her ear. "Hi, Owen. Yes, that sounds great. When? Yes, that's fine. OK, OK, see you then. Thanks." She put her phone away, clapped her hands together and bit her lip. "That was Owen. He wants to talk to me tomorrow about *Emma*." She noticed a questioning look on Max's face. "Owen Hughes is the director."

"Do you have the part?"

Daria's eyes sparkled. "I hope so. God, Max, I hope so."

"That's brilliant," Max said. "We'll have to go for a drink now to celebrate."

"I'm sorry," Daria said, checking her watch, "I have to meet my sister at six, I'll have to run. I didn't realise how late it was."

"Some other time, then."

"What?" Daria asked absently. She was thinking about meeting Owen the following day and what clothes to wear – should she go casual, or dressy, or arty?

"Nothing," Max said quietly. "I'll walk you to your car."

"I wish I had one. I got the train."

"To the train, so."

They packed away the kites together. Max wanted to ask her out for drinks or dinner or something, but decided he'd wait. She sounded busy what with the play and everything. There was no hurry, after all.

As they walked towards the DART station Daria hoped that Max would ask her out. She'd had a lovely afternoon and they'd seemed to get on. Maybe she'd read the signals wrong. But she didn't want to scare him off by coming on too strong and asking him out, not when she wasn't 100% sure.

"Thanks for a great afternoon," she said as they reached the station. "I really enjoyed it." She leaned over and kissed him on the cheek.

Max blushed. "Not at all. We should do it again sometime."

"I'd like that," Daria said. She bit the inside of her mouth, almost drawing blood. Ask me out, she willed Max, ask me out.

"Bye," Max said. "Hope you get the part. I'll courier the kite over tomorrow."

"Thanks. That would be great."

Sitting on the train, she could feel the windburn tingling her cheeks. She gazed at the beach out the window, watching the sea reclaim the sand in wet streams. Soon the tide would be fully in.

"What are you smiling at?" Mossy asked as Max walked through the door of the loft, a large grin plastered on his face.

"Nothing." He was damned if he was going to tell Mossy.

"A chick called in looking for you," Mossy drawled. "Nice-looking. Stayed for a coffee."

Max stared at him in amazement. There was only one 'chick' in his life at the moment, unfortunately, and a platonic one at that. He couldn't believe that Mossy had forgotten Lucy's name already. Or that Lucy had accepted a cup of coffee from him. She said she hated Mossy's lily-livered guts.

"Lucy," Max stated in disgust. "Her name is Lucy."

"Na, not Lucy," Mossy said lazily. "Jenny." He pulled a crumpled piece of paper from the back pocket of his jeans. "Here."

"Jenny? Let me see that." He grabbed the paper from Mossy's hand. "Hey!"

"086 8169933. Ring me, Mossy!" he read aloud. The 0's and the o in Mossy were drawn in the shape of love-hearts. Max cringed. "Why did Jenny give you her number? She was looking for me."

"Hey, don't get heavy, man. She was flirting with me," Mossy said defensively, "asking to feel my muscles and fluttering the old eyelashes like nobody's business. Didn't seem too concerned that you weren't here, to tell the truth." Mossy scratched his balls through his jeans. "So I asked her for her number."

"You can't go around stealing women from under my nose. It's not right."

70

"Settle your tights, man. You can keep that," he nodded at the paper. "You ring her."

"I have no intention of ringing Jenny," Max muttered, handing back the paper. "It's the principle of the thing."

"Good. I'll ring her then. Katia's away and I could do with a little action."

"Who's Katia?" He thought Mossy's latest was called Anka.

"Anka's mother. Anka went back to Sweden to finish her Masters. Her mum was a bit lonely so –"

Max put his hands over his ears, "I don't want to know!" He stomped towards the far end of the loft. "I'm finishing this kite, then I'm heading home. Keep out of my face."

"Get laid, man! I'm sick of your bad attitude. I'm sure Lucy would put out if –"

"Leave Lucy out of this," Max glared ominously.

"Only trying to help," Mossy mumbled before picking up a roll of blue sailcloth. "Give us a hand cutting this, will you?"

Max grunted and shook his head.

"Come on, man," Mossy pleaded, cocking his head, "a bit of co-operation, you know."

Max sighed. There was no point being annoyed with Mossy. He had absolutely no scruples and behaving morally was anathema to him.

"Stay away from my friends, especially the female ones," Max said, realising the futility of his plea.

"Sure," Mossy nodded, "sure." Won't be hard, Mossy thought to himself. They weren't exactly banging down Max's door. "Where'd ya find that Jenny chick? She's fine."

"Hand me the knife," Max snapped, ignoring his question.

Lucy stared at Lea Maxwell's pores through the large, brightly lit magnifying glass. She placed a mirror in front of the glass. "Now, look at your forehead and around your nose, Lea. Blackheads, loads of them."

"Yuck!" The teenager started to bring her hand towards her face before Lucy slapped it down.

71

"Do you want to make them worse? Your skin must be kept scrupulously clean. Keep your dirty hands away from it. And go easy on the sweets and chocolate."

"But Mummy says —"

"I don't care what your mother says. I'm the professional here and not your mother." She tried not to sneer when she said 'mother', but Mrs Maxwell was one of the most annoying clients she had. Rita Maxwell liked to think of herself as a 'Lady Who Lunched'. And lunch she did, and dinner, and breakfast, and brunch. She barely fitted any of her gaudy 'designer' clothes and her heavy gold jewellery hung in swaddles around her sagging, over sun-bedded neck. Rita was now sitting in the waiting-room, smoking her lungs black with More menthol cigarettes, although Lucy had told her time and time again that it was giving her pronounced wrinkles around her mouth and making her skin lose elasticity with every puff.

Lea was almost as bad. She was swiftly following in her mother's footsteps to the top of the most annoying clients' poll. The spoilt seventeen-year-old was the apple of her mother's eye.

The strange thing was, the more direct and just plain rude Lucy was about the Maxwells' skin and bodies, the more they seemed to respect her. They were suckers for punishment. And now she couldn't seem to get rid of them. She'd tried pawning them off on Paula, who fawned over them like they were royalty, but they always came back to her. Like bad pennies.

And if they weren't Max's mother and sister she would have told them both where to stick their cellulite and stretch marks many moons ago.

Because Max, as he liked to call himself, was really Sitric Maxwell, son of Rita Maxwell and brother of Lea Maxwell. And although he despaired of his socialite mother and bratty sister, he still liked to have some contact with them. But not direct contact. God forbid. He left that for Christmas, birthdays and Mother's Day. He saw his dad on a regular basis, for lunch or drinks after work, usually in Eric Maxwell's favourite haven – The Merrion Square Gentlemen's Club – where he hid away from his wife and daughter.

72

Lucy acted as a sort of secret agent, squirrelling away information on Rita and Lea that she thought Max might find interesting. And she reciprocated with news about Max, largely fabricated, to keep Rita happy.

Lea, on the other hand, had no interest in her brother as he wasn't 'cool' or even 'rich'. At least when he'd been in London he'd been a bit rich and Lea could lie to her Loreto schoolmates about his 'affair' with Tara Palmer-Tomkinson. And his warehouse apartment. And his collection of Habitat leather furniture. In Dublin, making kites and having no social life from what she could ascertain, he was of little or no use to her at all.

"Right, it's a face mask for you," Lucy said grimly, "followed by a strict cleansing regime. And are those milia I see?" She tut-tutted.

"What are milia?" Lea asked anxiously.

"Whiteheads. Extraction, I think."

Lea winced.

"Don't be such a baby. It won't hurt," Lucy smiled sardonically. "Wait till I pluck your eyebrows for the Debs, then you'll know what pain is. Who are you bringing anyway?"

Lea sniffed. "I'm not sure yet. I've a load of choices, I just have to pick one, that's all."

"I see." She had a feeling that Lea hadn't anyone to bring and, remembering her own better-forgotten Debs, she decided not to push the issue. "Well, there's plenty of time." Lea might be a pain in the rear but she was still Max's sister after all.

"Yeah," Lea replied gratefully.

Lucy put down the magnifying glass and mirror and handed Lea a thick white towelling headband. "Put this on. I'm going to use a fuller's earth and witch-hazel face mask to draw out the imperfections. It may feel a little cold when I first put it on." She mixed up the powder and liquid in a small plastic bowl and stirred it with a wooden spatula. "Keep your eyes closed and relax. You'll need to keep it on for fifteen minutes." She began to slather the mud-like mixture onto Lea's skin with her fingers.

73

"It's cold," Lea complained.

"I did warn you. Now, keep still."

Once she had Lea's face covered, except for the areas around her eyes and mouth, she left the room. "I'll be back in fifteen minutes. Keep still and try not to move your face or the mask will crack."

"OK."

Lucy closed the door behind Lea and breathed a deep sigh of relief. Just enough time for a quick phone call. She wanted to check on Hopper, who was working as a face-painter at a posh Foxrock children's party that afternoon.

"How's my baby?" Rita asked, stubbing out her cigarette in the earth of the Swiss cheese plant to her right.

Lucy winced. Poor plant. "Fine," she snapped.

"Good. She so wants to look her best for the Loreto Debs." Rita looked around her and lowered her voice. "I'm afraid she seems to be a little short of a partner though. What with all the studying for her Leaving Cert."

Lucy tried not to laugh. From what she could see, Lea did the bare minimum in the line of school work. If she spent as much time on French and history as she spent on painting her nails she'd be an A1 student.

"Anyway," Rita continued, "I was wondering if Max might have any suitable friends tucked away. Not too old, mind, mid-twenties at tops, I think. Someone professional, a lawyer perhaps or one of those computer men that are doing so well these days."

"I'm not sure –" Lucy began.

"You know my son so well. I'm sure between yourself and Max you could find someone suitable for my princess."

Lucy groaned inwardly. How was she going to get herself out of this one? "I'll talk to Max about it," she said half-heartedly. "I'm not promising anything, though. We don't know very many *suitable* single men." She saw a way out now and bolted for it. "In fact, they're all very unsuitable. The only one I know is my brother and he's practically a drug addict."

Rita looked shocked. "A drug addict! Does my Max know him?"

Lucy back-pedalled furiously. "No, not really. And Eugene isn't a drug addict. He's a student. I was only joking." She attempted a laugh.

Rita did not look amused. She raised her eyebrows. "Really, Lucy. It's not the kind of thing one jokes about. Drug addiction is a serious matter. We had a Ladies' Lunch for a Rehab Centre only the other week."

As far as Lucy could see, Rita and her cronies had 'Ladies' Lunches' for anything that moved or didn't move, so it was only a matter of time until drug addiction was the beneficiary of some of their collective husbands' hard-earned money.

Lucy didn't know how Eric Maxwell, an architect, was still solvent with Rita and Lea's legendary spending ability.

"I must remove Lea's face mask," Lucy said, dying to get away from Rita, and seeing her chance of using her mobile without being overheard by eager ears dashed.

"Don't forget about the Debs," Rita trilled after her. "Suitable ones only, of course."

"What was Mum on about?" Lea asked as Lucy opened the door of the cubicle.

"Sorry?" Lucy bluffed. "I didn't hear anything."

"You must have," Lea scowled, cracking the hardened mask on her forehead and around her mouth. "She said something about the Debs."

"Oh, that. She was just asking me to talk to you about suitable make-up, that's all."

"But it's ages away," Lea said suspiciously.

"That's what I told her," Lucy said, running the hot tap and soaking some fresh white face towels in hot water. "I'm going to remove the mask now with warm towels, OK?"

"That didn't seem like fifteen minutes. I was just getting into that Enya music."

"It's not Enya, it's 'Flute Tunes from the Brazilian Rain Forest'." She glanced at her watch. Lea was right, she'd only been out of the room for less than five minutes. But she had to get away from Rita. "I'll leave it on for a few more minutes while I prepare the towels."

"But I thought you said –"

"I must insist you keep quiet. I don't want to hear another word." She mixed a little more paste and lathered it around Lea's mouth and on her forehead. "Don't move either. I'm going to put cotton wool soaked in cucumber water on your eyelids to reduce the puffiness."

She did this and sat back, pulling a copy of *Hello* magazine from the cupboard under the sink. Twenty minutes later, when she'd read all about Madonna's latest look, she replaced the magazine and pulled the cotton pads from Lea's eyes.

"How long was that?" Lea asked, her mouth constricted by the thick, dried paste. "It felt like forever."

"Exactly ten minutes," Lucy lied. "Perfect timing."

When the Maxwell women had finally left, Lucy rang Hopper. She could hear high-pitched screams and an adult yelling in the background – "Darling, let go of India's pigtails immediately!"

"Hi, Lucy," Hopper said in a loud voice.

"Hopper!" Lucy bellowed back, forgetting it wasn't herself in the war-zone and nearly bursting her friend's eardrum in the process. She continued, lowering her voice,

"Are you all right?"

"Just about. Hang on a second." The noise gradually subsided. "That's better," she said finally. "I've locked myself in the loo. This is a nightmare!"

"I did warn you. I've done a few parties myself and they're no joke."

"I should have listened to you. They don't need a face-painter, they need a multi-functioning robot. If I have to do one more 'princess' or Britney face I'll scream. The parents are the worst. They're just standing around watching me being mauled by their precious offspring and ignoring it."

"At least it pays well," Lucy pointed out. Hopper had recently left Making Faces to go out on her own, specialising in film, television and stage make-up, including special effects. She did a mean car-crash victim, werewolf, or alien, as Lucy had found out playing guinea pig. But decent freelance work was hard to come by at the moment, so Hopper had to take what she could get until she became more established. Children's parties included.

"My mantra all day has been 'think of the money, think of the money'," Hopper said. "I feel like your man in Jerry Maguire – *show me the money.*"

Lucy heard a loud banging noise and a muffled voice in the background.

"Shit," Hopper muttered, "it's one of the Foxrock Fannies looking for me. I'd better go."

"See you later," Lucy smiled. Right at this moment she wouldn't be in Hopper's moccasins for all the world.

9

"Morning, early bird," Grace said, walking into the kitchen to grab a cup of coffee before leaving for work. "How long have you been up?"

"A while," Daria said. "I need to get myself organised for the audition this afternoon."

Grace gave her a hug. "Try not to worry. I'm sure you'll be brilliant. Just what they're looking for."

"Thanks." Yesterday she'd been confident of it herself, but today she wasn't so sure. She stood beside the kettle, watching it boil. She needed at least an hour to go over her lines.

"What time is the audition at?"

"Two. I'm getting my nails done this morning."

"Again?" Grace raised her eyebrows. It wasn't like Daria to be so concerned with her talons. If anything, she herself was the health and beauty fanatic in the family. Thermal strawberry face masks were her current weakness, along with Borie self-adhesive pore-cleaning strips that ripped the blackheads out of your nose. Grace loved inspecting the used strips under a bright light, delighting in the tiny dark specks of air-dried blocked sebum and poking them with her index finger. She always washed her hands thoroughly afterwards, of course.

"It brought me luck last time. Do you want coffee?"

"Yes, please."

Walking up Monkstown Road two hours later, Daria tried not to think about Max, but failed miserably. Maybe she'd find out more about him later. After all, it was the manicurist who'd first put them in contact – Lucy. Daria had asked for her by name when she'd made her booking. There was no point leaving these things to fate, she'd decided. You had to help destiny along now and then.

Lucy whistled as she walked to work. She was in better humour today than she'd been in for ages. Life without Brian was suiting her. She hadn't shaved her legs since Sunday which she was finding deliciously liberating. And she'd stayed in last night watching television with Hopper, Alan and Max without feeling an ounce of guilt.

Hopper had fallen fast asleep on the sofa at eight and was shortly afterwards tucked up in bed, lifted and cajoled there by the other three. Before passing out she'd made everyone promise to never, ever allow her to face-paint at a children's party again. Not if it paid a million pounds an hour.

Lucy reached Making Faces in record time and let herself in. Paula looked up from the reservations book and scowled.

"Morning, Paula," Lucy smiled. "Lovely day."

"Mumm," Paula muttered, her lips pursed. She picked up a white envelope and pulled out a bright red lipstick-stained More cigarette butt. "I found *this* in the pot plant."

Trust Paula to try and ruin her morning. "I don't smoke, Paula," she said evenly. She knew exactly whose offending butt it was and it certainly wasn't hers.

"It must be one of your friends then," Paula sniffed, holding the butt in her heavily lacquered fingernails.

"If you must know, it belongs to Rita Maxwell. I meant to remove it when she'd left but I forgot."

"I see," Paula said haughtily, knowing she was in the wrong. "Next time, don't forget. It's stinking the place out."

79

Lucy wasn't in the mood to argue. "Yes, fine." She pulled her mouth into a thin smile. "What's this morning looking like?"

"You have Missy Slater at ten for a wedding make-up practice and head and neck massage, Daria Delahunty at half eleven for a manicure, Cynthia Grahame at one for a full-leg wax, Tara Shiels at two for a pedicure, and Orla Nolan at three for a manicure and a pedicure.

Lucy looked over Paula's shoulder and noticed that Paula had given herself Pat Baker, RTE newsreader and local 'celeb', Mona Curry, TD's wife and all-round pain in the ass, and Elena Sugar, ex-model and former Dublin Rose. Typical!

But, to be honest, she preferred the 'normal' clients – they were far less demanding and easier to deal with, even if they didn't have quite the same so-called social standing or regular slots on the back pages of *Image* or *IT* magazines.

Lucy opened the door at ten to an anxious-looking Missy Slater. The young woman had lost weight and her face was pale. Lucy's heart went out to her. The wedding was next week and the last time she'd visited Lucy in Making Faces things hadn't exactly been going to plan. The florist had double-booked, the caterers had upped their already high prices at the last minute, and one of the bridesmaids had broken her ankle falling up the steps of a club on Leeson Street the night of Missy's hen. Lucy wasn't exactly sure how you fell up steps but she presumed the fall had been alcohol-fuelled.

"I'm so glad to see you," Missy tried to smile. "I don't think I could cope with Paula today. I'm too tired."

Lucy smiled. It was nice to be appreciated. "Let me hang up your jacket and I'll be out to you in one minute. Here." She handed her the latest copy of *Irish Bride* magazine. Missy sat down obediently and began to thumb through the pages.

"Right," Lucy said when Missy was sitting in the spacious cubicle a few minutes later. "Massage and practice make-up, is that right?"

Missy nodded silently.

"And how are the plans? Or should I ask?" Lucy said, washing her hands in the small white sink.

"Everything's finished now, touch wood," Missy said, reaching out and touching a wooden spatula. "Dad talked to the caterers and they agreed to compromise, the best man's mum is doing the flowers and Lauren's ankle is coming out of plaster the day before the wedding. The doctor said if it's strapped up tightly she can walk up and down the aisle but she'll have to keep the weight off it for the rest of the day."

"It's lucky you had your hen night early," Lucy smiled.

"You're telling me."

"I'm going to start the massage now. Can you remove your top?" She handed Missy a clean white towel. "Put this around your chest to keep you warm. "I'm going to cleanse your face and neck first." After cleansing Missy's face Lucy squeezed a blob of massage cream on her palms and began to slowly and gently massage the tense neck and face muscles.

"Try to relax, Missy. Clear your mind of any thoughts. Concentrate on how your head and neck are feeling and on the sensations of my hands."

She made calming criss-cross movements over the temples, followed by rhythmic circles and feather-light upward strokes. Missy melted under the experienced fingers. At the end of the massage she was practically asleep.

"Sit and relax. I'm going to cleanse your face and neck again and then apply the foundation. Before we start I'd like some idea of the type of make-up you'd like."

"Well," Missy began doubtfully, "I'm not really sure. What would you suggest?"

"You have lovely skin. How about a natural look, with lots of browns and tawny pinks? A touch of blusher and eyeshadow, nothing too heavy. What colour is your bouquet?"

"Pink. Pink tea-roses."

"And your dress? Ivory, white – ?"

"White. Empire-line."

"Sounds lovely." She wiped Missy's skin with cotton wool soaked in

81

cleanser. "I'm using a peach-toned foundation," she explained as she dotted the liquid onto Missy's cheeks, chin and forehead. She blended it carefully with a sponge and set it with translucent powder. Blusher and eyeshadow came next, followed by eyeliner, mascara, lipliner and lipstick.

When she had finished, she held a large round mirror in front of Missy's face.

"I don't know what to say," Missy whispered. "I look –"

"Beautiful." Lucy smiled. "You look beautiful."

Large tears began to form in Missy's eyes. Lucy offered her a tissue.

"My mascara –"

"Don't worry. It's waterproof. I always make my brides tear-proof."

"Hello again," Lucy smiled, letting her next client in the door. "Daria, isn't it?"

"That's right."

"Come right in." Lucy showed her into the cubicle. "Can I take your jacket?"

"Thanks."

"How's the painting going?" she asked when Daria was sitting down. She began to stroke each nail with cotton wool soaked in nail-polish remover.

"Fine. But I'm actually hoping to get a part soon. I have an audition later on today."

"You're an actor?" Lucy asked.

Daria nodded.

"Is the audition for *Mary Poppins?*"

Daria laughed. "No thank goodness, but well remembered. I was only working on the set for that. It's for *Emma*."

"I love *Emma*," she said, placing Daria's right hand in a bowl of warm water. "We read it in school. And the film was brilliant. It's one of my favourites. Good luck, anyway. If you get the part I'll definitely go and see it."

"You could bring Max," Daria said, regretting it the minute his name left her mouth.

"Max? I'm not sure theatre is quite his thing really."

"He mentioned that he liked *Emma* when he delivered my kites, that's all," Daria faltered. "I'm sure you're right. They were great – the kites, I mean."

"Good." She placed Daria's left hand in the bowl and began to push back the right-hand cuticles with an orange stick wrapped in cotton wool.

"How do you know Max?" Daria asked. "Is it through the kites?"

Lucy considered Daria carefully. She seemed very interested in Max. Maybe she'd set them up. She didn't think they'd be all that suited though. Still, she could always give it a go. Nothing ventured, nothing gained. Jenny hadn't exactly worked out after all – Max hadn't said anything about her calling into his office so she obviously hadn't bothered after all.

"We've been friends for years," Lucy said. "We were in playschool together and national school. We're practically related."

"You're lucky to have such an old friend. When we were in Boston we moved around a lot and it was difficult to keep friendships going. And when we moved to Ireland we had to start all over again."

"Do you have any brothers or sisters?" Lucy asked, working on the cuticles of the left hand.

"One younger sister, Grace."

"Do you get on?" She'd always wondered what it must be like to have a sister.

"Yes," Daria nodded, "very well. We live together."

"You're lucky. I have a younger brother and he's a disaster area."

"Boys, they're all the same!"

Lucy laughed. "No kidding! You must come over for dinner sometime. I think you'd get on brilliantly with my friend, Hopper."

"That would be nice," Daria said, not thinking for a moment that she meant it.

"How about Sunday evening?" Lucy suggested. "Bring your sister too."

"Are you sure?" Daria asked, a little startled. "I wouldn't want to put you to any trouble –"

"Not at all," Lucy smiled. "I love cooking, honestly. It'll be fun."

"Well?" Grace asked that evening, walking into the kitchen. "Did you get the part?"

Daria looked up from the carbonara sauce which she was stirring gently on the hob.

"Not exactly."

Grace sat down at the kitchen table. "Go on, tell me."

"Rosaleen O'Grady is going to be Emma. Owen said that the producers wanted a 'name' to play the lead part. He said that I was his first choice but he was outvoted."

"I'm sorry. I know how much you wanted it."

Daria attempted a smile. "Thanks. The good news is that I *am* playing Mrs Elton and I'm to be Rosaleen's understudy."

Grace jumped up and gave her sister a warm hug. "That's brilliant, well done! Now who's Mrs Elton?"

"She's married to the clergyman, Mr Elton, and she's an annoying snob and busybody. A real character part."

"Sounds like fun. I can't wait to see it. When does it open?"

"In eight weeks' time. There are rehearsals practically every day until then, not to mention costume-fittings and photo calls."

"Sounds busy."

"To be honest, I'm looking forward to it. My first 'real' part for a long time."

"But you'd have made a great Mary Poppins," Grace smiled. "I could have brought my class to see you."

"That's what I was afraid of. From the sounds of things they're completely wild."

"You're not far wrong," Grace giggled. "Wayne Matthews will be the death of me. Wait till I tell you what he did today . . ."

Daria rubbed her eyes. She'd been reading her copy of *Emma* for the last two hours and she was beginning to feel sleepy. She put her biro into the book to mark the page and placed it on her bedside table. She clicked off her reading-light and laid her head on the pillow. It had been a long day.

She was disappointed about not playing Emma, but at least she was the understudy. And maybe Rosaleen would fall over and twist her ankle at one of her 'luvvie' parties or something. She was well known for her partying. Daria didn't want any real harm to come to the woman, but a sprained ankle wouldn't hurt her too much.

She had a few days to finish up the *Mary Poppins* set and then she was straight into rehearsals on Monday.

Maybe things were finally going her way. Max had couriered over the kite today, as promised, which was disappointing. She was hoping he'd ring or even call into the Olympia himself.

She lay in bed, trying to think of a good excuse to ring him again but failed miserably. They didn't exactly need any kites for *Emma*, that was for sure. Maybe she could find out more from Lucy on Sunday night. It was strange really – being invited to dinner by your beautician – but Grace seemed keen, so she'd rung Lucy earlier to confirm.

10

"What's up?" Lucy asked Max. He was standing on her doorstep looking very dejected.

"Nothing," he muttered, walking inside.

"You can tell me over dinner," Lucy said, ignoring him. She was too busy for one of his moods. "First we have to plan our costumes for Friday night."

Max stared at her suspiciously. "You asked me over for dinner. You never said anything about costumes."

"Oops, I must have forgotten. Silly me." She pushed him into the living-room.

"Where are the others?" He was hoping for a quick 'manly' chat with Alan about cars or soccer or something.

"Hopper's working, some UCD drama thing one of her brothers is involved with, and Alan's at Paula's."

Max flopped down on the sofa.

"Careful!" Lucy said, pulling brown material from behind his back. "That's your costume."

"I'm not wearing a costume. No way."

"I'm sorry. You have to." Lucy smiled deviously. "It's compulsory. Everyone has to."

"What are you wearing?"

"I'm going as edelweiss."

"What's that when it's at home?"

"You know, edelweiss – the flower. I'm wearing green trousers, a green top, Hopper's painting my face yellow and I'm making petals with white tissue paper and wire for my head."

"You're nuts. You'll look stupid."

"Who cares?" Lucy was nonchalant. "It'll be a laugh. Mum's going as the Mother Superior."

"Unbelievable. Fucking unbelievable."

"Right, that's it. What's wrong?" This was obviously more than just a bad mood.

"Nothing! When's dinner?"

"You're not having dinner until you tell me what's up," Lucy insisted. She sat down on the sofa beside him and put her arm around him.

He shrugged her arm away.

"Max," she said gently, "tell me."

Max sighed. He wasn't going to win. He was useless at hiding his feelings. And besides, he really did want to tell Lucy.

"Jenny and Mossy among other things," he said finally.

"What about Jenny and Mossy?"

"I walked in on them today."

"Walked in on them?" Lucy said. "What are you talking about?"

"I was at the post office and when I came back I caught the two of them going at it on top of some of my pink rip-stop nylon."

Lucy suppressed a giggle. "Are you sure?"

"I've seen Mossy's naked ass so many times at this stage that, yes, I'm sure."

Lucy couldn't help herself. So Jenny had called into the loft after all – and met Mossy. She laughed.

"It's not funny," Max complained. "She was supposed to be into me, not him."

87

Lucy smiled. "She was, Max. But you weren't interested in her, were you? You never rang her."

"I know," Max frowned, "but that's not the point."

"What is the point?"

"I'm not sure. But they shouldn't have been at it on my nylon."

"I see. Let's eat."

Sitting at the kitchen table, Max munched on garlic bread while Lucy dressed the chicken Caesar salad.

"That girl was in again yesterday," she said, putting the plates on the table, "Daria."

"Really?"

"She was asking about you."

"What did you tell her?" Max asked suspiciously. Lucy wasn't exactly the most discreet of people.

"Just how we'd been friends since birth," Lucy smiled, "nothing bad, honestly."

"Better not have," Max murmured, loading his fork with chicken and lettuce and swiping it in the rich, creamy anchovy sauce.

"She's very nice. I might ask her over for dinner to meet you. What do you think?"

Max stiffened. He really liked Daria but he was afraid that Lucy's matchmaking might put her off. Lucy wasn't exactly subtle at the best of times. "She's not really my type, to be honest. Nice girl, though. I'd prefer if you didn't."

"Right," Lucy sniffed. Her plans for Sunday night were going out the window. But after Jenny she didn't really have a leg to stand on.

"You could always ask her over for dinner anyway, without me," Max said without thinking.

This sounded more hopeful. "I already have – Sunday night. I'm sure you'll have changed your mind by then."

After dinner, as Lucy made the coffee, Max cursed himself. How could he ask Daria out now without telling Lucy about everything? It was all getting a little confusing. And what if Daria told Lucy about their afternoon spent together? His head hurt just thinking about it. He'd better tell Lucy everything right now and ask her advice.

"Try not to think about Mossy's ass too much," Lucy smiled, handing him a mug of coffee.

"I wasn't. Anyway, you're a fine one to talk. I'm sure you've seen it yourself on several occasions."

"That's all in the past. I wouldn't mind seeing it again though," she grinned. "It's quite a sight."

"What's quite a sight?" Hopper asked, walking into the kitchen. They hadn't heard her come in.

"You don't need to know," Lucy assured her.

Later that evening Max stood glaring at Hopper and Lucy. He was wearing a large brown robe which trailed down to his feet. "I look ridiculous."

"It'll be black when I've dyed it," Lucy said, cutting a large rectangle out of a white sheet. She put the material over Max's head and placed a piece of white card around his face. "This will be your wimple. It'll be perfect."

"You'll be a babe-magnet," Hopper assured him. "Women love nuns."

"Are you joking?" Max said in disgust. "I'll look ridiculous."

"No, you won't," Lucy assured him. "Anyway, everyone'll be dressed up."

"Are you going, Hopper?"

"Yup," Hopper smiled, "and Alan. Paula's busy though. She's washing her highlights or something. I don't think Lucy really sold her on the idea."

"It's not really her thing," Lucy smiled angelically. She'd told Paula it was a charity choral evening in aid of the Austrian nuns.

"I would've thought she'd be well into dressing up as a nun though," Max smiled. "I can just see her in a tiny black leather number with black fishnets."

"It's not 'nuns and tarts'," Hopper sniffed. "I'm delighted she's not going."

"I know you are," Lucy grinned. "I wonder why."

"What do you mean?" Hopper asked, feigning innocence.

Max looked from Hopper to Lucy. "What are you talking about?"

"Nothing," Hopper said, staring frostily at Lucy. "Nothing at all."

"Take that off," Lucy said to Max. "I'll dye it tonight in the washing machine."

Max pulled the costume over his head and handed it to her. "Where did you get that anyway?" he asked, pointing at the brown robe.

"It's Eugene's," she explained. "He was Friar Tuck in *Robin Hood* in a school play a few years ago – with a lot of padding."

"Would he not mind you dyeing it?" Max asked hopefully. "Maybe you should ask him."

"Blanco?" Lucy snorted. "He wouldn't even notice."

"What are you wearing?" Max asked Hopper.

"I'm going as a mountain."

"A mountain?"

"You know – a green thing with grass and flowers on it," Hopper said helpfully.

"I know what a mountain is," Max said. "I'm just not sure how you dress up as one, that's all."

"You'll see," Hopper beamed. "Roll on tomorrow night."

Max never did get a chance to talk to Lucy about Daria.

Des, the taxi driver, got quite a fright when he collected Lucy, Max, Alan and Hopper on Friday night. Lucy's face was painted yellow and she had large, droopy white tissue petals framing her face, which had to be removed before she got into the back of the Volvo.

"Are you a daisy, love?" Des asked.

"No," Lucy smiled. "I'm edelweiss."

"Right," Des said thoughtfully. He looked at Hopper in amazement, cocking his head to one side. She was covered in a cone of fake grass, which had been dotted here and there with white flowers. "A teletubby?"

"No," Hopper replied, her green face grinning.

"Christmas tree?"

"No."

"I give up."

"She's a mountain," Alan laughed, "and I'm a mountain climber." He was wearing jeans, a fleece, hiking-boots and a woolly hat and was carrying a coiled rope over his left shoulder.

"I'm not sure if that mountain is going to fit in my taxi, but we'll give it a go. Is it a hen night or something?" he asked, looking at the suspiciously tall nun.

"We're off to the Olympia," Max explained. "To *Sing-a-Long-a Sound of Music*."

"Ah," Des grinned, "Julie Andrews. I love Julie Andrews." He burst into a rendition of 'Somewhere Over the Rainbow' while bundling Hopper's excess 'grass' into the front of the taxi. No one dared point out that Judy Garland sang that particular song – taxis were as rare as blue steak on Friday nights.

"Let's have a sing song," Lucy said as they passed Lawnsdowne Road. "How about 'Doh a Deer'?"

"Good idea!" Hopper beamed. Everyone groaned.

Lucy began 'Doh a Deer' and everyone joined in, including Des. As they reached St Stephen's Green they were launching into 'Climb Every Mountain'.

"I wish I was joining you," Des sighed as they got out of the taxi.

Alan had to help Hopper whose fake grass had stuck to the vinyl front seat. "Have a great night. It's back to the roads for me."

"Thanks," Lucy smiled, handing him some euro notes. "Keep the change."

"Cheers. Don't do anything I wouldn't do."

As they walked into the foyer of the Gaiety Theatre Lucy spotted her mother standing at the top of the steps.

"Hi, Mum," she yelled, making her way through the hordes. The others followed her. The foyer was filled with people in all kinds of get-ups. There was another mountain – a white, snow-covered one this time, lots of Marias and Baronesses, a troop of scary-looking Nazis leaning against the banisters and a group of rather large Von Trapp children, including several 'girls' in pigtails with bright pink cheeks and hideous dresses made of flowery curtain material.

"Lucy," Eileen shouted over the crowds, waving her arms enthusiastically. "I'll meet you in the reception upstairs." She pointed to the right-hand staircase.

"OK," Lucy smiled back, leading her gang towards the stairs.

The Tallaght Hospital reception was in the main bar beside the dress circle.

"There's a table over there," Alan said, nodding towards the elevated area opposite the bar.

"Excellent!" Hopper said. "I'm bloody boiling."

They sat down at the table and Lucy and Max went to the bar to collect the drinks.

"This is going to be so much fun," Lucy beamed at Max.

Max scratched the back of his neck. "This wimple is killing me," he complained. "It's worse than wearing a tie."

"Stop moaning. You look great."

"You said everyone would be dressed up," he picked up two glasses of red wine. "There's a couple over there who aren't."

Lucy ignored him and walked back towards Hopper and Alan.

"Hi, Lucy," she was interrupted by a woman who had a large cardboard box around her midriff, "it's me, Hilda."

"Hi, Hilda. Sorry, I didn't recognise you." Hilda Rowan was the Matron in Tallaght Hospital and a great friend of her mum's. "What are you?"

"I'm a brown-paper package tied up with string."

Lucy laughed. "Of course! You look brilliant. The nun is Max, a friend of mine."

"Hi, Max," Hilda smiled. "You're the one who makes the kites."

"That's right," Max said.

"Eileen's told me all about you," Hilda said. "And this is Dan, my son." A tall man wearing a black fleece, a wild, red and blue Jester-style hat, dark glasses and snow boots appeared beside her.

"Here's your drink, Mum." Dan handed Hilda a glass of white wine and nodded at Max and Lucy.

"Nice to meet you both," he said.

"You must be hot," Max sympathised.

"Yes," but at least this way no one can recognise me."

"Good point. I should have thought of that myself."

"But you make a great nun," Hilda grinned.

"Hi, guys," Eileen said, joining them. "You all look brilliant. Have you met Lucy and Max, Dan?"

"Yes, thanks," he smiled and removed his glasses, hooking them into his fleece.

"You might like to sit with them," Eileen continued, "unless you want to join me and your mother and some of the nursing staff."

Max's ears pricked up. "Nurses?"

Dan laughed. "A man after my own heart."

Hilda smiled. "It's mainly the staff nurses, I'm afraid, boys," she said, "and most of them are married. Sorry to disappoint you."

"Sit with us," Lucy said firmly, noticing Dan's rather gorgeous brown eyes. "I insist."

"That's settled, then," Max said, getting impatient to drink some free wine. "I'd better bring Hopper and Alan's drinks over."

Dan joined him.

"What age is your son?" Lucy asked trying to sound casual, after the two men had left.

Hilda smiled. "He's thirty."

"He's a chef," Eileen chipped in, delighted that Lucy had taken an interest in her friend's son. "Lucy loves cooking," she explained to Hilda.

"A chef," Lucy mused. "Where does he work?"

"He used to work at Tully's," Hilda said, "on Leeson Street. But he's just started his own catering company."

"I'd better go and make sure he's all right," Lucy smiled. She was going to find out all about Dan Rowan before the end of the night.

"Here," Eileen handed her five small white plastic bags. "Don't forget your Magic Moments bags."

"I can't believe you don't like Jamie Oliver," Lucy said, continuing her conversation with Dan from the bar. She took her seat in the Dress Circle between him and Max. Alan and Hopper sat directly behind the three of them. "He's brilliant!"

"I just think it's all been done before, by less good-looking blokes," Dan explained. "The only reason he was so popular was because he was cute. It had nothing to do with his food."

"Stop talking about him in the past tense," Lucy said. "You'd think the poor man had popped his clogs. He's still really popular."

Dan said nothing.

"And anyway, you're so wrong. Have you ever made any of his recipes?"

"No, but I've seen him on the telly."

"You don't know what you're talking about then, do you? Typical man, all mouth."

"That's a bit harsh," Dan said. "There's no need to get so defensive."

Suddenly the theatre was filled with the sound of James Brown's 'I Feel Good'.

"Hey, people," boomed a voice, "I'm the other James Brown." A tall, willowy man danced onto the stage. "Welcome to *The Sound of Music*." The camp host put his hands on his hips. "Are you ready to yodel?"

"Yes!" Lucy, Hopper, Alan, Dan and the rest of the packed audience yelled back.

Lucy dug Max in the ribs. "Join in," she hissed.

"Are you ready to boo the Baroness and hiss the Nazis?" James Brown asked.

"Yes!" everyone, including Max this time, shouted.

"First of all we're going to have a choral warm-up and then I'll award prizes for the best costumes," the host smiled. "Does everyone have their Magic Moments bag?"

"Yes!"

"Have a look inside – the bag I mean, missis," he joked, pointing at the front row. "Leave that poor Nazi alone. In the bag are cards to use during the 'Maria' song. Let me explain. There's a picture of the lovely Maria on the first card, a big question mark on the next – that's your 'how', and a little ghost on the last one – now who can tell me what that is?"

"Caspar, the friendly ghost," someone yelled.

"A will-o'-the-wisp," someone else suggested.

"Correct!" James Brown said. "A will-o'-the-wisp. And you also have the word 'flibbertigibbet' on the yellow card. And for the clown you need to hold your nose like this," he demonstrated, "and honk."

"Now for the other props. During the thunderstorm Maria will need a lot of help." He sighed. "The poor girl can't think how to make the kiddies' clothes so you have to yell 'use the curtains!' to her and wave the piece of fabric. No expense spared with that fabric, ladies, the best Hickey's had. I can see some of you were in Hickey's yourselves. Nice costumes. Oh, that's not a costume, missis, sorry."

"That's all a bit complicated," Max muttered.

Lucy glared at him.

"And finally," James Brown concluded, "edelweiss to wave during the song, an invite to 'The Captain's Ball', and a party popper to pull when Maria and the Captain finally kiss. Now could everyone who dressed up and would like a prize come down to the front."

"Come on," Hopper jumped up and dragged Alan by the arm. "Is anyone else coming?"

"Go on," Dan smiled at Lucy. "You should enter."

"No way!" Lucy exclaimed, looking at the stage. "There's your mum though." Sure enough, Hilda was climbing onto the stage, helped by an usher. She was followed by Eileen.

"Sisters are doing it for themselves," James Brown quipped as he saw Eileen, "and what's your name, my love?"

"Sister Orgasma, of the Tallaght Little Sisters of Mercy."

James Brown laughed. "Good on you, Sister. Join the other nuns please. And here's a green goat, I think," he said pointing at Hopper.

"I'm a mountain."

"Oh, sorry," he giggled, "it's all the hairy green bits."

"That's grass."

"Now line up, boys and girls, and I'll point to each of you. Now, audience, when I'm pointing at your favourite costume I want you to cheer, OK?"

"Yes!"

"Here goes," he said, walking along the row made up of the mountain (Hopper), the mountain climber (Alan), various Von Trapp children, nuns, kittens, mittens, Marias, Barons, Baronesses and Nazis. When he came to Hopper, Lucy, Dan and Max yelled as loudly as they could.

"The winner has to be the hairy-goat-mountain," James Brown yelled, "and here's your prize, a bottle of vodka. Don't drink it all at once, love."

"Thanks," Hopper grinned.

When she got back to the others, Hopper was still smiling. The audience were in the middle of a practice round of 'Doh a Deer'.

"Well done!" Lucy said.

"Good on you," Max said, interrupting his singing. He found to his surprise that he knew all the words of 'Doh a Deer' as they'd been made to sing it once at their Primary School prize-giving.

"Now let the fun begin," James Brown said. "And remember, boys and girls, you are the sound in *The Sound of Music*, so sing it loud and sing it proud."

The opening music began and soon they were all singing along with Maria to 'The Sound of Music', even Max. Lucy had forgotten what a strong tenor voice he had. He was actually very good. And Dan wasn't bad either. They were drowning out her own feeble attempts.

Alan and Hopper were in high spirits, literally – swigging shamelessly from the vodka bottle before handing it around.

Dan and Max put their arms around Lucy during 'Edelweiss' and they all swayed to the music, holding their fake flowers in the air, like lighters at a U2 concert.

96

"This is deadly," Max whispered to her, after barking enthusiastically (as instructed by James Brown) at Rolf, the Nazi postman.

"I knew you'd like it!" Lucy said, dead chuffed.

"Your man's nice," Max said lowering his voice and gesturing towards Dan.

"Humm," Lucy murmured. It was a pity he'd been so rude about Jamie Oliver though. Honestly, the cheek of him!

When it was all over and the final credits were rolling, Lucy fell back into her seat, exhausted. Alan and Hopper had disappeared.

"Where are the other two?" Lucy asked Max.

"They've gone home. I think they had one slug of vodka too many. Hopper wasn't feeling too well."

"That leaves me and you," Lucy smiled.

"And Dan." Max winked.

Lucy frowned at him.

"So did you enjoy that?" Dan asked, oblivious to Max's grin.

"It was great!" Lucy said. "I'm knackered from all the singing."

"Would you like to get something to eat?"

Lucy looked at her watch. "I don't think so, thanks," she said. "It's late. We'd better get home."

"Do you two live together?"

"God no," Max smiled. "Nothing like that. We're old friends. I'm in Monkstown and Lucy lives in Sandymount."

"I'm the opposite way, I'm afraid, in Clontarf."

Lucy stood up. "Des said we could ring him if we needed a cab," she said, pulling her mobile out of her pocket. Thank goodness for decent taxi men, Lucy thought to herself.

Sitting in the taxi after saying their goodbyes to Dan, Max turned towards Lucy.

"That was a bit rude."

"What?"

"We could have gone for a drink or something with Dan – it wouldn't have hurt."

"I'm tired. I didn't feel like it."

"He seemed like a nice bloke, that's all."

"You're a dark horse sometimes, Sitric Maxwell, do you know that?" Lucy said, swiftly changing the subject. "You sang your little heart out."

"I know," Max murmured, his eyelids getting heavy and his head dropping gently onto her shoulder.

Lucy smiled. It had been a great evening. She wondered if she'd ever see Dan again? She cursed herself. Max was right. They should have gone for a drink with him. She hated when Max was right.

11

"Did you have fun last night, love? I didn't see you afterwards."

"Yes thanks, Mum, it was brilliant. Did you hear Max singing?"

"Sure did, we were only a few rows in front of you. Wasn't he great?" Eileen laughed. "He seemed to enjoy it anyway."

"How much money did you raise?"

"Nearly ten thousand euro. The hospital is delighted."

"Well done!"

"Thanks for looking after Dan. I think he would have been a bit bored with us oldies."

"He's a nice guy. It was no trouble," Lucy said.

"Are you still OK to come over this afternoon?"

"Of course. Will Eugene be around?"

"I'm not sure. He said he'd be here for lunch, but you know Eugene."

Only too well, Lucy thought. "I'm sure he'll turn up, Mum. I'll see you around three, is that OK?"

"Perfect. See you later."

Lucy put down the phone and sat on the stairs in the hall for a few minutes thinking about her new 'brother' and 'sister'. Her thoughts were interrupted when she heard Alan's door open. Looking up the stairs, Lucy saw Hopper tiptoeing out.

"Hopper," Lucy said, "what were you doing in Alan's room?"

Hopper started. "Lucy, you gave me a fright."

Lucy patted the step beside her. "Come here," she said kindly. She looked at Hopper's sleepy but grinning face. "Did you spend the night with Alan?"

Hopper sat down. "Yes. And I feel really bad. I know I'm not a big fan of Paula's but –"

"It'll be fine," Lucy smiled gently, "you'll see. You were made for each other, yourself and Alan. It was only a matter of time. It's great."

"I guess so. But it was my fault."

"It doesn't really matter whose fault it was at the end of the day. What's going to happen now?"

"I'm not sure. We didn't really have a chance to talk about it."

"Oh, really?" Lucy smiled and raised her eyebrows.

"Stop smiling like that," Hopper said.

"What's he like in bed?" Lucy asked wickedly. "Go on, tell me."

"You're so nosy."

"I'd tell *you*."

Hopper laughed. "That's true. You told me absolutely everything about yourself and Brian's sex life, or lack of sex life, I should say. Whether I wanted to hear about it or not."

"Exactly! You owe me some juicy details."

Hopper knew she wasn't going to get out of this one easily. "Let's just say Alan would get an A in biology, OK?"

"A *big* A?"

"That's it. I'm not telling you one more thing."

"That's not fair," Lucy protested. "How many times did you do it? Go on, tell me."

"No! Stop!"

"OK," Lucy said reluctantly. She'd wait until later, when Hopper was more vulnerable.

"What are you up to today?" Hopper asked.

"I'm going over to Mum's to meet Jade and Aran. Should be interesting."

"That's a Japanese curse: *May you live in interesting times.*"

"Thanks," Lucy said. "Very reassuring."

"Hi, love," Eileen said, opening the door and giving her daughter a kiss on the cheek.

"Are they here yet?" Lucy asked quietly.

Eileen nodded. "They're in the sitting-room."

"Can I go on in?"

"Yes, of course."

Lucy and Eileen walked into the sitting-room where a small blonde girl was clinging to an older boy. Beside them was Agnes, the social worker who had talked to herself and Eugene previously about the fostering.

"Hello again," Agnes said, standing up and shaking Lucy's hand warmly. "I'm here today to help Aran and Jade settle in. They'll be staying the night and moving in properly on Monday for a little while." She turned towards the children. "This is Lucy, Eileen's daughter." The boy nodded. The girl noticed this and nodded too. "And this is Aran and Jade." Lucy smiled nervously at the two children who were huddled together on the sofa beside Agnes.

"I'll just go and make the tea," Eileen said, closing the door behind her.

Lucy sat down and smiled at the children again. There was a bedraggled-looking panda bear on the girl's knee. "Hi, Jade. I used to have a panda just like that called Spotty. What's your panda's name?"

"It's a she," Aran said quietly, answering for his sister. "And her name's 'Bear'." Aran was small and thin, with dark hair and intense, brown eyes.

"That's nice," Lucy said. "What's *your* favourite toy?"

Aran was silent for a minute. "Don't really have many toys," he said finally. "I have these though." He pulled some Harry Potter, Digimon

101

and Pokemon cards out of his pocket. They looked well-used. "I have more too, at home. These are my favourite ones."

"Can I see?" she asked.

Aran nodded gravely, walked over to her and handed her the cards. Jade hugged her panda to her chest as her brother stood beside Lucy.

Lucy studied the cards carefully. "You'll have to explain all about them to me," she smiled. "What does this mean – Technique: Poison Ivy?"

"That's how Palmon Digimon attacks," he said seriously. "She freezes her enemies."

"I see. This fellow looks scary."

"That's Ogremon. He's an evil Digimon."

"Eugene would love these," Lucy smiled. "He's my brother and he's mad into computer games. He'll be here soon."

"You're like us," Aran said quietly. "One girl, one boy and no daddy."

Lucy was taken aback. "I suppose you're right."

"Our mammy's sick," Jade said quietly. Her eyes filled with tears which began to run down her pale face.

Aran put his arms around her and held her tight. "Mammy'll get better soon, Jade. It'll be OK."

Lucy felt tears pricking her own eyes. She looked over at Agnes who was smiling gently.

"Your mum just needs some time to rest," Agnes said kindly, putting her hand on Jade's head and stroking it soothingly. "Your little brother is only a few weeks old and he needs a lot of attention. She'll be feeling better soon."

"And we can see Mammy whenever we want to, isn't that right, Agnes?" Aran asked, his voice timid and uncertain.

"That's right, love," Agnes assured him. "Every week for certain, and other days too if that suits Eileen."

Jade stopped crying. Lucy felt so sorry for the two children. She had only been eight when she'd last seen her own father and it still hurt.

The front door banged and Eugene bounded into the sitting-room.

"Hi, Agnes," he grinned, "and you must be Aran and Jade. He sat down on the arm of Lucy's chair. "Pokemon cards," he said, spotting the cards in Lucy's hand. "Deadly, can I have a look?"

"You'll have to ask Aran," Lucy said.

Eugene looked at Aran who nodded. Eugene then took the cards from Lucy and sat on the floor in front of Aran. "Now, have you got Charmander?" Eugene asked. "He's my favourite." He shuffled through the cards. "Digimon and Harry Potter ones too. Cool!"

Within minutes the two boys were sprawled on the floor, playing, Aran's cards set out on the carpet in rows.

Eileen stepped over them holding a loaded tray and smiled. "I see Jade and Aran have met Eugene."

"I think himself and Aran are going to have to be prised apart," Agnes said.

Jade was watching the two boys carefully, still clutching Bear.

Eileen put the tray down on the coffee table and began to pour the tea. She handed Jade a glass of milk. "Agnes said you'd like this."

Jade took the glass and mouthed 'thank you'.

"When Lucy was little I made her panda a set of clothes. A rain-coat and a jumper and a hat for when it was cold," Eileen said gently. "Do you think Bear might like some clothes?"

Jade nodded. A wisp of a smile formed on her lips.

"We'll measure him later then, after tea. I'm going to make chips and sausages. Do you like chips, Jade?"

Jade nodded again.

"I hope you've got lots of them," Eugene laughed. "I love chips."

"So do I!" Aran said enthusiastically.

Lucy smiled. Maybe this wasn't going to be so bad after all.

Lucy called in to Max on her way home. She'd said no to sausage and chips in her mum's earlier and was regretting it now – her stomach was gurgling away. It was raining heavily, the sky was already dark and it was getting really cold. She rang the bell impatiently and hugged her arms around herself to keep warm.

"Yes?" Max answered.

"It's me! Let me in. It's pouring out of the heavens."

Max pressed the buzzer and met her at the top of the stairs.

"You look a bit ropy," Lucy said as she walked into the kitchen, peeled off her wet jacket and plonked herself down at the kitchen table.

"It's all your fault," Max grumbled. "You were feeding me cocktails all last night."

"You weren't exactly saying no."

"I suppose," Max said reluctantly, leaning against the kitchen counter.

"What did you do this afternoon?" Lucy asked, shivering.

"Are you cold? I'll bring in the fan heater." He plugged it in beside Lucy and the air began to warm up. "It's supposed to be summer, so I don't have the heating on. Bloody Irish weather."

"This afternoon?" Lucy reminded him.

"I was messing on the internet, and I went shopping."

"Clothes?"

"Food."

"Exciting."

"Very. Sometimes I feel like I've no social life. No friends. What happened to them all, Lucy, all the college gang?"

"Marriage," she said decidedly. "Natalie and Jim, Ross, Mel, all of them except us really."

"The Two Musketeers," Max smiled.

"All for one and one for all."

Max suddenly looked lost. "What happens if *you* meet someone?"

"In the unlikely event of that ever happening, nothing will change. I'll still be here for you. Try getting rid of me."

"I'm serious."

"So am I. Now what are we going to do tonight?"

"Cinema? There's a special showing of *The Big Blue* at the IFC."

"You're on," Lucy said. "Jean-Marc Barr, the body to die for. What time's it on at?"

"Eight."

"Perfect."

"Jeeze!" Max said. "I'm sorry. I totally forgot to ask you. How did the meeting with the kids go?"

"Good, I think. Adam really took to Eugene, God help the poor lad. They were playing all afternoon."

"I can imagine."

"And the little girl, Jade, is a sweetie. Kind of shy though. All in all, I think it went well."

"Good."

"Adam said we were alike, both our families – because neither of us had dads."

Max looked at Lucy carefully. She hadn't mentioned her father for a long time.

"Anyway, what's in your fridge?" she said. She wasn't in the mood to talk any more. "I'm famished."

"Excellent!" Max grinned. "You're cooking."

"That was brilliant," Lucy said, walking out of the cinema. "Those diving scenes are something else."

"Rosanna Arquette is kind of cute too, in her own way," Max smiled.

"She does nothing for me," Lucy said. "Give me Jean-Marc any day. Those eyes, and that body in the wetsuit. Man!"

They walked towards the Temple Bar car park, where Max had left his grey BMW estate. He'd had a new one when he was working in London, but he rarely got to drive it. His current one was a 1990 model, which was always littered with kite and land-yacht 'bits'.

"I think your car could do with a wash," Lucy laughed as he put the key in the ignition. "It's almost black."

"I suppose it is due its annual wash soon. At least I have a car that works."

"I suppose." Her Audi was about to give up the ghost and she hadn't got around to replacing it yet.

As they drove along Nassau Street she stared out the window thoughtfully.

"Penny for them?" Max said.

"I was thinking about what I needed to buy for tomorrow night. For our dinner."

Max concentrated on his driving. "Your dinner."

"Are you sure you don't want to come?"

"And spoil your girlie night? I don't think so. Thanks all the same."

"Are you positive?"

"Yes," he said. "100%. Stop asking me. So what are you cooking?"

"I was thinking of starting with tomato and sweet chilli pepper soup," Lucy began, "then roast chicken. Followed by semi-freddo with strawberries."

Max cursed inwardly. He loved Lucy's roast chicken. "What's semi-freddo when it's at home?" he said, trying to take his mind off the roast.

"It's kind of like ice cream, only quicker to make. And richer. You'd love it."

"I'm sure I would," he said, tortured by thoughts of the dinner he was missing. But he couldn't change his mind now. Not if he wanted things with Daria to progress. He hoped that Daria would keep quiet about the kite-flying though. And that Lucy wouldn't put her off or ask her too many probing questions.

As they pulled up outside Lucy's house his mind was made up. He'd tell her all about meeting up with Daria and how much he liked her. As they walked up to the front he decided he'd definitely come clean.

But as they approached the door they heard shouts from inside.

"What's that?" Max asked.

"Sounds like Paula." Lucy quickly put the key in the lock and shouldered the door open.

"You bastard," they heard Paula scream as they stepped into the hall. "I'll fucking kill you."

Paula was standing at the top of the stairs outside Alan's room. The door was closed and Max and Lucy could see why. Paula was holding

106

a kitchen knife in one of her hands and was waving it around dangerously.

"I can explain," Alan's voice shouted from inside his bedroom. "Put the knife down."

Paula hacked at the door frantically, gouging deeply into the wood.

Lucy stood at the bottom of the stairs and shouted up angrily before Max could stop her. "Paula, watch the door. We'll have to pay for that!"

Paula spun around and glared at Lucy, sparks flying from her eyes. "Keep out of it. This has nothing to do with you." She staggered and steadied herself by putting one hand on the door. She was clearly drunk.

"Paula," Max said calmly, "put the knife down. Let Alan come out and you can both talk."

"Talk! We don't talk. We've never talked." She began to cry. "I don't think he's ever really loved me at all. We just shag, that's all. Shag, shag, shag."

"That's not true," Alan shouted through the door. "I did love you, Paula. And I'm still very fond of you. As I told you, you're a great girl. I just don't think we should be together."

Paula sat down on the carpet and rested her back against the bedroom door.

Max began to climb the stairs slowly.

"Max," Lucy hissed, "be careful." She followed behind him.

"She's upset," he whispered back. He reached the top of the stairs and smiled gently at Paula. "Give me the knife, please."

Paula stared at him for a few seconds. "You like me, don't you, Max? You think I'm attractive, don't you?"

"Yes. Very attractive. Now give me the knife."

Paula sighed, released her fingers from around the knife's handle and it dropped onto the carpet. "I wouldn't have hurt him. I love him."

Max picked up the knife and handed it to Lucy who was standing

107

at the top of the stairs. He put his arms around Paula and held her tightly. "You'll be fine."

Lucy ran down the stairs and hid the knife in one of the kitchen drawers. She went back up the stairs and stood beside Max. "Is she OK?" He nodded.

Alan's door opened a crack. Lucy stepped in. Alan looked terrible. His eyes were red and blotchy.

"Thank God you guys arrived," he said, slumping onto the bed. "I've been holding that door closed for the last hour – the lock doesn't work."

"What happened?" Lucy asked, sitting down beside him.

"I'm not sure. One minute we were talking and she was fine, and then she just flipped the lid."

"What were you talking about?" Lucy asked.

"Breaking up. I was trying to let her down gently. At first she just cried. Then we had a few more drinks and she lost it. Ran into the kitchen and started waving that knife around like a madwoman. I didn't know what to do."

"Did you tell her about Hopper?"

"No! And I'm not going to either. Things are bad enough without rubbing salt into her wounds. She'll go ballistic."

"You're probably right," Lucy said. "Listen, I'll get Max to bring her home. I'll go with him, OK?"

"Thanks. I'd really appreciate that."

"Will you be all right on your own? I could stay with you if you like."

"Thanks, Lucy, but I'm fine, honestly. Look after Paula."

Lucy went back outside. "I told Alan we'd take you home," she said to Paula.

"I want to stay here with Alan," Paula sobbed.

Max looked at Lucy. 'Help!' her eyes said.

"I'd like to bring you home," he crooned. "Make sure you're safe. Will your flatmate be there?"

"Yes, I think so."

"I'll help you up," Max said, putting his arm around her shoulders as she stood up.

"Bye, Alan," Paula said to Alan's door. "Ring me tomorrow."

"Shoot me if I ever get like that," Lucy said as they drove back towards Sandymount from Paula's house.

Claire, Paula's flatmate, had been shocked to see Paula in such a state. She had promised to look after her and to ring Lucy the following day.

"She wouldn't have done anything," Max said. "She was just really upset."

"I guess so. It was scary though."

"Listen, do you mind if I don't come in?" he said as they pulled up outside her door for the second time that night. "I'm kind of tired."

"Of course not," she smiled, kissing him on the cheek. "You were great. I don't know what would have happened if you hadn't been there."

"Anytime."

Hopper was sitting on the end of the stairs. She jumped up as soon as she saw Lucy come in the door.

"What the hell happened this evening?" she asked quietly. "I came in a few minutes ago from the pub and saw Alan's door. I asked him about it but he won't talk to me. He muttered something about Paula and then told me to get out of his room."

Lucy put her arm under Hopper's elbow and guided her into the sitting-room. "It was terrible," she said flicking on the lights and closing the door behind them. "Alan broke up with Paula and she went mental. She was stabbing his bedroom door with one of my kitchen knives. Max managed to calm her down and we dropped her home."

"Holy shit! I know I don't like the woman but she must have been really upset."

"It's all over now. I'm exhausted. I'm going to bed."

"You can't! I need to talk to you about Alan."

"Not now," Lucy said gently. "Please? Tomorrow, OK?"

"OK," Hopper replied listlessly. She wondered if she should take a knife to the curtains or sofa or something, maybe then people would listen to *her*.

After Lucy had gone to bed Hopper sat in the sitting-room with the lights turned off, thinking about Alan. In the space of one night she'd fallen helplessly in love with him and it was all Lucy's fault – she'd encouraged it. But, with Paula's behaviour, Alan was unlikely to want a girlfriend ever again.

At one o'clock in the morning she heard the door open. It was Alan.

"I was looking for you. You weren't in your room," he said.

Her heart leapt. "No."

He sat down beside her. The moon shone in the window, illuminating the room enough to make out her face and her damp, tear-stained eyes.

"I'm sorry about earlier."

"You don't have to explain," she said generously. "You've had an upsetting night. I'm the one who should be sorry."

"Why?" He sat down beside her and took her hands in his. "You didn't do anything wrong."

"But last night, and Paula. I feel really bad."

"She doesn't know about that. We would have broken up anyway. I don't love her. I don't think I ever did."

"Really?"

"I want to be with you. I know that now."

Hopper was speechless.

"Can I kiss you?" he asked.

"Of course you can."

"I forgot to tell you," Hopper smiled at breakfast. She'd been beaming all morning. She couldn't help herself. Her mouth ached from smiling so much. Alan and herself had had an amazing night of mind-blowing sex. They'd both felt a little guilty about Paula, but not guilty enough to stop themselves eating the face off each other. "Brian rang yesterday."

"Brian?" Lucy asked, stirring the scrambled eggs. "What did he want?"

"Don't know. Said he'd ring again."

"That's all I need. And what are you so happy about this morning? You look like the cat that got the cream."

"I did," Hopper admitted, "and he's in the shower."

"No way!"

"Shush, keep your voice down. He'll hear you."

"That was quick," Lucy said trying not to sound disapproving.

"I know, and I feel bad about it really."

"That's why you're so chirpy this morning?" Lucy asked archly.

"I *do* feel bad, honestly," Hopper said, "but it's not my fault. Fate brought us together. It was meant to be."

"Fate my ass! It was me. I take all the credit for this one, thank you very much. Who got you both the tickets for *The Sound of Music?*"

"OK, fate and Lucy – satisfied?"

"And does love's young dream want any scrambled eggs?" Lucy asked. "There's salmon in it."

"She most certainly does."

"Hello there, Prince Charming," Lucy smiled as Alan walked in the door, rubbing his dark hair with a hand-towel. "Would you like some eggs?"

"Please," Alan said, a grin plastered from ear to ear. He sat down at the kitchen table and kissed Hopper on the cheek. She positively purred. "Hopper told you then?"

"Yes, and I can't say I'm all that surprised, to tell the truth. I could see the potential from the very beginning. There were just one or two obstacles in the way."

Alan frowned. "You don't approve, do you?"

"After seeing Paula in such a state last night, I'd have to say I'm not sure about your timing," Lucy said honestly. "I'm delighted for the pair of you, of course. Just a little worried about Paula."

111

"She's always been a bit of a drama queen. I'm sure it'll all blow over. It's not the first time she's done something like that."

"Really?" Hopper asked bursting with curiosity.

"Let's just leave it at that, but I think she'll be fine. She'll bounce back quickly, I hope."

"Claire said she'd ring me today," Lucy said, "to tell me how Paula's doing."

"Good," Alan said, noticing Hopper's face. He didn't really want to have this conversation right now, not in front of her. It wasn't fair. "Now where are those eggs?"

They had munched through eggs, toast, bacon sandwiches and drank three pots of tea before Max called in at two with the Sunday papers.

"You'll never guess who's coming to town next Wednesday," he said, coming through the front door and waving *The Sunday Tribune* in Lucy's face.

"Who?" Lucy asked with interest.

"Only Mr Jamie Oliver! In person."

12

"Will you not come this evening?" Lucy asked as she selected a large free-range chicken in SuperValu. "Please?"

"No!" Max said. "And that's my final answer."

Lucy sulked for a few minutes. "Pretty please?"

"Lucy!"

"OK," she sighed, "I'll stop. It's such a wasted opportunity though. You may not find Daria attractive, but her sister might be cute."

"There is no way I'm going to dinner with four girls," he said, raising his voice. "Especially if you're trying to set me up with one of them."

"Keep your pants on," she said, moving to the fruit and vegetable area with Max straggling along behind her. "If Grace turns out to be nice, can I arrange a dinner for the two of you?"

"What is wrong with you?"

"It was just a suggestion. No need to get shirty."

She picked up a carton of fresh basil leaves and placed them in her basket. "Weigh these for me, will you?" She handed him three heads of garlic.

As he queued to use the scales he wondered how he always got tricked into going shopping with Lucy. Usually he had a nice meal to look forward to but today that wasn't the case.

"If there's any chicken left over can I have it?" he asked hopefully, handing her the weighed and stickered garlic.

"Not a scrap of chicken will pass your lips unless you come tonight."

"You're a hard woman."

"I take that as a compliment," she grinned.

"Come in," Lucy opened the door to Daria and Grace.

"This is Grace," Daria said, "my sister."

"Hi, Grace," Lucy smiled, "nice to meet you."

"Thanks for having us over," Grace said. "It's very kind of you."

"I like making new friends," Lucy said, leading them into the sitting-room, "and I like to cook, so any excuse. Let me take your coats."

Hopper flicked off the television and stood up. "Boy, does she love to cook!" she grinned. "I'm Hopper."

"Daria," Daria stood forward and proffered her hand. Hopper shook it warmly.

"And I'm her sister, Grace." They also shook hands.

"Lucy tells me you work in the theatre," Hopper said. "I'm a make-up artist. We may bump into each other at some stage. I live here too. Sit down and make yourselves comfortable."

"Where do you work?" Daria asked, lowering herself into the generous-sized armchair.

"I'm freelance at the moment. But I'm hoping to get some work over Christmas in the Olympia."

"I've just finished a set there," Daria said.

"Really?" Hopper asked. Soon they had launched into a full-on 'do you know so and so' session.

"She's just got a part in *Emma* at The Gate," Grace said proudly, after they'd exhausted familiar names.

"Congratulations!" Hopper said warmly.

Lucy poured glasses of wine and handed them around. "I'll just check on the food. Won't be a sec."

When Lucy had left the room Daria turned towards Hopper. "Do you know Max too?"

"Yes. He practically lives here. Nice guy."

"Yes, he is," Daria agreed. She was dying to find out more about him. Grace looked at her strangely.

In the car on the way over Grace had questioned her sister's motives about going to Lucy's house. She accused her of only accepting the invitation to find out more about Max.

"And you teach, Grace?" Hopper asked.

"That's right. Senior Infants. They're mad little characters."

"Who's mad?" Lucy asked, rejoining them. The chicken was nearly done and she'd given the soup a stir.

"My pupils," Grace giggled. "Completely bonkers! The boys are the worst."

"Are they much different to the girls at that age?" Hopper asked, taking a sip of her wine.

"Like you wouldn't believe. They can't keep still, always fidgeting and squirming in their seats. The girls are a lot less physical and better behaved. They play kiss-chase in the playground and get the boys backs up. It's really funny."

"Kiss-chase?" Lucy gasped. "What age are they?"

"Five and six," Grace laughed. "They mature very early these days."

"No kidding," Lucy said. "We were playing that in sixth class. I remember Max being terrified of a girl called Carol. She used to race after him in the playground and floor him. She was a strong girl."

Daria listened with interest. She intended to store away all the information she gleaned about Max.

Grace laughed. "Sounds scary. Max is your friend who makes the kites, isn't he?" She knew exactly who Max was but she didn't want to give the game away.

"Lucy was trying to set him up with your sister this evening but he refused to come," Hopper smiled.

The room went silent for a moment.

Lucy glared at Hopper. "That's not quite true," she said quickly. "He was busy, that's all."

"Oops, sorry. I'm always putting my foot in it. I didn't mean to imply –"

"It doesn't matter," Daria said, crushed. She tried to laugh it off. "He isn't really my type."

Grace glanced at her sister who had gone quite pale. "Daria's rehearsals start tomorrow," she said hurriedly, trying to take the heat off her sister. "The director, Owen, is really cute – you should see him. And he's always had a bit of a crush on her."

"Really?" Hopper asked with interest. "Tell us more."

"He's only twenty-four!" Daria protested. "And it's all purely professional."

"A toy boy!" Lucy smiled. "I approve. Now let's eat and you can describe this Owen to us, Daria."

The dinner went swimmingly. Lucy kept off the subject of Max, and Hopper managed to mention him only once, while describing their trip to the *Sing-A-Long-A-Sound-A-Music*. They talked about the theatre, men, Grafton street shops, Irish men, fancy-dress parties, American men, and food.

"That was amazing," Grace enthused, pushing her finished dessert plate away from her. "You're a great cook, Lucy."

"Thanks."

"We'll have to have you both over soon," Daria said. "It's been fun. But be warned, it might be takeaway. There's this great place near us called The Szechuan Pantry."

"I've heard of it," Hopper said. "I've always wanted to try the food. Your man in *The Sunday Tribune* swears by it."

"Hopper loves her Chinese and her curries," Lucy smiled, "bless her. You'd swear she was a boy sometimes. Would anyone like more wine?"

"Please," Daria said. "Grace's driving so I may as well make the most of it. It'll have to be my last glass though – I have my first rehearsal in the morning."

"You'll both have to come with me to see her in *Emma*," Grace said.

"We'd love to," Lucy said.

Hopper nodded. "To the first rehearsal," she said, raising her wine glass.

They all clinked glasses and cheered.

"To Daria," Lucy said. "Wishing her every success."

"You're very quiet," Grace said to Daria on the way home. "Was it the Max thing?"

"I've been trying to push it to the back of my mind all evening. I can't believe he said that."

"Said what?"

"That he didn't like me."

Grace sighed. "He just couldn't make it for dinner," she said gently. "That's all. Maybe he was embarrassed or something. Maybe he wants to take you out alone, without an audience."

"If that's the case, why hasn't he rung yet?"

Grace had no answer for that one.

Max rang Lucy's at midnight. Hopper answered the phone.

"Hopper, sorry to bother you. Are your guests still there?"

"No, it's OK. They've just gone," she said.

"Good, is Lucy there?"

"She's in the kitchen. I'll go and get her."

"Hang on a sec," Max stalled, "how was your dinner?"

"Lovely," Hopper said, holding back a hiccup. "Daria and Grace are really nice. We all got on like a house on fire."

"Did Daria," Max began cautiously, "did she ask about me?"

Hopper was silent for a second. "Why would she?"

"No reason – I just made some kites for her, that's all."

"Don't worry," Hopper laughed. "Lucy told me about trying to set the two of you up and you're safe there. We told Daria you refused to come to dinner. She didn't seem too bothered."

Max was flabbergasted. "Listen, I have to go. Tell Lucy I'll ring her tomorrow." He put down the phone.

"Was that Alan?" Lucy asked as Hopper walked into the kitchen.

"No, it was Max."

"Max? What did he want?" she asked, licking some semi-freddo off a spoon.

"I'm not sure," Hopper said. "He said he'd ring you tomorrow. Is there any more of that ice cream stuff left?"

"Here." Lucy passed her the bowl and a spoon. The two wine-sozzled women sat down at the table and finished it off.

Max sat staring at the phone. Daria must think I'm the rudest man on the planet, he thought to himself.

He flicked on the CD player. U2's 'Stuck in a Moment You Can't Get Out Of' filled the room. He lay back and listened to Bono.

* * *

"Lucy, it's Brian. Sorry to ring so early. Can you talk?"

"Hang on a sec," Lucy said, moving from the reception area to the kitchen. She hated taking personal calls in work – Paula was such a nosy bat. Luckily she hadn't come in yet, which was unusual as she was never late. "Right, fire ahead." She hoped he didn't want to 'talk' talk. She wasn't in the mood. Her head was throbbing like nobody's business and her hands were shaking slightly. Thank goodness she wasn't doing any eyebrow-plucking or moustache-waxing this morning.

"I'm sorry to bother you. There's just something I wanted to tell you."

Get on with it, Lucy muttered to herself. She'd forgotten how drawn-out Brian could be. "Yes?" she said, slugging down some black coffee.

"I'll get straight to the point, shall I?"

"Yes."

"I've met someone," he said and then hesitated. When there was no response from Lucy he continued. "Her name's Bertha and she's an accountant too. We were at a tax seminar together and really hit it off. I wanted to tell you myself. You know how small Dublin is."

"Thank you for telling me." What did he expect her to say? She was delighted. It stopped any lingering sense of guilt (not that there was much, she hadn't thought of him for days), and it meant that he was completely out of her hair for good. "I'm so pleased for you. That's great. You'll have loads to talk about – money and spreadsheets and things."

"I'm so relieved," Brian said. "It's all happened so quickly. I was concerned that you'd think I'd forgotten all about you, about us. I miss you, you know, but life must go on."

"Absolutely! Thanks for telling me. I hope you'll be very happy together."

Brian laughed. "Steady on, we've only known each other a few weeks. How are you anyway? Have you thought any more about what I said?"

"Yes. But you're wrong, Brian."

"Lucy?"

"Yes?" She was getting irritated now.

"You have to let people in. You never let me get close to you."

"That's not true," she protested.

"It is. But maybe –"

"Listen," Lucy interrupted, "I'm dead pleased for you. You deserve someone nice. But there's a client at the front door. I'm sorry. I have to go."

"See you, Lucy. Think about what I said."

"See you," she whispered. He wasn't the worst. In fact she felt strangely empty now. It was comforting knowing that someone fancied you, even if it was only your recently dumped ex.

Paula walked into the kitchen. "Lucy," she sniffed, "can I talk to you for a second?"

"Sure," Lucy replied. First Brian, now Paula – she's be glad when this day was over. She hadn't seen Paula since the knife incident on

Saturday night. Claire had rung Lucy on Sunday afternoon and said that Paula was really hungover and mortified at her behaviour. She blamed the drink and the shock for all the drama.

"About Saturday night," Paula began, her cheeks reddening under the heavy make-up. "I'd prefer if it was never mentioned again. I was very drunk and emotional. I'm sorry about your door," she couldn't look Lucy in the eye, her gaze wandering all over the room. "I blame *him*. I thought we were going to get . . ." Tears began to form in the corners of her eyes. "Never mind. I'll pay for the door."

Lucy felt sorry for the overwrought woman. She hadn't done anything wrong, not really – apart from being her annoying self and you couldn't really blame her for that. She and Alan should never have been together in the first place.

She pulled off a piece of kitchen roll and handed it to Paula. "It's forgotten already," she smiled gently. "And don't worry about the door. I'll get Max to have a look at it. I'm sure he can fill it with some of his plastic-padding stuff or something."

Paula looked at the kitchen roll, her blue eyes now rimmed by streams of black mascara which had stained the Winnie the Pooh design. "I should have used the waterproof mascara this morning – how could I have been so stupid? I'll have to fix my make-up. Can you take Mrs Stanley? She's due in five minutes for a pedicure."

Lucy sighed. She couldn't stand Ethel Stanley or her feet. But Paula was upset. "Just this once, OK?"

"Thanks. Tell you what. I'll do Mrs Evans' bikini line for you later. Deal?"

"Deal." Now that she had something on Paula, maybe working at Making Faces wouldn't be so bad after all. Until Paula found out about Hopper that was. Then the shit would hit the proverbial fan.

Owen Hughes clapped his hands. "If you could all find a chair, please, people, and sit down." The excited chatter and laughter gradually stopped as the actors sat down in a semicircle facing him. They were in the St Peter's Church Hall on Parnell Square, the nearest affordable rehearsal space the producer could find. Not very glamorous, and the fluorescent striplighting left much to be desired, but at least it was warm. And a local cafe had promised to provide coffee and tea on tap, which was most important if he was going to get these people to work before lunchtime.

Owen looked at the sea of faces in front of him. He smiled at Daria who was clutching a large yellow notebook and a pen eagerly. Everyone seemed to be present except for Rosaleen, which wasn't surprising. It was only eleven o'clock after all.

He coughed to clear his throat. "It's good to see you all here. We have a busy few weeks ahead of us, and I'll need your full co-operation in order to make this production gel. Antonia will hand out your scripts. This will take a few minutes, so if you could just bear with me while that is being done. Dublin has never seen this version of *Emma* and I want to make it a play to remember. Something sensational, unforgettable. I want people to talk about this production in years to come – like Steven Berkoff's *Salome*. I want –"

"Owen, darling!" a voice cried, and a tall, red-haired woman launched herself through the swing doors of the hall. "Am I late? Don't tell me you've started without me? How naughty!" She swept towards him and kissed him dramatically on the lips, red and purple velvet scarves following behind her. She clicked her fingers at Antonia, Owen's assistant. "Seat, there's a good girl."

Antonia dragged a chair towards the centre of the semi-circle, the metal legs making an unpleasant noise on the wooden floor. Daria and John Davis, the actor who was playing the male lead, Mr Knightley, moved their chairs to allow room for another seat.

Rosaleen swiped a finger over the chair's top and, satisfied that there was no dust, sniffed and sat down.

"Now," Owen said, hoping there wouldn't be any more interruptions, "as I was saying, I hope this production will be as memorable as Berkoff's *Salome* –"

"Darling," Rosaleen butted in, "you're so kind. You know the critics said I gave a faultless performance. I wouldn't like to say so myself, but the critics said I was wonderful." She turned towards the other actors in the hall. "I played Salome, you know. But of course, you probably all realise that. I was in every newspaper in the country and Gay Byrne —"

Owen coughed loudly. He realised he'd have to take control of things right now or rehearsals were going to be an ego-fest for Rosaleen and nothing would get done. "I'm sorry, but we must start now, Rosaleen. Have you all got your scripts?"

Rosaleen glared at the young director.

John winked at Daria. "She'd make a great Mrs Elton," he whispered. "It's a pity you can't swap roles. "You're far too pretty to be Mrs Elton."

Daria smiled. She could feel herself blushing. "Thanks."

"*Emma* was one of Jane Austen's last novels," Owen said. "It was written in 1816 and reflects life at that time in England. It's full of comedy and social comment and its heroine, Emma, is one of Austen's most engaging heroines." Rosaleen preened herself and smiled knowingly at everyone at the mention of her character's name. Owen hoped she wouldn't do this every time he mentioned 'Emma'. He wished he'd been allowed to cast Daria in the lead role. She would have been so much easier to deal with, and she had real talent, not like the old ham in front of him.

"Can everyone turn to page one hundred and seven of their scripts? I'd like to start at one of the key scenes of the play. By this day next week I'd like you all to have read Jane Austen's book and also my notes on the text which are at the back of your scripts." Everyone groaned.

He continued. "It's important to get a feel for the period, women's place in society, education, or the lack of it, the class system — that sort of thing. In the Box Hill picnic scene Emma slights and hurts one of the female characters, Miss Bates, a harmless woman with a good heart. Mr Knightley is shocked by this flaw in Emma's character and tells her so. It is here she begins to recognise both her feelings for him and her own thoughtlessness and moral ambiguity. All the main characters have come together for a picnic and are sitting and chatting companionably. Emma and Mr Frank Churchill are flirting and the mood is light and frivolous until she says something unforgivable." He looked around at the cast. "I'm throwing you all in at the deep end here, I'm afraid, but bear with me, please. The first readings are always the hardest but let's see what we can do, shall we? Rosaleen, can you begin?"

"Of course." She stood up.

"You can stay seated," Owen said.

Rosaleen raised her eyebrows and sat down again. "Highly irregular," she muttered to herself . She began to read Emma's lines.

Owen listened carefully, nodding his head. "Good," he murmured. "You come in here, Daria."

Daria took a deep breath and read her lines.

"Excellent," Owen smiled. "Wonderful."

Daria felt a wave of relief flood through her body. She began to feel less nervous.

Later that morning, Rosaleen, as Emma, fell to her knees, put her hands to her face and pretended to cry noisily.

Owen frowned at her. "Rosaleen, it says 'contrite' in my script. Emma is speechless, astounded, confused. And she realises that what her dear friend, Mr Knightley, has said is true."

"Owen, darling," Rosaleen looked up at him from her postulant pose. "It clearly says in my copy of Emma that tears ran down her cheeks." She scrambled in her black velvet bag, and pulled out a well-thumbed copy of the book. She found the relevant page and read it out.

"Jane Austen's Emma may have cried, but mine won't. She's too angry at herself to cry. It's her epiphany."

Rosaleen sniffed and sat down once more. "It's such a burden being classically trained."

John smiled at Daria. "Time for coffee, I think. That was excellent, people, excellent!" He ran his hands through his hair. He had his work cut out for him with Rosaleen.

Daria felt a wave of adrenaline flow through her body. She was finally involved in a proper play in the most prestigious theatre in Ireland. She was so happy she could cry herself, Jane Austen or no Jane Austen.

"Daria, is that you?" Grace called from the kitchen. She wiped her damp hands on a tea towel and put on the kettle. The washing-up could wait.

Daria came into the kitchen, a huge smile on her face. She dumped her bag unceremoniously onto the kitchen counter.

"Hi, Grace," she said, throwing her arms around her sister. "I had a brilliant day."

"Good. I'll make you a cup of tea and you can tell me all about it. Sit down."

Daria sat at the table and her eyes were accosted by the huge bouquet of red roses in a bucket on the floor by the window.

"Where did those come from?" she asked in amazement.

"Here," Grace handed her a small envelope. "I'm really sorry. I couldn't bear the suspense so I opened it."

"Congratulations on getting a part, Max." Daria read. She looked up at her sister who had a grin plastered from ear to ear.

"Lucy or Hopper must have told him," Grace laughed. "Sorry about the 'vase'. I didn't want to break up the bouquet before you saw it and nothing was big enough."

"I think they look quite nice in the bucket," Daria laughed.

"So, you still think he doesn't like you?"

Daria wrinkled her nose. "I'm not sure. I'll wait and see if he rings."

Grace laughed. "You're joking? You're going to ring him and thank him for the flowers, right?"

"No, he has to ring me. It says so in my library book *The Rules : Time-tested Secrets for Capturing the Heart of Mr Right.*"

Grace shook her head. "You've finally lost it, you know that," she smiled.

"Pass me my bag," Daria said. She delved in her bag and pulled out a battered red paperback book with arrows and hearts embossed in gold on the cover. *"Rule 5 : Don't Call Him and Rarely Return His Calls. There is no reason to call him. He should be calling you, and calling you again and again until he pins you down for a date."*

"You're having me on," Grace said nervously. "You don't really believe any of that, do you?"

Daria laughed. "Of course not, idiot! I had you going there for a second. Damn right I'm going to ring him. Try stopping me. The book's a good laugh though. I bet Lucy and Hopper would get a kick out of it."

Grace smiled. "Why don't we have them over and you can test them out on 'the rules'?"

"Good idea. How about Friday evening?"

"Perfect!" Grace said. "Who's cooking?"

"The Chinese takeaway!" Daria grinned.

13

"Did you ring the florist's?" Eric Maxwell asked Max. They had just sat down at their window table at Posh Grub in Dun Laoghaire for lunch.

Max had rung him that morning, ostensibly to ask him out for lunch. But Eric had got the feeling that there was something on his son's mind other than food, and after a few perfunctory questions Max had admitted that a particular female was in danger of never wanting to see him again. Eric had suggested roses. "Always works with your mother," he'd explained.

"I rang just after I talked to you this morning," Max said anxiously. "They said they'd deliver by twelve." He looked at his watch. "It's half past one now."

"Will she be at home to collect them?"

"Shit! Sorry, Dad," he added sheepishly. "Of course she won't be there. If fact, there won't be anyone there. Why didn't I think of that?"

"Calm down, Max," Eric said levelly. "They'll leave them with neighbours or something. I'm sure they're well used to it." He picked up a long, fire-engine red rectangular menu and began to read. After a few seconds he looked at Max. "I'm having grilled swordfish with tomato salsa. How about you?"

"That was quick! I'm not sure, the sea bass I think, or maybe the fisherman's pie."

Eric stared out the window. Posh Grub was situated just off the main street, looking onto a pedestrian walkway. "Not a bad location for a restaurant, really," he said thoughtfully. "Dun Laoghaire can only get better."

Max smiled again. He didn't want to spend the whole of lunchtime talking about local planning or the lack of it. A tall, dark-haired waitress took their order and soon they were tucking into some tasty home-made tomato bread.

"So who's this new woman?" Eric asked, sipping a glass of Walker Bay Chardonnay.

"Her name's Daria." Max picked at the crumbs on his side plate. "She's an actor."

"An actor? An actress, you mean."

"No, Dad. They all like to be called actors now – male or female. She's American, well, Irish-American really – her dad's Irish."

"Sounds interesting," Eric smiled. He cocked his head. "Pretty?"

"Very," Max nodded, smiling back.

"I hope it all works out for you. Maybe I'll get to meet her some day."

"Maybe."

"Hi, Max. This is Daria."

Max sat down. He had been pacing his living-room, flicking through the television stations trying to find something to hold his attention. Anything to stop him obsessing about the fact that Daria hadn't rung him and to prevent himself from ringing her. He didn't want to seem desperate, even though he was feeling it.

"Daria, how are you?" He'd begun to feel embarrassed about sending such a lavish bouquet of flowers. He'd gone over and over it all afternoon and had decided that roses were naff and that she'd think him old-fashioned and out of touch.

"Great, thanks," she said. "I'm just ringing to thank you for the

127

roses. They're beautiful. We don't have enough vases to hold them all. It was sweet of you."

Max realised that he'd been holding his breath and took a deep gulp of air. "I'm glad you like them. I wasn't sure about roses –"

"I love roses!" Daria interrupted. "They're my favourites. I'm an old-fashioned girl at heart."

Max was relieved. He was glad he'd listened to his dad. "How are your rehearsals going? Have they started?" He was anxious to keep her on the phone.

"They're going well, I think," Daria said. "The leading lady is a bit of a prima donna but everyone else seems really nice. The guy who's playing Mr Knightley, John Davis, is a panic. He's in *Fair City* sometimes. He plays one of the barmen. Do you watch it?"

"No." He hoped this John guy wasn't *too* nice. "How was dinner at Lucy's?" he asked before thinking.

"Fine. Great, actually. Lucy's a brilliant cook."

"Yes," Max agreed. He didn't know if he should bring up Hopper's comments. He decided not to. He was embarrassed enough as it was.

"Max? Are you still there?"

"Yes, sorry. I was wondering, if you're not too busy –"

"Yes?"

"Would you like to have dinner with me this week sometime?" He coughed nervously.

"I'd love to. How about Thursday? Lucy and Hopper are coming over on Friday."

"Thursday is good. I'll collect you from your house at sevenish. Does that suit?"

"Sounds great," Daria smiled. "Our house is just beside Monkstown Church – Monkstown Terrace. The one with the yellow door, number nine."

"Perfect. I'll see you then."

Max put down the phone and leant back on the sofa. A huge wave of relief surged over his whole body. He smiled to himself. Then he remembered one of the last things that Daria had said – about Lucy and Hopper. He'd have to tell Lucy everything, and fast.

Lucy looked at her watch. Max was late. She was getting more and more agitated by the minute. Where the hell was he? He'd promised to be there at six on the dot and it was now twenty past. There were loads of people queuing in front of her outside the door of Hanna's Bookshop and it was boring waiting on her own. The two women behind her were discussing the best way to cook a turkey, which, as it was May and not December, was slightly disconcerting. The designer-suited man in front of her looked very out of place – he was probably getting a book signed for his wife or girlfriend or something.

She was very, very nervous. Meeting Jamie Oliver was number one on her wish list, way above owning a Prada coat or even staying in The Motu Hotel on Bora Bora in the South Pacific, a small hotel anchored just off the tropical island, which she'd seen on a travel programme and had lusted after ever since.

Meeting Jamie Oliver. The very words sent shivers down her spine. She could see his face right now, hair tousled, twinkling eyes, luscious full lips smiling. He'd be swept away by her Irish accent, charmed by her tinkling laugh and her . . .

"Lucy?"

Lucy was snapped out of her daydream and plunged back to the grey, damp evening. It was Dan Rowan.

"I thought it was you," he said. "Waiting for the man himself?"

"Yes," Lucy said curtly. "And you're here to slag him off, are you?"

Dan looked hurt. "No. I'm here to get a book signed."

Lucy raised her eyebrows.

"Don't look at me like that," he smiled. "I picked up a copy of *The Return of the Naked Chef* last weekend. You'd recommended him so highly I thought the least I could do was to give the bloke a chance. And you were right. I tried a couple of the recipes and they were good, bloody good."

Lucy stared at Dan in amazement.

129

"What?" he asked.

"You're admitting you were wrong?"

"Yes."

"Good!" she said, thawing slightly. "I might let you into the queue in that case." She leant over towards him. "I think the women behind me are mad," she whispered. "They probably won't even notice."

"They're talking about cooking seaweed," he whispered back after listening to them for a couple of seconds.

"It was turkey a few minutes ago," Lucy giggled.

"What time is the signing?"

"Half six. I'm expecting Max but he's late."

"Is he getting the Dart by any chance?"

Lucy nodded. "I think so, why?"

"There's another landslide in Killiney and the trains are running behind. I heard it on the news."

"So it's just you and me for the moment."

"I guess so," Dan said. "How's your mum? Did she survive the nun-fest?"

"She had a great time."

"Mum told me about the fostering." Dan continued. "I think it's brilliant, fair dues to her. I'm sure it's not easy taking on two kids like that."

"No. But she's well able for it. And Jade and Aran are little dotes."

"What age are they?"

"Jade's five and Aran's seven," Lucy replied. "Their mum's only twenty-two. She's just had another baby and she can't cope with them all."

Dan sighed. "That's really sad. How long will your mum have them for?"

"It depends. Until their own can cope, I suppose."

The queue moved forward a few feet.

"Looks like Jamie's here," Dan smiled. "Are you excited?"

"Of course." In fact she felt decidedly faint. Her head was spinning and her palms were hot and sticky.

The queue moved again.

"Are you all right, Lucy?" Dan asked with concern. "You look a little pale."

"I'm fine," she assured him, loosening her scarf and opening her jacket. "I'm just a little hot, that's all."

As they moved inside the front door Lucy could see the bright flashes of cameras.

"It's a bit mad in there," Dan said. He was a good foot taller than Lucy. "I can see Jamie at a desk. There's a couple of photographers buzzing around him."

"Is Jules there?" Lucy stood on her toes but still unable to see.

"Jules?"

"His wife."

"What does she look like?"

"Tall, with long dark hair," she said. "Pretty," she admitted reluctantly.

"Don't think so. There's a couple of guys in suits and a blonde woman with glasses. No tall pretty girls, unfortunately."

Lucy laughed. The queue moved again.

"I can see him!" Her hands began to shake. In real life Jamie looked better than anything she could ever have imagined. From what she could see he was wearing a red shirt with funky silver cufflinks. He was smiling and talking to a woman in a beige raincoat and signing her book. Twenty minutes later there was only the businessman in front of them.

"It's for my wife," Lucy heard him say as he handed Jamie a copy of *The Naked Chef* to sign. "She loves you. Watches all your shows."

"What's her name, mate?" Jamie asked.

"Dee."

Jamie signed the book and exchanged a few pleasantries about Dublin with the man.

"You're next," Dan smiled. Lucy's eyes were glued on her idol. Her heart began to race. She pulled her well-thumbed copies of Jamie's cookery books out of her bag in preparation.

Dan pushed her forward as soon as the man had moved away. "Go on."

"Hi," Jamie smiled up at Lucy.

Lucy could feel blood rushing to her face. She put her books onto the large mahogany table and pushed them towards him.

He opened one, exposing the light blue fly-leaf which was splattered with a large red stain.

Lucy was mortified. "Sorry," she muttered. "It's spaghetti sauce."

"Good to see the book's being used, love," he smiled. "Which sauce? Tomato?"

"Red onion and tomato. The one with balsamic vinegar."

"Ah," Jamie nodded. "How did you find it?"

"Good," Lucy said. She couldn't believe she was talking to Jamie himself. "But I preferred the seafood Tagliatelle sauce."

"One of my favourites," he said enthusiastically. "Do you make your own pasta?"

Lucy nodded. "I love making pasta. I have a deadly pasta-machine which helps, but I adore kneading the dough. There's something really sensuous about pasta dough," she babbled.

"I know what you mean, mate," he grinned. "All that lovely strong flour, giving it a real go with your palms." He leant towards her conspiratorially. "I wish I was having a good old knead right now, tell the truth."

Lucy laughed.

"I suppose I'd better get on with the old signing or me publishers will sack me." He glanced up and winked at one of the suited men who was loitering behind him. "What's the name, love?"

"Lucy," she said eagerly.

When Jamie opened her copy of the original *Naked Chef* book he was greeted by a fine shower of white powder.

"Flour," Lucy grinned. "I was making your scented rolls the other day."

"You're a real foodie, my girl," Jamie laughed. "Are you a chef?"

"No. I'm a beautician."

132

"Pity," Jamie mused. "If you love cooking, you should cook."

Lucy looked at him properly for the first time. She couldn't make out if he was teasing her or not.

"I'm serious," he said, smiling at her, the corners of his eyes crinkling. "Life's too short. Go with your heart. If you love it, do it! That's what I say."

"You might be right," Lucy said thoughtfully. "Thanks."

"Any time, Lucy. Nice to meet you." He handed her the books.

"And you."

He reached over and placed his hand on one of hers. "Good luck," he said sincerely.

Waiting beside the desk for Dan to get his book signed, Lucy's heart began to gradually slow down. She watched Jamie as he interacted with Dan. Jamie was quite delicious, but a really nice guy too. Dan wasn't bad either.

When they stepped out of the door into the cool air Lucy saw Max immediately.

"Sorry, Lucy," he smiled ruefully, running his hand over his tightly-shorn head. "The trains were delayed and my mobile's out of juice. I forgot to recharge it last night."

"Not to worry. Look who I bumped into."

"Hi, Dan," Max grinned. "Another Jamie fan?"

"A recently converted one," Dan admitted, smiling at Lucy.

"Seeing as I'm here now," Max said, "how about a drink?"

"Good idea," Lucy said. "I think I need a large brandy. Keogh's?"

"Suits me," Dan said. Max nodded.

"And how was Jamie Oliver?" Max asked her as they walked up Dawson Street.

"Delicious," Lucy said.

"Still smitten?" he asked as they crossed the street.

"A little," Lucy admitted.

"They were chatting for ages," Dan said. "Much longer than anyone else."

"Really?" Max said, staring at Lucy.

133

"It's not what you think. He was giving me career advice."

"Sorry?" Max asked.

"I'll tell you inside," Lucy said as they walked in the door of Keogh's. "You have to buy me a drink first."

"Bribery and corruption," Dan laughed.

"No better woman," Max said.

"So what's this about Jamie giving you career advice?" Max asked with interest after they'd settled themselves into the snug with their drinks.

"He said I should be working with food as I loved cooking so much, that's all. And something about life being too short to do work you don't like."

"He's right there," Dan said. "I'd agree with that wholeheartedly. Why spend forty hours or more every week doing something you don't like? Makes no sense."

"That's why I left London," Max said. "I hated my job – it was stressful and boring and, at the end of the day, no one appreciated my work, not really."

"What line of work are you in?" Dan asked.

"I was an engineer. But I make kites now."

"Kites? What type of kites?"

"All kinds. Power-kites, quads, stunt-kites, the works."

"That's fascinating. I'm a surfer myself. Been doing it since college. But I'd love to try flying a kite. I've heard there are quads that can pull you along the water, they're that powerful."

"Too right!" Max said. "Have you ever been to Bull Island in Clontarf?"

"No."

"They have sand-buggies there that are pulled along by kites. It's quite something." Max took a slug of his Guinness.

"We've spent whole afternoons watching them," Lucy added. "They're quite a sight."

"I'm definitely going to find out more about the surfing-kites," Dan said.

"I could make you one," Max said. "You'd have to give me a few weeks to work the measurements out, but I'm sure I could do it."

"Excellent," Dan grinned. "And could you teach me how to fly it?"

Max laughed. "You teach me how to surf and I'll teach you how to fly."

"Deal," Dan said, holding out his hand. They shook on it.

Lucy sipped her pint as they talked about kites and surfing. She wasn't sure that she wanted Dan and Max to become friends. It complicated things. A lot.

The following morning Lucy answered her mobile phone in the kitchen of Making Faces. Paula was late again and she was having a quick cup of coffee. She was surprised to find Dan on the other end.

"Lucy, I hope you don't mind me ringing. Max gave me your number. I've just been booked for a christening on Sunday. Another catering company let them down. I was wondering if you'd be interested in helping me at it? Doing some prep work, cooking and a bit of serving. What do you think?"

"I'm not sure."

"I was thinking about what Jamie said to you," Dan continued, "and I think you should give it a shot – cooking, I mean."

"Give me a few minutes to think about it and I'll get back to you," she said. As she put down the phone a myriad of thoughts tumbled into her mind. Cooking for your friends and family was one thing, getting paid for it was quite another. She wondered if jumping in at the deep end was a good idea – what if she drowned? And working with Dan. She was beginning to warm to him and she'd certainly like to see him again. But perhaps a hot, sweaty kitchen wasn't exactly the ideal environment.

Paula popped her head round the door. "Rita Maxwell's here. She wants to have a word with you."

"Right. I'll be out in a second." About bloody time Paula was in, Lucy thought to herself – she was getting a little sick of her boss's tardiness at this stage. It had been going on all week.

"Lucy," Rita gushed, hugging her warmly and pecking the air on either side of Lucy's head dramatically, with a loud popping sound, taking care not to upset her thickly applied orange-red lipstick, "how nice to see you."

"Hi, Rita," Lucy replied cautiously, well aware that Rita wanted something.

"I was in the area and I just popped in to see if you'd found anyone for Lea's Debs," Rita beamed, the lipstick on her teeth glowing in the light.

Shit, thought Lucy, I'd completely forgotten. "It's under control," she assured Rita. "Max and I have been discussing it and we may have someone suitable. Give us a few days," she stalled.

"Wonderful," Rita gushed. "Now don't let me down, will you? Little Lea's happiness depends on you and Max, my dear."

Damn, Lucy said to herself.

Thinking about it afterwards, Lucy realised that she should have been honest with Rita and said that they couldn't find anyone. She'd really landed herself and Max in it now. At lunchtime she picked up her phone and rang Max.

"Max?"

"Yes?"

"You're not going to believe this." She explained about Rita's request.

"A Debs partner for Lea? Are you mad?" Max said, his voice rose to a dangerous level. "What the hell are we going to do? You'll have to ring my mother and explain."

"I can't do that! And after all, Lea is your sister. You want her to enjoy her Debs, don't you?"

"I suppose," Max muttered. He wasn't actually sure if he did want his bratty little sister to enjoy anything, but he couldn't admit that to Lucy.

Just then Mossy lumbered into the loft, gnawing on a greasy pepperoni sausage.

"Hang on, Lucy. Leave it to me, I've had an idea. I'll ring you back

136

later."

"Lucy, it's Mum."

"Hi, Mum."

"Are you all right, love?" Eileen asked. "You sound tired."

"I am tired, I guess. I've had one hell of a day at work and it's getting to me, I suppose."

"You work too hard," Eileen said, an anxious tone in her voice. "I worry about you. That salon is taking a lot out of you."

"I know. But enough about me. How are you? How are the kids?"

"I'm great. And Aran and Jade are beginning to settle in, I think. They are going to the same school which is a bit of a drive in the mornings, but the teacher, Miss Begley, has been really supportive. She's overlooked our late mornings and is helping me with the homework, telling me how to settle them down to do the work and how to help them without doing it for them."

"Homework," Lucy laughed. "I'd forgotten all about that. Do they get much?"

"Jade has some reading every evening and worksheets usually – colouring in letters or numbers, that kind of thing," Eileen explained. "Aran gets quite a lot – sums, English, reading. It can take him up to an hour."

"An hour! But he's only a baby!"

"He's seven, Lucy. And I think, to be honest, he's a little behind. He may take more time than normal. He finds it difficult. But I've found he loves books and I've been reading to them in the evenings, Roald Dahl, Harry Potter, the Narnia stories, that kind of thing. He'd love to be able to read for himself, so luckily he applies himself."

"That's great," Lucy said. "You're really enjoying this, aren't you, Mum?"

"Yes, love. It's given me a whole new lease of life. Eugene's not around much these days and I don't see you that often –"

"I'm sorry, Mum."

"I didn't mean it that way. It's normal for your children to move away and to get on with their own lives. But it's not easy to let go."

"I don't suppose it is." She'd never given it much thought before now.

"Anyway, I rang for a reason."

"Yes?"

"Linda has to go into hospital on Saturday morning to have two moles removed and I'd like to go up to see her." Linda was Eileen's younger sister who lived in Bangor with her husband and two children.

"Is she OK?"

"It's nothing serious. She'll only have to have a local anaesthetic and the doctors have said she'll be out by lunchtime. But I'd still like to see her all the same."

"Of course."

"But I don't want to bring Jade and Aran if I can help it. I know it's a lot to ask but could you look after them from Saturday morning till Sunday morning? I'll be back first thing, I promise."

"Of course," Lucy said. "I'd be happy to help. If you think I'm up to it."

"Absolutely!" Eileen laughed. "I checked with Agnes and she said it was fine and to ring her if there are any problems."

"I have to work on Sunday. But I won't need to leave till about eleven."

"I'll leave early and be back by then," Eileen promised. "Are Making Faces open on Sundays now?"

"No," Lucy said. "Thank God. If Paula had her way we would be, though. I'm helping at a christening."

"A christening?" Eileen asked.

"I'm helping with the food," Lucy said grudgingly. For some reason she wasn't keen on her mother knowing she was working with Dan. Eileen was bound to jump to all sorts of conclusions and once herself and Hilda, Dan's Mum, got together who knows what would happen? They'd be married off within minutes and Dan would be mortified and probably never speak to her again. "Listen, I have to run. I presume

138

you'd like me to stay in Dun Laoghaire on Saturday night?"

"If that's OK."

"It's fine. I'll ring you tomorrow to go over the details. I have to go now, sorry."

"You can tell me all about the Howard christening tomorrow," Eileen said firmly before putting down the phone. She wasn't going to give up that easily. She'd been talking to Hilda that very morning who had said Dan was doing the catering at Dr Howard's son's christening and that he was going to ask Lucy to help. Minna Howard was one of the consultants at Tallaght and Hilda had got Dan the 'gig'.

Lucy smiled wryly as she put down the receiver. Dublin was far too small for her liking.

Max was working late that evening and Alan and Hopper had gone into town to catch some obscure American singer/songwriter in Whelan's. She fetched the large tube of sour cream and onion Pringles from where she'd hidden them behind the fridge and settled in to watch a double episode of *Sex in the City*.

14

Max stared at his watch nervously. Ten to seven – he was early. He flicked on the radio and listened to the end of *The Last Word* on Today FM. The presenter was pontificating about the latest scandal – a sexual harassment case involving a senior politician and his secretary.

Max checked his appearance in the mirror. There wasn't much he could do with his hair – what was left of it. In the last year he'd favoured a tight, shaved cut as it seemed to suit his thinning blond locks. His eyes looked a bit red and he had a spot on his neck, but there was nothing he could do about those imperfections now. He'd ironed his navy shirt and teamed it with his beige combats, a pair Lucy had given him. So he hoped he looked half-decent anyway.

On the dot of seven he clicked off the radio abruptly. Then he decided it would seem over-enthusiastic if he appeared at seven on the button so he turned it back on again. At seven minutes past seven he was standing on Daria's doorstep, his palms sweating and his pulse racing. He hadn't been this nervous in a long, long time.

"Hi, Max," Daria said, opening the door. "Come in. I'll just get my coat. I'll be two seconds." She ran up the stairs. Max stood in the hall, noticing the bright, modern pictures on the yellow walls and the jaunty, bright-red velvet-covered chair.

On her return she smiled at him broadly. "So where are you taking me?"

"You'll see."

Half an hour later they were standing in semi-darkness, on damp, dark-grey concrete, surrounded by a salty, fishy smell.

"Well?" Max asked. "What do you think?"

"I love it!" Daria smiled, looking around her. She squeezed his arm. "It's brilliant!"

They were standing in front of the Bay of Rays and watching the fish swim backwards and forwards, gliding through the water using their wing-like fins. Now and again the flat grey and dark-brown fish swam along the surface, poking their 'noses' through the water.

"They look like dogs," Daria laughed, "the way they seem to be sniffing the top of the water."

"Or kites," Max said. The large fish were kite-shaped – a triangular body with a long, thin tail.

"You're right," she smiled. She moved on to the next tank. "What are these?"

"Tomato Clownfish and Yellow Tangs," he read from the plaque on the wall beside the tank. "Both native to the coral reefs of the Indo-Pacific."

"They're lovely," she said, gazing through the glass. "The colours are so intense."

"It's to camouflage them in the coral," Max explained, an expert after reading the plaque.

"And these are amazing!" she stared into the next tank where a host of tiny blue fish with bright yellow tails were swimming. "Yellow-tailed Blue Damsels," she read.

He put his arm around her and looked into the tank. She smelt delicious – of freshly mown lawns and summer evenings. He breathed in the delicate scent.

Daria turned towards him and kissed him gently on the cheek.

"Thanks for bringing me here. How did you get them to open the aquarium just for you?"

Max smiled. "The manager is a friend of mine. He sells my kites in the aquarium shop and we often go for coffee or lunch."

"You have some interesting friends. A beautician, an aquarium manager and a make-up artist."

"Yes. I suppose I have." He didn't really want to talk about Lucy – not yet. "Are you hungry? I've booked a restaurant called Marina nearby."

"I'm starving. Is it a fish restaurant?"

"It is," Max said. "How did you guess?"

"A themed evening," Daria laughed. "What fun!"

After they'd ordered and relaxed into a bottle of Spanish Merlot, Daria told Max all about her week of rehearsals.

"So, let me get this right," he said after listening intently for a few minutes. "You're playing Mrs Elton, but you're also the reserve for Emma."

"The understudy. You only have reserves in rugby and soccer."

"OK, the understudy," Max smiled. "And the woman playing Emma is a lush."

"Max!" Daria laughed.

"Well, from what you say she is. So there's a good chance you'll get to play Emma after all, if she's hungover or drunk or something."

Daria laughed again. "I guess so. But that's terrible. I don't wish Rosaleen any ill –"

"Of course you don't," Max smiled, putting his hand on hers. "It hadn't even crossed your mind. Here comes the food."

A young waiter was walking towards them with two large plates. Tantalising smells wafted up from the white ceramic. "Salmon blinis?" he asked. Daria smiled and nodded. "And the mussels in white wine sauce for you, sir."

"Thank you," Max said. They began to eat.

"These are gorgeous," Daria enthused, loading a small blini

pancake with lots of sour cream and topping it off with a generous slice of dark pink salmon. "How are the mussels?"

"Great." Max wiped some butter from the edges of his mouth with his linen napkin.

"Have you been here before?"

"No. It got a great write-up in *The Sunday Independent* a few weeks ago so this was a good excuse to try it out."

"So that's all I am? A good excuse."

"Sorry," he smiled sheepishly. "I didn't mean it that way."

"I'm only joking. I'm glad you asked me out and I'm having a really nice evening. You're lovely."

Max could feel himself blush. He wasn't used to compliments from people other than Lucy. "So are you. You're great company." He bit the bullet. "Hopper told me what she said at dinner – you know about me not wanting to be there because of you."

"Oh?" Daria said, tilting her head to one side and looking at the table. She was a little embarrassed that he'd brought it up.

Max felt uneasy. "It's hard to explain. Lucy has a habit of trying to matchmake and – well, I guess this time I didn't want to risk it. She can be very – how can I put this?"

"Direct?"

He nodded gratefully. "Yes, direct. I hope you weren't offended. I wanted to ask you out in my own time, without Lucy's involvement."

"That's what my sister, Grace, said," Daria said. "Anyway, don't worry. It's forgotten."

"Good," Max said, "and about Lucy – ."

"Yes?"

He took a deep breath. "I'd like to tell her about us myself."

"Us?" Daria smiled. "Is there an us?"

Max could feel himself blush again. "Well, um –"

"It's OK, Max," Daria laughed. "I'm only teasing you. I'd love to go out with you again."

"You would?"

"Yes! And what were you trying to say about Lucy?"

"I know you're having herself and Hopper over to dinner tomorrow."

"And?"

"I was hoping to talk to her on Saturday, so would you mind not mentioning anything about this evening until then?" he said, trying very hard not to sound too desperate. He got the strange feeling that Lucy wasn't going to take too kindly to being kept in the dark about things, but hopefully she'd be happy for him. After all, she and Daria were becoming friends – that should help, he thought rationally.

"Sure," Daria agreed, "no problem. I understand. You've been friends for a long time, I know. Of course you should tell her yourself." At the back of her mind Daria wondered whether 'friends' covered Max and Lucy's relationship, but decided not to dig too deeply.

Max breathed a sigh of relief. "Thanks."

While the waiter cleared their plates, Max told Daria about his latest project – making a surfing-kite for Dan.

"And this kite can pull you along the water?" Daria asked in amazement.

"It would probably pull *you* straight out of the water. Sometimes even Lucy is pulled off her feet by the bigger kites."

"It sounds brilliant I'd love to watch," Daria said. "I really enjoyed our afternoon on the beach."

"I'm going to test Dan's kite on Sandymount beach on Sunday, as long as it's not too windy," Max said. "Would you like to come along?"

"Sure," Daria nodded. "I'd love to."

"Grilled turbot with chervil?" the waiter asked.

"Here," Max said.

"And the baked monkfish for you," the waiter smiled at Daria. She smiled back. "*Bon appétit.*"

After their meal they strolled along the Bray seafront. Daria took Max's hand and held it firmly, her palm and fingers warm against his. There was a gentle breeze and the air was warm.

"It's a beautiful evening," she said as they approached the bright, twinkling lights of the amusements.

"Yes," he agreed. They sat down on a wall and looked out at the sea which was gently lapping the pebbly beach below them.

"Penny for them?" Daria said after a few seconds' silence.

"I was thinking how lucky I was to be here with you."

Daria leaned over and kissed him gently on the mouth. "I'm the lucky one."

Max brushed her short fringe off her face and kissed her forehead tenderly. "Thanks." He then cupped her chin in his hand and lifted her face towards his. Their lips touched, gently at first, then more firmly. Max put his arms around Daria's slim body and held it closely to his own. In the background, they could both hear the rhythmical sound of the waves breaking on the shore.

"How did last night go?" Lucy asked Max on the phone the next morning.

Max was silent for a second. How the hell?

"Dan's kite," Lucy prompted. "You said you were working on it last night."

"Oh, yes," Max said, relieved. For a moment he thought that he and Daria had been spotted. "Fine, it's nearly finished."

"When's the test run?"

Shit, Max thought to himself. "I'm not sure. Maybe Sunday."

"Pity," Lucy replied. "I'm helping Dan out at a christening all day."

"Dan?"

"Yes, Dan," Lucy replied irritably. "I know what you're thinking and don't!"

"What?"

"Stop acting the innocent. You and my mother. You're each as bad as the other."

"You mean you don't like Dan?" Max teased her.

"I'm not answering that. As if I'd tell his new best buddy anyway."

"Me?" Max laughed.

"Yes, you," Lucy grumbled. "The surfing and kiting boys."

Max laughed again. "You're just jealous."

145

"Of smelly wet suits and the icy-cold Irish sea?" she sniffed. "I don't think so! What are you up to on Saturday?"

"Depends," he said cautiously.

"Good! We're taking Aran and Jade to the Italian circus and then you're helping me feed them and put them to bed."

"You're joking! No way!"

"You'll love it and I won't be taking no for an answer," she said firmly. "I'll see you at ten at my house – you're driving."

Max sat at the table in the loft with his head in his hands. He was tired after last night. He and Daria had talked till one in her kitchen, sharing a bottle of wine and some brandies. He'd left his car there and walked home. He had to collect it later – before Lucy and Hopper arrived.

The way he was feeling at present, the very idea of a circus with its animals, noise, crowds and smells was enough to turn his stomach. Still, he mused, at least I'll have a chance to talk to Lucy.

15

"Tell me about last night," Grace said as she helped her sister set the kitchen table.

"It was great!" Daria smiled. "He's a sweet guy, really interesting to talk to and a real gentleman. First we went to the aquarium in Bray and we were the only people there."

"That's original," Grace said. She loved to see her sister smile and Daria had done nothing but all morning.

"And then we had dinner in a place called Marina in Bray."

"And then?"

"We went for a walk and came back here."

"And?"

"Stop being so nosy, Grace!"

"So I take it that you like him then?"

"Yes," Daria admitted. "And before you ask, we're meeting up on Sunday afternoon. Oh, and don't say anything to Lucy or Hopper, OK?"

"Why not?"

"Max wants to tell Lucy about us himself."

"Us?" Grace said, lifting her eyebrows. "So there is an us?"

147

Daria smiled, remembering teasing Max about the very same thing. "I hope so."

"I won't open my mouth," Grace promised. "But I hope he tells Lucy soon, otherwise it could cause problems. And besides, it'll be fun to compare notes with her about the two of you."

"Charming," Daria laughed. "Now are you going to ring the Chinese or will I?"

"Hi, Lucy." Daria gave her guest a kiss on the cheek and ushered her inside. "Hi, Hopper," another kiss.

Hopper handed her a clinking Oddbins bag. "You might want to put the bottle of white in the fridge. It isn't chilled."

"How have you been?" Lucy asked as they followed Daria into the kitchen.

"Really well, thanks."

"I like the yellow in the hall," Hopper said. "It's lovely and warm."

"Grace chose it," Daria said. "I think it's a little bright myself but –"

"What are you saying about me now, sister dear?" Grace asked. She smiled broadly. "How are you both?" she asked Lucy and Hopper. Being a little more reserved than her sister she didn't kiss Lucy and Hopper.

"Excellent!" Hopper enthused. "And all the better for seeing the two of you."

"Sit down," Daria said, gesturing at the table. "Our living-room is tiny so we thought we'd stay in here if you don't mind. It's much bigger."

"I love kitchens," Lucy said. "So you'll have no argument from me."

"I'm afraid we probably don't use ours in the same way as you use yours though," Daria smiled ruefully. "I can't remember the last time we used the oven for anything other that heating pizzas. And we don't own anything like the amount of kitchen appliances you do."

"That reminds me of a joke," Lucy said. "Why do brides wear white?"

"Go on," Grace said. "Tell us."

"So they'll fit in with the rest of the kitchen appliances after the wedding."

Everyone groaned.

"That's terrible," Hopper squealed. "Who told you that one?"

Lucy thought for a second. "Mossy, I think."

"That'd be right," Hopper grimaced. "Mossy is the most sexist man I've ever met. He works in the Loft with Max. Lucy went out with him for a while and they spent the entire time either in the kitchen – she'd cook and he'd eat, he was the original human dustbin – or in the bedroom. It was sad."

"It's true," Lucy admitted. "I don't think we had a decent conversation in the whole time we were together. It's terrible how a nice body can suppress all your intelligence and common sense."

"Tell me about it," Daria smiled. "I once went out with an Italian actor who talked about himself night and day. He was gorgeous, like a cross between that dark-haired guy from *Traffic* and Rob Lowe."

"Rob Lowe?" Hopper asked in disgust. "He's mank."

"He most certainly is not!" Daria insisted. "Have you never seen *About Last Night* or *St Elmo's Fire*?"

"You eighties girl, you," Hopper laughed.

"You're right, Hopper," Grace said. "She's very sad. But Romero was very good-looking. A complete egotistical bastard however."

"Do we ever learn?" Lucy asked.

"Maybe," Grace said, looking at her sister.

Daria stood up, ignoring her sister's gaze. "I'm so rude, I never offered anyone a drink," she said. "Who'd like a glass of wine? Red or white?"

"Red for me," Lucy said.

"Me too," Hopper added.

"And one white for Grace," Daria said, opening the fridge and pulling out a chilled bottle of Chardonnay. She poured the wine and handed around the glasses. "Now I'm just popping out to collect the Chinese. We got a bit of everything. I hope that suits?"

"Sounds great," Hopper smiled. "Would you like some company?"

"Yes," Daria smiled, "that'd be nice. It's just across the road."

After they had left the kitchen Grace stood up. "I'm just going to top up my glass. It's going down rather quickly."

"It's Friday," Lucy laughed. "No school for you tomorrow."

"Thank God."

"I don't know how you do it," Lucy said. "I vaguely thought about primary-school teaching when I was in sixth year. I would have been woeful though. I have no patience at all. A classful of children would have scared the living daylights out of me."

"You'd have been well able for them," Grace smiled. "Anyway my lot are small. At least I'm bigger than them. By the time they reach sixth class some of the girls are so tall and glamorous it's scary."

"Glamorous?" Lucy asked incredulously. "Are you serious?"

"Yes. They are all confirmed Britney Spears addicts, with long hair and glittery make-up and pink nails. You should see them!"

Lucy whistled. "All with boyfriends no doubt. Any of them have cars?"

"No. They have some pretty excellent scooters though. But you're right. They all have boyfriends, the cool ones anyway. Makes us single teachers feel a bit inadequate really."

"I can imagine," Lucy said. She took a sip of her wine. "Have you met any nice Irish men? Or do you prefer Americans?"

Grace smiled. Lucy certainly was direct. "I like both, I guess, in different ways. Irish men have a great sense of humour but Americans treat you like a princess. In America the whole dating thing is very different. It's kind of like a game with set rules – you know, first date kissing but no tongues, second date tongues –"

"Are you serious?" Lucy asked. "That sounds really old-fashioned."

Grace shrugged her shoulders. "It is, I suppose, but at least you know where you are with American men. Irish men could be all over you like a rash within the first minute of meeting you or they could ignore you all night. You just wouldn't know."

"You're right there. It took my last boyfriend, Brian, ages to get the message that I fancied him. I had to practically throw myself at him."

"Are you still together?"

"No. We broke up a short while ago. Nice guy but it wasn't quite right, if you know what I mean."

"Completely," Grace said. "I broke up with Miles just before Christmas. He's American, from New York and we were attempting to have a long-distance relationship. I met him when he was in Dublin on business."

"What happened?"

"We were together nearly a year but the constant travelling and long, wistful phone calls got to me in the end. I didn't love him enough to move over there and he didn't love me enough to move to Dublin. Sad really."

"That must have been hard."

"It was. But I'm fine now. It was for the best."

"You'll probably meet some nice Irish man and be swept off your feet. You wait and see."

"I'm not holding my breath. To be honest I'm enjoying being on my own at the moment. I'm in no hurry."

"Good woman. You're dead right."

"What about you? Any new men on the horizon?"

Lucy smiled sheepishly. "There is someone. But –"

"Go on."

"I'm not sure if he likes me." She told Grace about meeting Dan at *The Sound of Music* and at the Jamie Oliver signing. "He's asked me to help him on Sunday at a christening, so I'll see him again then."

"He's a fool if he doesn't fall for you – a beautiful woman with an exceptional talent in the kitchen."

"Being a chef, I'm not sure it's my kitchen talent he'd be after," Lucy laughed. "But thanks all the same."

"Hello!" they heard Hopper call from the hall. "Food's coming."

Daria and Hopper walked into the kitchen laden down with brown-paper bags with cardboard handles. "So, what have we missed?" Daria asked.

"Nothing," Lucy smiled angelically. "We were just discussing Irish and American politics."

"And world trade agreements," Grace added. "The usual."

"This is chicken chow-mein," Daria said putting a steaming red ceramic dish in the middle of the table. "This is Szechuan king prawn, and these are the house special, Singapore noodles, my favourite. There's sweet and sour chicken, some kind of beef and black-bean thing and boiled and fried rice. Please help yourselves."

"It all looks delicious," Hopper said, her eyes gleaming. "I don't know where to start."

"Try a bit of everything and see what you like best," Daria suggested. "The Szechuan sauce is quite spicy – it's got chilli in it, so be careful."

"I'll definitely have that then," Hopper grinned. "I love hot food."

"It's also laced with garlic," Lucy warned. "Alan won't be too impressed."

"I wouldn't worry too much about my darling boyfriend. He has some English mates over and they are hitting the Bhai Curry House in town. I don't expect to see him till tomorrow at the earliest."

"Men and their curries," Daria laughed. "I mean I like curry, don't get me wrong. But they seem to have some sort of strange curry fetish. Do you think it has some sort of hormonal effect on them or something? Maybe it's like chocolate to us girls."

"I know what sort of effect it has on Alan," Hopper laughed. "But I'm not sure if flatulence counts as hormonal, does it?"

"Hopper!" Lucy said.

"No, Lucy," Grace smiled. "She's right. It does cause flatulence."

"Can we talk about something else while we're eating?" Daria giggled. "Please?"

"I was asking Grace about Irish and American men earlier," Lucy said, "and she was telling me about the dating rules. We only got as far as the first date though."

"The second," Grace corrected her. "But nothing much changes until about the third month when you might be allowed to sleep with him if he was showing signs of commitment and really respected you."

"What?" Hopper asked, nearly choking on her noodles. "Three months? Are you serious?"

"Wait!" Daria said suddenly. "That reminds me. I wanted to show you both my library book." She jumped up and picked a book up off the kitchen counter. "Here we are – *The Complete Book of Rules : Time-tested Secrets for Capturing the Heart of Mr Right*. It's by two American women."

"I watched a programme about this a couple of years ago," Lucy said. "It's really old-fashioned and all the men were calling it devious."

"It is a bit devious," Daria laughed. "I'm not sure it would work on Irish men either."

"Why's that?" Grace asked, trying not to sound too interested.

"Well, the first rule is 'Be a creature unlike any other'," Daria smiled.

"A what?" Lucy asked.

"Let me see," Daria said, scanning the type. "Right, it's to do with smiling and lighting up rooms. Boring really. I'll go to rule two – 'Don't talk to a man first'."

"So you just have to stand and stare at them until they talk to you?" Lucy asked in bemusement.

"The whole thing seems to be that the men have to pursue you," Daria explained. "So not only can you not talk to them first, you can't phone them ever, you can't accept dates for the weekend after Wednesday and you never pay for anything."

"I've totally blown it then," Hopper said. "In all respects."

"Don't tell me you've slept with Alan already?" Lucy asked jokingly.

"I'm ashamed to say I have," Hopper said with mock humility. "On the first date. Which wasn't even a date. And I instigated the entire thing."

"Shame on you," Daria giggled. "Right, I think we've had enough of this book. Anyway, as they say, rules are meant to be broken." She threw it onto the kitchen counter.

Grace topped up all the wine glasses which had started to empty at an alarming rate.

"Maybe we should make some of our own rules," Hopper said, taking a large slug of her red wine.

"Like what?" Daria asked with interest.

"Let me see," Hopper mulled it over. "OK, rule number one – always have knock-out sex on the first date, that way they won't forget you. Actually, forget that. Always give a knock-out blowjob on the first date. They never forget that!"

"Hopper!" Lucy squealed.

"Are you speaking from experience?" Grace asked.

"Of course," Hopper smiled wickedly.

"You do that on a first date?" Daria asked. "Oral sex. Do you not think it's a bit – you know – personal?"

"Would you sleep with someone on the first date?" Hopper asked.

"Depends," Daria replied. "Maybe not on the first, but when it felt right." She took a sip of her wine. "Or if I was really feeling in the mood." She grinned.

"Good woman!" Hopper said animatedly. "But what about blowjobs?"

"No," Daria said, wrinkling her nose slightly. "I'd have to know them better to get that intimate."

"Intimate!" Lucy shrieked. "But you'd sleep with them!"

"Yes. But that's different."

"How is it different?" Hopper asked.

"Just is," Daria replied.

"I think Daria's right," Grace interjected. "Using your mouth just seems a lot more – oh, I don't know –"

"Intimate!" Daria insisted. "Like I said."

"Yes," Grace agreed, nodding vehemently.

"You're both mad," Lucy laughed.

"It's just as well neither of you are with my Alan," Hopper grinned. "He loves his –"

"Too much information!" Lucy screamed, putting her hands to her ears theatrically. "We've only just met Daria and Grace! They'll think we're brazen hussies."

"As the only one here having sex to my knowledge," Hopper continued, "I'd like to –"

"Bitch," Daria interrupted good-naturedly.

"I'd like to propose a toast to good sex," Hopper continued. "Blowjobs or no blowjobs."

"To good sex," Lucy said raising her glass. Everyone joined in.

"I have another rule," Hopper said. "At the beginning, you must wear nice underwear at all times."

"Unless it's all in the wash," Daria added. "Then you shouldn't wear anything."

"Nothing is good," Lucy smiled. "I like nothing."

"I'm a 'Ruby's Drawer' girl myself," Grace smiled. "I used to buy it all the time in the States. Now I use the Web site."

"Isn't it great!" Hopper agreed. "I bought these amazing purple knickers recently that have little ribbon ties holding them up and a cute matching lacy bra."

"That explains the brown parcels. Me and Alan thought you were having sex-toys sent to the house," Lucy laughed. "How disappointing!"

Hopper glared at her and then laughed. "Nosy gits. But I wouldn't examine my post too carefully these days. You never know what you might find."

"Ice cream, everyone?" Grace said, trying to keep the conversation on safer ground. She stood up.

"Ice cream and sex," Hopper grinned. "Interesting word association."

Grace laughed. "Is there anyone not having ice cream? Speak now or forever hold your peace."

"That was very legal," Lucy giggled.

"I'm a very legal kind of gal," Grace smiled.

"Unlike me," Hopper insisted. "I'm totally illegal."

Grace spooned large dollops of chocolate ice cream into bowls and placed them on the table.

"While we're on the subject, Hopper," Lucy said, "the underwear subject, I mean. What does Alan go for? Is he your typical male – black basque, suspenders and high-heel boots?"

"They're so predictable, aren't they," Daria agreed.

Hopper cocked her head to one side and thought for a second. "Yes and no. He likes the usual all right. But he also likes things with fluff and feathers on them. Pink girlie things. To be honest, we haven't been together that long and I haven't fully tested the waters yet."

"Have you tried your pink fake-fur padded handcuffs?" Lucy asked.

"No!" Hopper laughed. "Although he might like those all right!"

"This is all making me very jealous," Daria said wistfully.

"But you have a –" Grace held her tongue after Daria kicked her under the table.

"A ghost of boyfriends past," Daria said smiling.

"What's that?" Hopper asked.

"Don't know," Daria admitted. "I just made it up. It's the drink talking."

"It's just funny because I think Alan's bedroom is haunted," Hopper said. "Maybe it's the ghost of his ex, Paula."

"But she's still alive," Lucy pointed out.

"Unfortunately," Hopper muttered.

Lucy glared at her.

"Why do you think the room's haunted?" Grace asked.

"It's developed a really funny smell this week," Hopper began. "Sweet but acidic. We can't find where it's coming from. And his things keep moving around the room. The other day he found his hairbrush on the bedside table and he always leaves it on the window-sill."

Lucy laughed. "Some scary ghost you have there, Hopper."

"OK, smart-ass. Listen to this – he found fingerprints on his mirror and they weren't his or mine, and one evening he came in and there was the impression of a head on his pillow."

"And?" Lucy asked with interest.

"We'd had a pillow fight that morning. His pillows are feather. We left the pillows on the floor."

"So your ghost makes the bed?" Daria asked, trying not to laugh.

"It's not funny," Hopper said. "It's freaking Alan out."

"There *are* ghosts that leave smells and move things around, come to think of it," Grace said.

Hopper looked at her carefully.

"I remember reading about this haunted house in America a few years ago," Grace said. "It had a poltergeist."

"You think Alan's room might have a poltergeist?" Hopper asked.

"Maybe," Grace said thoughtfully. "You should try to video it. That's what the people in the book did."

"Great idea. I think I will."

"That was really nice," Lucy said after they had settled themselves into the taxi and were under way. "They're great fun."

"Nice food too," Hopper said. "I'm stuffed."

"It's been good catching up with you, too. I haven't seen you all week. And you never told me about Alan's room being haunted."

Hopper was silent for a few seconds. "I'm sorry. I guess myself and Alan have been a bit caught up in each other." She put her hand on Lucy's. "We'll do something next week, I promise. Just the two of us. Go to the cinema or something."

Lucy sighed. "I'm sorry, I didn't mean to make you feel bad. I'm just not in great form. Ignore me."

"Anything wrong?"

"Nothing I can put my finger on. Just a general less than one hundred per cent feeling. Maybe I'm coming down with something."

"How's work?"

"Fine, I suppose. Same as usual."

"And Paula?"

"Back to her usual annoying self," Lucy said. "When is Alan going to tell her about the pair of you?"

"Do you think she suspects something?"

"Doubtful. She's so caught up in her own little selfish world she tends not to notice what's going on around her. But she'll find out eventually. And then she'll probably fire me."

"Are you kidding?" Hopper said. "You're the one who keeps the place running. She's such a little prima donna, spending hours with the models and the politicians' wives and ignoring the bread-and-butter regulars. The clients like you. There's no way she'd let you go, unless she's even stupider than I thought."

"Thanks," Lucy replied gratefully. At least someone appreciated her. "I hope you're right. But I really think Alan should talk to her, and soon."

"I'll have a word with him over the weekend," Hopper promised. "What have you got planned for Sunday? There's football on – want to watch it with us?"

"Thanks but no. As you're aware I have less than no interest in the game. And besides, I'm helping at a christening with Dan."

"Dan from *The Sound of Music?*"

"Yes."

Hopper was silent. Lucy looked at her. She was grinning broadly.

"What?" Lucy demanded. "Not you as well."

"I'm not saying anything," Hopper said evenly.

"Keep your smirks to yourself. I'm just helping out a friend."

"A friend?"

"Yes, a friend. Now can we change the subject?"

16

Max pulled up outside Lucy's house. He was tired and grumpy. He'd stayed up far too late watching bad television and drinking whiskey, and his body was punishing him for it. He needed to spend the morning in bed, not entertaining two children. How did he let himself get talked into these things? But at least he'd get to tell Lucy about Daria.

He beeped his horn for a brief second to let her know he was outside. It was nearly ten after all – if he was awake the neighbours bloody well deserved to be too.

Lucy waved from the door and went back inside. She came back out a few minutes later carrying a large grey travel-bag, a small black rucksack, and a jacket. Max got out of the car and kissed her on the cheek.

"I though you were only staying one night at your mum's," he said as he swung her heavy bag into the boot.

"I am," she replied, letting herself into the car.

He walked around to the driver's side and opened the door. He would never understand women and packing, never. If he was staying

159

the night somewhere he might bring a spare pair of boxers and his toothbrush in the pocket of his jacket. But what the hell was in her bag?

"I'm going straight to the christening tomorrow, so I need extra things. Work things, like an apron and stuff."

Max grunted non-committally.

If the truth be known, Lucy couldn't decide what to wear the following day. She wanted to look smart and efficient yet sexy and it wasn't an easy one to call. In the end she'd thrown all her favourite clothes into her bag and hoped for the best. Not to mention her make-up, hairdryer, choice of three perfumes (Coco Chanel, Envy or Cabotine, depending on her mood), and two pairs of shoes.

"What's wrong with you?" she asked, after several minutes of silence.

"Nothing. I'm just tired."

"You've been working too hard," said Lucy. "What were you up to last night, anyway?"

"I stayed in." Max turned onto the dual carriageway at Ballsbridge. "Watched crap telly, fell asleep on the sofa, woke up at four and went to bed."

"Sounds lovely," she said. "A bit of football in the park with Aran will wake you up."

"Um," Max grunted.

"Listen, if you don't want to help –"

"No," interrupted Max, "it's fine. Ignore me. Once I've had some breakfast I'll be grand."

"We'll stop and get some bacon and sausages on the way and I'll make you a fry in Mum's, OK?"

"Sounds good," he said, suddenly beginning to feel better. "Hey, I talked to Mossy about going to Lea's Debs."

"Mossy?" Lucy asked incredulously. "No way! What did he say?"

"He's agreed to do it."

"Excellent!" she said. "How much do we have to pay him? I presume there are conditions."

Max laughed. "How did you guess? We have to pay for a limo, the flowers and the chocolates and . . ." Max stopped as he navigated some roadworks.

"And?" Lucy asked impatiently.

"He wants a session of massages at Making Faces."

"What?" Lucy shrieked.

"My head," Max groaned. "Don't yell."

"I thought you said you were in last night," Lucy said suspiciously.

"I was. I just had a few whiskeys."

Lucy raised her eyebrows. "Anyway, what's with Mossy and the massages?"

"Himself and Jenny have broken up. She caught him kissing a Dutch girl in Lillie's and she wasn't impressed. But he said he really misses the massages so he wants more."

"There's no way I'm massaging Mossy."

"There's always Paula," Max said hopefully.

"Paula doesn't do massage. She says it wrecks her nails."

"She might make an exception for Mossy."

"I wouldn't bet on it."

"He's calling in on Monday for his first session. So you'd better be nice to him."

Lucy said nothing.

Ten minutes later, after a flying visit to a mini-market in Dun Laoghaire, they pulled up outside Eileen's house and hopped out. The front door swung open before they were halfway up the path.

Jade ran out. "Hi, Lucy," she said. "Are we really going to the circus?"

"Yes," Lucy smiled.

Jade looked up at her. "I've never been to the circus."

Aran was waiting at the front door with a black and white football in his arms. He was wearing a Manchester United tracksuit.

Lucy looked at Max and smiled. "I guess we're going to the park then."

"Can we eat first?" Max pleaded. "I'm starving."

"OK. I wouldn't like the new David Beckham to have to play on an empty stomach."

Eileen came down the stairs. "Thank you so much, Lucy. And Max too." She gave Max a kiss on the cheek. "How nice to see you! I'd better get going. I want to get to Bangor as soon as possible and I'm sure the traffic in town is going to be terrible, even at this hour."

"You should go over the East Link," Max suggested. "It makes sense to avoid town if you can."

"Good idea," Eileen said. She kissed Jade and Aran. "Now be good for Lucy and Max, you two. Aran, make sure you help Lucy this evening with finding pyjamas and everything. And bed by eight, mind. I'll ring this evening to see how you're getting on."

"We'll be good, Eileen, honest!" Aran smiled as if butter wouldn't melt in his mouth.

Max carried Eileen's bag out to the car. It was much lighter than her daughter's.

"Thanks, Max," Eileen said. "Have a good day with the kids." She smiled widely. "It'll be good practice for you, when – you know."

"Bye, Eileen," Max laughed. He watched as the car pulled away. Lucy, Jade and Aran waved from the doorway.

"Who'd like some sausages?" asked Lucy, making her way towards the kitchen.

"We've already had breakfast," said Aran, trying not to sound impatient. He was dying to get to the park. It wasn't often he got to play football, especially not with a man. He'd never met his dad. He thought he'd be playing with Lucy but this was even better.

"Ages ago," Jade added.

"But I'm sure you could fit in a sausage or two," said Lucy. "Am I right?" They both smiled and nodded.

Max brought up the rear. He'd never seen Lucy with children – she was really good with them. She seated them down in the kitchen and poured them each a glass of Sunny Delight.

"Eileen makes me have a plastic cup," said Jade, "but I like this one better." She held up her glass tumbler on which Bart and Lisa Simpson were swimming with dolphins.

"Eileen got that one free with the Nutella," Aran said knowledgeably. "Be careful you don't drop it."

"I won't drop it," Jade insisted nervously. "I'll be real careful. I promise."

"It doesn't really matter if you do break it," said Lucy. "We can always get another." She put a plate down in front of each of them. Max was leaning against the kitchen counter holding the plastic shopping bags and feeling a little out of place.

"I forget to introduce you all properly," she said, taking the bags from Max and placing them on the table. "This is Max, my friend. Say hello."

Jade and Aran said, "Hi, Max."

"And Max, this is Jade and Aran."

"Hi, Jade and Aran. Nice to meet you." He waved at them lamely and smiled a little too broadly.

"What football team do you support?" asked Aran with a little frown. Max wasn't wearing any club's T-shirt so it was hard to tell.

"Well, if I had to pick one I'd choose Manchester United," Max said kindly. He actually supported Leeds, sad person that he was, but he could see that Aran was a mad United fan and he didn't want to disappoint him.

"Cool!" Aran grinned. "Who's your favourite player?"

Shit, Max thought. "Um, Roy Keane."

"Mine's David Beckham."

"He's got a baby," said Jade. "There was a picture in one of mam's magazines."

"It's called Brooklyn," said Aran. "Becks has the name tattooed on his back."

"I'd forgotten that," said Max. He remembered thinking that it was a lot safer than getting your girlfriend or even wife's name, if you had to do it at all.

163

They heard a sizzle as Lucy placed the sausages and bacon in a frying pan. "Now, how do you all like your eggs?"

"Scrambled!" Jade said quickly before anyone else had a chance.

"Mam always makes scrambled eggs," Aran explained. "They're Jade's favourites."

"Scrambled it is then. Is that OK with you, Max?"

"Perfect," Max smiled. "So Aran, what position do you play?"

Lucy zoned out as the boys discussed the Premiership. After a few minutes she noticed Jade looking a little left out. "Are you excited about the circus?" she asked, interrupting the football talk.

"Yes! Aran's been but I haven't."

"When did you go, Aran?" asked Max.

"When I was four. Mam took me to Booterstown to see it. There were tigers. And llamas. I liked the llamas." His eyes lit up. "And I had candy floss. Can Jade have some candy floss today, Lucy?"

Max looked at Lucy. What a nice child! He couldn't recall ever thinking of his own sister, Lea, before himself at that age. Maybe that was because Lea was so spoilt that he resented her right from the very start.

"Max? Aran just asked you do you like candyfloss?"

Max smiled. "I sure do. I love the way it sticks to your mouth and then disintegrates. Yum."

"Candy floss for everyone, then," Aran said decidedly. "This is going to be so cool."

Lucy piled the sausages and bacon onto a large plate and put the scrambled egg saucepan on a mat in the middle of the table. "Help yourselves," she grinned, handing everyone cutlery. "Can you give Jade a hand, Max?" He nodded and she stood up to fetch some more Sunny Delight and some normal orange juice for herself and Max from the fridge.

"I thought you said you'd eaten already," Max said to Aran who was shovelling food into his mouth and washing it down with gulps of orange.

"I have," Aran replied, his mouth full of food.

"Aran!" Lucy scolded good-naturedly. "Don't eat with your mouth full."

Aran swallowed and grinned. "I have to eat with my mouth full, Lucy."

Max laughed. "He has a point."

Lucy sighed. "You know what I mean."

Aran nodded. "I know, I know. Don't talk with my mouth full."

"That's right," Lucy smiled. "Just what I said."

They all laughed. Jade looked at her brother admiringly. She thought he was very clever.

Aran took another gulp of his drink and looked at Max beseechingly. "Can we go to the park now? Please?"

"Let Max finish," Lucy said, looking at Max's plate.

"But we won't have time before the circus," Aran pleaded.

"Give me two minutes," Max said, eating quickly.

"Don't give yourself indigestion," Lucy said.

"Don't worry. I've a strong stomach – I'll be fine."

A few minutes later Max stood up. "Right," he said to Lucy. "I'm done."

"Are you sure?"

"Yes. Listen, I'll go on with Aran and you two can follow."

"Great." She put her hand on Jade's head. "I need Jade to be my little helper, don't I, pet?"

Jade smiled up at her. "I like helping."

"I know you do," Lucy said gently. "Eileen told me you're a great little worker." She also told her to make sure Jade was included in things on her own as Aran tended to be very protective of her and did everything for her. Jade needed to find her own place in the world, Agnes, the social worker, had explained. She wouldn't always have her older brother to look after her.

"See ya later, alligator," Aran said as he ran into the hall and opened the door.

"Wait for me!" Max shouted after him. "I hope my heart is up to this," he said, holding his chest theatrically and grinning at Lucy.

"Go on, you old ham," she laughed. "Catch up with him and we'll see you in a minute."

"Is Max your boyfriend?" asked Jade as she passed Lucy the glasses from the table. Lucy squirted some more Fairy Liquid into the washing-up bowl and swirled it about with her yellow-rubber-gloved hand. There was a dishwasher but she wanted to give Aran and Max some time alone and washing-up was a good delaying tactic. She'd decided it would be good for both of them to have some male company.

"No, love," said Lucy. "He's my friend. My best friend."

"He's very nice. Does he not love you? Mam had a boyfriend called Terry and she said he didn't love her."

Lucy was silent for a second. She didn't know what to say. Jade was only five and it wasn't fair that she was privy to such adult things at such an early age.

"He loves me the same way as Aran loves you," Lucy began cautiously. She didn't know if a five-year-old would understand what many people of her own age didn't. "Like a brother. We've grown up together, you see."

Jade stared at Lucy. "I want to marry Aran. So he'll never go away."

Lucy sighed. She didn't want to upset Jade. "That's nice. But he'll never go away. He loves you a lot."

"Dad went away," said Jade.

Lucy didn't know what to say. But she wanted to be honest with Jade. "But your mum and Aran will always be there for you."

"Mam has a new baby," said Jade, tears beginning to form in her blue eyes. "She won't want us back now."

Lucy took off the washing-up gloves, put her arms around the little girl and held her tight. "Your mum's getting better all the time. Eileen said the baby's not crying so much now and your mum's not so tired. You'll both be home soon. You saw her last week, didn't you?"

"Yes, but I'd like to see her every day," Jade said into Lucy's shoulder. "I like Eileen. She's nice. But I want Mam."

"I know you do," Lucy crooned, rubbing Jade's back gently. "It'll be

OK. Why don't you run up to the bathroom and wash your face? Then we can join the boys in the park, OK?"

Jade looked at Lucy. "Don't tell Aran I was crying, will you? He told me I have to be a big girl and not to cry."

"Of course I won't. Tomorrow, when Eileen's home, I'll ask her can you visit your mum again. And you could give your mum a ring before we go if you like."

Jade looked doubtful. "She's not in. Aran already tried ringing."

"Tell you what. Why don't you write to her or draw her a picture or something, and we could drop it in on the way to the zoo?"

Jade began to smile. "I'd like to draw Mam a picture later. But can I give it to her when I see her instead?"

Lucy smiled at her. "Of course, that's a great idea. Go and wash your face and I'll get the jackets."

"And how's my football star?" Lucy asked Max in Dun Laoghaire Park. Aran and Jade were climbing on the monkey bars in the playground. She and Max were sitting a little distance away on a metal park bench which was giving her a very cold bum.

"Honestly?"

Lucy nodded.

"I'm knackered. Being goalie isn't all it's cracked up to be. Where does your man get his energy?" He gestured towards the playground.

"Jade's upset about her mum," said Lucy. "We were talking when you and Aran left."

"I thought her eyes looked a little red," said Max.

"It's hard to know what to say," she sighed. "It's a difficult situation for everyone."

"But they'll be back in their own house soon, right?"

"Yes. Well, mum hopes so anyway. But she'll miss them."

"It must be hard building a relationship like that and then having to let go," Max mused. "I couldn't do it."

"I don't think I could either. But mum's very pragmatic about the whole fostering thing. She says she wants to give something back."

167

"I really admire what she's doing. Aran and Jade are great and they deserve every chance in life."

"You're right," said Lucy. She put her head on his shoulder. "They do."

"Is it time for the circus?" Aran shouted over from the monkey bars. Lucy looked at her watch. "Not yet."

"Cool. More time to play. Are you ready, Max?"

Max groaned. "Give me a few more minutes. I'm wrecked."

Lucy and Max sat in companionable silence, watching Jade and Aran hanging off the wooden bars like real chimpanzees. Max thought about talking to Lucy about Daria but as he was about to bring up the subject Aran came running over, eager to start another punishing game of footie.

Never mind, Max thought to himself as he picked up the football. There'll be plenty of time later.

"Are you both strapped in?" asked Lucy, turning around to survey the back seat.

"Yes, Mummy," Max quipped from the driver's seat.

Jade and Aran giggled.

"I wasn't asking you, idiot."

Max turned the key in the ignition. "Is everybody ready for the circus?"

"Yes!" Jade and Aran chorused from the back.

"Lucy? Are you ready?"

"Yes, Daddy," she smiled. He seemed to be really enjoying spending time with the children. Although she suspected most guys relished the chance to act like kids whatever age they were. She gazed out the window at a good-looking young father who was pushing a pram.

"Earth calling Lucy. Come in, Lucy! Jade asked you about the animals. Do you know if there *are* lions and tigers at this circus?"

"Sorry, I was miles away." She thought for a second. "I'm not sure. They don't have as many wild animals as they used to in circuses though. So maybe not."

"Why not?" asked Aran.

"It's not good for the animals to be cooped up in small spaces," Lucy explained. "They're used to wide open plains where they can run around. It'd be like keeping yourself and Jade in one small room all day, I guess."

"I wouldn't like that," said Aran.

Lucy glanced at Jade in the rear-view mirror. The little girl looked disappointed. "I tell you what, if there are no lions and tigers in the circus I'll take you both to the Safari Plains in the zoo next weekend, OK?"

"Can they run around there?" asked Aran. "The animals, I mean."

"Yes. It's specially designed for them, with lots of open space. Anyway, the zoo is fun."

"I've never been to the zoo," said Jade.

"I haven't either," said Aran.

"That settles it. We'll go next weekend even if there *are* lions and tigers today. How's that?"

"Cool!" Aran grinned. Jade nodded.

"Can I come too?" asked Max. He was feeling a little left out. "I haven't been for years. I hear they've really improved it in the last while."

"Of course you can," said Lucy. "That would be fun."

"It's like you're the Mammy and Daddy," said Jade. "And we're the children. Like a real family."

"Yes, love," said Lucy. "I suppose it is."

Max concentrated on the road. He thought about what Jade had just said. He supposed one day he *would* be driving his own children to the zoo with his lovely (he hoped) wife. Maybe settling down wouldn't be so bad, he mused as he drove along Monkstown seafront.

"Do you think all these cars are going to the circus?" asked Jade as they were stopped at traffic lights in Blackrock.

"Some of them might be," said Max. They drove past Roches Stores and the blue iron railings of Blackrock College.

"I see it. I see it!" Jade squealed as the large red and white tent came into view. There were ornate wooden steps leading into the tent's enclosure and tall, swarthy men in red uniforms were collecting the tickets. Max parked the car down a side street. Jade took Lucy's hand as they walked towards the booking office.

"I just have to collect the tickets," said Lucy. "Then we can go inside."

Jade pulled excitedly out of her arm. "There's pictures of tigers on that caravan! Look, Lucy!"

"So there are," Lucy smiled. "And elephants."

They queued to get their tickets. Lively Italian organ music played in the background, giving a festive air.

"Look!" Jade exclaimed in awe. Her eyes were focused on the ornate merry-go-round beside the tent. Wooden horses snaked up and down golden poles, their manes fanning out behind them and their eyes wild and exciting. She pulled her hand out of Lucy's, ran towards it but stopped at a safe distance from it, much to Lucy's relief.

"Reminds me of *The Magic Roundabout*," Max grinned. "Dougal and Florence and all the gang."

"I don't think their roundabout was quite like that," Lucy laughed. "I seem to remember it being just red and blue."

"I think you're right. Hey, look at Jade!" Jade was swaying backwards and forwards to the music, watching a lavender-coloured horse as it revolved. The merry-go-round stopped and she turned to look at Max and Lucy.

"Can I have a go?" Jade asked quietly, nervous that they'd say no. She'd never seen such a beautiful horse and she so wanted to sit on it.

"Of course," Lucy smiled.

"Here," said Max. He held out his hand and helped Jade step onto the wooden platform beside the lavender horse. It seemed to tower above her and he had to lift her on, his arms securely around her waist. He was amazed at how little she weighed. He'd lifted Aran in the park and thrown him over his shoulder, fireman style, but Jade was less than half her brother's weight.

Lucy paid the young attendant. Aran stood beside Max and stared at his sister with a slightly worried expression on his face.

"Would you like a go too?" Lucy asked kindly.

"No thanks. I think I'll just watch."

"Not really a boy's thing," said Max, "is it, Aran?"

"No," Aran said gratefully. After a few seconds the merry-go-round started to move. "You don't think she'll fall off, do you?" he asked, biting his lip.

"She'll be fine," Lucy assured him. "She's holding on really tightly. Don't worry."

Jade had a huge smile plastered from ear to ear. She bent forward and hugged the horse around its neck.

The ride didn't last very long and in a way Lucy was glad. Aran didn't stop frowning until his sister was safely back on solid ground.

"That was brilliant!" Jade smiled as Max helped her down. "My horse was the best! Thanks, Lucy."

"My pleasure," said Lucy. "Now let's go inside."

They made their way to the entrance of the tent. As soon as they stepped inside their noses were accosted with the sickly sweet aroma of buttered popcorn and sugared-to-the-max candyfloss.

"Food time," Max rubbed his hands together as soon as he saw the large wooden stand. "Who's for candy floss?"

"Me!" said Jade and Aran simultaneously.

"Back in a second," said Max. "Will you come and help me, Aran?"

Aran looked at Jade. She nodded. "Sure," he said and loped off with Max towards the stand.

Lucy and Jade watched the glamorous Italian women who were collecting the tickets. Their fishnetted legs and gold and silver high-heeled sandals contrasted violently with their buttoned-to-the-neck red and black fitted long-sleeved jackets. The overall effect was unnervingly sexy. Each girl was dramatically made-up with heavy pan-stick foundation, vivid blue or green 70's style eyeshadow, luscious red lips and the *pièce de résistance* – black, spider-like false eyelashes. Jade was entranced. She couldn't take her eyes off one particular woman

171

who was swinging her waist-long white-blonde ponytail in the air and flirting with all the men, who, being mostly married middle-aged fathers, were more than delighted with the attention.

"Here we are," said Max, as he arrived back with Aran, both laden down with goodies. "We'll carry this lot until we get to the seats." Jade looked perturbed. "Don't worry, Jade. I won't eat any of your candy floss, I promise."

He dug Lucy in the side as their tickets were checked by one of the fishnetted ushers. "This wasn't a bad idea at all."

"Behave yourself!" Lucy laughed.

Their seats were just beside the ring and Aran was most impressed.

"We'll be able to see everything, and maybe the animals will even jump on top of us," he said excitedly.

Jade squealed.

"Don't worry," said Aran. "I'm sure they'll put the lions and tigers in a cage or something."

"Don't scare your sister like that, Aran," Lucy scolded.

"It's OK," Jade insisted. "I don't mind the animals coming close as long as they don't eat my candyfloss."

Lucy and Max laughed.

In a few minutes the lights grew dim and smoke came billowing out from behind the heavy red-velvet curtains. The tent was filled with loud Italian music. Suddenly the curtains opened and a host of entertainers burst through, juggling, dancing, tumbling and jumping. Behind them, a flock of white geese followed, cackling and flapping their snowy wings. Fire-eaters spurted flames from their mouths, clowns ran along the top of the wooden ring, bending down and waving at Jade and Aran. The air was loaded with exotic promise. And as suddenly as they came on, the entertainers exited.

"Wow!" Lucy breathed to Max as the tent fell into a hushed, expectant silence. Max squeezed her hand. She looked at Jade and Aran. Their eyes were glued on the curtains, waiting to see what was coming next.

The spotlight focused its moony gaze on the curtains. One long, lithe fishnetted leg came through the red velvet, followed by a bare, bronzed arm. They writhed snake-like to the slow, sensuous music. The body followed. It was the blonde woman with the amazing plait. She was sheathed in a glittering silver leotard which left little to the imagination.

Lucy glanced at Max whose eyes were fixed on the Italian woman. Lucy wasn't surprised. The woman attached her plait to a wire and was pulled slowly skywards by her hair.

"That must hurt," Jade whispered to Aran.

The woman contorted her toned body to the music, swinging her legs into impossible-looking positions. She then began to swing her body in circular movements, building up speed so that soon she was moving in a wide arc. The audience clapped loudly. Lucy was too amazed to clap. She'd been to circuses before, but never one like this. She was impressed.

Next came wild white stallions that careered around the ring, changing direction suddenly and abruptly, and sending sawdust flying with their thundering hooves. A strongman lifted unbelievable weights, a tiny dark-haired woman spun golden hoops on her arms and legs, a tightrope walker balanced on one leg while holding a dog on his shoulder and, unlike Irish clowns, the Italian clowns acted out pieces of drama, dressed in Charlie Chaplin-style black suits. Some acts were introduced in broken English by the ringmaster who was also the strongman, which added to the exotic atmosphere.

"I've never seen anything like this," said Max at the interval. "It's more like theatre than the circus."

"I know," said Lucy. "Isn't it amazing? The kids seem to be enjoying themselves too." Jade and Aran, along with lots of other children, were petting a tiny brown pony which was in the middle of the ring.

"Do you want anything to eat?" asked Max, spotting an ice-cream vendor. He waved her over.

Lucy laughed. "I'm fine, thanks. You obviously do though. And I'm sure Aran and Jade would manage an ice cream."

He bought three Cornettos and began to pull back the foil

173

wrapping of his own. He took a bite and handed it to Lucy. "Go on. You know you want to."

Lucy smiled and took the cone from him. "You're a bad influence, Max." She bit into the vanilla and chocolate top.

Jade and Aran came running back and climbed over the wooden ring. "The pony was so cute," said Aran. "He licked Jade's fingers."

"I've ice creams for you both," said Max.

"Max!" said Lucy. "They'll have to wash their hands first."

"We'll only hold the wrapper," said Aran. "Honest."

"Oh, go on." Lucy sighed. "Max will open them for you. Make sure you don't get your licked fingers near your mouth, Jade."

"OK," said Jade.

The lights dimmed again and they settled into their seats. Lucy hoped that the kids wouldn't catch worms or something!

Camels were first out, huge elegant animals snorting hot, moist air from their pink nostrils. Next were the tumblers, a troupe of smaller than average men who threw themselves around the ring in an alarming manner. They climbed on top of each other to produce a towering human pyramid to much applause.

Aran and Jade drew back slightly as a stocky man in a tiger-skin carrying a whip came into the ring alongside a gigantic tiger. He held the tiger by the collar, as if it were a pet dog. The tiger was on a long thick chain which the trainer also held like a lead. The tiger leapt from metal platform to metal platform, as commanded by his trainer. He was rewarded by 'treats' just like a dog.

Jade had clambered onto Lucy's knee as soon as she'd seen how large the tiger was and Aran was leaning back in his chair, towards Max.

"That tiger's so well-behaved," Max whispered to Lucy.

"I'd say he was reared in captivity," she replied. "He's probably never been in the wild."

"Beautiful animal," said Max.

Next were the jugglers, followed by the trapeze artists. Lucy had always loved watching the men and women flying through the air and these performers were true artists. Their manoeuvres were faultlessly timed, each twist and dive perfectly executed.

"They're flying!" Jade said, her eyes open wide in amazement.

"That's why it's called the flying trapeze," said Max.

At the end of the show the whole troupe joined together in the ring, providing a stunning tableau of magnificent animals and artists. Jade and Aran clapped along to the music as the parade passed in front of them.

When the parade had finished and the last claps had died out, they stood up and prepared to go.

"Look!" said Aran. "They're going to have dinner." He pointed to the middle of the ring.

A long table had been carried into the ring and had been covered with a red and white chequered tablecloth. A huge bowl of steaming spaghetti sat on the table and beside it were white bowls and forks. The performers came back on stage. A large, rotund woman began to serve them spaghetti. And they all sat down to eat at the table, completely ignoring the audience's stares.

The ringmaster announced, "Mamma Tante her circus family dinner. *Buon appetito* and goodbye!"

"Wow!" said Max as they walked to the car. "That was incredible."

"Do you think they always have dinner at the end?" asked Aran.

"They probably do," said Lucy, holding Jade's hand firmly. The traffic on the Blackrock dual carriageway was moving past them at an alarming rate and she wanted to keep her ward safe.

Driving back to Dun Laoghaire they talked about the circus.

"What was your favourite thing, Jade?" said Max.

Jade thought for a second. "The horses, I think," she said quietly. "They were beautiful."

"Mine was the strongman," said Aran. "He was cool!"

"I liked the trapeze artists the best," said Lucy. "I've always loved them. What about you, Max? What did you like? Or should I ask."

Max laughed. "The tiger, I think. And the woman with the hair, of course."

"Of course," Lucy smiled. "Now who'd like Burger King for tea?"

"Me!" Jade and Aran shouted.

Eileen rang Lucy later that evening from Bangor. "How are you getting on?" Eileen asked. Max had collapsed in front of the television, Jade and Aran sitting at his feet. They were all watching a nature programme about hippos, while empty, tomato-ketchup-smeared plates and Burger King drinks cartons were strewn on the floor in front of them.

"We're exhausted," said Lucy, "me and Max that is. The kids are full of beans."

Eileen laughed. "They're bundles of energy all right. Keep you on your toes. How was the circus?"

"Brilliant!" Lucy enthused. "We all loved it. Jade was a little scared of the tiger but liked everything else. You should go. It's well worth seeing."

"But you've stolen my excuse for going," said Eileen.

"I'm sure Jade and Aran would be well on for going again. Or you could go with a friend. They have evening shows for adults."

"I might just do that."

"How's Linda?" asked Lucy.

"Good. The operation went without a hitch and she's back home now. She said to say hello."

"Tell her I was asking for her and I'm glad it went well."

"I'll be back early tomorrow, well before eleven. I know you have to work. I haven't forgotten."

"Thanks, Mum. I'll see you in the morning."

"That was Eileen," Lucy said as she walked into the sitting-room. "She hopes you're both being good."

"We are," said Aran, a flicker of doubt on his face. "Aren't we?"

Lucy ruffled his hair. "Of course you are. Now will you help me carry the plates into the kitchen like a good lad? Max?"

She looked at Max. His eyes were closed and his mouth was open.

"He's having a nap," said Jade.

Lucy smiled. They'd all had a busy day. "Once I've tidied up in the kitchen it's bath time for both of you."

Aran and Jade groaned.

"Once you both have your pyjamas on you can watch television for a little while, OK?"

"Yippee!" Aran whooped.

Max murmured and moved a little on the sofa.

"Oops, sorry," said Aran. "I didn't mean to wake Max."

"Don't worry," said Lucy. "It would take more than that to wake him up."

At nine o'clock Aran and Jade were safely tucked up in bed and Lucy was watching a new series about an Irish family who had moved to the south of Italy. Max was still asleep. She decided she'd better wake him.

"Max," she said, shaking his shoulders gently. No response. She shook him more firmly "Max, wake up."

Max opened his eyes slowly and groaned. "Have I been asleep long?" he asked groggily. "What time is it?"

"Time for you to go home to bed by the looks of it. You've been asleep for ages."

"Where are Aran and Jade?

"In bed. Where you should be."

Max sat up. Lucy was right. He should go home. "Listen, will you be here in the morning?"

"Yes, but I've a christening in the afternoon, remember? I'll be leaving here at elevenish."

"Right," Max said yawning. He didn't know why he was so tired. Must be a combination of late nights and the energetic football in the park, he thought. "I'll talk to you in the morning. I'll call in around ten, OK?"

"Is everything all right?"

"Fine, there's just something I wanted to talk to you about but it'll wait."

Lucy saw him to the door. She kissed him on the cheek and gave him a hug. "Thanks for helping me with the kids today. I really appreciate it."

"No problem," he smiled sleepily. "I enjoyed it." Walking to his car the fresh air woke him up slightly. Maybe he should go back and talk to Lucy now. He yawned again. Maybe not. He'd see her tomorrow after all.

17

Max reached out and grabbed his mobile from the bedside table. "Hello?" he said groggily.

"Hi, Max. It's Daria. Sorry, did I wake you up?"

"I'd be lying if I said no. What time is it?"

"Nearly twelve."

"Twelve?" How the hell had he managed to sleep so late? He'd gone to bed just after eleven. Damn. He must have slept through the alarm.

"Is there something wrong?" she asked.

"No. Sorry. Ignore me."

"I was just ringing to say I'm going to Wicklow with Grace for lunch. I know we'd planned to meet on the beach at two but is four OK? Tell me if it's too late."

"Four's fine," Max said. "But there's no point in both of us driving. Why don't I collect you?"

"That'd be nice. I'll see you at four, then."

Max put the phone back down on the bedside table and glared at his alarm clock. Stupid thing, he muttered to himself.

* * *

"So what's on the menu?" Lucy asked Dan. They were sitting in his dark-blue Honda jeep, on the way to Killiney where the christening lunch was being held.

"There are forty guests," Dan said, "and it's a buffet, so I've kept it simple. A choice of chicken tikka, pork in mustard sauce, or mushroom, potato and spinach bake for the vegetarians. And then a range of salads – fried potato salad, normal potato salad with spices, tomato salad, apple, walnut and celery with blue cheese, and – hang on a sec." He avoided a double-parked car and turned left at the top of Dalkey village, up Sorrento Road. "Where was I? Oh, yes, salads. The last one's a green salad with one of your mate Jamie's dressings – honey whole-grain mustard and garlic."

"Sounds great. And dessert?"

"Pavlova, fruit salad, and buckets of cream."

"Excellent!"

"A lot of the prep work is already done. And the main dishes just need to be heated. But the salads need to be put together and dressed. And the desserts need to be garnished."

"Sounds fine. You tell me exactly what you'd like done and I'll do it."

"Might take you up on that," Dan said suggestively.

"Anything other than cooking will be extra, of course."

"I have loads of cream after all," Dan continued, sending goose bumps down Lucy's spine. "It would be a shame not to use it."

"Would you stop!" Lucy laughed. She was enjoying herself already.

Dan pulled the jeep onto a leafy drive off Military Road in Killiney. Gravel crunched under the tyres. "Here we are. Silva House." Two tubby black Labradors came out to meet them, wagging their tails.

"Impressive," Lucy said, gazing at the large, redbrick house in awe.

"Doug Howard is a stockbroker," Dan smiled. "I must be in the wrong business."

"And his wife's a consultant," Lucy reminded him.

"True."

A tall, slim blonde woman followed the dogs onto the white

gravelled drive. She was wearing a pair of dark blue Earl Jeans and a white shirt. A red and yellow flowered scarf was knotted jauntily at her throat. She smiled broadly at them as they got out of the jeep.

"You must be Dan," she said warmly, shaking his hand. "And this is —"

"Lucy, She's helping me cook."

"Nice to meet you, Lucy." They shook hands. The woman had a firm, strong handshake. "I'm Minna Howard. My husband, Doug, is inside with Alfie. Thanks for doing this at such short notice."

"No problem," Dan smiled. "And who's this?" he bent down to pat one of the dogs who wagged his tail furiously.

"That's Wrigley. He seems to like you. The other one is Fenway."

"They're lovely," Dan smiled, standing up. "I adore Labradors. We had a golden one called Phoebe when I was growing up."

"Unusual names," Lucy said. "Where did they come from?"

"Doug's a huge baseball fan," Minna said shaking her head. "Don't ask."

"Baseball stadiums," Dan whispered to Lucy.

"What time is the service at?" Dan asked.

"Twelve." Minna looked at her watch. "Heavens, it's twenty past eleven and I haven't even got changed. I'll show you where the kitchen is and leave you to it, if that's all right."

"Fine," Dan said. "And you'd like to eat at one thirty?"

Minna nodded. "The bar staff and your waitresses should be arriving at any minute. They're from Con Collins Catering."

"I'll look out for them," he promised.

"Follow me," Minna said as she led them into the house. The hallway was painted in a warm cream, and original paintings and etchings hung in heavy gold frames. There was a huge, ornate mirror over the marble-topped hall table and the luxurious deep-pile cream carpet sank under Lucy's feet as she stepped on it. "The reception rooms are to the left and right," Minna said, gesturing to the open doors on either side of the hallway. Lucy looked in. The rooms were huge, with high ceilings and marble fireplaces. "And the kitchen's down here." The kitchen was to the back of the house, down three small steps. "I've cleared all the worktops and you're welcome to root around to find anything you need."

Dan had a quick recce of the room. It was a cook's heaven. A large, stainless-steel Smeg cooker, an Aga, a huge, American-style chrome larder-fridge, chunky wooden chopping-blocks, two sinks – huge Belfast ceramic ones – and an array of copper and stainless-steel pots and pans hanging from a rack over the central work-space.

"This is an amazing kitchen," he said. "You lucky things!"

"I have to admit it was like this when we bought the place," Minna said sheepishly. "I'm not much of a cook myself, don't have the time. But Doug loves it. You can't get him out of here at the weekends."

"I'm not surprised," Dan said. "Now, you go and get ready and we'll make a start. If I have any questions maybe you could give me a minute or two before you leave?"

"Perfect," Minna smiled, turning on her heels and bounding up the steps.

"She's really nice," Lucy said in a low voice. "And what a house!"

"Never mind the house," Dan said. "Look at the kitchen!"

Lucy sighed, running her fingers over one of the polished granite worktops. "Life is so unfair."

Dan laughed. "One day. Now, we'd better get cracking. We don't have much time to get ready. They'll be back from the church before we know it."

They walked out towards the jeep. "Where's the church?" Lucy asked as they lifted the first plastic case out of the boot.

"Up the road, in Killiney village. It's the modern one on the hill."

"I've been there," she said as they carried the heavy box through the hall door. "It's beautiful, all white with stained glass and dark wood inside. I went to a christening there a few years ago."

"Friends or family?" They placed the box on the terracotta-tiled floor of the kitchen.

"Family. One of my cousins. My aunt and uncle used to live in Killiney before they moved up north."

Back at the jeep, Dan climbed into the boot, lifted the second box down and handed it to Lucy. "This one's quite light – can you take it on your own?"

Lucy nodded. Dan jumped out of the boot, reached back in and pulled out another box.

"You have a brother, right?" Dan asked.

"Yes, Eugene. He's away in Brittas at the moment with 'the lads'." She tried not to snort as she said 'the lads'. "They're camping, apparently."

"Do you get on with him?"

"Yes and no. He drives me mental some of the time. He's so irresponsible and he gets away with murder. Mum's very easy on him. It's a mixture of being a boy and being the youngest, I suppose. It's always been one rule for him and another rule for me. But we get on OK, I guess. Sorry for the rant."

"Don't worry," Dan smiled. "I have two sisters, and what with them and Mum, I grew up having to fight to get a word in edgeways. The women in my family do love to talk!"

Lucy laughed.

They put the last box down on the floor in the kitchen. Dan had brought everything he needed with him, from kitchen knives to tinfoil and clingfilm. He'd explained that often kitchens were woefully ill-equipped and you could never take anything for granted.

"Let's unpack the crates first and get everything laid out," Dan said. "Then put the main dishes in the oven and the Aga on a low heat to get them out of the way, put the rice in the pots ready to boil and get stuck into finishing the salads, OK?"

"Sounds good, boss!" Lucy smiled.

Dan looked her in the eye. "I'm really glad you're here today. Thanks for saying yes."

"Glad to be of service." Lucy tried not to blush under his gaze. He really did have the most lovely eyes. She was glad she'd decided on her new black top with the tie around the waist and her beige lycra stretch jeans and black sandals. You'd never know the whole outfit was from

Dunnes and she felt comfortable yet sexy. She'd plonked her sunglasses on her head, tied her hair back for cooking and brought her new, black apron with the useful front pocket which tied around her waist professionally. She'd made sure to wear it while baking last week just to break it in a little. She didn't want Dan to think she'd bought it specially or anything.

"Maybe I can bring you out later, dinner or something, to say thank you?" Dan suggested. "As well as paying you, of course."

"Dinner would be nice. Thanks." Excellent, she thought to herself. Now she wouldn't have to spend all day wondering whether he was going to ask her out or not.

"How are my chefs?" Minna walked into the kitchen, a small white-fleece-wrapped bundle in her arms that Lucy presumed was baby Alfie. She was wearing a simple but elegant pink Whistles outfit – a flowing, velvet skirt and matching cardigan. Her long blonde hair was caught up in a large pink gardenia hair-clip.

"Fine, thanks," Dan said. "Just one thing, how do the temperatures in the lower and upper Aga oven differ?"

"The upper one's the hottest. About mark 4 or 5. The lower one's about 2 or 3."

"Perfect!" Dan smiled. He thought for a second. "That's it, I think. We have everything we need. Can you just show me where the food will be served from upstairs?"

"Of course." A little noise came from Minna's bundle. "Hush, Alfie," she said, rocking the baby slightly.

"Can I have a peek?" Lucy asked, her hormones getting the better of her. She peered into the halo of white blanket. The baby had a tiny, scrunched-up pink face. "How old is he?"

"Eight weeks."

Lucy stroked one of his tiny clenched pink fists gently. "He's so tiny. I love the little fingernails."

Dan looked over Minna's shoulder. The baby opened his eyes. They were bright blue.

"Sorry," Lucy said, "I didn't mean to wake him up."

"Don't worry," Minna smiled. "He was already awake. Weren't you, my little pet?" She kissed Alfie on the cheek. "Now we'd better get going. I'll show you the set-up in the dining-room."

Dan and Lucy followed her. A tall, well-built man was standing in the hall. He was wearing an expensive-looking dark suit, a black shirt and a dark purple tie. Lucy was impressed. Irish men were not exactly famous for their snappy dress sense.

"Hi, I'm Doug." He held out his hand to Lucy and then Dan. He had a strong London accent and piercing blue eyes.

That explains the clothes, thought Lucy.

"Dan and Lucy," Dan explained. "The caterers."

"Excellent!" Doug boomed. "I'm starving."

"Honestly, Doug," Minna said. "You've just had breakfast. You never stop thinking of your stomach."

"Too right, mate," he said, smiling.

"Doug, can you hold Alfie while I show Dan and Lucy the dining-room?"

"Sure. Hand the little blighter over. If he pukes on my suit he's dead." He took Alfie from his wife, the tiny size of the baby making him look even more imposing.

The dining-room, like the rest of the house, was magnificent. Dark green walls, dark wood furniture and a huge, mahogany table stretching from one end of the room to the other with matching, high-backed mahogany green-leather chairs. Dark blue velvet curtains swathed the huge bow windows which looked out to the garden. Lucy spotted an old-fashioned round greenhouse in the middle of the grass, next to a small pond.

"You can put the food on the table and these sideboards," Minna said, pointing at the gleaming mahogany. "If you need mats for the hot things, they're in there. And serving spoons are in here." She pulled out two large drawers under a glass cabinet to show them.

"Great," Dan said. "Now we'd better let you go or you'll be late."

* * *

185

"Chantal, would you mind not flicking your nail polish into my food, thank you." Dan glared at the young waitress in front of him. She was standing behind one of the sideboards, scratching the purple nail polish off her nails with a knife. Her long black hair, with peroxide-blonde highlights, thankfully was tied back, but her white shirt could have done with an iron. Con Collin's Catering staff left a lot to be desired.

It was twenty past one and the guests were beginning to hover hopefully outside the dining-room door, glancing in and licking their lips. Most of the food was already *in situ*, the main courses in clever metal dishes, kept warm by low gas flames underneath. The salads were lined up along the dining-room table in large ceramic bowls. All was ready bar the rice, which was simmering away in huge pots in the kitchen and the pavlovas which Lucy was adding the finishing touches to in the kitchen.

Dan was half-tempted to serve the food himself but he knew he had to finish cooking. Chantal wasn't exactly what he'd expected when he'd been promised an experienced silver-service waitress. Still, at least he could concentrate on the food.

"Stay there, Chantal," Dan instructed the scowling girl. "I'll be back in two minutes. And don't start serving until I say so, OK?"

He popped his head round the kitchen door. Lucy was piping cream onto the top of four large meringue bases. "How are you getting on?"

"Fine," said Lucy. "I'm nearly done. I'm not going to put the fruit on till the very last minute. It's all in the fridge, chopped and ready to go."

"Brilliant!" Dan said warmly. He really couldn't have coped without Lucy. The last half an hour had been spent carrying up the salads and setting out the table upstairs with the 'help' of Chantal. Lucy had been invaluable. She also looked damn cute. Her long dark hair was tied back with a red scarf and her cheeks were gently flushed from the heat in the kitchen.

Dan stood and watched her and was reminded of his ex, Mary. Quite a different sort of girl altogether. Mary was tall, thin and elegant, with a sleek hard-edged jet-black bob and impeccable and with expensive taste in clothes. They'd been together for nearly three years but she'd given him a 'live-together-and-get-more-serious-or-break-up' ultimatum three months ago and he'd chosen the latter. It wasn't that he was a commitment-phobe or anything; it just didn't feel right. She'd become career-obsessed, in the office before seven-thirty and never out before six in the evening. She'd recently been made a partner in her law firm, the youngest and only woman partner, of which she was rightly very proud. But with the new role came extra responsibilities, both directly and indirectly. Not only was she expected to put in the hours in the office, she was also expected to attend business lunches, dinners and social occasions at the weekends.

Dan hated her work 'do's' and had refused to attend any more after a particularly bad experience with an obnoxious lawyer, a self-proclaimed European Law 'whiz kid' who had insulted his earning-power as a chef, before depositing a glass of red wine all over Dan's shirt while gesticulating wildly about the euro.

Mary had certainly changed. When he first met her she was energetic, lively and fun. She wasn't afraid of doing outrageous things, like flashing her bra (usually bright orange or red) in the pub or paddling in the fountain on Dun Laoghaire's new promenade. But he'd changed too. In a way it had come full circle. He was much more open now to trying new things than he'd been a few years ago. The surfing, for example. He'd met some German tourists in a pub in Galway who'd persuaded him to give it a go. Mary thought he was mad, freezing his ass off in the Atlantic with people he'd just met, foreigners for that matter. But he'd loved it and a year later was reasonably proficient. And the next thing he was going to try was kite-surfing, thanks to Max.

Dan felt very comfortable with Max. He'd only met the guy twice but he was really looking forward to seeing to him again. They had a lot in common. Meeting new friends wasn't as easy as it used to be. Married blokes were a dead loss. Always running home to put shelves up or to replace washers. And as for married blokes with kids –

"Dan?" Lucy interrupted his thoughts. "Would you like me to bring up the rice now?"

"Sorry? Yes, that would be great. I'll give you a hand."

Chantal was looking for split ends when Lucy and Dan entered the dining-room. "Listen," Lucy said quietly, realising that the young girl wouldn't exactly give Dan's food the right 'image'. "Why don't I help Chantal serve? You can finish off the pavlovas – you'd be quicker than me. I don't mind."

"Are you sure?"

Lucy nodded. "It'll give me a chance to check out the crowd for rich husbands."

Dan hugged her. "Lucy, you're brilliant. Thanks. I'll just send Minna up to you and I'll come up and help serve myself when the pavlovas are finished."

"I think she's out by the glasshouse," said Lucy. She was a little taken aback by the hug, but she liked it all the same.

"Thanks."

Lucy gazed out the window. She watched Dan walk towards Minna.

"Is that yer boyfriend?" Chantal asked with interest.

"No."

"Nice ass," Chantal commented, cocking her head to get a better look.

"Yes, I suppose it is nice," she agreed. "I'm going to be helping you serve."

"So I heard," Chantal said testily. "I'm not deaf."

"Right," Lucy sighed.

"Ah, listen," Chantal said. "I didn't mean to snap, I'm sorry. I just broke up with me boyfriend, you know the way."

"I'm sorry," Lucy said.

"Ah, jeez," Chantal smiled, "don't worry. He was a little bollox anyway."

Lucy laughed. Maybe serving with Chantal wasn't going to be too bad – if she could just keep the girl's language in check.

"What can I give you, sir?" Chantal asked politely, smiling attractively. "Chicken tikka, pork in mustard sauce or there's a vegetarian option."

Lucy nearly fell over. Where had this polite girl with the plummy south Dublin accent come from?

"The salads are over there, sir. Help yourself. Enjoy."

"Charming girl," the man said to Lucy. "Charming."

When Dan joined them he was equally amazed. "What's happened to *her*?" he asked Lucy as Chantal flirted with a small, rotund man with a bright red face and matching shiny red bald head.

"Isn't she great?" Lucy smiled. "She told me she wants to act. Daniel Day Lewis is her role model. Method acting is her thing apparently."

"Wonders will never cease," Dan smiled. "How are things going?"

"Great. Most people are going for the chicken and they love the salads. Compliments all round."

"Excellent! Anything I can do?"

"You could remove the fried-potato bowl. It's all gone – Doug ate practically the whole lot himself."

"Will do," he said, picking up the bowl.

"So Chantal," he said after he'd returned from the kitchen. Everyone had finally been served, but from the way the table was being eyed up from the hallway and through the windows from the garden, many were gearing up for seconds. "Lucy tells me you're into acting."

"Yep," Chantal nodded, pushing a long dangling lock of hair behind her ear. "I waitress to make a bit of money when I'm not working."

"What type of work do you do?" he asked as he fluffed up the remaining rice with a metal spoon.

"I want to get into films. I've done mostly plays so far, comedies – Andrew's Lane mainly. But I've an audition for an English film next week."

"I hope it goes well. Best of luck."

"Thanks," Chantal said gratefully. "They're looking for someone with a strong Dublin accent to play a waitress, so you never know, I may be in luck."

"One of my friends acts," Lucy said. "Daria Delahunty. She's in *Emma* in The Gate which is opening in a few weeks. Do you know her?"

"Na," Chantal said. "Lucky bitch though. The Gate's a great theatre. Real classy."

"How are my wonderful cooks?" Doug boomed from the hallway. He walked in the door clutching an empty plate. "I've come for seconds. Any more of that fried-potato salad?"

"Hi, Doug," Lucy smiled. "You cleared us out of it, I'm afraid, but there's plenty of the other potato salad."

"Splendid," he beamed. "Everyone loves the food. Minna's delighted. And Edna Woods wants to book you, Dan, for a fork supper in a few weeks. She'll ring you later. Minna gave her your number, I hope you don't mind."

"Not at all," Dan said. "I'm glad you're happy with it. Wait till you see the desserts."

Doug's eyes brightened. "I'll be back for thirds before that, mate."

"I'm sure you will," Lucy laughed.

The pavlovas were a big hit. Chantal stayed serving in the dining-room while Lucy and Dan began to clear away.

"That went well," said Dan, putting a large pottery salad bowl into one of the plastic crates.

"Are you pleased?" said Lucy.

"Very," Dan smiled. He walked towards her and put his hands on her cheeks. They felt deliciously cool. He kissed her on her forehead. "Thank you for all your help."

"It was nothing –" she began.

Dan interrupted her. He kissed her on the left cheek. "You cook like an angel," he said. He kissed her on the right cheek. "And you're beautiful." Lucy could feel herself blushing. She looked into his eyes, trying not to squint as he was so close. She could feel his breath on her face. She smiled and lowered her gaze. "Look at me," he whispered. She raised her eyes again. "You're lovely," he kissed her firmly yet tenderly on the lips.

190

"Ahem."

They jumped apart.

"Sorry to interrupt but is there any more cream?" Chantal asked, grinning from ear to ear.

"I'm knackered," Lucy complained, sitting back in the jeep. "I haven't had so much exercise in years." They had spent the last hour clearing up and lifting the crates back into the jeep. As they drove, the windows were open and the warm air was stroking her face and bare arms deliciously.

Dan patted her thigh. "You'll be fine," he smiled. They drove onto the Dun Laoghaire coast road.

"You're quiet," Dan said as they past the East Pier. "Is there anything wrong?"

No," Lucy said. "I'm just wiped out. Looking after Jade and Aran yesterday took it out of me, I guess."

"And you've been inside working all day," Dan pointed out. "How about we go for a walk? It's lovely out."

"That would be nice. What about Sandymount Strand? It's just beside my house so I can call in and grab a jumper first."

"Perfect."

"Do you want to come in and check out my kitchen?" Lucy smiled as they pulled up outside her house.

"No," Dan laughed, "but I'd kill for a glass of water."

"I might just be able to manage that, if you're good!" She jumped down and pulled her key out of her pocket. "Follow me."

Lucy led the way down the steps towards the kitchen. She could see Hopper and Alan through the open kitchen door, sitting on plastic chairs in the garden, drinking cans of Bulmers.

"Hi, guys," Lucy said. "You remember Dan?"

"Of course," Hopper said. "Nice to see you again."

Alan nodded at Dan and smiled.

"Enjoying the sun, I see," Dan said, crouching down on his hunkers.

191

"What would you like to drink?" Lucy asked Dan. "And can I get anyone else anything while I'm at it?"

"We're grand, thanks," Hopper smiled. "We've only just opened these cans."

"Water is fine," Dan said. Lucy looked at him quizzically.

"Are you sure?" she asked. "There's apple juice or Ribena."

"Ribena," Dan smiled. "I don't think I've had that since I was a child."

Lucy grinned. "It's my favourite. My mother tried to wean me off it in my teenage years but I'm a confirmed addict."

"One Ribena, so," Dan said. Alan fetched two more plastic chairs and handed one to Dan.

"Thanks," Dan said, sitting down, face into the late-afternoon sun. "Have you been out here all afternoon?"

"Most of it," Hopper nodded. She sat up and grabbed a white floppy hat from the ground. "I suppose I'd better put this on. My cheeks are beginning to tingle."

Dan noticed that her nose was scattered with freckles and her cheeks were bright pink. She was wearing gigantic pink-tinted shades, a white bikini top and cut-off denim shorts. Her toenails, which peeped through blue Diesel platform sandals, were painted turquoise. Silver toe-rings glinted on both little toes.

"How was the christening?" Alan asked.

"Fine," Dan replied, reaching into his shirt pocket and putting on his sunglasses. "Lucy was brilliant. I couldn't have done it without her."

"Really?" Hopper asked with interest.

"Are you talking about me?" Lucy interrupted. "My ears are burning." She was carrying a tray on which a large purple-liquid-filled jug and four glasses sat. The ice in the Ribena clinked against the sides of the glass.

"I was just telling Hopper how helpful you were today," Dan said.

She smiled beatifically, remembering how, in Minna and Doug's kitchen, he'd said she was lovely.

"Who'd like Ribena?" she asked. "I brought extra glasses just in case."

"Oh, go on then," Alan smiled. "It'll make a change from the cider."

"Do you think you could mix them?" Hopper asked. "Cider and blackcurrant?"

"We used to make things called 'Black Witches' in college," Alan said. "Cider and Pernod and blackcurrant. They were lethal."

Hopper jumped up. "Great idea! I think we have some Pernod in one of the kitchen cupboards. Lucy needed it for some recipe or other recently."

Lucy laughed. "Count us out, Hopper. We're going for a walk."

"That's far too healthy," Alan said. "Stay here and have a few drinks."

Lucy looked at Dan. He shrugged his shoulders. She was very tempted. But she wanted to spend some time with Dan – alone.

"No, honestly," Lucy insisted. "Thanks all the same."

"Are you around for dinner?" Alan asked hopefully. He didn't fancy cooking and Lucy made wicked barbecue spare ribs.

"No," Lucy said, "we're going out."

"Really?" Hopper asked, staring through her sunglasses at Lucy. "Where to?"

"Haven't decided yet." She was eager to stop Hopper in her tracks. She knew if she stayed any longer Hopper would start to interrogate Dan about his background, pets, family, past girlfriends, you name it. In fact, Lucy was surprised Hopper hadn't started already – the sun must have slowed her curiosity-gene down.

"Where do you live, Dan?" Hopper asked.

Lucy started moving towards the kitchen door nervously.

"Clontarf," Dan smiled, standing up.

"And who do you live with?" Hopper continued. "On your own or with others?"

"Well," Lucy interjected. She smiled at Dan. "We'd better go before the sun disappears. See you later, guys."

"But —" Hopper said as Dan's back disappeared inside.

"Damn," she said to Alan. "I'd only just started."

"He'll be back," Alan said, sipping his Ribena. "Did you see the way he was looking at Lucy? He's mad about her."

"I suppose," Hopper said. She stretched her arms above her head and yawned a deep sun-yawn. "I'm going to make a jug of that 'Black Witch' stuff. Will you give me a hand?"

Alan looked over at her and smiled. "I'll give you more than a hand," he said. He reached out and began to gently stroke her leg.

"What will you give me?" Hopper purred.

"I'll give you some ice," Alan said, standing up. He picked a piece of ice out of his drink, held it in his fingers and knelt in front of her. "Close your eyes."

"I don't think —" Hopper began.

"Now!" he said forcefully.

Hopper closed her eyes. She shivered as Alan ran the ice up her arm, along her shoulder and down her chest. He slithered it inside her bikini top and began to tease her right breast with its coldness. She gasped as he touched the melting cube against her nipple.

"Alan," she breathed, "the neighbours."

He ran the ice up her chest again and toyed it against her lips. Hopper couldn't take any more. She jumped up, threw her arms around his neck and began to kiss him deeply and passionately. Their bodies were crushed tightly together. Hopper could feel his hardness through his cotton shorts and she moved her body against it sensuously.

"Kitchen," he gasped. "Quick!"

18

"Hello? Yes, this is Dan Rowan. Hang on one second." Dan turned towards Lucy. "I'm really sorry. It's the lady from the christening, Edna Woods," he said in a low voice.

"Go ahead," Lucy said. "It's fine."

As they continued walking slowly towards Sandymount Strand, Dan made delicious-sounding menu suggestions involving seafood.

Lucy dithered as to whether she should put her fleece jumper on or not. It was getting a little cooler. She'd changed into jeans and runners before they'd left the house and given her teeth a perfunctory brush and her wrists a tiny dab of perfume. Luckily Hopper hadn't followed Dan into the hall to interrogate him any more. Thank goodness for Alan – a great distraction if ever there was one.

Lucy was delighted that Hopper and Alan were getting on so well. They were incredibly relaxed with each other, but had managed not to lose the spark of attraction that had brought them together in the first place. In fact, as far as Lucy could see, they were as besotted with each other as they had been in the beginning – if closed bedroom doors were anything to go by. She was trying not to be jealous, but it was hard sometimes living with a couple. But now with Dan on the scene, maybe things would be different.

"Sorry about that," Dan said, putting his small Nokia back into the pocket of his denim jacket. "It's early days with the catering, so I have to take any work going until I'm established."

"From what I saw today," Lucy smiled, "that won't take very long."

"I hope you're right," he said. "But let's not talk about work."

"What would you like to talk about then?"

He put his arm around her shoulder. "You," he said sincerely. "I want to know everything."

"OK, you asked for it. I was born in the Rotunda Hospital on the nineteenth of March and I was six pounds three ounces."

Dan laughed. "That's tiny! I was nearly nine pounds."

"A small and very difficult baby," Lucy grinned. "So I'm told. My mum had a devil of a time trying to get me to sleep, apparently. But you don't want to hear all this. I was only joking!"

Dan was silent for a second. "I don't mind what we talk about, to be honest," he said finally. "I'm just really enjoying being with you."

Lucy's heart melted. She didn't know what to say. "Thanks," she mumbled. "Hey, the tide's out!"

Dan looked towards the strand on the other side of the road. "So it is," he smiled. "Excellent."

They crossed the road and walked along the path, down the steps and onto the sand.

"Is that a kite flying over there?" Dan asked, squinting into the sun. "Where?"

He pointed towards the distinctive red-and-white striped towers. "There." Lucy saw a large blue and white kite in the clear, blue sky. She could just make out two tiny figures in the distance.

"It is! Let's go over and have a look."

"Watch the water!" Dan warned as they strolled along the beach.

Lucy stepped over the puddle of sea water. "I should have worn my wellies."

"Do you have any?"

"Oh, yeah! Big green ones with buckles on the top. Perfect for gardening on the estate. They match my dark green Range Rover and my Barbour jacket."

He laughed. "So, no wellies then."

"No," she smiled. "No wellies."

"Your garden's not bad though. I'd love a garden."

"We're lucky. Mum comes over now and again to weed and we make Alan cut the grass 'cause he's a boy."

"That's most unfair!" Dan protested. "What about your dad? Does he have to cut the grass too?"

"No. He lives in England. So, when is Edna's dinner party?"

"In two weeks. She was going to cook herself, but she's changed her mind. Her husband's company are paying for it as it's for clients mainly."

"Sounds good." They were getting closer to the kite-flyers now, a man and a woman. Lucy looked up at the kite. It was massive. The man flying it was having trouble keeping himself on the ground and the kite in the air.

"That looks like Max," Dan observed. Suddenly the kite crashed to the ground and the woman ran over to the man who was lying on the sand. She leant over and kissed him. He threw his arms around her and pulled her to the ground.

Lucy stared at the couple and began to walk faster and then run towards them, her eyes glued to the embracing couple.

"Lucy? Hang on. Wait for me!"

Lucy's heart was racing. That man looked too much like Max. As she grew closer she saw it was Max. With Daria on top of him. And they were kissing passionately on the damp sand.

She stopped dead in her tracks. What the hell was going on here? What was Max doing with Daria?

Dan came up behind her. She could hear his deep breathing.

"Lucy?" He looked at the couple on the sand. "Hey, Max!" he shouted.

Lucy turned around. There were tears in her eyes and her face was screwed up and flushed in anger. "I'm going," she muttered.

She began to run away from him, sending water flying under her feet.

As soon as Max heard Dan's voice he had stopped kissing Daria and looked up, to see Dan staring down at him and the back of what looked like Lucy running towards the shore.

He pushed Daria off him whispering "Sorry," and ran after Lucy.

"Lucy! Come back! I can explain."

She kept running.

"Lucy!" he shouted. "Stop!"

He kept running but it was no use. His jeans and fleece were damp from the romp on the sodden beach and his Timberlands were not the best for sprinting in. He stood, panting and trying to catch his breath, watching her until she disappeared. He should have told her. It was all his fault. He felt sick to the stomach. He'd never had a falling out with Lucy, not really. But he knew how stubborn and unforgiving she could be – he'd witnessed it with other people. She wouldn't even talk to her own father for goodness sake, even now, twenty years on.

"Max?"

He heard Daria's voice behind him.

"Are you all right?"

"Not really. Lucy will never forgive me."

She put her arm around him. "It'll be fine. Go and talk to her."

"It won't be fine. You don't get it – she'll never trust me again. I'm so bloody stupid!"

"Max, you've known each other for years. You're practically family. She'll understand. You're overreacting."

"No, she won't understand," Max snapped. "Listen, I have to go. I'll get the kite and give you a lift home."

Daria said nothing. She followed him towards the kite. Dan was crouched over, sorting out the lines.

"Thanks," Max said.

Dan smiled gently. "I presume you'd forgotten to tell Lucy about your girlfriend."

Max nodded. "Something like that. Stupid really. Just never got the chance. Lucy's funny about things like that."

"We're going out to dinner later," Dan said thoughtfully. "At least we're supposed to be. I'll talk to her for you if you like."

Max sighed. "No, thanks all the same. I'd better talk to her myself. I'll drop Daria home and then I'll call into the house. I presume that's where she is."

"Sure," Dan said, "no problem."

The three of them packed up the kite and began to walk back towards the shore.

Max dropped back to walk beside Daria who hadn't uttered a word since he had bitten her head off.

"Listen, I'm sorry," he said. He bit his lip. "I had no right to take things out on you. I don't know what to say."

"You're right," she agreed. "You didn't. But you were upset. It's over now. Forget about it." She tried a smile but one side of her mouth refused to co-operate, leaving it lopsided.

"Thanks," he whispered. He put his arm around her shoulder and they walked back to the car in silence.

"I'll go on to Lucy's," Dan said. "We walked. My jeep's there."

"Do you want a lift?" Max asked.

"No, it's fine. But thanks anyway."

"That was your kite by the way, the one I was testing," Max said. "I've one or two adjustments to make on it before it's ready. I'll give you a ring when it is."

"Great," Dan said. "See you. Good luck with Lucy."

Dan knocked on the door of Lucy's house. Hopper answered it.

"Hi," she said nervously.

"Is Lucy there?" he asked.

"Yes and no. She's not feeling too well. She's really sorry. She's in her room and can't be disturbed," she gabbled.

"We were supposed to be going out to dinner this evening. Are you sure?"

"I'm really sorry," Hopper leant forward and whispered. "She's in a bit of a state and she doesn't want to see you. Something about Max apparently."

"Right," he said, defeated. "Bye." He turned away.

"Will I give her any message?" Hopper asked hopefully.

"No. No message."

Hopper watched him get into his jeep. He was a really nice guy and Lucy was mad to let him go. She had to do something. "Wait!" She yelled, running down the steps and knocking on the jeep's window. Dan pressed the window down. "Wait one second," Hopper pleaded. "Please. I'll go and talk to her."

"OK," Dan said. He turned off the motor.

Hopper ran up the stairs and tried to open Lucy's bedroom door but it was locked. "Lucy," she shouted. "Dan's outside and he's about to drive away. Please come and talk to him."

Lucy turned the key in the lock and opened her door. She looked dreadful – her eyes were red and blotchy and mascara had run down her face in tiny black rivulets.

"I can't," she said quietly. "I just can't. Tell him I'm sorry."

"Lucy –" Hopper began sternly.

Lucy began to cry again.

"OK," Hopper said. "I'll tell him you'll ring him. I'll be back up to you in a minute with some more tissues."

She went back out to the jeep.

"I'm sorry," she told Dan. "I tried talking to her. She said she'll ring you."

"No problem," Dan said, starting his engine again. "I guess dinner's off then."

"I guess so," Hopper nodded. "See you."

Dan fixed his eyes on the road ahead and began to drive home.

* * *

"Lucy," Max stood outside her bedroom door, "open the door, please."

He knocked again, more urgently this time. "Don't be stupid." He immediately regretted calling her stupid. He was the stupid one. "I'm sorry, Lucy," he continued. "I should have told you. Please –"

He was drowned out by the heavy guitar sound of the Manic Street Preachers.

"Lucy!" he yelled.

The music was turned up even louder.

Hopper appeared beside him. "Jeez," he jumped. "You gave me a fright."

She regretted letting him in. Lucy had told her not to, in any circumstances, but she'd paid no attention. Lucy and Max had had lots of arguments and they'd always made up pretty quickly. Although she couldn't remember Lucy crying over them before. Mostly she was annoyed with him. Not upset.

"You'd better go," Hopper shouted over the music. "That's my CD, so I don't mind, but I don't think the neighbours will be that impressed."

"No!" Max shouted back. "I want to talk to her. Lucy!" he yelled again, banging on the door.

Alan joined Hopper. "What's going on?" he shouted.

"Max and Lucy are having a fight."

"Why?" Alan asked.

Hopper looked at Max. "Why?" she asked.

He looked at them both and pointed downstairs. They followed him downstairs and into the kitchen.

The music upstairs stopped.

"So," Hopper said, sitting down at the kitchen table. "Go on. Spill." She stared at Max.

"She saw myself and Daria on the beach," he began.

"And," Hopper said impatiently.

"Well," Max sighed, "we were kissing."

"What?" Hopper exclaimed. "I don't understand. You bumped into Daria on the beach and kissed her?"

"Not quite," Max said.

"You idiot," Hopper said after Max had explained that he and Daria hadn't exactly met by accident.

"You're in trouble now, mate," Alan said. "You know what Lucy's like."

"Only too well," Max grimaced.

"She's upset, Max," Hopper said. "Why don't you go home? You could try ringing her later. Myself and Alan will keep an eye on her."

"I'm not sure," Max said doubtfully.

"Where's Daria?" Hopper asked.

"At home," Max said. "I dropped her off before coming here."

Hopper looked at Max carefully. "I presume she knows where you are now?"

"Yes. Why?"

"Nothing," Hopper said, shaking her head. "Don't mind me."

"What?" Max demanded. "Tell me. You've obviously got something on your mind."

"Well," Hopper began slowly, "I just feel sorry for Daria, I suppose. She's probably not feeling all that special right at this moment." Hopper sighed. "You've abandoned her to be with Lucy. How does that look?"

"It's not like that!" Max spluttered. "Me and Lucy are friends. Daria knows that."

"Does she?" Hopper asked. "Are you sure?"

"Of course," he insisted. "And anyway, Daria saw how upset Lucy was."

"And why was she so upset, exactly, Max? Think about it. Is it just because you hadn't told her about your new girlfriend? I don't think so."

"That's unfair," he said standing up. "You're jumping to all sorts of conclusions, Hopper. I thought you of all people would understand." His face began to redden and he was clenching his fists tightly. "I don't like Lucy that way, you know that. She's my friend, that's all. It's different with Daria." He glared at her.

"I don't know why you're being so defensive," she said. "It was just a suggestion, but it seems to have hit home with you. Maybe you should wake up and smell the coffee, Max."

"Speaking of coffee, would you like a cup, Max?" Alan asked, trying to defuse the situation. "Or a drink?"

"No," Max muttered. "I'm going."

He walked towards the kitchen door and was startled to find Lucy standing behind it.

"Lucy!" he said. "How long have you been standing there?"

She walked into the kitchen, opened the fridge, took out a can of Coke, turned around and walked back out again, completely ignoring Max's question. "I'm glad I'm giving you all something to talk about," she said, before glaring at Max and returning to her bedroom.

"Now look what you've done," Max pointed at Hopper accusingly.

"Me?" Hopper said, her voice raised. "Don't blame me. I'm not the one sleeping around behind Lucy's back."

"What are you talking about? I'm not sleeping with anyone behind Lucy's back. How dare you!"

Alan stepped in. "You'd better go now, Max," he said, ushering him towards the door. "Please. Everyone's a bit upset."

"Upset," Max yelled. "Too bloody right I'm upset. Tell your girlfriend to keep her mouth shut in future."

Hopper moved towards Max, her eyes sparking with anger. "I can't believe –"

"Max!" Alan warned. "Out, now. Before someone says something they'll regret. Please!"

"Too late," Max muttered as he slammed the front door behind him. "Too bloody late."

"Lucy?" Hopper asked. Lucy's bedroom door was open and she stepped inside gingerly. "Lucy, love, I'm so sorry."

Lucy was lying on the bed staring at the ceiling. Hopper sat down on the bed beside her. "Please talk to me. I shouldn't have said those things to Max. I'm sorry." She waited for a response. "You have every right to be angry with me, I know. But please talk to me."

"Did you hear what he said?" Lucy said eventually.

"Who? Dan?"

"No, Max. He loves her and he doesn't love me."

"That's not what he said, pet. You know that."

"It's what he meant."

"Lucy," Hopper said, stroking her hair, "you have to let him go. Daria seems nice. He'll still be there for you."

"No, he won't," Lucy said, sounding like a petulant child. Hopper tried not to smile. "He'll be off doing things with *her*."

"And what about Dan? You can do things with him instead. I think you're overreacting, to be honest. It'll all seem better in the morning, I promise."

"I don't know," Lucy sighed. "I can't believe he lied to me. My head hurts thinking about it."

"Ring Max tomorrow," Hopper said, biting her tongue. She wasn't sure if withholding information constituted lying, but now wasn't the time to get into it. "Talk to him."

"Maybe," Lucy said.

Hopper scrunched up her nose. She needed something to take Lucy's mind off Max. "Would you like to see the new toy I got for Alan's computer? It's really cool."

"Not right now," Lucy said. "I'm too tired."

"Suit yourself," Hopper sniffed. "I was only trying –"

"Sorry, Hopper," Lucy said, sitting up slowly. "I'd love to see your new toy, really. What is it?"

"A web-cam."

"A what?"

"Come into Alan's room and I'll show you."

"What do you want a web-cam for, Hopper, or should I ask?" Lucy raised her eyebrows.

Hopper laughed. "Nothing seedy, honestly. Just a spot of Nancy Drew-ing."

19

It was three in the morning and Lucy couldn't sleep. Everything kept spinning around and around in her head.

She'd trusted Max. More than anyone else in the world. Hopper had let it slip that Max and Daria had been seeing each other for a few weeks now. This had made Lucy even more angry – he'd had weeks to tell her.

She couldn't escape the feeling that she was losing Max. Like she lost her father.

"Lucy, look at me." She could still remember almost every word her beloved daddy had said that night, over twenty years ago.

"Your mother and I have decided to call it a day. Don't cry, sweetie. You have to be brave." He'd wiped the tears from her eyes with his large, white cotton hankie. *"I'm going to be living with Stella and Amanda, in Liverpool. It'll be like having a new mummy and a new sister."*

"Stella and Amanda from Galway?" Lucy had been confused. Why would her daddy be living with them? She didn't understand .

"Yes, love."

Stella and Amanda Cody rented the house next door to them in Roundstone in Galway where they all went on their holidays every year.

205

Stella was small and blonde, like her pretty daughter, Amanda. Lucy played with Amanda and had always been jealous of her clothes and her huge collection of Sindy dolls. Amanda had seven Sindy dolls, a Sindy house, horse and caravan. Lucy had two Sindys and one's hair had all been cut off during a hairdressing game, so it didn't really count. They'd used the shorn-Sindy as a boy doll, a kind of Sindy 'Ken'.

Amanda did have a daddy but he lived in London with another family. He was always sending Amanda presents. Amanda always said how lucky Lucy was to have a daddy living in her house.

Lucy had liked Amanda until now – until Amanda had stolen her daddy away.

Stella and Daddy hadn't meant to fall in love, Eileen told Lucy later, as she cried in her bedroom. It had just happened. But he'd still love Lucy and visit her lots.

"No!" Lucy had screamed at her mum, not knowing what she meant exactly. But from that moment on, she had never talked to her father again.

After a few years Eamonn White had given up visiting, ringing and sending presents as it was a waste of time. Lucy had never forgotten him and how he'd replaced her with a new improved daughter in the form of Amanda.

Max was the only one Lucy had ever told about her dad, the only one she'd ever really let in. And now he too had let her down.

* * *

"Kathleen O'Mara wants a bikini wax first thing this morning," said Paula, looking up from the appointments book. "Are you up to it? Lucy?"

"I heard you," said Lucy. "That's fine."

"And you've an eyebrow-shaping with Rita Maxwell and a pedicure with Mrs Nugent senior." Paula slammed the book shut. "And then there's a massage with a Mrs Mossy. I took that booking from Max last week. He said it was a corporate client." Paula sniffed. She doubted if Max had any 'corporate clients' but as he'd paid up front with his credit card, who was she to argue? "Who's Mrs Mossy?"

Lucy groaned inwardly. Her murderous feelings towards Max increased tenfold.

"It's not Mrs Mossy, it's Mossy."

"Mossy is her first name?"

"Yes, I mean no," Lucy sighed. "It's *his* first name."

Paula raised her eyebrows. She tapped her pen on the outside of the appointment book impatiently. "Go on," she said.

"Mossy works in Max's office," she began. "He's a professional sailor, kind of."

"And?" Paula was getting impatient at this stage.

"Max owes him a favour so he offered him some massages, that's all," Lucy said. "And, knowing Making Faces is the best in the business, he sent him here."

Paula cocked her eyebrow. She couldn't tell if Lucy was being serious, but she was willing to let it go.

"He's very attractive," Lucy added as an afterthought. "Tall and blond, very tanned. It'll be quite a physical massage. He's built like a brick, muscles all over the place."

Lucy could see Paula's mouth begin to twitch. Bingo!

"I don't mind at all, in fact –" Lucy continued.

"I couldn't let you take him," Paula said smoothly. "No doubt Rita will want a little chat. You know what she's like. I'll do him."

"But –" Lucy pretended to be aggrieved.

"I'm afraid I'll have to insist," Paula said, putting her hand on Lucy's shoulder. "I'm the boss."

Stupid cow, Lucy thought to herself as she prepared the wax for Kathleen O'Mara. She fell for it. The last thing Lucy wanted to do today was massage Mossy!

"Are you sure about this, Kathleen?" asked Lucy anxiously.

Kathleen O'Mara nodded solemnly. "It's a birthday present for Dessie. It's his sixtieth on Saturday and I thought I'd give him a little surprise."

Lucy tried not to giggle. He'd certainly get a surprise, if surprise was the right word for it!

Kathleen was in her late thirties and was Dessie Thompson, the 'Carpet King's' second wife. A devoted new wife and mother of Dessie Junior, their one-year-old son, she wore Gucci and Prada and was always popping into the local salon for 'little treats' to keep her body and face in shape.

A big fan of Botox, Kathleen had been dismayed to find that Making Faces was Botox-free. Although Paula had promised to look into it. Lucy dreaded the day when she'd have to inject her clients with the muscle-freezing formula, even if it did eradicate their wrinkles. However young Cliff Richard looked, he still couldn't frown.

"Lie back and try to relax," said Lucy. "I'm going to apply the wax in two stages. It may feel hot at first."

Lucy checked that the beeswax and resin mixture was the right consistency and tested it on the inside of her wrist to make sure it wasn't too hot. Satisfied, she gave it one final stir.

"I'm going to apply the wax now, Kathleen," she said. She smoothed the wax onto the right-hand side of Kathleen's naturally dark blonde pubic hair with a spatula, against the hair growth, with the natural growth and against it once more, ensuring that each hair was coated in the syrupy substance. She kept the edges of the wax thick, to make sure it would tear off in one smooth, swift movement. It was going to be painful enough as it was.

"I'll remove it in sixty seconds," said Lucy.

She waited, took a deep breath and, holding the edge of the wax firmly, ripped it off in one quick stroke.

"OWWW! Shit!" yelled Kathleen.

Paula stuck her head in the door. "Is everything all right?" she asked anxiously. Looking at Lucy, hairy wax strip in her hand she grimaced. "Brazilian?"

Lucy nodded solemnly.

"Always a killer," said Paula, closing the door behind her.

"Sorry about that," Lucy said, carefully checking to see that no wax particles were left on her client's skin. She applied some antiseptic lotion to the area on a piece of cotton wool.

Kathleen looked down at her newly bared nether regions. "I hope Dessie appreciates this."

"I'm sure he will," said Lucy, trying not to laugh. *Sex and the City* had a lot to answer for.

"Darling, he sounds ideal," Rita Maxwell purred. "Tell me more."

Lucy placed a little moisturising cream on her ring-fingers and massaged Rita's eyebrows for a few minutes. She moved her fingers in small circles, increasing the pressure as she went along.

"Lucy!"

"Sorry?"

Rita looked up at her. "Mossy. Tell me more."

Lucy removed the cream with damp cotton wool. "He's tall, with blond hair. Very good-looking."

"Lea will love him," Rita giggled. "And a professional sportsman to boot. Wait till I tell the girls."

Lucy hoped to goodness that Mossy didn't arrive for his massage early. His long shaggy hair was definitely in need of a cut. How were they going to make him do that? She stopped herself. Not my problem, she thought. Max's problem. It's his bloody sister.

She placed cotton wool pads on Rita's eyes and began to pluck.

"Don't make them too thin, will you, dear?" Rita said.

"No."

Rita waffled on about the Debs and Lea's dress while Lucy continued with the tweezers. When finished, she handed Rita a mirror for inspection.

"Wonderful," Rita said. She picked up her bag and prepared to leave. "And I hope you'll come to our little Debs drinkie-poos. Max will be there, of course." Rita raised her new eyebrows. "It's only two weeks away now."

"Sure," Lucy said, cursing herself inwardly for being such a coward. She showed Rita out. As she walked past Paula's cubicle towards the kitchen she heard a low moan. Intrigued, she opened the cubicle door a crack and peeped in. Mossy was lying on the massage table, an indecently small white hand-towel just about covering his buttocks. He was covered in massage oil, his tanned skin glistening in the lights. Paula was putting her full body-weight onto him, rolling the skin and muscles on his back. As Lucy watched she noticed that Paula was smiling.

"Mossy," she heard Paula say, "you must work out a lot. You have wonderful muscle tone."

"I do my best," Mossy lied. "I like to look after myself. I think it's important to respect your body."

Lucy nearly choked with suppressed laughter. She half-expected to see Mossy reach out and grab one of Paula's toned legs while she was working on his back. But he seemed to be behaving himself.

"This is the best massage I've ever had," Mossy said. "You're very talented, Paula."

"Why, thank you," Paula said in a deep, husky voice, one that Lucy had thankfully been spared so far.

Lucy shut the door quietly and leant against it. What had she done?

* * *

Max rang Lucy several times on Monday. And every time she'd ignored it. By Wednesday, after many more calls, two door-steppings and one hand-delivered letter, he'd given up.

* * *

Max stared out at the sea. It was a dull evening but at least it wasn't raining. He was sitting on the end of Dun Laoghaire pier, hoping for inspiration. He didn't know what to do about Lucy and it was driving him crazy. He'd tried everything he could think of, except flowers. In the mood she was in, he figured that a dozen red roses might do more harm than good.

210

He leant back and stretched his legs out in front of him. He hadn't been sleeping too well and his body felt stiff.

He looked at his watch. If he didn't get a move on he'd be late for Daria.

As soon as he walked into the brightly-lit restaurant he saw her. She was sitting at a table in the window and she looked stunning. Her hair had been teased into dark twists and her mouth was a slash of crimson red. She was wearing a black-leather top which had no back, unless you counted the thin straps which criss-crossed over her even, pale skin.

"Daria," he said, approaching her. She looked up and smiled. He kissed her on the cheek before sitting down. "You look amazing. I love the top."

"Thanks. It's new."

Max sat down. "Nice place," he said, looking around.

"You've never been to Mao's?" Daria cocked her head to one side.

"No," Max said, picking up the menu. "Not this one. I've been to the one in town. Great food." His stomach rumbled. He hadn't eaten all day. "I'm starving. Have you ordered wine?"

"No. Not yet. You choose – I'm easy."

"Oh yeah?" Max smiled.

"Stop!" she laughed.

Max smiled again. "Is red OK?"

Daria nodded.

"How about a Merlot?"

"Fine."

Daria watched him as he ordered the wine. She'd spent the last few days replaying Sunday's events in her head. Things had been a little strained between them over the last week which had made her all the more determined to make tonight a success.

"How was your day?" Max asked.

"Great. Rosaleen was late, so myself and John got to rehearse the last scene together. When Emma and Mr Knightley admit their love for each other. It was fun. Halfway through Rosaleen stormed in and

211

gave out to everyone for starting without her. Owen made her sit and watch while myself and John finished the scene."

"I'll bet she was fuming," Max laughed.

"She was."

"Are you ready to order?" A young waitress stood beside their table, notebook and pen ready. She looked at Daria.

"I'll have the Mao salad to start and then the chicken satay," Daria said.

"And I'll have the chilli soup and the Thai green curry," Max said, handing her the menu. "Thanks."

Daria picked up her wineglass and took a large sip. "So what have you been up to today?"

"The usual. I finished Dan's kite, the one we were testing on Sunday. He's calling in to collect it next week." Max cursed himself for bringing Sunday up. Too late now, he thought to himself. He bit into a prawn cracker which he'd dipped into the spicy red chilli sauce, took a long sip of wine and smiled. "It's good to see you. Sorry about the last few days. I haven't really felt like going out."

"That's OK. It's Friday. We have the whole weekend ahead of us. Forget it."

"And about Sunday –" he began. It's already out there, he thought to himself, may as well deal with it.

"Don't. It's fine, honestly. Lucy was upset. You were upset. It's over, period."

"Are you sure? I feel really bad about it. I shouldn't have dropped you home like that. I should have –"

"Please," she said, putting her hand on his. "Leave it."

"OK," he said, relieved. He'd presumed that Daria would want to talk about it but he'd obviously read her wrong. And that suited him just fine – he could concentrate on enjoying himself instead.

"The wine is lovely. Good choice." She took another sip.

Max looked at the bottle. They had already drained over two thirds and they hadn't even started eating yet. "It's certainly going down well."

As they ate their starters, Max realised that he hadn't thought about Lucy for at least twenty minutes. He smiled at Daria.

"What?" she smiled back, dipping her skewer into the peanut sauce.

"Nothing." He poured her some more wine and topped his own glass up, finishing the bottle.

"I'm going to have to leave the car here and get a taxi home," he said, after ordering another bottle.

"You can always stay at my place."

"Are you sure?"

"Yes." She ran her leg up his under the table, her suede trousers rubbing against his jeans suggestively. His heart began to beat faster.

"That would be good."

The rest of the dinner went in a blur of wine, spicy food and flirtatious conversation. Daria was in flying form and by the end of the evening Max felt on top of the world. Walking back to Monkstown, they stopped several times.

"We'll never get home at this rate," Max laughed as she pushed him against the wall of Fish Antics and kissed him deeply, sending shivers down his spine.

"What's the hurry? We have all night." She pressed herself firmly against him and he could feel his body responding.

"That's it!" he said, sweeping her up in his arms and running down the road.

"You're going to give yourself a heart attack. Put me down!"

"Never," he puffed, crossing the road at Monkstown church.

As they approached Daria's house he had to put her down. He bent his body over to catch his breath.

"I'm impressed," she said, rubbing his back. "But I hope you haven't used up all your energy." She bit his ear playfully and ran towards her front door, opening it and stepping inside.

Max followed slowly, his heart racing and his breath staggering in short gasps. When he walked inside Daria had disappeared. He closed the front door behind him. In the gloomy darkness he could just make out her red jacket at the bottom of the stairs. He picked it up. Halfway up the stairs was her little black top. Max could feel his pulse racing. At the top of the stairs, outside a door, were her suede trousers.

He took a deep breath and opened the door expectantly. The curtains were open and the streetlights outside illuminated the room in a soft, yellow glow.

Daria was lying on the bed wearing nothing except a black G-string, matching black bra and black high-heeled sandals, whose delicate leather laces criss-crossed her ankles and her lower calves, accentuating her slender legs. She smiled up at him lazily.

"Come in. Care to join me?"

Without taking his eyes off her face, he took off his jacket and threw it on the floor, followed by his shirt. He lowered himself onto her bed and unlaced his boots. Once they were discarded, he leaned towards her, grazing her lips with a soft kiss.

"You're beautiful," he smiled.

She pulled his head towards hers and gave him a deep, erotic kiss. He moved his hands gently over her cool skin, arms, chest and stomach, finally lingering just above her breasts. He touched these slowly with his fingers, pushing aside the fine mesh of her backless-bra, tracing tiny circles on the sensitive skin.

Daria ran her hands up and down his back, her short fingernails grazing his skin.

Max gasped as she began to undo his trousers and pull them down his slim thighs. He helped her and kicked them onto the floor.

"Going commando, Max?" Daria smiled.

"Absolutely." Truth be told, he couldn't find any clean boxers this evening so he'd decided to go without.

As they kissed he caressed her buttocks, moving his hands over the smooth skin.

"Have you got condoms, Max?"

Shit, he thought to himself. "No," he admitted. "Sorry."

"Not to worry," Daria said, reaching one arm towards her bedside table. She couldn't quite reach. "Move over a second."

He rolled off her.

"Thanks." She pulled a packet of Mates from the drawer and looked inside. "Loads left."

"Good," he said, kissing her ear playfully. "Now where were we?"

"About here." She took his hand in hers and moved it down towards her G-string.

"Really? I would have thought we were more here." He gently pulled her G-string down her thighs.

"I'd have to agree," she said, lifting her hips to allow him to slide it off.

As their bodies came together for the first time that evening, all thoughts of anything else flew out the window.

* * *

Max opened his eyes. Bright morning light was streaming in the window. He turned and looked at Daria. She was still asleep. He wasn't surprised. They hadn't stopped all night. She was quite something.

He sat up gingerly, aware of a faint throbbing in his temples. At least they'd been drinking decent wine last night, so the hangover shouldn't be too bad. He got out of the warm bed and pulled the curtains closed. He stood and looked at Daria. Her dark hair contrasted starkly with the white pillowcase, her face was lightly tanned and there was a smattering of freckles on her nose and cheeks. Max smiled. He got back under the covers, put his arms around her and drifted back to sleep.

20

"Are you sure you want to come?" asked Lucy. "It's the zoo, Eugene. There're no bars there, you know. Not the sort you're used to anyway. No chicks, no loud music, no –"

"That's unfair, Sis," Eugene grinned. "I want to have a laugh with the kids. It'll be rockin'."

"If you're positive," said Lucy doubtfully.

"Listen," said Eugene, stirring even more sugar into his tea. "They won't be with ma all that much longer. So I'd like to do stuff with them now, OK? They're good kids."

"OK, OK, I believe you." She took a sip of her own tea. "You would have enjoyed the circus last weekend. It was deadly."

"Deadly?" Eugene grinned. "You're fierce trendy, Sis."

"Shut up!" she smiled, flicking his ear with her finger.

"Feck off!" he said, rubbing his ear. "That hurt."

"Language, Eugene," said Eileen, walking into the kitchen.

"Sorry, Ma. Lucy attacked me."

Eileen looked at her daughter. "I don't know which of you is worse!"

Lucy pointed at her brother. "Definitely him."

"That's a compliment coming from you, Granny-pants."

"Eugene!" said Eileen, exasperated. "You should be setting a good example to the children. You and your sister should be nicer to each other."

"Aran and Jade aren't here, Ma," said Eugene. "And besides, I love me sis, don't I?" He put his arm around Lucy's shoulders.

"Get off!" said Lucy, shrugging his arm off.

"And stop calling me Ma," Eileen sighed. "You know I hate it."

"Sorry, Mother dearest," said Eugene in his poshest accent.

Eileen swatted him on the head with a damp tea towel.

"That's not fair!" Eugene protested. "You just gave out to Lucy for hurting me."

"Sometimes, Eugene," said his mother, "you deserve it!"

"Are the kids ready?" asked Lucy.

"Yes," said Eileen. "They're so excited. Jade's sitting at the bottom of the stairs, waiting. And Aran's in the living-room watching a Pokemon video."

Lucy stood up, put her own cup in the sink and swiped Eugene's from under his nose. "Come on, Bro," she said. "Time to mosh."

Eugene shook his head. "You're so sad."

* * *

"What's in your handbag, Eugene," Jade asked innocently as they walked to the car.

Lucy laughed.

Eugene glared at Lucy. "It's not a handbag, Jade. It's me record bag, for all me records."

"Can we see your records?" Aran asked.

"I don't have any with me today," Eugene said, looking a little sheepish. "But I do usually."

"Are you a DJ?" Aran asked.

Lucy snorted.

"Yeah, man," Eugene said, ignoring her and nodding his head. "I've a couple of gigs every week in the Union."

Aran stared at him, a blank expression on his little face.

"The Students' Union," Eugene explained. "It's a bar in college."

"Do you get paid for it?" Lucy asked as she unlocked the doors of her mother's car. Eileen had lent it to them for the day. Lucy didn't trust Eugene's driving.

"Not exactly. But I get paid in kind. Free pints."

"What's a DJ?" Jade asked, climbing onto her car booster seat.

"Someone who would like to be a musician but has absolutely no talent," Lucy said, clicking in her seat belt.

"Balls!" Eugene said.

Jade and Aran giggled.

"Sorry, kids," he said. "Pay no attention to Lucy. A DJ is the maestro of the music. The groove-master. The trendsetter."

"He puts records on a record-player," Lucy said.

"Go back to the 80's, dinosaur," Eugene laughed. "Record-player, yeah, right!"

"I think I'd like to be a DJ when I'm big," Aran said.

Lucy groaned.

"What music do you like, Aran?" Eugene asked.

Aran thought for a moment. "Anything except boy bands and silly girls. And I hate Britney Spears."

"My man!" Eugene said, putting his hand in the air and giving Aran a high five.

"I like Samantha Mumba," Jade said in a small voice. "Mam said she used to live near us when she was little."

"I like her too," Lucy said, backing her up. "Why don't you sing a Samantha Mumba song? Do you know any?"

Jade nodded. She began to sing.

"You have a great voice," Eugene said. "Maybe you could be a singer when you grow up."

"Do you think so?" Jade asked, delighted.

"Yeah," Eugene. "Absolutely!"

Lucy smiled. Sometimes her useless brother surprised her.

"What are you going to be, Eugene?" Aran asked. "A DJ?"

"Maybe," Eugene said. He looked at Lucy who was staring at the road straight ahead, trying not to laugh. "Or maybe an actor. I'm in the DramSoc and we're doing a modern adaptation of *Romeo and Juliet*. I'm Romeo."

Lucy couldn't help herself this time. She snorted again and began to laugh. "You! Romeo! I don't believe you."

"I am! And you should see my Juliet." He kissed his fingers. "*Bellissimq*! She's going to be my new mot."

"What's a mot?" Aran asked.

"There's no such word," Lucy said. "He means his new girlfriend."

Jade giggled. Aran looked put out.

"What's wrong, Aran?" Eugene asked.

"Don't like girls," Aran muttered, his arms crossed in front of his chest.

"That'll change, mate. Wait and see. Speaking of which, Lucy, Mum tells me you're grooving on down with Hilda's son, you dark horse you."

"What!" she said. She'd kill her mother.

"Oops, sorry. Raw nerve?"

"No!" she insisted. "I helped him on a catering job, that's all. I can't believe she said –"

"Go easy," he said. "That's all she told me. I was just fishing. Got you!"

"You little b –"

"Now, Lucy you'll have to watch your language in front of the children!" Eugene grinned.

Lucy wondered how she'd cope with *three* children all day. She wished Max was there to help her. He found Eugene really entertaining for some bizarre reason.

"How's Max?" Eugene asked, as if reading her mind.

"Fine. Busy."

"Are you in a snot with him?"

"No! Why would I be?"

"Dunno. Just asking. Keep yer knickers on."

Aran and Jade giggled at the mention of knickers.

"Have you been to the zoo before, kids?" Lucy asked, scrambling for something to change the subject.

"You already asked us that, remember?" Aran said. "Last weekend when we were out with you and Max."

"Yes, of course. How could I be so stupid?"

* * *

Lucy sat outside an 'authentic' African hut sipping a Coke. Eugene had kindly offered to take Aran and Jade around the Savannah Plains on his own, motivated no doubt by the rather attractive driver of the Safari Train, a zebra-striped covered trailer pulled by what looked like a small tractor. Lucy appreciated the time out. It was hard work keeping up with the kids – their energy would give Sonia O'Sullivan a run for her money.

She was trying not to think about Max, but it was proving difficult. Everything seemed to be reminding her of him, from the penguins (his favourite zoo animal) to the bright flags flying at the entrance (which looked like kites). She knew in her heart that she should stop being so stubborn. But it was too late now. She'd spent the week ignoring his calls and even his impassioned letter, which had made her cry, and she could hardly just ring him now as if nothing had happened.

Lucy sighed. The thing was – she really missed him. Hopper was there for her, but it didn't seem the same somehow. Lucy bit the skin around her thumb, making it bleed. She hadn't bitten her nails for years, not since she'd been lambasted in beauty college by her tutor, Mrs Allen, for having 'the most unattractive nails she'd ever seen, and on a beautician!'. It'd been the way Mrs Allen had said it, making her feel like the lowest of the low. So she'd given up cold turkey and hadn't put a finger near her mouth since.

But this week she'd demolished all of the nails on both hands except the one on her left little finger. She'd even been giving her cuticles a going-over.

She finished her Coke, put the cup back down on the table, sat back and closed her eyes.

"Lucy!" Jade yelled from almost beside her, making her jump. "We saw lions!"

Lucy sat up and rubbed her eyes. She must have dozed off. "Did you?"

Jade nodded enthusiastically. "And giraffes and hippos and zebras." She stopped to catch her breath. "The lady on the train said that hippos are really dangerous. Did you know that?"

Eugene and Aran appeared beside Lucy. Eugene ruffled Jade's hair affectionately.

"I was just telling Lucy about the hippos," Jade said.

"They can rip your head off," Aran smiled. "Imagine that."

"No thanks!" Lucy laughed. "I'd rather not. Now who'd like a drink?"

"Me!" Jade and Aran replied in unison.

"Any beer?" Eugene asked her hopefully.

Lucy smiled at him and raised her eyebrows. "Coke, Eugene?"

* * *

"I've a few messages for you," Hopper said as Lucy walked in the door that evening. She's obviously been sitting on the stairs waiting to pounce, Lucy thought.

"Max rang twice," Hopper said. "He said to ring him. And Dan rang. He wanted to check how you were. He sounded worried. And Eugene rang just a few minutes ago. Something about RTE ringing your mum's and leaving a message. I couldn't really make out what he was on about. He was very excited. Said your mobile's switched off."

"Thanks," Lucy said evenly. "I'm going upstairs."

"No, you're not," Hopper said, blocking her way. "You're going to talk to me. You've been avoiding me all week and I'm worried about you."

"I'm fine," Lucy insisted. "I'm just tired."

"Don't give me that. I know you." She held Lucy's arm firmly. "Come into the kitchen and I'll make some coffee. Alan's watching football in the pub with some work friends, so we have the place to ourselves."

"OK," Lucy said admitting defeat. She sat down and thumbed through Delia Smith's *How to Cook, Book One* which lay open on the table. "Whose is this?" she asked, holding up the white-covered book.

"Mine," Hopper said as she filled the kettle. "I got it from the library this morning. You haven't been cooking all week and myself and Alan have been having withdrawal symptoms. We're sick of Super Noodles. I thought I might have a go at cooking a roast tomorrow."

"I'm sorry."

"Don't be daft. I hadn't realised how much cooking you actually do before this week. It's not fair to rely on you so much. And anyway, you won't always be around –"

"Are you kicking me out? Has it got that bad? Is that what you're trying to tell me?"

Hopper laughed. "Are you mad? Of course we're not kicking you out, you big thick. But things change, you know. Myself and Alan were vaguely thinking about buying a house, that's all."

"A house! Are you serious?"

"About what? About Alan or about buying a house?"

"Both!"

Hopper spooned coffee into the two mugs. She waited until the kettle stopped boiling and poured the steaming water into the mugs.

"Hopper!" Lucy said impatiently.

"OK, OK," Hopper said, putting the mugs on the table. "One second." She pulled a carton of milk from the fridge and splashed a dollop into each, spilling some on the table in the process, then mopping it up with kitchen paper. She sat down and pushed one mug towards Lucy.

"I suppose I'm serious about both," she said finally. "Alan's just Alan. You know him as well as I do –"

"Hardly!" Lucy grinned.

"You know what I mean. He's one of life's good guys. He makes me happy and he seems to feel the same way about me, God love him."

"I knew you were getting on well, but I hadn't realised how well. It's all happening very fast. Buying a house together is a big step."

Hopper crinkled her nose. "I know. It sounds so grown-up, doesn't it? And to be honest, I'm not exactly sure what we can afford. Probably a one-bedroom shed in Bally-Go-Backwards. But Alan's really keen on the idea. He thinks renting is like throwing money down the drain."

"He's probably right," Lucy said. "Does this mean he's thinking of staying in Dublin?"

"Yes," Hopper nodded. "For the moment anyway."

Lucy sighed. "So you'll both be moving out soon."

"Not for ages," Hopper assured her. "If it even happens at all. You know what my track record with men is like."

"But Alan's not your average man."

"True," Hopper agreed.

Lucy took a sip of her coffee. "Anyway, I'm glad it's all working out."

"So am I. Finally. Speaking of which, what are you doing, girl? Max is going crazy trying to contact you. *And* you haven't rung Dan, have you?"

"Hopper, I'm not really in the mood."

"In the mood? Get with the programme. You'll lose both of them if you persist in being so damn stubborn."

"Stubborn! I'm not being stubborn."

"Yes, you are," Hopper replied, trying to keep her cool. Lucy could be completely exasperating sometimes. "You should have talked to Max and Dan last Sunday. Instead you let it drag on and on all week. And now it's the weekend and you still haven't talked to either of them."

"Why should I?" Lucy asked petulantly. "I don't have to."

"Jeez, Lucy, isn't it obvious? I know Max wasn't exactly truthful with you about his little fling, but in the grand scheme of things, is it really such a big deal?"

223

"Yes!" Lucy said emphatically. "He was seeing one of my friends behind my back and neither of them had the decency to fill me in. *And* we were in Daria's house having dinner last week for goodness sake – she could have said something."

"Max probably wanted to tell you himself. I'm sure it's not Daria's fault."

"And you didn't exactly help things, Miss Big Mouth," Lucy continued. She was picking at her last remaining nail as she spoke.

"Sorry? What are you talking about?"

"Sunday night in the kitchen. What was that all about?"

"I'm glad you brought it up. I'm sorry I upset you. But you have to face facts. It's true, isn't it?"

"What?" Lucy demanded.

"You're in love with Max. That's why you reacted like that on the beach."

"That's ridiculous!" Lucy said.

"Is it? Maybe you should think about it. Because you've blown this whole thing way out of proportion. You seem to think you've got some God-given right to know every little thing about his personal life. I hate to break it to you, but you don't. Max is not your boyfriend."

"I know that!" Lucy said, her voice dangerously loud. "He's my best friend and he's never lied to me. Until now. Of course, I can't expect you to understand about friendship and loyalty, can I, Hopper? Some friend you are."

"That's not fair. I'm only trying to help. You're impossible to talk to. I don't know why I bother."

"Don't then," Lucy said, standing up. "And I'm *not* in love with Max." She walked out of the kitchen, slamming the door behind her.

* * *

A little later Hopper knocked gently on Lucy's bedroom door. "Lucy, are you OK? I've brought you a cup of tea."

Lucy blew her nose. She was tempted to shout "Go away" at her but she didn't have the energy. Instead she sniffed "I'm fine, come in."

Hopper noticed her red eyes and sat down beside her on the bed. She put the cup of tea on the bedside table and gave Lucy a hug. "I'm sorry. I shouldn't have been so hard on you."

"That's OK. I'm not annoyed with you. Can we just forget it?"

"Sure."

"And please, I don't want to talk about Max or Dan. Not right now."

"Fine. But will you at least ring Eugene? I'm dying to know what he was on about."

"Yes, I'll ring him," Lucy said, fishing out her mobile from her bag and turning it on. She punched in his number. "Eugene, it's Lucy. What's up?" She listened for a few seconds before screaming "Are you serious? I don't believe it!"

Hopper stared at her quizzically. "What?" she mouthed.

"That soon?" Lucy continued, ignoring Hopper. "Brilliant! Listen, I'd better go. Hopper is dying to know what we're talking about. I'd better put her out of her misery. Bye."

"Well?"

Lucy grinned. "You know that show *Strike A Match?*" Hopper nodded. "A woman from RTE rang this afternoon. Eugene has been chosen as a contestant. And myself and Mum get to choose his date."

"No way!"

"I'm deadly serious," Lucy said. "It's recording the week after next. And I'm going to find him the most painful girl I can!"

Hopper laughed. "You wouldn't!"

"Just watch me!"

21

Hopper bounded up the stairs. There was something on the web-cam today, she just knew it.

For the past week she'd been recording images of Alan's room when they were out, using the new web-cam, but nothing had shown up. Hopper was disappointed. There hadn't been any poltergeist-type occurrences all week – no strange smells, moved objects or ghostly fingerprints. Maybe they had both been imagining it.

She opened Alan's bedroom door slowly and walked in. Everything seemed just as they had left it – the duvet thrown haphazardly on to the bed, the window ajar, the chair in the corner piled high with Alan's discarded clothes.

Hopper stood still and sniffed. There was definitely some sort of sweet smell in the room that hadn't been there before. She felt decidedly nervous. She pulled out her mobile.

"Alan?"

"Why are you whispering, Hopper?"

"I think it's been in the room again."

"The poltergeist?"

"Yes."

"Has anything been moved?" Alan was whispering now too.

"I don't think so," she said, "but there's definitely a funny smell."

"Did the camera record anything?"

"I haven't checked."

"Well, go on," Alan urged.

"Will you stay on the phone while I have a look?" Hopper said nervously. "In case I see anything."

"Sure. But hurry up."

"OK, OK. I'm having a look now." She lodged her mobile between her ear and her shoulder and clicked on the mouse, scanning the images recorded on the computer. The web-cam had recorded images of the room every few seconds which it had then built up into moving pictures.

"See anything?" Alan asked.

"No. Nothing yet. Hang on." She gasped. An image had just appeared on the screen – a small blonde image that certainly wasn't a poltergeist! She watched in astonishment, her eyes glued to screen.

"Hopper? Hopper? Is there something there?"

"No, I thought I saw something, but it was the sun coming in the window," Hopper lied. "Listen, this could take a while. I'll ring you back."

"Are you sure? You sound a bit spooked."

"I'm fine, honestly," Hopper smiled broadly. The mystery was solved. "Just fine and dandy." She said goodbye and then punched a familiar number into her mobile.

"Hello, Making Faces Beauty Salon. Can I help you?"

"Yes, you can. Do you know who this is, Paula?"

There was a squeak on the other end of the phone. "Sinead. What the hell do *you* want?"

"Call over to the house at lunchtime. I want to talk to you."

"Don't be ridiculous," Paula said scathingly. "Unless you're going to apologise for your horrid behaviour we have nothing to say to each other."

"I'll see you at one, unless you want me to tell all your clients that you're a witch. I have pictures."

"What?" Paula said in a strangled voice.

"You heard me. I'll see you at one."

* * *

"Sit down," Hopper said to Paula, pointing at the chair beside the window.

Paula moved one of Alan's jumpers out of the way and sat down gingerly.

"I want you to explain to me exactly what you thought you were doing," Hopper said calmly.

Paula opened her mouth to speak. "But –"

"Stop!" Hopper said, enjoying herself immensely. "I don't want any excuses. I just want the facts."

"You're not going to tell anyone, are you?"

"That depends on how co-operative you're going to be." She'd spent the last hour scouring Alan's room from top to bottom after seeing Paula pull out some strange items from all over the room – under the bed, sewn into the curtains and tucked behind a picture frame.

Hopper held up her first find – a small wooden skewer which had been driven through two halves of an apple. She'd found it under the chest of drawers. The apple halves were held together by a light-blue ribbon. "What's this?"

"A love spell," Paula whispered.

"What?"

"A love spell," she said, louder this time.

"And this?" Hopper held up a small muslin bag full of dried petals, which she'd found under the mattress.

"A magic pillow."

"And these?" Hopper held up two pennies that had human hair wrapped around them which had been tucked under the carpet.

"Another love spell."

"And what are they all for exactly?"

Paula blushed and stared at the floor. "Do I have spell it out?"

"Unfortunate choice of words, but I guess not. How are your clients going to react to the news that their beautician of choice is a witch?"

"I'm not a witch!" Paula said vehemently. "I just thought . . . it was stupid really. I went in this morning to take it all away but I obviously forgot those ones."

Hopper sighed. "I really don't know what to do with you, Paula."

"None of it worked. I read it in a book – *Princess Candy's Love Spells*. I was going through a bad patch – I really wanted Alan back. But I'm fine now."

"And you were willing to try anything? Even magic?"

Paula nodded silently.

For the first time ever Hopper admired her. It was a mad thing for Paula to do, but Hopper kind of respected that.

"What are you going to do?" Paula asked after a few minutes.

Hopper smiled. "Nothing. It's what you're going to do. Or *not* going to do," she added cryptically.

* * *

Lucy hummed The Boomtown Rats' 'I Don't Like Mondays' as she walked in the door of Making Faces the following morning, even though it was actually Tuesday. It felt like a Monday.

"Morning, Lucy," said Paula, glancing at her watch.

"Morning, Paula," said Lucy through gritted teeth. She was two minutes late at most. Lucy slid her fleece jacket off and hung it up on the back of the kitchen door on top of a black calf-skin leather coat.

"Careful of my coat," said Paula, frowning. "It was expensive."

Stupid bitch, Lucy thought as she made herself some coffee.

"Make me a cup, will you?" asked Paula, examining her nails for imperfections. She scratched at a sliver of polish, held it up to her heavily dark-brown outlined mouth and blew it away. For someone who ran a beauty salon, she rarely took her own make-up advice, like blending your lip-liner to the shade of your lipstick.

"Do anything interesting last night?" Before Lucy had the chance to answer she ploughed on. "I went sailing with Mossy," she giggled. "It was wonderful. We went to Dalkey Island on a sailing ship and –"

"Yacht," Lucy interrupted.

"Whatever. And we had dinner in The Royal Irish Yacht Club. I wore my backless Gucci. It's such a lovely place, and the men are such gentlemen. Have you been there?"

Lucy shook her head.

"Shame, but it wouldn't really be your scene, would it?"

"Alan and Hopper are buying a house," Lucy blurted out. Paula was being such a bitch she couldn't stop herself.

"What?" Paula asked, staring at her coldly.

"You heard me."

"Together?"

"Yes."

"And why would Alan buy a house with *her*?"

Lucy smiled. "Because he's crazy about her," she began, savouring every word. "In fact, he's so madly in love with her that he's decided to stay in Dublin and settle down with her."

Paula's face went white. Everything started to slot into place. She'd made Hopper a solemn promise yesterday afternoon not to interfere in Alan's life ever again. She could kill Hopper. "Is this some sort of sick joke? Because if it is –"

"It's not a joke," Lucy said, starting to feel a little guilty.

Paula sat down. "I see." She sighed. "I suppose he was going to meet someone sooner or later. But *her*. Are you sure?"

"Paula, I live with the two of them."

"Of course." She was silent for a few seconds. "I guess life goes on."

"You're taking this very well," Lucy said suspiciously.

"I suppose," Paula said, tying her hair back with a bright red gardenia-decorated clip. "But there's no point worrying about it. Anyway, Mossy's coming this morning. So I've given you Mona Curry."

Mona was one of Paula's most important clients. Paula had never let anyone else near the local TD's wife. Lucy was astonished. "Are you sure you're all right, Paula?"

Paula looked at her carefully. "I don't know what you mean." The bell went outside. "That'll be Mona. Chop, chop."

I'll give you bloody chop, chop, Lucy muttered to herself as she answered the door.

"Mrs Curry." Lucy plastered a smile on her face. "How nice to see you. Won't you come in?"

"Mona," Paula said, coming into the reception area and kissing the tall thin-faced woman on both cheeks, "Lucy's going to look after you this morning. She's a make-up expert. I have to do the books. Tedious but necessary, I'm afraid."

Books, my ass, Lucy thought to herself.

Mona raised her eyebrows. "I *was* expecting you, my dear," she said to Paula.

"There'll be a reduction, of course," Paula said hastily. "To cover the inconvenience. Say ten per cent?"

"That would be fine," Mona said, handing Lucy her bottle-green suit jacket. Ten per cent was ten per cent after all.

Lucy hung it up on the back of a kitchen chair. She couldn't believe Paula had given the woman a discount like that in front of her. How insulting. She was glad she'd told Paula about Alan and Hopper now. Stupid cow. She went back outside.

"This way, please," she said to Mona, showing her into the small cubicle and sitting her down.

"I have a big charity ball this evening and I want my make-up to be perfect," Mona explained. She was holding her small black handbag protectively on her knee.

"What's it in aid of?" Lucy asked politely, opening up the large make-up tray and getting everything ready.

"Oh, don't ask me," Mona sighed wafting her hands in the air. "We go to so many. Children, or the homeless, I think. Homeless children maybe. I can't remember."

"I see. And what are you wearing?"

"A dark blue Paul Costello dress."

"And what type of make-up were you thinking of, Mrs Curry."

"Oh, call me Mona. Mrs Curry sounds so old. And just make me look beautiful, darling."

Lucy bit her lip. That wasn't going to be easy. The woman had skin the consistency of leather from baking herself in the sun. Too many political junkets to the Caribbean. Mona's pencil-thin eyebrows didn't do her long face any favours, and her sharp, protruding chin would open beer bottles. It was going to be an interesting morning.

Half an hour later, Lucy left the cubicle to get Mona a coffee. She heard the doorbell ring and stuck her head around the kitchen door to see who it was. A blond man wearing dark glasses stood outside, casually leaning against the wall. Lucy immediately went to let him in. Attractive men were a rarity at Making Faces. Maybe he was a gigolo, on a secret rendezvous with Mona Curry, Lucy smiled to herself.

"Hiya, Lucy," the Chippendale lookalike drawled as she opened the door.

"Mossy!" Lucy said, startled. "Your hair."

He ran his hands through his newly shorn locks. "Paula brought me to Red's – what do you think?"

Lucy stared at him in amazement. He was wearing a freshly ironed shirt, denims with no rips and a pair of spanking new docksiders.

"You look great, Mossy, very different. Come in." She ushered him into the reception area.

"Paula likes me to dress a bit smarter, you know."

"My ears are burning." Paula came out of her office. "Was someone talking about me?"

"Mossy was just telling me about his new image."

Paula stood on her toes and gave Mossy a dainty kiss on the cheek. "Doesn't he look handsome?" she trilled. "He's going to see Tikki in Assets today. So I'm giving him a facial and a massage."

"Assets modelling thingy?" Lucy asked. This was all getting a little surreal.

"Agency, darling," Paula said. "Not thingy. Patagonia are looking for a new face for their Irish ads and I suggested Mossy."

Lucy grinned. "Mossy?"

"And why not?" Paula glared at Lucy. "Look at his bone structure." She grabbed Mossy's chin in her hands and turned his head sideways for Lucy to survey.

"I guess," Lucy said doubtfully. As Mossy still had his dark glasses on it was hard to see what he was thinking. Not that he did much of that anyway. "It requires a lot of sitting around, killing time. Do you think you'll cope with that, Mossy?" She was trying to keep a straight face.

"It'll be hard," Paula answered for him, "being such an active person, so sporty. But he'll get used to it, won't you, darling?"

Mossy nodded.

"Anyway, Patagonia will pay through their teeth for the right image. Tikki said he'll pull in about a thousand euro a day if he gets it."

Lucy drew in her breath. "A grand a day?"

Paula smiled triumphantly. "Not so stupid now, is it?"

Lucy had to admit that it wasn't.

"Lucy!" Mona Curry's voice cut through their conversation.

"I'd better go," Lucy said glumly.

"Later," Mossy smiled as he was led into a cubicle by Paula.

* * *

Paula gave Mossy a lot more than just a facial. By the end of the morning he had been plucked, massaged and manicured to within an inch of his life. He'd even had his chest hair waxed. Lucy had feared the worst as sharp cries had emulated from the cubicle. She'd been afraid to open the door, so she'd plastered her ear against the thin wood instead.

"Just one more strip," she'd heard Paula say. "Tikki said she wanted a completely smooth chest for the swimsuit shots. You're being so brave, darling."

Wait till I tell Max about this, Lucy had smiled to herself. Then she'd remembered.

22

Max was sitting in the loft, describing his new kite, the Maxfoil Magic, on the website. 'A *stunning piece of kite engineering*', he wrote. '*A power kite for the more experienced flyer, a combination of raw power and rapid response. This adaptable kite can be stacked with other Max Foils –*'

"Yo, Max," Mossy strode towards him.

Max looked up. If he hadn't recognised the voice he would have been in trouble. The man in front of him looked nothing like the Mossy he knew.

"Mossy! What's happened to you? You look almost respectable."

"Thanks, man," Mossy smiled, taking off his sunglasses. "I'll be out this avo. Would you mind taking my messages?"

"Sure." He wasn't used to Mossy being so polite. "Listen, you haven't forgotten about Saturday night, have you?"

"Lea's Debs, of course not. I talked to her on the phone the other night. She seems like a nice kid."

"She's all right. I'm going to the pre-Debs drinks party in Mum and Dad's. Do you want a lift?"

"That'd be good. The limo is collecting us from there. And, listen, man, I'll pick up the chocolates and the corsage for Lea."

"Are you sure?" said Max. "I don't mind –"

"Paula's already booked a white orchid. So it's under control." He put his sunglasses back on. "Have to run. See you later."

"See you," Max said to Mossy's back. He had no idea what had happened to Mossy, whether aliens had landed and taken over his body or whether the Mormons had got him. But whatever it was – Mossy wasn't Mossy any more. He tried Lucy's mobile – he was dying to tell her what had just happened.

"Hi, this is Lucy. I can't take your call right now. You know what to do." He put down the phone, stared at his computer screen once more and began to type. '*The Maxfoil Magic has a wingspan of . . .*'

* * *

"What are you doing tonight?" Max asked Daria early on Friday evening.

"I've no plans," said Daria.

"Why don't I make us dinner at my place?"

"Sounds great. What time?"

"Around eight."

"Red or white wine?"

"Either," said Max. "Both."

Daria laughed. "I'll see you later."

Daria pulled off her clothes and stepped into the shower. As she smoothed perfumed body lotion over her chest and arms she smiled, remembering how Max's hands and fingers had felt on her skin. Sex with him was good, no, great. Now if they could only talk more, things would be perfect.

* * *

Max sliced the Italian sausages and added them to the pan. He was making one of his signature dishes – pasta with spicy sausage. He'd made it so many times it was like second nature to him now. Lucy had taught him three dishes to impress 'the ladies' – this one, lasagne, and chicken with cashew Nuts. God help him if he ever dated a vegan. There was a carton of Ben and Jerry's Phish Food in the freezer, and he had already started piling into the red wine.

He was really looking forward to seeing Daria. He'd forgotten how much fun flirting was. And as for the sex, his breath quickened just thinking about it.

He heard the buzzer and let Daria in.

"Good to see you," she smiled as he answered the door. She put a clinking O'Brien's bag on the hall table and handed him her coat. She was wearing her black leather top again, with a pair of tight-fitting jeans and high-heeled sandals.

"You look lovely," he said. She kissed him firmly on the lips.

"So do you." She moved away and he grasped her wrist.

"Not so quick." He pulled her towards him and kissed her again. He pushed her gently against the closed hall door and pressed his body against hers.

"Max!" she protested, as one of his hands made its way inside her top and skimmed her breast.

He stood back and grinned. "I can't help myself."

"I'd love a glass of wine."

"Can't we just –"

"Later," she smiled. "Food first. I'm starving."

"You're a hard woman," he laughed.

She followed him into the kitchen. He poured a glass of wine and handed it to her.

"Is there anything I can do?" she asked.

"No," he said, stirring the sausages which he'd caught just in the nick of time. "It's all under control."

Ten minutes later they were eating.

"This is delicious," said Daria. "And you said you couldn't cook."

"I can't," Max insisted. "Not really. This is one of Lucy's recipes."

"How is Lucy?"

"Fine, I think."

"You haven't talked to her?"

"No, we've both been busy."

"It's almost two weeks now, Max," said Daria carefully.

"I know that," said Max, trying not to get riled. "I've been ringing every day. She won't talk to me."

"Sorry," she mumbled.

"No, I'm sorry. I didn't mean to snap. It's not your fault."

Daria took a sip of her wine. They didn't say anything for a few awkward seconds.

"Do you want to talk about it?" she asked finally.

"Not really. Maybe later."

"OK." She stared at her plate.

"How are rehearsals?" asked Max, pouring her some more wine.

"They're going really well. We had some more dress-fittings today. Olive, the costume designer, told Rosaleen that she'd have to make separate Emma costumes for me as I was two sizes smaller. Rosaleen nearly had a canary. She insisted that I tried on one of her dresses, so I did and it was like a tent on me."

Max laughed. "She must hate you by now."

"She does," Daria smiled. "But she hates everyone else as well, so it's no big deal." She filled him in on what Rosaleen had been like at rehearsals the previous week, about her temper tantrums and her by-now legendary erratic behaviour.

After a few minutes Max speared a piece of sausage on his fork and held it in front of Daria's mouth. She slipped it off the fork and into her mouth. He reached out and stroked the side of her face.

She smiled. "Eat, Max!"

"OK, OK," he grinned back. "So when's opening night?"

"The third of July. Would you like to go? There's a party afterwards."

"I'd love to. And I want to sit in the front row so I can gaze at my beautiful girlfriend all night."

She smiled. "I'll see what I can do."

They chatted about the week, both carefully avoiding mentioning Lucy's name again.

"Would you like some more?" asked Max a little later.

"No, thanks," said Daria. She pushed her almost-empty plate away from her. "That was really nice but I'm stuffed."

"How about ice cream?"

Daria cocked her head. "What flavour?"

"Chocolate."

"Now you're talking."

He placed several generous spoonfuls in two bowls and placed them on the table.

"What?" asked Daria as she finished her first spoonful. Max was staring at her.

"Close your eyes," he said.

"Max."

"Go on. Please. Humour me."

She could feel his chilled lips on hers, and as she opened her mouth she could taste ice cream. She swallowed the ice cream and kissed him back before pushing him away.

"You're such a teenager," she laughed, licking her lips. He stood behind her, playing with the lacing at the back of her leather top.

"Max, stop! Sit down."

His hands moved towards her neck, gently rolling the skin and muscles under his fingers.

"That's nice," she said.

His hands moved over her shoulders and down towards her chest. She slapped them away. "You're incorrigible."

"And you're no fun," he complained, taking his hands away and sitting back down.

Daria laughed. "Let me finish my ice cream, you big bully."

He sat and watched as she spooned the ice cream into her mouth. As soon as she'd put her spoon down for the last time he pounced.

"Max!" she squealed as he put his arms around her, lifting her out of her seat. He pressed his body against hers and kissed her passionately. Her body began to respond to his and she could feel her resolve weaken.

I guess we're not going to talk this evening, she thought to herself as he threw her down on his bed and began to kiss her neck.

* * *

"Mossy, I'm outside in the car. Answer the door will you?"

"Sorry, man, I didn't hear you." Pearl Jam were going full throttle in the background. "I'm just coming."

Max laid his head against the steering wheel. He was knackered. Daria had stayed the night and they hadn't got much sleep. Not that he minded. They were getting on famously and he couldn't stop thinking about her, especially naked. Man, she had a great body. Slim and lithe, with a rounded, womanly belly and . . .

"What were you thinking of?" Mossy asked as he opened the car door. "You have a filthy big grin on your mug. Don't tell me it was a girl?"

"None of your business," Max said, pulling out.

"You're getting some, aren't you, man?"

"Have you got the chocolates?"

"Max is dipping the salami. Good on you, man!"

"The chocolates, Mossy? And the corsage?"

"Chill, Max, I haven't forgotten," he said, in an annoyingly calm voice. "Swing by Paula's."

"Fine," Max said shortly. It was on the way to his parents' house, but he still found this irritating. "She's still talking to you then?"

"Talking," Mossy laughed, "and the rest. She's some woman, Max." Mossy flicked through Max's CD case, finding some Frank Sinatra. He slipped it into the player and began to sing along to 'It Had to Be You'.

"You like Frank Sinatra?"

"Sure. The Rat Pack. Music, money, beautiful women. What's not to like?"

When they pulled up outside Paula's door the curtains twitched and Paula's smiling face peeked out. Seconds later she was standing on her tiptoes on the doorstep kissing Mossy. She was wearing a light, chiffon dressing-gown. Her hair was piled on top of her head and she seemed to have a lot of sparkling make-up on. Interesting attire for eight o'clock in the evening, Max thought as he watched her. He beeped the horn as Mossy's hands began to roam inside Paula's gown.

Paula glared at Max. Mossy laughed.

"Chocolates and corsage!" Max shouted at him. Mossy nodded and disappeared inside, closing the door behind him.

Fifteen minutes later Mossy got into the car. Max was fuming. He'd beeped the horn until one of the neighbours had asked him to stop. Then he'd banged on the door, but Mossy and Paula had ignored him. He'd even tried ringing Mossy's mobile, to no avail.

"You're treading on very thin ice, Mossy," Max said as they finally drove away. Paula was waving from the doorstep with a big smile on her face. "Have you got the chocolates and the corsage?"

Max glanced at Mossy who shook his head.

"I'll fecking kill you if you get out of the car again," Max said as he turned the car dangerously, doing a sweeping U-turn on the road. Luckily there was no traffic. "You're not going in this time. I don't trust you."

As they pulled up outside Paula's house again, she came to the car with two boxes in her hands, kitten-mule slippers clacking. "Looking for these?"

"Don't open that door," Max snapped at Mossy. He opened the passenger window halfway using his automatic window button.

Paula scowled at Max and slotted the boxes in the window. "You're such an old man, Max." She blew a kiss to Mossy. "Behave yourself, big boy," she trilled. "See you later, my darling."

"I'm surprised you didn't bring her with you," Max said as they drove away.

Mossy said nothing and looked out the window.

* * *

240

"And this is Max, my son," Rita said, picking some imaginary fluff off his jacket collar. He'd worn Black Tie as requested on the invitation, not because he wanted to but because he had a clean tuxedo in the back of his wardrobe left over from his London days. His only suit (the pinstriped) hadn't been pressed since his friends' Heidi and Don's wedding last summer. After coming back from the city he'd given all but one suit to Oxfam as he hoped he'd never need them again. "Max, this is Hannah Graham, my dear friend from the Golf Club. Her daughter is in Lea's class. Max is a businessman, aren't you, darling?"

"Um, yes," Max smiled at the attractive blonde woman who was wearing an eye-catching red dress. His mother always introduced him as a 'businessman'.

"What type of business are you in?" Hannah asked.

"He's in manufacturing," Rita quickly answered for him. "I must introduce you to Lea's date, Maurice. He's to die for. A professional sailor too. Isn't that glam?" Rita steered Hannah away by the elbow.

"Bye, Max," Hannah said cheerily.

Pity, Max thought to himself as he helped himself to more red wine. Hannah seemed almost normal. Most of his mother's friends were painful. And he was looking forward to calling Mossy 'Maurice' later. He'd always wondered what his real name was.

"Can you top me up, please?"

Max heard a familiar voice and turned around.

Lucy was standing in front of him, glass held out.

"I thought you were the waiter," she said, blushing. "Sorry," she mumbled, turning away.

"Lucy." He put down his glass and held her arm. "Don't go."

"I'm not in the mood." She scowled at him, her forehead wrinkling unbecomingly.

"This is stupid. Can't we just talk?"

"No!" she snapped. She picked up an open bottle of red wine and walked away.

"Shit," he muttered to himself under his breath. He looked around. Lea and Mossy were standing in the bay window, surrounded by adoring parents, mostly of the female variety. From around the room the other debutantes were eyeing up Leas's partner jealously. Their own Debs partners, seventeen-year-olds from Blackrock College and St John's paled into insignificance beside the glowing Mossy. Max watched Lucy walk outside to the deck.

"Is that your girlfriend?"

Max looked around. Standing beside him was one of the most stunning women he'd ever seen. She was tall, with long raven-black hair which fell like a sheet of silk down her left shoulder. Her dress, if you could call it that, barely covered her tanned and toned body, swooping generously at the front to display her perfect cleavage and coming dangerously close to displaying another cleavage at the back.

"No," Max said. "Just a friend."

"I see," the woman said, flicking her mane from one side to the other. Max felt tendrils of scented hair brush his cheek. "Are you here with anyone then?"

"No," he said, finding it hard to talk to this delicious creature.

"The strong and silent type. I like that," she smiled. "I'm Emily. And you are –"

"Max," Max managed.

"And what's your favourite sexual position, Max?"

Max gulped. "Sorry?"

"I can't stand small talk," Emily grinned. "Sorry. I'll ask you a more conventional question if you like."

"That would be good. If you don't mind."

"Not at all. Do you like younger women? Because I just love older men."

Max gulped again. "Um, I –"

"I see you've met my daughter," Hannah interrupted.

Thank God, Max thought to himself. He was running scared. "Yes," Max smiled.

"Doesn't she look stunning?" Hannah put her arm around Emily protectively. "Such a perfect Debs dress."

"You're in school?" Max asked Emily incredulously.

"Yes," she nodded. "But I'm hoping to study medicine in UCD in September. Fingers crossed."

"Hard to believe, isn't it?" Hannah sighed. "My little baby, all grown up." She waved at a face in the crowd. "There's Cynthia. Do excuse me."

"And who are you here with?" Max asked Emily, looking around hopefully.

"Henry. Henry Fisher. He's outside throwing around a rugby ball with some of the guys."

"Captain of the Blackrock rugby team?" Max asked.

Emily nodded and winked at him. "How did you guess? He's a puppy dog. I can easily give him the slip later."

"Actually I've got a girlfriend," Max blurted out.

"Pity," Emily sighed. She stroked his arm.

"How about my friend, Mossy?" Max said gesturing towards the window.

Emily eyed Mossy up and down. "I don't think so. He's not my type."

"Really?" Max asked, delighted.

"Too good-looking, no character in his face. I'd hate to go out with someone who was more attractive than I was."

"Yes, quite," he said, deflated. He'd had enough. He gazed towards the open door longingly.

"Go and talk to her. Bring her a drink," she said.

"Who?"

"The woman outside," said Emily. "The one who's not your girlfriend. I may be seventeen but I'm not stupid. I presume you've had a row or something."

Max smiled. "It was nice talking to you."

"You too," she beamed. "Good luck."

Max grabbed an open bottle of wine on his way outside. "It's a Debs, Jim, but not as we know it," he said, sitting down beside Lucy on the white garden two-seater.

Lucy glared at him.

"Smile," he cajoled. "You know you want to."

"Go away, Max," she muttered. She fixed her eyes on the boys playing with the rugby ball on the lawn in front of her.

"They're going to ruin their suits," Max said. He noticed the bottle Lucy had taken with her earlier was nearly empty. "More wine?"

"No, I'm fine."

Max put his arm around her shoulders. She shrugged it off.

"A gorgeous seventeen-year-old just tried to pick me up," Max said. After getting no response he continued. "She said she liked older guys." He took a sip of his wine. "Man, was she beautiful! Then she spoiled it all by saying she preferred ugly men."

"Really?" Lucy asked, curiosity getting the better of her.

"Practically. I offered her Mossy and she said she liked her men less good-looking."

Lucy snorted.

"Now, was that so hard?"

"What?"

"Laughing."

"That wasn't a laugh." Lucy went quiet again.

Max took a swig of his wine. "This is decent stuff," he said. He read the label out loud. "Edgewood Estate, Napa Valley Cabernet Sauvignon 1995. Nice bottle too. Let me see, smooth but tangy, a touch of –"

"Max! Shut up! You're boring me."

"Sorry," he mumbled.

They sat in silence for a few minutes. "Nice evening," Max observed finally. "Good for sitting outside, don't you think?"

Lucy ignored him.

"For heaven's sake, Lucy, would you stop it? This is ridiculous."

Lucy stood up and strode purposefully towards the house.

"Where are you going? Lucy!"

"What's up, man?" asked Mossy a little later, finding Max sitting outside alone.

"Nothing," said Max. "It's a bit too much for me in there." He nodded towards the French doors.

244

Mossy nodded. "I know what you mean, man. This woman accosted me on the stairs. Old enough to be my mother. Said she knew where the spare room was."

"You didn't –"

"Na," said Mossy. "She scared me. Nice-looking woman though."

"Tall? Blonde? In a red dress?"

"How did you guess?" Mossy smiled.

"I met her daughter earlier. She's as bad."

"But your sister's all right, for a kid. Are you going to the hotel?"

"No," said Max. "Mum and Dad are though. You'll be sitting with them."

Mossy groaned.

"Sit beside Dad if you can," Max advised. "You can talk about sailing or something."

"I suppose," said Mossy reluctantly. He looked around. "Where's Lucy?"

"Is she not inside?"

"Na. Lea was looking for her earlier. Something about her make-up running. She wanted Lucy to fix it for her. Maybe she's gone home."

"I would have seen her leave from here," Max mused. He stood up. "I'd better go and see if she's OK. Red wine doesn't always agree with her."

Mossy stayed sitting. "I think I'll stay here, man. It's going to be a long night."

"What time are you leaving at?"

Mossy looked at his watch. "Shit! Very soon." He took a large gulp of his wine and pulled out his mobile. "Have to ring Paula."

As Max walked inside he could hear him say "Hi, babe, miss you already."

He scanned the living-room, but Lucy was nowhere to be seen.

"Are you all right, son?" his dad asked. Eric was standing beside the pot plant in the hallway, trying to keep out of the way. He wasn't a great man for parties.

"I've lost Lucy. Have you seen her?"

Eric nodded. "I was talking to her. She went upstairs a few minutes ago. She was feeling a little unwell, I think."

"I'll just go up and check on her," said Max. He bounded up the stairs. The bathroom at the top of the stairs was unoccupied. He walked into the spare room. A light was on in the en suite, it glowed gently through the glass blocks which made up the 'wall'. Max knocked on the door. "Lucy?"

"Go 'way," Lucy muttered. She was kneeling over the bath, a cold, damp facecloth pressed to her forehead and she did not want to be disturbed.

"Lucy?" he tried opening the door but it was locked. "Come on. Let me in."

She ignored him.

"I'm staying here until you let me in," he insisted. "I don't care how long it takes."

"Don't be stupid, Max," she wailed. "Go away."

"I keep telling you, I'm not going anywhere. So get used to it. I just want to make sure you're OK. Look, I'll bring you home and I won't even try to talk to you, I promise."

Lucy's eyes welled up with tears. She'd been sick, her throat and stomach hurt, her head throbbed and she felt awful. And now Max was being far too nice to her. She began to cry.

Max, ear to the door, heard her. "Open the door, please."

She crawled over and turned the key in the lock. He pushed the door open. Lucy was slumped in a heap at his feet. He kneeled down beside her and began to stroke her head. "Hey, don't cry." He brushed the tears away from her eyes tenderly with his hands. Her mascara was running down her cheeks and her eyes were shockingly red and bloodshot. He reached over and pulled the toilet-paper off the holder, tweaking a muscle in his shoulder in the process. He dabbed Lucy's face with the tissue.

"Thanks," she hiccupped.

He pushed her hair away from her face. She closed her eyes.

"Just having a little sleep," she murmured.

After ten minutes of Lucy sleeping on his lap, Max's legs had begun to go to sleep themselves. He wriggled them out from underneath her, supporting her head with his arms. He then pulled her up against his chest, put his arms around her and carried her out of the bathroom and onto the bed in the adjoining room. He removed her black sandals and folded either side of the bedspread over her body, enveloping her warmly. Then he went back downstairs.

His father was still standing in the hall, but now he had his coat on. "How's Lucy?" he asked.

"A little drunk," Max admitted. "She's sleeping it off."

Eric frowned. "I'm afraid we have to go now. The limo's here."

"Don't worry. I'll drive her home later when she's feeling better and I'll lock up."

"Thank you, son," said Eric. Rita came rushing towards him.

"Into the car, Eric," she flustered. "We're already late. Where are Lea and Mossy?"

"Here, Mum," Lea said from behind her mother. "Don't fuss."

"Where's your coat, Lea?" Rita asked. "It's warm now, but there may be a chill –"

"Mum," Lea muttered.

"I'll give her my jacket later," Mossy beamed, "if it gets cold."

"You're such a gentleman," Rita purred. "My Max has such lovely friends."

Mossy grinned at Max. "Anything for a mate."

"And some hard cash," Max said under his breath.

Max watched the black limousine drive away. He closed the door and rested against it. All the other guests had left and the house was silent as a grave, but the hall still had a warm, smoky atmosphere. He walked into the living-room. His mother's (and they were definitely his mother's and not his father's) blue velvet drapes were still open and late evening light snuck into the room. He poured a glass of wine, slumped down on the sofa and stared out the window.

A couple of glasses later, he got restless and rang Daria's mobile but it was powered off. Then he remembered – she was at the cinema with

247

her sister. He looked at his watch. Nearly ten. Not the most exciting way to spend your Saturday night, he thought to himself as he went back upstairs to check on Lucy. As he walked into the spare room he could hear her in the bathroom and thought the worst.

"Lucy?" he said, anxiously walking towards the bathroom door. He fully expected to see her leaning over the toilet again.

"In here," Lucy replied in a garbled voice. He walked in and she was brushing her teeth fervently, her mouth awash in white foam. She'd cleaned the remainder of the streaked make-up off her face and pulled her hair back with a piece of what looked like dental floss.

She spat out a mouth full of toothpaste. "I borrowed a new toothbrush." She gestured towards the basket of guest toiletries beside the sink. "I hope your mum won't mind."

"She won't even notice. How are you feeling?"

"I've been better." She splashed some water on her face.

He watched as she dried her skin with a towel. Her cheeks glowed and she looked remarkably well, considering. He reached out and touched her hair.

"What are you doing?" she asked.

"I don't know," he mumbled. "Sorry."

She looked him in the eye and a blush began to form on his cheeks.

"I'll drive you home now," he said quickly. Then he remembered he couldn't drive now as he'd polished off the bottle of wine. "Actually I've had a few drinks, I'd better order a taxi."

"Thanks. And I'm sorry."

"For what?"

"For being rude to you earlier."

"Lucy, this has gone on long enough. I want us to be friends again. I miss you."

"I miss you too," she said, burying her face in his shoulder.

He held her against him and began to stroke her hair. He was feeling a little drunk himself. He kissed the top of her head, breathing in the vanilla scent of her hair. He held her face in his hands and kissed her forehead firmly.

"Welcome home, honey," he smiled.

"You're mad, you know that?" she laughed.

"I take that as a compliment," he said.

She yawned.

"I'd better order that taxi now before you fall asleep on top of me."

She yawned again and rested her head on his shoulder. "But I'm not tired, Max," she insisted.

Max smiled. "Of course you're not."

23

"How was the Debs thing last night?" Hopper asked at breakfast the following morning.

"I'm still suffering," Lucy sighed. "Shouldn't have drunk so much wine. I'm a sucker for free booze."

"Was Max there?"

Lucy looked at her. "You know he was. It was Lea's Debs, after all."

"And?"

"And what?"

Hopper sighed theatrically. "You're impossible."

"And you're worse than the Spanish Inquisition. If you must know we talked and everything's back to normal."

"I'm so glad," Hopper smiled. She gave her a hug. "That's great news. Did you tell Max about Eugene and *Strike a Match?*"

"No," Lucy smiled. "I didn't actually. I'll give him a ring later. We have a lot of catching up to do."

"Hi, Max, how are you this morning?"

"What time is it?" Max grunted.

"Nearly twelve."

Max looked at his alarm clock. "Lucy, it's only just gone eleven."
Lucy ignored him. "What are you doing today?"

"Depends," Max said. "If it involves anything healthy or energetic then I'm busy."

"Eugene's on *Strike a Match* tonight. I promised I'd go into town with him this afternoon to buy some new clothes. Will you come and help?"

"*Strike a Match?* The dating thing on RTE?"

"Yes."

"Eugene?"

"I know," Lucy laughed. "Gas, isn't it? Come shopping and I'll tell you all about it."

"I don't think I'd be much help. I'm not exactly all that hot in the fashion stakes myself."

"I'll choose the clothes. You deal with Eugene. Please?"

"OK," he sighed. "I'll pick you up at two. Tell Eugene to meet us at your house."

"Perfect." Lucy smiled to herself as she put down the phone. It was nice to have things back to normal.

"You're sweet to do this," said Lucy. "I really appreciate it."

Max unlocked the back door of the car and Eugene lowered himself in. "Yeah, thanks, man."

"No problem. Now where to first?"

"We need a shirt and a leather jacket," said Lucy. "So I guess Alias Tom or somewhere like that. Grafton Street area."

"I'm not wearing a shirt," Eugene complained. "Next you'll have me in a suit and tie and then where will I be?"

"In a job?" Lucy quipped. "Like most grown-ups."

Max started the car. "No squabbling, please. Not in *my* car."

"Anyway I have a shirt," said Eugene.

"You have a white dress shirt that was left over from an Arts Ball in first year," said Lucy. "You wore it last Christmas. I asked you did

251

you have another shirt to wear instead and you said no. We had to tie together the shirt-cuffs with wool, 'cause you didn't have any cuff links, remember?"

"Oh, yeah. But you're not putting me in any funny colours, right?"

"Of course not," Lucy lied. "Wouldn't dream of it."

"Are you excited about this evening, Eugene?" Max asked.

"Suppose."

"What type of woman are you after?"

"Whatever type we give him," Lucy interrupted.

"Leggy, blonde, good teeth, loaded," Eugene grinned.

Lucy snorted.

Eugene stared at her. "You set me up with some dog and you're dead."

"Sorry, Eugene, but there won't be a thing you can do about it. Tonight's my revenge for twenty-odd years of misery as your sister."

"She's not serious, is she, mate?" Eugene asked Max.

"No," he said. He glanced over at Lucy who was still smiling. "At least I don't think so."

"This shirt is purple," Eugene moaned. "I'm not wearing purple. Can we not get the black one? I liked that. Or the grey one?"

"Eugene," Lucy said, "you looked like something out of *The Sopranos* in the black and a teacher in the grey. Trust me. Just try it on."

Eugene looked at Max. Max shrugged his shoulders.

"OK." He went back into the dressing-room cubicle.

"Be kind to him," Max whispered to Lucy. "He's probably really nervous about this evening."

"You're right. I'll try. It's just so easy to get a rise out of him and much more fun."

Max dug her in the ribs. "That's not nice."

Lucy giggled. "I know. I know. I'm only joking."

Eugene pulled back the curtain of the cubicle and walked out. Lucy smiled. The shirt fitted him beautifully. "It really suits you. The colour's great. What do you think, Max?"

"I like it."

"Really?" Eugene asked suspiciously. He wouldn't put it past Lucy to stitch him up but he trusted Max. "I'm not sure." He turned around and looked at his back in the mirror.

"No," Max smiled, "your bum does not look big in that shirt."

"What?" Eugene asked in confusion.

"Oops, sorry, that's what I have to say when I'm shopping with Lucy. I lost the run of myself for a second there."

Lucy thumped him on the arm.

"Ow!"

"When you two have quite stopped I'd like to buy this and get out of here," Eugene said. "I hate shopping."

"You'll wear it?" asked Lucy.

"Yeah," said Eugene sheepishly. "I quite like it."

"Result!" said Max as they walked out of the shop. "Where next?"

"Marks & Spencers," said Lucy, "for a jacket."

"Granny-knickers!" said Eugene loudly.

"Eugene," Lucy warned, "lower your voice! And what are you talking about?"

"Marks and Spencers – you wouldn't see me dead in there. It's for old people."

"Actually I sometimes get things in there," said Max evenly.

"Need I say more?" Eugene smirked.

"Are you calling me old?" asked Max.

"I'm only messing."

"Listen," said Lucy, "you can't afford an expensive jacket and I've seen some nice ones in Marks & Spencers, so we're going there. And that's final." She glared at Eugene.

"OK, keep your granny-knickers on," he said.

"Eugene!" she hissed.

Max walked on ahead.

"I'm exhausted," Max sighed as they drove back to Sandymount.

"But Eugene will look great tonight," said Lucy, "and that's all that matters. Hopper and Alan are watching it in our place and then we're all meeting in Blackrock. Do you want to join us?"

"Maybe. I'll have to check with Daria. We'd planned to go out for dinner."

"Of course," said Lucy, a little too quickly.

"But I'm sure she won't mind. What time are you meeting at?"

"The show's on at eight, so say tennish in Blake's."

"Perfect," he smiled. He hoped Daria wouldn't mind the change of plan. "And you're sure it's OK to bring Daria?"

"Why wouldn't it be?"

"No reason." Max stared at the road ahead. It was just a little awkward, he wanted to say, after the 'beach scene', but he didn't want to go into it in front of Eugene.

"So what time do you have to be in RTE?" he asked.

"Half six," Eugene said. "Mum's collecting us at six."

"I hope she realises what she's let herself in for," Max laughed.

"Ladies and gentlemen, it's Saturday night. We're live from Studio One, and it's *Strike a Match*, the dating game with a difference," boomed the host, Havana Bacardi. She was wearing a figure-hugging gold lamé dress and a white-blonde wig. Her false eyelashes glittered gold in the lights.

Lucy, Eugene and Eileen were sitting in make-up waiting to be 'done'. They were appearing in the second half of the show, after the interval.

"Is that a boy or a girl?" Eileen asked Lucy, nodding at the screen.

"Shush, Mum," Lucy giggled, "it's a drag queen. You know, a man dressed up as a woman. Have you not watched this before?"

"I've been watching it religiously. I thought it was a man all right but I just wanted to be sure."

Lucy patted her hand. "Don't be nervous. It'll be fun."

"I hope so, and I'd love to find a nice girl for Eugene."

Eugene laughed. "I'm not sure they do 'nice' girls on this show, Mum. You just choose me the prettiest one, OK? Pay no attention to what Lucy says."

"Eugene White?" one of the make-up women called.

Eugene stood up. "Here!" he put up his hand.

"You're not in school," Lucy teased.

He glared at her.

"Leave your brother alone," Eileen sighed. It was going to be a long evening.

The make-up lady swathed Eugene in a huge black robe and began to pat foundation on to his face.

"You have lovely skin," she said as she worked. "Nice and smooth. Do you exfoliate?"

"Yes. But don't tell anyone."

"I won't," she promised, winking.

Lucy sat in front of a large, well-lit mirror as her own make-up was being applied. She watched as the practised hand placed a powder-puff under her eye-socket to collect any stray particles of eye-shadow as her eyes were coloured and contoured.

"Look up please," the woman said, rimming Lucy's upper lids with dark brown liquid eye-liner.

"Look straight ahead. Try not to blink." The woman coated Lucy's eyelashes with mascara, pulling at each lash gently as she stroked the wand over them expertly.

Lucy began to relax. She was enjoying this immensely. She felt light-headed and there was a tingling sensation all over her body. Adrenaline, she decided.

The make-up woman patted her face and neck with powder, setting the foundation. "Finished! What do you think?"

Lucy gazed at herself in the mirror. Her skin looked flawless, her eyes were smoulderingly gorgeous – heaped with toffee browns and glittering golds, and her lips glistened dew-pink in the lights.

"Fantastic!" she beamed. "Thanks."

She felt like a million dollars. She hoped her own clients felt exactly the same way as she did when they looked in the mirror at Making Faces at their own newly-made-up selves.

The make-up lady helped her take off the black robe. Lucy was

255

wearing her favourite little party-top – a fitted silk vest covered in carnival-coloured red, yellow, fuchsia and blue silk fake-flowers. "I love your top," she said to Lucy. "It's fantastic. Where did you buy it if you don't mind me asking?"

"In a second-hand shop in Sandycove. It's actually Gucci. It used to belong to an Irish rock-chick apparently – Katie Long"

"Clever old you. It's probably worth a fortune. Good luck this evening. I hope you find a lovely man."

"I'm only here for my brother. I'm not actually on the show."

"That's what they all say," the woman smiled. "Good luck anyway."

"Lucy, your make-up is beautiful," Eileen said as they met again in the show's waiting-room down the corridor. Eugene was sitting beside her, his eyes darting around the room nervously. There was another young man sitting in the far corner of the room with what looked like his own mum and sister. Those two women were arguing noisily about Ireland's chances in the World Cup while the man stared at his feet. Eugene knew just how he felt.

"Thanks, Mum," Lucy said, "so's yours. And you're looking good, Eugene. How are you feeling?"

"OK," he said, picking up a piece of paper from the small table beside him and ripping it up. "A bit nervous, I guess."

Lucy looked at him carefully. She felt sorry for him – he seemed more than just 'a bit nervous'.

"Think of it as a play. We're all acting in a big play that just happens to be televised. Mum's playing the gentle and fair mother character. I'm playing the kind and considerate," Lucy paused for a second, "successful, attractive and sexy sister, and you're playing the suave, funny and adorable young man who just happens to be looking for a woman to equal his considerable talents."

Eugene looked at her with interest. "Go on."

"The characters are all taking part in a slightly silly, but humorous television programme, which, of course, is slightly beneath them."

"And what's my motivation?"

Lucy thought for a second. "You want to make your television debut. You want a good story to tell your mates in the pub. And maybe meeting a nice 'mot' while you're at it wouldn't be such a bad thing."

Eugene began to smile. "I'm in a play called *Eugene and the 'Strike a Match' Babe* and I'm going to knock them dead!"

"Exactly!"

Eileen smiled at her daughter. For all her bravado, Lucy really did understand her brother very well.

"Three minutes, people," Joe, the assistant producer, said. "Follow me please. We're going to the studio now. Eugene White, you're up first. Your mum and sister are up next, OK? They'll wait in the wings until you've finished your first bit."

Eugene nodded. "*No problemo*, boss."

"And you're on in the second half, O'Malleys, after the second break," Joe said to the other group.

"Fine," one of the women said. "We'll be ready."

Lucy could feel butterflies in her stomach. She squeezed Eugene's shoulder as they waited in the wings to be called on to the set.

"They'll love you," she whispered.

"Pick me a good one," he pleaded.

Lucy listened to the applause as Eugene strode on to the set and took his place behind the red and pink heart-decorated podium.

"Isn't he lovely, audience?" Havana asked. "A fine figure of a man. This is Eugene White from Dublin and he's looking for a girl with a good heart who looks like Pamela Anderson. Naughty, naughty, Eugene!"

Eugene smiled broadly. "That's right."

"And I believe you're in college, Eugene. Tell us about that."

"I'm in UCD, doin' Arts." There was a loud cheer from someone in the audience. "And that'll be me mate, Derek. Hi, man." Eugene waved up at the audience.

"And what do you do for fun, Eugene?"

"I'm a DJ. I'm into me music. *Comprendo?*"

"Oh, I'd comprendo with you any time, my dear," Havana flirted. "You're darling. Isn't he darling, audience?" Everyone cheered. "And now, let's play *Strike a Match*. Bring on the Whites!"

"Go, go, go," Joe whispered.

Lucy and Eileen were ushered on to the set. Lucy was momentarily blinded by the bright lights but managed to find her place beside Eugene and her mother at the podium.

"Hello, Eileen, hello, Lucy," Havana said. "Lucy is Eugene's sister. Doesn't she look glam tonight? And Eileen is Eugene's Mum, another very glam lady. Give them a round of applause." Lucy and Eileen smiled as the audience applauded. "Now Eugene, baby, it's time for you to leave. Put on the headphones in the waiting room like a good chap while we choose a lovely lady for you. Do you have anything to say before the delicious Gloria spirits you away?"

"Do me proud, Lucy and Mum. I'm counting on you."

"I'm sure they will pick you an absolute beauty," she said. "Everyone say goodbye to the lovely Eugene!"

The whole audience roared "Goodbye" as he left the set.

"Now I have you both all to myself, so tell me the truth, ladies. Is he as lovely as he looks?"

Lucy laughed. "Not always."

"Lucy!" Eileen spluttered.

"No, no," Havana insisted. "Do go on, Lucy. We like to know the truth on this show, don't we, audience? Tell all."

"He's a bit of a chancer," Lucy said, "likes to think of himself as a lady's man." Shit, Lucy thought to herself, what have I just said?

"Really?" Havana asked, raising her eyebrows to the heavens. "Oh, we like that, don't we, audience? We don't like the boring ones, do we? Go on, I'm dying to hear more."

"But he's very kind," Lucy continued, back-pedalling. "He's great with kids and animals." She grinned. "And more than anything – he wants world peace."

"You are naughty!" Havana scolded, slapping Lucy gently on the

258

arm. 'But we like Lucy too, don't we, audience? She's got a bit of spunk. Spunky Lucy, that's what we'll call her."

The audience cheered.

"And what would you like to say about your son, Eileen?"

"He's a good lad. And he has great respect for women."

Havana clapped. "We like that, Eileen. We like that. Now, without further ado, let's bring on the girls."

Lucy watched carefully as three girls paraded onto the set.

"Hello, the girls," Havana cooed. "Sit down now and make yourselves comfortable. This is Eugene's mum, Eileen, and his sister, Lucy. They're going to ask you a few questions, but before they start could you each introduce yourselves?"

"Hello," one of the girls stood up immediately. She was tall, with dark-auburn hair which cascaded in sausage-like ringlets down her strong back. She was wearing a red-velvet dress which clung to her voluptuous six-foot frame. You wouldn't mess with her, Lucy thought to herself. "I am Rowie De Young. I am Dutch, and I am doing a Doctorate in Psychology in Trinity College, Dublin." She sat down smartly.

"Thank you, Rowie," said Havana. "You next, Maxi."

A small, pretty dark-haired girl stood up. "I'm Maxi," she said in a high-pitched voice. "I'm from Dublin and I'm a waitress and a singer – I'm into karaoke. And I collect pigs," she giggled. "Not real ones, of course. Ornamental ones." She looked at Eileen and Lucy. "And I'd love to date Eugene. I'd make him very happy. I hope you pick me."

Lucy looked at her mother. Eileen was trying very hard not to laugh.

"And finally, Nessa."

"Hi, I'm Nessa. I'm from Kerry and I'm studying French and Business in Ringsend College. I like going to the gym, swimming, skiing and having fun. But I have a serious side too." Nessa blinked rapidly in the bright lights like a startled rabbit.

"Thank you, Nessa. And join us after the break to hear Eileen and Lucy's questions."

"Two minutes, people," Joe said. "Everyone stay in their places."

"Would you look at the state of your one," Havana whispered to Lucy in a decidedly male voice, "I'd like to see a bit less-a-Nessa if you know what I mean."

Lucy smiled. "No kidding." Nessa was blonde – very blonde. Her hair was piled on top of her head in an elaborate chignon and she was wearing a turquoise lycra dress, her generous bosom threatening to burst out of the tightly stretched material.

"Are you OK, Mum?" Lucy asked.

"Yes, thanks. It's all a bit strange though – it's not what I expected at all. Have you got the questions in case I forget mine?"

"Yes, don't worry. They're here." She handed her mother a sheet of paper. "There's yours. But you won't forget. Stop worrying."

"Places everyone," Joe said. "Back in ten, nine, eight, seven, six, five, four, three, two –"

"Welcome back to *Strike a Match*," said Havana. "And now Eugene's mum and sister, Eileen and Lucy, are going to ask the girls some questions. And then we'll have 'the talents'. Ready, girls?"

"Ready, Havana," Maxi and Nessa giggled. Rowie nodded.

"Fire ahead, Eileen."

Eileen coughed nervously. "My son is very fond of music. What sort of music do you like and why?"

"Good question, Eileen," said Havana. "Maxi?"

"I like Destiny's Child, Robbie Williams and anything with a nice tune I can sing along to. Will I give you a song, Havana?" Maxi burst into a spirited version of Robbie Williams' 'Angel' much to the amusement of the audience.

Havana put her hands up in the air. "Enough, enough, you'll have them weeping in their seats, love. We know what your talent is going to be. And Nessa? Could you answer Eileen's question."

"Destiny's Child again," Nessa smiled broadly at the camera. "And ballads, anything slow and smoochy." She shimmied her body suggestively, giving Eileen a bit of a fright.

"Nessa!" Havana exclaimed. "You'll give Eugene's mum a heart attack. And finally, Rowie."

"I love classical music," said Rowie, looking Eileen straight in the eye. "I also listen to American jazz, Cuban music and I like dance music – mainly trance."

Eileen looked at Lucy and shrugged her shoulders.

"Eugene likes that too," she assured her mother.

"Thank you, Rowie," said Havana. "Next we have Lucy's question. Lucy, fire ahead."

Lucy smiled. "In your opinion, what is the most important invention in the world and why?"

Havana fanned herself with her hand. "Hard question, girlfriend. I wouldn't like to have to answer that. But we'll see how the girls get on. Nessa first this time."

Nessa looked a little confused. "Invention? I'm not really sure. Um, um, maybe clothes. They're important. You'd get cold without clothes."

The audience laughed kindly.

"Quite right too, Nessa," said Havana. "Couldn't have you getting cold, could we?" She looked the contestant up and down.

The audience laughed again.

"And Rowie?"

"The printing press," said Rowie firmly. "Before the printing press was invented in the 1430's, books had to be copied out by hand. But after Johannes Gutenberg's invention books were a lot faster to produce and more accessible to everyone."

Lucy smiled at the woman. Rowie had brains and she wasn't afraid to use them.

"Excellent, Rowie," said Havana. "And finally, Maxi."

"Music. Like Eugene, I love my music. It's the greatest invention in the world." She began to sing Abba's 'Thank You for the Music', before being interrupted by Havana.

"Thank you, Maxi. And now we have what we like to call 'the talents'. If you've watched this show before you'll know that each

261

young lady has to display one talent for the audience, and for Lucy and Eileen. Maxi, I wonder what your talent is. Do I need to ask?"

Maxi smiled. "I'm going to sing, Havana."

"How did I guess? Fire away, girl."

The backing-track came on and Lucy winced as she heard the familiar strains. Maxi threw herself into the performance.

"What's she singing?" Eileen whispered to Lucy.

"A Madonna song called 'Ray of Light'."

"Is it supposed to sound like that?"

"Like what?"

"Like a scalded cat."

Lucy laughed.

Havana looked over at them and winked. "Lovely, lovely," she said as Maxi finished. "Thank you, Maxi. And what will you be doing, Nessa?"

"I'm going to dance." She gyrated her toned body to an S Club 7 track expertly, earning huge applause from the audience.

"Well done, you," said Havana. "Have a little rest now, pumpkin. And now Rowie, what's your talent?"

"I'm reciting a poem by Seamus Heaney."

"Really?" asked Havana, a little taken aback. This was a first for the programme. One girl had attempted to strip a few weeks ago, now that had been interesting. But culture – no one had ever attempted culture before.

"Yes, really. It's one of my favourites. It's called 'Mother of the Groom'." She began to recite the poem, her silky voice embracing the words, giving them poignant meaning. The poem was about a mother remembering her son when he was small. It took the audience a few stunned seconds to clap, but their applause was warm and genuine.

"That was beautiful," said Havana. "Thank you. Now Maxi, Nessa and Rowie, please leave the studio while Eileen and Lucy make their decision.

When the three women had departed, Havana turned towards the Whites. "Eileen, Lucy, what did you think? Maxi first."

"I don't think so," Eileen began uncertainly. "She was a bit –"

'Much," Lucy finished for her. "Not Eugene's type really. Too full on."

"And Nessa?"

"Very attractive," said Eileen.

"But not right for Eugene," said Lucy firmly. "He'd run rings around her. He needs someone stronger, more self-confident, more like –"

"Rowie?" Havana smiled.

"Exactly! I pick Rowie."

"And Eileen?"

Eileen looked at her daughter. "If Lucy thinks Rowie's the right one for Eugene, then Rowie it is."

"We have a match! Bring back Eugene."

Eugene walked on and smiled at Eileen and Lucy.

"Have I got a girl for you," Havana said to Eugene. "Hand-picked by your mother and sister and all the way from Holland, here's Rowie."

"You should have seen his face when saw Rowie," Lucy laughed in Blake's pub later that evening. "He looked terrified. She gave him such a mammoth hug – I thought she was going to crush him."

Hopper and Alan laughed.

"They showed that bit all right," said Hopper. "The whole show was a panic. And what was that blonde girl wearing? It looked like a swimsuit."

Lucy grinned. "Eugene nearly killed me afterwards. 'Why didn't you pick the one with the nipple dress?' he asked."

"The nipple dress?" asked Alan.

"Let's just say it left nothing to the imagination," Lucy explained. "Absolutely nothing."

"Here you all are. Television star and all."

Lucy looked up. Max was standing behind their table.

"Hi, mate," said Alan. "Come and join us." He patted the seat beside him.

"Can I get anyone a drink?" asked Max.

"Lucy's just bought a round so we're all set, thanks," said Hopper. Max sat down beside Alan.

"Where's Daria? I thought she was joining us," asked Hopper.

"She's at the bar. She'll be over in a second. So what did everyone think? We were watching the show at home. Lucy, you looked amazing!"

"Thanks," Lucy smiled. "They had a great make-up department."

"I can't believe you chose that mad Dutch one," he said. "Did Eugene not murder you afterwards?"

"It's funny but they actually seemed to be getting on quite well in the hospitality room afterwards."

"Apparently Eugene was disappointed that they didn't pick Nessa," said Alan.

"Which one was Nessa?" Max asked. "The blonde one with the big –"

"Max!" Lucy and Hopper exclaimed.

"Hair, I was going to say hair, honestly."

"Yeah, right," said Lucy.

"Here's your pint, Max," said Daria, stretching over Hopper's head. "Don't move, Hopper." She passed Max his pint and sat down beside Hopper on a bar stool.

"You were great on the show, Lucy," she smiled. "Did you enjoy it?"

"Yes, it was actually really good fun."

"And here's the man of the moment." Alan looked towards the door. They all started cheering and clapping.

Lucy was glad of the distraction. Seeing Daria again, after the recent 'episode', was a little embarrassing.

"Eugene! Eugene! Eugene!" Derek, who was beside his friend, chanted, thumping his closed fist into the air.

Everyone in the pub stared over at the door. But it wasn't Eugene and Derek they were looking at – it was Rowie de Young.

24

"Are you and Alan all set for tomorrow?" Lucy asked Hopper.

"Kind of," Hopper smiled. She looked out the kitchen window. The sky was full of dark, threatening clouds. "I hope the weather picks up a bit." She dunked her biscuit into her tea. "I thought July was supposed to be bloody summer."

"Baltimore's miles away," said Lucy. "They probably have different weather patterns there. The Gulf Stream and all that."

Hopper snorted. "Good try. Has Eugene made up his mind yet about coming?"

"No," Lucy smiled, "but Rowie has. She's put her foot down. Apparently she spent some of her summers as a child in Schull and she loves West Cork."

"Who would have thought?" Hopper laughed. "Eugene being bossed around by his girlfriend! I'm dying to meet her again. I didn't really get to talk to her in the pub the night after the show. How long ago was that?"

"Nearly a month. I've met her a few times since and I really like her. She's very good for Eugene and, what's the word? Formidable."

"Good word," Hopper grinned.

"What are you girls talking about?" Alan asked as he walked down the stairs to the kitchen.

"Our trip to Baltimore," said Hopper.

"What else?" Alan smiled, sitting down at the table. "So what's the final head count?"

"You two, myself and Max, Eugene and Rowie – six," said Lucy. "And Daria's joining us for two days – she's getting the train down on Sunday. So seven."

Hopper was staring at her with a strange expression on her face.

"What?" asked Lucy.

"Nothing." Hopper broke her gaze and concentrated on the table instead. "Now that Eugene and Rowie are definitely going, it just makes things interesting, that's all." Hopper smiled at Lucy. "You'll have to share a room with Max and Daria."

Lucy sat up poker-straight. "What?"

"Calm down, Lucy," Alan soothed. "She's only winding you up. Aren't you? There are four bedrooms – you'll have a whole room to yourself."

Hopper bit her tongue.

"I'm going to finish packing," Lucy said sharply. "Then I'm going to Mum's, so I'll see you both later."

"Listen, I'm sorry. I was only messing. What are your plans for dinner?" Hopper asked.

"I'm making moussaka. Max is coming over as Daria's working. You may as well join us."

"Are you sure?" asked Hopper. "We wouldn't like to put you to any –"

"It's fine. But no smart comments, OK?"

"Moi?"

Lucy frowned as she walked out of the room. Hopper was infuriating.

"What's up with her?" asked Hopper. "She's very tetchy."

"Leave it. She's obviously finding things a little difficult at the moment. She's used to having Max all to herself. I'd say you just got a bit too close to the bone."

She looked at Alan carefully. "You don't miss a trick, do you?"

Alan shook his head. "I watch and listen."

"And I don't?"

"No," Alan smiled. "You ask personal questions."

Hopper punched him on the arm. "Thanks a lot."

"I'm only joking. We're as bad as each other. I'm just more subtle. Why do you think we get on so well?"

"I've no idea," she said. She stood up and sat back down on his lap, legs straddling him, and kissed him firmly on the mouth. "It must be pheromones."

"Or animal lust," he murmured. He pulled her long-sleeved T-shirt out of her trousers and snaked his hands up her back. "No bra?"

"No underwear at all. My boyfriend doesn't like it."

"Lucky man," Alan murmured as he kissed her neck. "Very lucky man."

* * *

"Hi, Mum," Lucy kissed Eileen on the doorstep. "How are things?"

"Good. Come into the kitchen. I'm just making some tea. Would you like a cup?"

"No thanks, I'm all tea-ed out. Myself and Hopper have been drinking it all morning."

"How's Hopper? Still with that nice Alan?"

"Yes," Lucy nodded. "They seem really happy together."

"That's good." She poured boiling water into her cup. "Sit down. Take the weight off your feet."

"It seems really quiet without the kids," Lucy said. "Do you miss them?"

"Of course," Eileen said quietly.

"I'm sorry, Mum. I didn't mean to –"

"It's fine. Their mum is much better and it's only right they should

267

be with her." She took a sip of her tea. "You should have seen the look on little Jade's face when Agnes told her she was going home. Poor wee thing started crying and couldn't stop – she was so happy."

"And how are you, Mum?"

"OK. Getting better. Agnes said letting go the first time was the worst and then it gets easier."

"Any news on the baby?"

"Babies," Eileen corrected her. "Twins. They arrive the day after tomorrow."

Lucy whistled. "That's quick!"

"I've been out stocking up on baby wipes and nappies. You forget how much equipment babies need – the house is full of cots and buggies and highchairs."

"What about work?"

"They've given me unpaid leave. But, to be honest, I don't think I'll go back. Not for a while anyway. I'd like to foster for as long as I'm able."

"You really love it, don't you, Mum?"

Eileen nodded. She was silent for a moment. "When you and Eugene were small I was working as many hours as I could just to keep us afloat. I wish I could have spent more time with you both. It's easier now – the mortgage has been paid off and money isn't such a problem. Sometimes I wish I could turn back the clock."

"Mum, you were always there for us. And we loved being with Gran when you were working. She spoiled us rotten. Especially Eugene."

Eileen smiled.

"It's true," Lucy insisted. "He always got more potatoes than me and more chocolate biscuits."

"He was a foot taller than you, love," Eileen laughed. "He needed more fuel."

Lucy decided to let it go. "And when Gran died, we were in secondary school and able to look after ourselves."

"I wish things had been different," Eileen sighed. "Your dad –"

Lucy stared at her. "Don't!"

"I know you don't like talking about him, but he's still your dad."

"Some dad," Lucy snorted. "Running off with that floozy and her daughter. Abandoning his own children."

"Lucy! That's unfair. We'd been having problems long before he met Stella and Amanda. You know that. It was for the best really."

Lucy had a lump in her throat. She hated talking about her father; it always made her emotional. "But he left us, Mum."

Eileen put her arms around her daughter. "I know, love. And maybe you were too young to remember but your dad was heartbroken when you refused to talk to him. He rang every day for almost a year and visited every month but you refused to stay in the same room as him. The poor man gave up after that. But there's something I've meant to tell you. He keeps in touch with Eugene. They're often on the phone and Eugene's been over to see him quite a few times."

"I don't want to talk about this," Lucy said, her mouth set in a firm line. She remembered all right, but she'd managed to block it all out of her mind for years and years. But she'd had no idea Eugene was still in contact with their father – she'd kill him.

"You have to," Eileen said gently. "He's sick. That's why I asked you to come over today."

"Eugene's sick?" Lucy's eyes opened.

"No, not Eugene. Your dad. He's had a heart attack."

Lucy caught her breath. "I'm not interested. The sooner he dies the better."

Eileen gasped. "You don't mean that!"

"Yes, I do. I'm sorry, Mum. He ruined my life and I hate him."

Eileen sighed. "You have to make your peace with him."

"Why? He's done nothing for me, nothing!"

"That's not exactly true," Eileen said slowly.

"What do you mean?"

"He paid your school fees and Eugene's, he paid for you to go to Beauty College and Eugene's college fees, and –"

Lucy put her hands over her ears. "I don't want to hear any of this! He doesn't care about me. He doesn't."

"Yes, he does. You've pushed him away all these years, but he still loves you."

Lucy began to cry. "He doesn't love me. How could he love me? He went away." Eileen handed her a tissue and Lucy wiped her eyes.

"Will you ring him, Lucy? He's in hospital in Liverpool. Eugene says he's been asking for you."

"Is he very bad?"

"Yes, love. I'm afraid he is. Will you please ring him?"

"No," Lucy said standing up. "I'm sorry. I can't. I have to go now."

Eileen watched her daughter's back as she walked out the door. She lifted the phone off the kitchen table.

"Eugene," she said, "I need to talk to you."

* * *

"I presume you'll have seconds?" said Lucy, taking the moussaka out of the oven and placing it on the hob.

"Of course," Max smiled.

"Alan?"

"Please."

"What about me?" asked Hopper.

"Sorry, Hopper. Would you like some?"

"No, but thanks for asking."

Lucy snorted. "You're a lunatic." She took Max and Alan's plates and spooned on a generous amount of the steaming lamb dish.

"What's in it anyway?" said Max. "The moussaka, I mean. The restaurant type is always smothered in tinned tomatoes."

"Are you saying mine is better?" she asked as she handed the boys their plates and sat down again.

"Isn't it always?" said Max.

Lucy beamed at him. "Good answer." She thought for a second. "It's mainly minced lamb, with aubergines, herbs, red wine, cinnamon, and ricotta and parmesan over the top."

"That's my favourite bit," said Hopper, helping herself from Alan's plate. "The top."

Alan hit her fork away with his. "Get your own, you brat!"

Hopper stuck her tongue out at him.

"Later, Hopper," he smiled.

"Please," said Lucy. "Not at the dinner table."

"Have you finished packing, Max?" asked Alan.

"Kind of. I have to collect a kite from the office in the morning and then I'm pretty much set."

"How many are you bringing?" Alan spooned coffee granules into the cafetière.

"Only three. Maybe four. And the land yachts."

"Max!" Lucy grinned. "There'll be no room for me in the car."

"That's the general idea." Lucy scowled at him. "Only joking. Most of it will fit in the boot, and the rest can go on the roof. It'll be fine."

"You know we're only going for few days?" said Hopper.

Max nodded. "Don't want to be bored though, do we? It's quite a sleepy little town really."

"I have a feeling that you won't be bored," Hopper grinned. "Not with Daria there."

"Coffee's up," Alan said quickly. "And I found Lucy's stash of chocolate biscuits."

"Hey!" Lucy protested. "They're for Baltimore."

"They have shops there, Lucy," Alan smiled. He looked at Max. "Don't they?"

"You'd think we were going to Outer Mongolia," said Max. "Of course they have bloody shops." He stopped for a second. "Well, a shop anyway. And Skibbereen is only down the road."

"Skibbereen?" asked Hopper.

271

"The capital of West Cork," Max explained. "Now, hand me a chocolate biscuit."

* * *

"I thought you said six o'clock, Max," Lucy complained. "It's now nearly seven and I've been ready for ages. Where are you?"

"I'm just leaving," Max lied. He rolled over and looked at his alarm clock. "Lucy, it's only ten past six," he groaned.

"I know," she said. "And you said six o'clock. Which makes you officially late. So get out of bed!"

"How did you know – ?"

"Just hurry up," Lucy interrupted. "I'm going to have a cup of coffee. If you're not here by the time I've finished it, there'll be trouble with a capital T." She slammed down the phone.

"Jeez, she's narky this morning," Max muttered as he dragged himself out of bed. Maybe he shouldn't have stayed up till one drinking with Alan. Hopper and Lucy had been canny and gone to bed early. It would have been easier to stay on the sofa but he'd staggered home instead.

He looked in the full-length mirror, opened his mouth and examined his gums. Just as he expected – stained dark blue-red from the port. Alan's great idea, of course. Port and Stilton. No wonder his stomach felt a little queasy. They'd finished off practically a whole Stilton – one Lucy had bought in Sheridan's to bring down to Baltimore – not to mention a good half of the bottle of port.

He turned sideways and held his gut in his hands. He'd have to watch it. His stomach was looking decidedly flabby. He leaned forwards and ran his hands through his hair. It definitely seemed thinner. He drastically needed another haircut, or shave. He didn't have enough hair for a haircut any more. He glanced down. At least his penis seemed normal – no change there.

He pulled a white long-sleeved T-shirt out of his wardrobe and dragged it over his head. He picked his jeans up off the floor, gave them a quick sniff and put them on. Ten minutes later, after throwing some clothes into a bag, he opened the door and lowered his sunglasses over his wincing eyes. Thank goodness he'd packed most of his toys yesterday or it would have taken him forever to get ready.

As he pulled up outside Lucy's house, the front door opened immediately and she bundled down the steps, loaded down by two large bags and a vanity case. He jumped out of the car to help her.

"Here," he said, taking one of the bags and the vanity case off her, "I'll take these."

"Great," she said, dumping the other bag on the steps and running back up the steps.

"Where are you going?"

"To get my other bag," she said.

Max groaned. He threw her bags into the boot, on top of his own.

"Will you need this during the drive?" he asked Lucy as she walked back down the steps. He held up the small black-leather case.

She looked at him curiously. "My vanity case? Of course not. Why would I need that?"

"I don't know. I thought it was a handbag. It's heavy – what's in it?"

Lucy cocked her head. "Do you really want to know?" Max nodded.

"Four perfumes, two types of hair spray, manicure set and two nail-polishes, nail-polish remover, shampoo, conditioner, moisturiser, make-up, false tan, eyelash curlers –"

Max put up his hands. "Enough!" He'd never understand girls. They were going to a cottage in the wilds of West Cork, not to Hollywood for goodness sake. Mad, the lot of them!

Lucy opened the car door. "What are these?" she pointed at the side of her seat where long pieces of black carbon and what looked like sails poked forward and blocked her entrance.

"New land-yacht sails," said Max sheepishly. "Climb under them. Or you can get in my side if you like."

"How kind of you," she said acerbicly. She looked into the back of the car. Land yachts, kites and boxes of spares covered the back seats. "I see you've left plenty of room for me to lie down. Such a considerate man."

"Um, are you getting in?" he asked carefully.

"I suppose I'll have to," she snapped. She opened her last bag which lay at her feet, pulled out a pillow and handed the bag to Max. She then ducked under the sails, muttering when her hair got caught in one of the masts, and finally settled herself in the passenger seat with the door closed.

Max tossed her final bag into the boot unceremoniously. He got in beside her and smiled.

"Ready?"

"Yes," she muttered, jamming the pillow between her head and the window. She was leaning heavily on one of the new sails, but he didn't have the nerve to ask her to move. By the time they had reached the M50 she was fast asleep and snoring gently.

Max rubbed his eyes. He didn't want to miss the turn-off the motorway for Cork and it was easy enough to do. Lucy was now dribbling onto her pillow as well as snoring. Lucky for some. He wouldn't have minded a bit of a kip himself. But at least the traffic was light at this hour of the morning and they'd be in Baltimore by lunchtime. His stomach groaned as he thought about food. Hangover or no hangover, he was bloody starving. He'd really fancy a full Irish breakfast right at this minute – chips, bean, mushrooms – the works. He'd find a cafe soon and stop. He'd even leave Lucy in the car if she was still asleep. In the mood she was in it would be far more relaxing. And anyway, he thought rationally, she didn't like fried breakfasts.

"Why didn't you wake me?" Lucy grumbled as they came into Portlaoise. "I'm starving. I would have loved some breakfast."

Max groaned inwardly. He was hoping they'd have a pleasant drive down. Chatting, listening to music. But Lucy wasn't exactly being Little Miss Sunshine. "Sorry," he said evenly. "I didn't want to wake you."

"We'll have to stop for lunch in Cork city then. I can't wait till we get to Baltimore."

"I'm not stopping in Cork. We're meeting Alan and Hopper at twelve in Read's Pub, remember?"

"I don't care," Lucy said petulantly. "I'm starving."

Max ignored her.

"Do you hear me?"

"Yes!"

"Well?" Lucy demanded.

"Well what?"

"Can we stop in Cork city?"

"No!"

"What?"

"I said no."

"Why not?"

"Lucy," he sighed, "please stop this."

"Stop what?"

Max put his foot on the brakes and pulled the car into the side of the road. Rocks flew up from under the wheels. She was thrown forward against her seat belt. Luckily there was nothing behind them.

"Stop acting like a child," he said firmly. "What is wrong with you?"

"Nothing," she muttered, folding her arms in front of her. "I'm just hungry."

"I'll stop at the next shop or garage and you can get a sandwich, OK?"

"I don't want a sandwich. I want a proper breakfast."

"Fine. We'll get your usual breakfast – a KitKat and a cup of coffee. OK?"

Lucy stared out the passenger window and then realised most of her view was blocked by the damn sails. She blinked back the tears.

Max, not noticing, pulled out and drove on.

Lucy closed her eyes. Talking to her mother yesterday had really unnerved her. She wanted to talk to him about it so badly. She

275

wanted him to ask her what was wrong. What was upsetting her. Why she was crying. Why she hadn't slept one wink last night. But he didn't even seem to notice.

Typical, Max thought to himself. Now she's sleeping again. He fixed his eyes on the road and put his foot down hard on the accelerator. The BMW started to tick rhythmically as it always did when it went over sixty miles an hour. Max had had several garages look at it but there was nothing they could do about it. Usually the noise annoyed him but today he was glad of the distraction. He focused on the ticking and tried to clear his mind of murderous thoughts towards his passenger.

"We thought you'd never get here," said Alan slapping Max on the back.

"My car's not as new as yours," Max smiled. Alan drove a new black Volkswagen Golf with all the trimmings.

"What are you having?" asked Alan.

"A pint of Guinness."

Alan grinned. "This is Cork, remember. You have to drink Murphy's instead of Guinness. Two Murphy's, please, and a glass of Bulmers," Alan said to the barman. "Where's Lucy?"

"In the car. She's asleep. I didn't want to wake her."

Hopper waved from the back of the pub. At least, Max thought it was Hopper. The light was dim and his eyes were only starting to adjust. Max ran his hand over the smooth, dark wood of the bar. "Great place."

"Now this is what I call a real Irish pub," Alan smiled. "Leather seats, snug, roaring fire," he leaned towards Max, "great-looking girls." Alan gestured towards his right.

Max checked out the German girls who were sitting there. At least he thought they were German – short blonde hair, sallow skin, multi-coloured Patagonia rain-jackets. One of them winked at him and he smiled back at her.

"I think you've made a new friend, mate," Alan laughed.

"What are you two laughing about?" Lucy asked, appearing at Alan's side.

"Nothing," Max assured her. "How are you feeling?"

"You should have woken me."

"Sorry," he said. He felt like he was stuck in *Groundhog Day*.

"What would you like to drink?" Alan asked Lucy as their own pints and Hopper's drink were placed in front of him.

"A Coke, thanks."

"Is anyone hungry?" Alan asked as soon as he sat down beside Hopper. "I have some menus here." He handed them around.

"Starving," Lucy said, looking at Max meaningfully.

25

"A real fireplace," Hopper sighed. She crouched down beside the fireplace in the cottage. "They've left briquettes, firelighters and matches. Cool! I'll light one tonight. Let's go upstairs and check out the other bedrooms," Hopper said excitedly, grabbing Lucy's arm. "Come on."

As the two girls disappeared up the wooden staircase Alan slumped onto the sofa. "I'm knackered after that drive."

Max sat down beside him. "No kidding. The roads are —"

"Crap," Alan added helpfully. "Although the roads in Dublin aren't much better."

"Let's not talk about roads or traffic," Max said.

"Or house prices," Alan added. He stuck out his hand and Max shook it.

"Agreed."

They were silent for a few minutes. "So what will we talk about?" Max asked finally.

"What we usually talk about when the girls aren't here. Them. And other women."

"I'm sure they can hear us," Max said. "In fact, they're probably listening right now, ears pressed against the floor."

"I wouldn't be surprised. So cars it is then."

"And music," Max laughed. "Don't forget music."

"What were you two talking about?" Hopper asked a few minutes later after checking out all the bedrooms both upstairs and downstairs.

"The usual," Max said. "Cars."

"And music," Alan said trying not to laugh.

She didn't believe them for one second, but gave them the benefit of the doubt. "The bedrooms are nice. We're in the one upstairs to the right. And Max and Daria are in the one directly at the top of the stairs. Lucy, Eugene and Rowie are in the rooms on this floor."

"Do we have any say in the matter?" Max asked.

"No!" Hopper and Lucy said in unison.

Max looked at Alan who shrugged.

"Fine," Max said. "Whatever."

Hopper threw herself on top of Alan, her elbow catching him in the ribs.

"Hey, watch it!"

Hopper kissed him on the arm. "Don't be such a baby."

Max watched them enviously.

Lucy was staring out the window, looking at the view. "You can see Sherkin Island from here."

Hopper jumped up. "Where?"

"There." Lucy pointed at the island which was peeping through the fog.

"I see it," Hopper said excitedly. "Can you get onto it?"

Max nodded. "They have ferries across. We can go over at some stage if you like."

"Great," Hopper enthused. "Is it big?"

"Not very," he said. "You can easily walk across it. There are beaches over the far side."

"I hope we get some decent weather," Alan said. "I fancy a swim."

279

"Me too," Lucy said. "If it's sunny. Eugene'll swim regardless of the weather. He goes down to the Forty Foot Bathing Place in Sandycove with Max every December for his Christmas morning dip."

"I'd forgotten that," Alan smiled. "Maybe I'll go with you this year. When are Eugene and Rowie arriving?"

"This afternoon," Lucy said. She wasn't looking forward to seeing her brother after her mum's revelations yesterday. Maybe she wouldn't bring it up at all – it was bound to spoil the holiday.

"I suppose we should unpack," Hopper said.

Alan groaned and sat up. "Why don't I get my stereo out and we can leave the rest till later?"

"Good idea," Max said. "I'll help you."

Outside, Alan turned to Max. "What's up with Lucy? She's not her usual smiling self. Have you two had a fight?"

"Not really. She was in a foul mood all morning, so I just let her sleep it off. I think she's just tired."

"Are you sure you didn't say anything to annoy her? You know what women are like."

Max sighed. "I don't know. Maybe I did."

"Well, I hope she snaps out of it soon. Try talking to her. Go for a walk or something and sort it out."

"Good idea. I will." Alan passed him two speakers to carry inside. "You brought the whole system?" Max asked incredulously.

"Of course," Alan smiled. "I don't travel without my music."

"I hope you haven't brought all your weirdy stuff."

"What do you mean? Surely everyone likes The Zombie Bloodsuckers and Amy's Death Proxy?"

"Yeah, right!"

The boys put the stereo components up on the kitchen table and began to set it up, untangling the muddled snakes of multi-coloured wires.

"You're not leaving it there," said Lucy.

"Why?" asked Alan.

"Where will we eat?"

Alan looked around the room. There was only one table. He looked at Max.

Max shrugged. "She has a point. How about over there?" He pointed to the left of the fireplace where there was a square coffee table.

"OK," Alan conceded. Max took the lamp off the coffee table and placed in on the floor. They then began to carry the stereo over to its temporary home.

Half an hour later the cottage was filled with the sounds of Moby, and Alan and Hopper were dancing, throwing each other around in elaborate moves and laughing.

Max looked out the window. "The fog seems to be lifting now," he said to Lucy who was sitting opposite him, flicking though a copy of *Now* magazine that some other holidaymaker had left behind. She was reading all about Jamie Oliver's new haircut.

"Fancy a walk?" he continued.

She looked up. "OK."

"We're going for a walk," Max said to Alan and Hopper, shouting over the music.

"Fine," Alan shouted back. "See you later."

As soon as the door closed Alan moved his hands down, caressing Hopper's buttocks through her thin velvet skirt. She moved her body against his and kissed his ear gently.

"Those two are incorrigible," Lucy said to Max as she marched up the driveway. "They can't keep their hands off each other."

"Doesn't bother *me*."

Lucy ignored him. "Which way?" she asked as they came to the top of the drive. "Left or right?"

"Right."

Lucy strode off, leaving him standing.

"Slow down," he said. "It's not a race."

She paid no attention to him and kept on walking.

Max stared at her back and sighed. He watched her for a few minutes and then ran after her and grabbed her arm.

"Lucy, what's wrong?"

"Nothing!" She stared straight ahead. "Why would there be anything wrong?"

"I know you," he said, trying to get her to look at him. "And there's definitely something up. You're in one of your moods."

"I am not!"

"I'm not going to argue with you. Does it have something to do with me. Have I said something –"

"What!" she spat. "You arrogant bastard! How dare you! It has nothing to do with you. Nothing at all."

Max felt like he'd been stung. There was no need for her to be so bloody rude. But at least he'd established that there *was* something wrong. That was a start. "I'm sorry," he said. "I just presumed –"

"Well, don't presume. Ever." She began to walk on.

Max refused to let go of her arm. "This is stupid. I know there's something upsetting you." He looked into her eyes. "I can't help you if you won't tell me," he said gently. "Please."

Lucy began to cry. She couldn't help herself. Max was being too damn nice. Even when she'd been impossibly nasty to him all day.

Max put his arms around her. "What is it?" he asked, stroking her hair.

She shook her head. "I can't," she murmured through the tears.

He held her for a few minutes until the sobbing and heaving had stopped. Then he passed her a tissue from the packet in his pocket. "Here. Dry your eyes."

"Thanks," she sniffed, dabbing them gently. She felt like a huge weight had been lifted from her shoulders and most of the tension had dissolved away.

"Do you want to go back?" he asked kindly.

"No, I'm OK."

They walked down towards the village. "The fog's lifting," Max commented as they passed the harbour. It might even be nice tomorrow."

Lucy nodded.

282

Max put his arm around her shoulders. "You'll be grand."

She turned towards him. "I'm sorry," she said, tears forming in her eyes again. "I'm ruining your holiday."

"It's OK," he smiled. "I'm used to you, you old bat."

She smiled back and the tears receded.

They walked past the Mariner restaurant, stopping to look at menu. The sun threatened to fight through the clouds and they could feel its warmth on their faces. They walked a little further in silence and stopped beside a small cove.

"Want to paddle?" Max asked.

Lucy stared at him. "Are you joking?"

"No. I will if you will."

"Deal." They climbed down the marram-grass slope and stopped a few metres from the water. The beach was stony and they sat down on the shingle and removed their boots and socks.

"It looks cold," she said standing up and walking gingerly towards the tiny waves which were lapping the shore.

He followed her. The stones felt cool beneath his feet. "You can try it first," he said.

"I thought you were the brave man who swims in the sea at Christmas?" she said, looking back at him.

"Paddling is different. At the Forty Foot you just jump in. There's no subtlety about it."

"I must come and watch you this year," Lucy said.

"I'd like that."

"Just to see your willie shrink, you understand," she laughed.

"Nice," he laughed, "very nice." He walked forward, grabbing her arm and forcing her into the water with him.

"It's freezing," she squealed.

"You'll get used to it."

Lucy bent down and pulled her jeans up further. Max watched her.

"What?" she asked. A smiled lingered over his lips.

"Nothing."

"I'm getting out. My toes are turning to ice."

"You big baby," Max smiled.

They sat down on their jackets. Max stretched his legs out in front of him and wiggled his toes.

"You have really long toes," Lucy said. "I hadn't really noticed before." She picked up a small stone and rested it on top of his right foot.

"You know what they say about men with long toes." He winked at her.

"That's long feet, not toes," she laughed. "You're only a size nine."

"Nine and a half," Max corrected her. "Don't forget the half."

She put more stones on his feet, building little pyramids on each. "Now, don't move!"

Max closed his eyes and raised his face to where the sun would be if it wasn't obscured by the clouds. "It's actually quite warm now." He pulled his fleece over his head, collapsing and scattering Lucy's pyramids in the process. The fleece caught his T-shirt, exposing several inches of his bare flesh.

"Penny for them?" Lucy had a peculiar expression on her face.

She turned away and stared out at Sherkin Island. "The sun. I was wondering whether it would come out later."

They sat in companionable silence for several minutes. Max tossed some stones into the sea. He tried skimming some, but it was hard to find flat stones from his prostrate position.

"Are you ready to talk yet?" he asked eventually.

"No. Not really."

"Try," he cajoled.

Lucy took a deep breath. "My dad's really sick and Eugene's kept in contact with him all these years without telling me."

"Your dad's sick?"

"I've been trying to tell you all day."

Max was tempted to snort or laugh but thought better of it.

"He had a heart attack," she continued. "He's in hospital in Liverpool."

"I'm so sorry," Max said. "I had no idea. Have you spoken to him?"

"Of course not! You know how I feel about him."

"But –"

"But what? It doesn't change anything." She tried to hold back the tears but it was no use. Her tear-ducts had a mind of their own. "I don't care," she sobbed. "I don't care."

Max put his arm around Lucy and held her tight. He wanted to tell her to ring her dad but he didn't dare.

"I'm sick of crying. Have you any more tissues?"

"Here," he handed her the whole packet. "Keep them."

"Thanks. I feel better now. I just wanted to tell you."

"I know," Max said. "I understand. Have you talked to Eugene?"

"No. I'm so annoyed with him for lying to me all these years."

"It's not his fault, you know. I'm sure he never meant to hurt you."

"I suppose not. But he has."

"And anyway, he didn't exactly lie to you –"

Lucy glared at him.

"Do you want to go back now?" Max asked quickly. "Alan and Hopper will be wondering where we've got to."

"I'm sure they'll find plenty to do," Lucy said. "I'd like to sit here for a while, if that's all right."

"Of course. Do you want to talk more?"

"No." She squeezed his arm gently. "I'm all talked out for now. And please, don't say anything to Eugene. I'll talk to him when I feel it's right."

* * *

"Where have you two been?" asked Hopper. She was curled up on the sofa with her head on Alan's lap.

"We went paddling," said Lucy.

"Are you mad? It's freezing."

"It's colder in here than it is outside," said Max. "The sun's even threatening to come out." He sat down on one of the armchairs. "What have you two been up to anyway? Or should I ask?"

"No," Hopper laughed. "Probably not."

Just then Eugene's car pulled up outside and he jumped out, followed by Rowie.

"Here we go," said Hopper. "Earplugs in, everyone."

"Hopper!" Lucy hissed. "Behave yourself."

Rowie strode into the cottage with Eugene trailing behind her. She approached Lucy, who was the only one standing, and held out her hand.

"Lucy," she boomed in heavily accented English, "nice to see you again. And all your friends." She looked around the room, nodding at each of them.

Lucy tried not to gasp at the boa-constrictor handshake. She half-smiled at Eugene, walked towards him and gave him a hug. "Good to see you."

"And you, Sis," said Eugene. He turned towards the others, who were sitting on the sofa. Hopper's eyes were glued on Rowie's dark-red velvet bustier, figure-hugging jeans and black leather platform boots.

"Everyone, you've met Rowie," Eugene beamed. "Rowie, you remember Alan, Hopper and Max."

"Darling boy," she gave the astonished Max an all-encompassing hug. "How could I forget. Just like my little brother, blond and beautiful, no?"

Max blushed furiously. Lucy stifled her giggles. Rowie was taller than Max and swamped his slender frame.

"Come here, woman," Eugene laughed. "Leave poor Max alone."

Rowie bounded over and gave Eugene a kiss on the cheek. "Isn't he wonderful?"

"Would you like some tea?" Lucy asked them. "Or something to eat? Or a drink?"

"No," Rowie smiled. "I think we might have a rest, if that is OK." She raised her eyebrows at Eugene. "How about it, little man?"

Eugene blushed and nodded.

Alan jumped up. "We were just going to the pub," he improvised.

Max stood up too. "That's right."

"I'm not," Hopper complained.

"Yes, you are," said Lucy, glaring at her. "Rowie, I'll show you your room."

Eugene went to the car to fetch the bags, Max and Alan trailing him.

Rowie sat down on the double bed and bounced up and down. "Fantastic," she smiled.

"Are you and Eugene – ?" Hopper began, lingering at the bedroom door.

"Come on, Hopper," Lucy interrupted. "We don't want to keep the boys waiting, do we?"

"But I was just going to –" she protested.

"You can talk to Rowie later. Right now, we all have a date with a pint."

"I can't believe you dragged me away like that," Hopper complained as they walked towards the village.

"Stop moaning," Lucy smiled. "You'll have plenty of time to give Rowie the full treatment later."

"I just wanted to –"

"I know! Find out what age she is, what she sees in my brother, how long she plans to stay in Ireland. I can just imagine."

"That's unfair!"

They caught up with Max and Alan who were standing by the gate waiting for them.

"What do you think of Rowie's outfit?" asked Alan.

"Not you as well," Lucy laughed.

"You have to admit," said Max, "it's very, how will I put this, striking."

"Very striking," Alan nodded. He raised his eyebrows at Max.

"What do you mean by striking?" asked Lucy.

"Nothing," said Alan. "Which pub are we going to?"

"Stop trying to worm out of it," Lucy continued. "Tell me."

"It's –" Max began, grinning. He shook his head.

"Very –" Alan added.

"For heaven's sake," Hopper said. "Spit it out, guys."

"Sexy," Alan smiled.

"Very, very sexy," Max agreed.

"If Eugene wasn't your brother –" Alan began.

"Hey!" Hopper protested, pinching his side between his ribs and his hipbone and making him jump.

"Hopper! Stop!"

"Make me!"

Alan grabbed both her arms together with one hand, lifted them over her head, and began to tickle her armpits.

"Stop!" Hopper giggled. "That's not fair."

Hopper and Alan fell to a heap on the pavement, laughing hysterically.

"Get up, the pair of you," Lucy smiled. "You're making a show of us."

"Don't be such a mammy," Hopper said. "We're on our holidays."

"Who are you calling Mammy?" She launched herself on top of the sprawling couple.

"Ow, get off," Alan yelled. "Max, help! Lucy's squashing me!"

"Love to." He put his arms around Lucy to help her up but Hopper grabbed him.

"Get his legs, Lucy," Hopper said. "Behind the knees."

Max collapsed on top of Lucy.

"Watch my ankle," he yelped. "That's not funny."

"Oh, it is," Alan grinned, the back of his head resting on the concrete. "And if you all get off me, the first pint's on me."

"My elbow hurts." Lucy rubbed the throbbing joint tenderly.

"Let me see," said Max.

She pulled the sleeve of her shirt up.

"It's red, all right," he said. "I'll get you some ice. It might stop it bruising too badly."

"Thanks."

Hopper and Alan were propping the bar up, talking to a local couple about the traffic problems in Dublin. Lucy watched them as she waited for Max. Alan had his arm draped lazily around Hopper's shoulder. Now and again he caressed the back of her head with his fingers, and she leant back into his hand, giving him a whisper of a smile.

"Are you OK?" Max asked. He had a teatowel in his hand.

"Fine. Just thinking."

"Don't do too much of that. Bad for you. Here, give me your arm."

"You don't have to –" Lucy began.

"Let me," Max said. "Please."

Silently Lucy put her arm out in front of her. Max shifted the ice around in the teatowel and placed it gingerly against her elbow. "How does that feel?"

Lucy winced. "Cold. Here, I'll hold it."

He took his hand away abruptly and coughed. "Would you like another drink?"

"Please. A pint of cider and a packet of crisps. Cheese and onion."

Lucy stared at Max's back as he stood at the bar. He reached into one of the back pockets of his faded denims to retrieve his wallet, put his wallet on the top of the bar beside him and leaned forwards on his tanned arms, resting his head on his hands and gazing out the pub window.

She felt strange. He was being his usual kind self but somehow things were different. She didn't like it one little bit. It made her feel decidedly nervous. Maybe he was just being extra nice to her because of her dad.

"Can we join you?" Hopper said, bouncing onto the leather seat beside Lucy.

"Be my guest," Lucy said, moving over. "Just watch my elbow."

"Did your mother never tell you not to play on the street?" Alan smiled. "It can be dangerous, you know."

"Only when you lot are around," Lucy said. "Bloody terrorists."

"Who's a terrorist?" Max asked, placing a pint of cider on the beer mat in front of Lucy.

"Thanks," she said.

He sat down and took a sip of his own pint. "Murphy's. Can't beat it. So, come on, who's a terrorist?"

"Lucy was just complaining about her elbow," Hopper said. "She was blaming us."

"Too right," Lucy said.

"It's a pity we weren't drunk," Max said. "Then we might not have felt it at all. Natural anaesthetic."

"We can always have a repeat performance later," Alan suggested. "And maybe Rowie could join in."

"Bags be under Rowie," Max said.

"Max," Lucy laughed, "I won't be able to look Eugene in the face if you don't stop."

"I wonder if Rowie looks Eugene in the face," Hopper said thoughtfully. "When she's –"

Alan put his hand over Hopper's mouth. "Don't go there," he warned. He picked up her glass. "No more drinks for you."

"I'll behave. I promise."

"So what's the plan for tonight?" Alan asked.

"Dinner, I guess," Max said.

"The couple at the bar recommended a place called The Mermaid," said Alan. "It's run by an English couple and it's just up the road apparently."

"Sounds good. What do you think, Lucy?"

"Fine by me. I'll text-message Eugene and check with him. But he'll eat pretty much anything."

"Including Rowie, I imagine," said Hopper.

"Hopper," Alan said. He was trying not to laugh. "I think I'm going to take you for a walk and sober you up. It's only six." He turned towards Max. "Maybe we'd better eat early."

"Good idea. I'm starving anyway."

"But you've only just had lunch," Lucy smiled.

"That was ages ago."

"I'll get the number of the restaurant from the bar," Alan said standing up. "How about I make a booking for seven o'clock?"

"Perfect," said Max.

After booking, Alan dragged a protesting Hopper outside for some fresh air. Max and Lucy watched them walk towards the pier. It was bright but not warm enough to sit outside as the wind had a cold bite to it.

"Make sure Hopper sits well away from Rowie tonight," said Lucy. She opened her second packet of crisps and began to tuck in. "Want one?"

"No, I'm OK, thanks. How's the elbow?" Lucy had removed the teatowel as it had started to drip.

"Not too bad. I think the ice helped."

"I was wondering," Max began. He sounded a little nervous.

"Yes?" Lucy turned towards him.

"Are you going to talk to Eugene later, about your dad?"

Lucy looked at Max for a few seconds. "I told you. I don't want to talk about it. OK?"

"I know. It's just –"

"Stop."

"And about earlier –"

"Max, I said stop," Lucy stared at the table. "Why can't you just leave it?"

"Fine, have it your way. You always do."

"What do you mean by that?"

"Nothing. You're right, forget it. I'm going to the bar. Do you want another drink?"

"No," Lucy mumbled. He left the table.

Her phone beeped. "Wave. I'm outside," the text message read. She looked up. Eugene had his face pressed up against the glass. He was grinning at her. She waved and smiled back.

He bounded in the door, followed by Rowie who had pulled a moss-green chenille cardigan over her shoulders, the collar a fiesta of fluffy green strands. Lucy recognised it immediately as a Lainey Keogh design. Paula had pointed it out in VIP magazine in the salon one day, and Lucy had lusted after it ever since.

"Hiya, sis," Eugene kissed her on the cheek. Rowie had disappeared. "What are you drinking?"

"Not for me, thanks. I'm having a rest."

Eugene lifted up her almost empty glass and looked at the light-brown dregs.

"A pint of cider, so. No rest for the wicked."

Lucy laughed. "Go on then. You're a bad influence."

"I see how it is," Max smiled. "You'll let your brother buy you a pint but not me. I'll try not to take it personally." He stood up. "We can't have impoverished students buying drinks. What are you having, Eugene?"

"It's fine," he protested.

"I insist," Max smiled. "You can get the next ones in."

"Grand. Mine's a pint of lager and Rowie will have a Jack Daniels straight up."

"Cider, lager, straight Jack Daniels, got it."

"Where's Rowie?" Lucy asked as they waited for Max who was chatting amicably to the barman.

"In the loo. She always takes hours. Something to do with re-styling her hair apparently."

Lucy smiled. "You really like her."

He nodded. "She's amazing. I've never really met someone who's so totally together. She's got a really good head on her."

"She's not your usual type."

"I know. She's heaps better."

"The boys are very impressed," Lucy couldn't help adding.

Eugene was chuffed. He grinned from ear to ear. "Good. Listen, while I have you alone, mum rang me yesterday."

"I don't want to talk about it. Please, we're on holiday, OK?"

Eugene looked at her carefully and then nodded. "OK, but I really think you should ring dad," he said gently. "He's in a bad way. It would get all this out of your system. He's only a bloke trying to get on with his life, that's all. He'd love to talk to you, honestly."

"I'll see," she said, pressing her eye-sockets with her knuckles. "Now can we change the subject."

"Is that a yes?"

"Don't push it."

"Lucy, here's your pint," Max said putting it down in front of her. "Where's Rowie?"

"Here I am, sweet boy," said Rowie, laying her head on his back affectionately.

"Um, Rowie," he stammered, straightening up. "Your Jack Daniels. And lager for Eugene."

"Thanks, man," Eugene smiled.

Max sat down beside Lucy. "Cheers, everyone," he raised his glass.

"Cheers!"

26

"Are you sure it's up here?" said Hopper. "This is more of a lane than a road."

"The barman said second on the right after the bright pink house," said Alan.

"Yes, but –" she said, navigating a large muddy pot-hole.

"I think there's something around the corner," said Lucy. "I see lights." She was leading the pack, impatient for her food. All the afternoon's drinks had gone to her head and she was dying to eat. "Yes, definitely a house."

The others caught her up. The large white house was set back from the road. Parked outside were several cars with Cork registrations and a battered old bottle-green Range Rover.

"Hallelujah," said Hopper.

A large blue and white sign saying 'The Mermaid' hung over the door. They made their way inside and were greeted in the hallway by a young woman who was perched on a stool behind a wooden desk.

"Welcome to 'The Mermaid'," she smiled. "Can I help you?"

"We have a reservation for seven o'clock," Alan stepped forward. "Under 'Alan'."

"Ah, yes. For six. Follow me please." She took some large plastic-covered menus from a holder at the side of the desk and strode through a doorway. Walking inside the restaurant Lucy was hit by the heady aroma of garlic.

"Smells good," she said to Max.

"Here's your table," the woman said. When they had all sat down she passed around the menus and the wine list.

"What's everyone drinking?" asked Max. "Red or white?"

"White," said Hopper.

"Same for me," said Alan.

"We'll have red," Rowie smiled.

"And Lucy and me are red," said Max, "so a bottle of each to start with and we'll see how we get on. Hopper, would you like to choose the white?"

"Sure." She scanned the menu. "Let me see. The Pinot Grigio please."

"And I'll order the Merlot, I think." Max looked at Rowie for confirmation. She nodded.

"Good choice. We can try the Shiraz next."

Max ordered the wine and they all surveyed the extensive menu.

"I'll never be able to pick a starter," Lucy complained. "There are so many things I want to try."

"It's buffalo mozzarella for me," said Hopper. "Yum."

"Me too," Rowie smiled. "And carpaccio of beef."

"Where's that?" asked Eugene. Rowie pointed it out on the menu.

After a few minutes a waiter came over. "Ready to order?" He pulled a notebook and a pencil out of his pocket.

"Just about," said Lucy.

"I'll start with yourself," the waiter smiled.

"I'll have the blackened peppers with olives, please. And then the seafood risotto."

The waiter went around the table taking orders.

"I'm starved," Rowie said as soon as he'd left. She took a piece of tomato bread out of the basket in the middle of the table and bit down on it firmly.

"Delicious."

"So, Rowie," Hopper said as soon as Rowie had finished her bread, "yourself and Eugene have been together a while now. Is it quite serious?"

Lucy kicked her under the table. But Hopper ignored her and continued staring intently at Rowie.

"You don't have to answer that," Lucy quickly interjected. "Don't mind her."

"But I like direct questions," said Rowie, unabashed. She smiled at Hopper. "Serious?" she thought for a second. "Maybe, maybe not. Eugene is Eugene and I like him very much. We will have to wait and see." She paused as the waiter poured her a small taster of wine. She tasted it and nodded at him. "That's fine, thanks."

"We hit if off from the start," Eugene said, joining in. He'd been eavesdropping with interest. "It's like we've known each other all our lives."

"I know what you mean," Alan said, smiling at Hopper.

"Oh, please," Lucy whispered.

Max, who was sitting beside Lucy and had heard her, laughed. "Lucy can't handle the love-fest, Rowie," he said. "You'll have to talk about something else."

Lucy glared at him. If she'd meant to share her cynicism with everyone she would have. She didn't need Max to do it for her. "Where did you get that idea, Max? I don't mind at all."

"Sorry," Max murmured.

"And how long have yourself and Max been together?" Rowie asked.

"We're not –" Max began.

"We're just friends," Lucy interrupted. "Max has a girlfriend called Daria. She's an actor. Did Eugene not tell you?"

"Perhaps he did," Rowie said evenly. "I may have forgotten. Interesting."

"What? What's interesting?"

"Nothing. Ignore me."

"No, go on. I want to know," Lucy demanded.

"So," Max interjected, sensing trouble. "What are we going to do tomorrow? Is anyone on for checking out the Beacon? There's a great view from up there."

"I was asking Rowie something," Lucy glared at him. "Why did you interrupt me?"

"Lucy," Eugene said, "go easy. Max probably thought –"

"I don't care what Max thought!"

Hopper leaned towards Lucy. "Lucy, you're a little drunk. Max didn't mean anything. Let it go." She put her hand on Lucy's and leant over. "Don't ruin the evening, OK?"

"Sorry, everyone," Lucy said. "The drink's going to my head. What were you saying about the Beacon, Max?"

"Just that we should go there tomorrow, if the weather's fine. Daria will be arriving at lunchtime – we could go after that."

"Good idea," Lucy said. She stood up, wobbling. "Excuse me for a second."

"Are you all right?" Hopper asked, looking up at her.

"Sure," Lucy smiled. "Just going to the loo."

In the loo, Lucy put the seat of the toilet down, sat on it and lay her head in her hands. Why had she jumped at Rowie and Max like that? She was so embarrassed. She felt raw and prickly – as if all her nerve endings had come to the surface.

"Lucy," Hopper's voice drifted through the door, "are you in there?"

"Yes." She stood up and flushed the chain. "Just coming." She opened the door.

"I was worried about you," said Hopper. "You've been gone for ages."

"Sorry." Lucy washed her hands. "I was in a bit of a daze, must be the wine."

"You keep blaming the drink. It's not just that, is it?"

"No. I've got a few things on my mind, that's all. I'm fine, honestly."

"You know I'm here if you want to talk about it," said Hopper.

"I know. And I do appreciate it, thanks."

"Girls and their communal toilet visits," Alan laughed as Lucy and Hopper took their seats again. "Nothing changes."

"I go alone," Rowie stated firmly. She winked at Eugene. "Usually."

Eugene coughed. "Not in front of my sister."

"I don't mind, Eugene," Lucy said. "I'm saving it all up to tell mum."

"Ha, ha." Eugene stuck his tongue out at her.

"Here's our food," said Max. Their waiter dished out the plates.

"Smells good," said Lucy, breathing in the strong aroma of her peppers.

"Anyone for more wine?" Max asked, holding up the bottle. He poured the last of it into Eugene's glass and ordered another. "It's going to be a long night, I fear," he smiled.

"I didn't mean to unnerve you earlier," Rowie said to Lucy later in the evening. They had finished their main courses and were waiting for their desserts. Eugene had swapped places with Max and they were discussing cars. "I'm sorry."

"There's no need to apologise," Lucy said. "I overreacted. Everyone always assumes myself and Max are together. It just gets annoying."

"I see. And why do you think people assume that?"

Lucy shrugged. "Because we get on so well, I suppose. We do a lot of things together, spend a lot of time together."

"Why?" Rowie asked gently.

"Why what?"

"Why do you spend so much time together?"

"Because we're friends," said Lucy, trying not to get defensive. "We always have been. We've known each other since we were kids. We've grown up together."

"Ah," said Rowie, "I see. That may be part of it."

"Part of what?"

"I was watching your body language."

"Body language?" Lucy laughed. "Eugene should have warned me."

"Part of my doctorate deals with body language, in the workplace mainly. But I've studied the subject extensively."

"Go on," Lucy said with interest.

"Are you sure?"

"Yes."

"You and Max hold each other's gaze for longer than normal. And from what I can make out both your pupils dilate when you are talking."

"Meaning?"

"There's sexual attraction there."

"Really?" Lucy asked incredulously.

Rowie nodded. "Women are far more adept at using body language than men are. You display some of the classic preening gestures – touching your hair when you're talking to him, exposing your wrists, flipping your shoe on and off."

"How do you know what I'm doing with my shoe under the table?"

"I dropped my napkin at one stage and I happened to notice," Rowie smiled. "And you've been running your finger up and down the stem of your wine glass –"

"Rowie! You're making this up. What I'm doing with the wine glass and my shoe has nothing to do with Max. And anyway, I've never noticed any of the other things you're talking about."

"You're both doing it subconsciously. If I may ask another direct question," Rowie said, fixing her gaze on Lucy's face. "Why are you not together? It seems strange that two people who enjoy each other's company so much and are attracted to each other –"

"I'm not attracted to Max!" Lucy said, a little louder than she intended.

Eugene and Max looked over. "Could you have said that any louder?" Eugene said sarcastically.

Lucy looked at Max. He had a strange expression on his face. "She tells me that all the time," he said. "It's nothing new. I'm used to it by now." He picked up the bottle of red wine. "Anyone for a top-up?"

"I didn't mean –" Lucy began.

"It's fine," he said. "No need to explain. As you well know, I feel the same way. I can see that you're a fine-looking woman but I have no interest in you, personally. No offence."

"None taken." She picked up her wineglass and took another sip.

The whole table was listening to Max and Lucy's exchange in silence with unabashed interest.

Hopper broke the tension. "This is all getting far too serious. I think we should sing a song. Any suggestions?"

"'Summertime'," Eugene said. "It's the only one I know. Oh, that and 'American Pie'."

"You start 'Summertime' and we'll join in," Rowie said.

Eugene began to sing. He had a clear, strong voice. Soon everyone had joined in. In the middle of the second chorus the waiter came over.

"Sorry," Lucy said. "Do you want us to stop?"

"Not at all. As long as the songs don't get X-rated it's fine. The owners are pretty laid back. I was just coming over to see if anyone wanted dessert."

"I'll ask them before the next song," she promised. He handed her six dessert menus. "Do you live down here? You're from Dublin, right?"

"Can't deny it," he smiled. He had a wide, open smile which lit up his face. "My parents have a house down the road and I work here in the summer. I'm in college in Dublin."

"What are you studying?"

"Engineering. In Bolton Street."

"My brother's in UCD. He's the noisy one over there." She pointed at Eugene.

"Are you in Baltimore for long?" he asked.

"Just till Wednesday, unfortunately. It's such a beautiful place."

"You'll have to come again."

"Absolutely!"

Eugene and his choir stopped singing and some of the surrounding tables clapped. He stood up and took a bow.

"Does anyone want dessert?" Lucy asked when he'd sat down again. "This nice man is waiting for our order." She looked up at the waiter. "I'm sorry, what's your name?"

"Conor."

"Conor is waiting for our order," Lucy said again. She handed round the menus. "So be quick."

"Ice cream, please," said Hopper.

"Nothing for me," said Rowie. "I'm stuffed."

"Toffee and fudge cake," said Max, "with extra cream. Thanks."

"Pig," slagged Alan. "Same for me, please."

Eugene shook his head.

"And ice cream for me too," Lucy smiled. "That's it, Conor."

"Would anyone like coffee?" Conor asked. He took the order.

As soon as Conor had left the table Eugene pounced. "You should be ashamed of yourself, chatting up the waiter like that. He's a bit young for you."

"I wasn't chatting him up!"

"That's not what it looked like to me."

"I wonder does he sing?" Hopper asked. "We should ask him later. Anyone want to suggest the next song?"

"Me," Rowie said, "'It's Raining Men'."

"Good choice," Lucy nodded.

Hopper got the song underway. Some of the girls at the next table joined in enthusiastically. "Hallelujah," they all screamed, waving their hands in the air. One of them eyed up Alan and Max, winking at both of them.

301

"You're in there, mate," Alan laughed.

"She's not really my type," Max grinned. She was small and buxom, with an unruly mane of dyed-blonde curly hair. Her black dress was stretched precariously over her ample breasts, which threatened to escape at every shimmy.

When Conor came back with the desserts they had just finished a lively version of 'La Bamba', accompanied by Hopper on the spoons and Lucy and Eugene on the 'drums' – tapping the wine glasses, salt and pepper pots and anything else they could find that would make a noise with their 'drumstick' knives.

"Can you sing?" Hopper asked him.

"I guess so," he said.

"Give us a tune so," Eugene said.

"OK. Give me one minute."

"Come back," Hopper shouted at his back. "We didn't mean to scare you away. Lucy wants –"

Lucy clamped her hand firmly over Hopper's mouth. "Stop! Leave the poor guy alone."

He came back a few minutes later brandishing a guitar. "Tina, the owner said I could take a few minutes off. So what's your poison?" He pulled the guitar's shoulder strap over his head and began to strum a few chords. "How about David Gray?"

"Brilliant!" said Eugene. "Do you know 'Babylon'?"

"Sure do," Conor played the opening bars.

"He's really good," Lucy whispered to Hopper.

As he began to sing everyone listened in awe. His voice was strong and it had a husky, Tom Waits edge.

As he finished Eugene started to cheer. "Good on you, man! More!"

"I'd love to. But I have to get back to work. Sorry. Maybe later."

"We'll hold you to that," said Eugene. "Would you mind if we borrowed your guitar?"

"Not at all," he replied, taking the shoulder strap off and handing it to Eugene.

"It's not for me, man," Eugene said. "It's for Rowie."

* * *

"I can't believe they let us stay in the restaurant so late," said Lucy. She was slumped in front of the fireplace on the sofa. Alan was re-kindling the fire in front of her.

"Amazing, isn't it," he said. "There's no way you could do that in Dublin. Or sing all night."

"I don't know," said Max. "Remember that St Patrick's night at Ralph's in Donnybrook – we were singing then."

"And at PD's in Dalkey," said Lucy. "I remember a particularly brutal rendition of 'Bohemian Rhapsody' by Eugene."

"I don't remember that," Eugene said.

"I'm not surprised," she laughed. "You'd polished off more jugs of the house wine than the rest of us put together."

"Must have been thirsty, man."

"You're always thirsty," Rowie smiled. She stretched her arms over her head and yawned. "My throat is sore from singing. But I had a wonderful night. Thank you all so much for inviting us down here."

"You're more than welcome," said Lucy stifling a yawn. "Now you have me yawning, Rowie."

"Sorry," said Rowie. She looked at her watch. "It is nearly two, I suppose. I might go to bed."

"It's only early," Eugene complained.

"Come on, young man," Rowie stood up. "Goodnight, everyone. Don't wake us up till at least lunchtime."

"No fear," said Alan. "I might call it a night too." He stretched his arms over his head. "I'm wrecked. Hopper, bedtime."

"OK, boss."

A few minutes later Max looked over at Lucy. She was curled up on the sofa, her head on a cushion and her eyes closed. Everyone else had gone to bed. He sat and watched her. Her hair was tumbling over her face and her breathing was rhythmical and slow. He went upstairs, fetched a blanket and placed it over her.

He leant over and kissed her gently on the cheek. "Goodnight, Lucy," he whispered.

Lucy listened to him climbing up the wooden stairs. She pulled the blanket around herself tightly, opened her eyes and stared at the fire.

27

"Where did you learn to play the guitar?" Hopper asked Rowie. It was just after midday and they were all sitting at the kitchen table in recovery, except for Lucy, who was upstairs taking a shower.

"In school," said Rowie. She licked her buttery fingers. "I still play quite a lot. I even brought my guitar this weekend just in case. It's in the boot of the car."

"You're very good," said Hopper. "You'll have to play for us again."

"Of course. I'd like that. Does anyone want the last piece of toast?" She held out the plate.

"Fire ahead. I'll make some more," Alan said, standing up. "I'm sure Lucy would like some."

"If there are no other takers," said Rowie. She took the toast off the plate and smothered it in butter.

"I might walk down to the shop and get the papers before I go and collect Daria," said Max.

"Good idea," said Rowie. "Can I come with you?"

"Please do," Max smiled. They grabbed jackets and Max pulled the door behind them with a sharp bang.

"I think I'll have a little rest," Eugene said lazily. He loped towards the sofa and lay down, his long legs dangling over the end.

"Hi, Eugene," said Lucy a few minutes later. Her hair was damp and she was rubbing it gently with a towel.

"Hi, Sis. How did you sleep? I hear you conked out on the sofa."

"I know. It was comfortable enough though. And the fire kept me nice and warm. It was still glowing this morning." She sat down on the armchair. "My head isn't the best."

"Mine's not too bad," said Eugene.

"I must be getting old."

"Would you like some toast, Lucy?" Alan called over from the kitchen area.

"Love some." She sat down at the table and helped herself, slathering it with butter and jam. She poured herself some tea from the pot and sat back. "That's better. I'll be human again in no time. Where are Max and Rowie?"

"Gone to get the papers," said Hopper. "They'll be back in a minute."

"So what's the plan for today?" asked Lucy.

"Plan?" Hopper smiled. "I'm going to do absolutely nothing all afternoon. If the sun comes out I'm heading outside with a rug and some cushions, otherwise that sofa over there is mine. I have three magazines and the new Tina O'Reilly to read and I'm not moving till I've finished them all."

"Sounds good," Lucy grinned. "I think I may have to join you."

"Girls," Alan said, "there's a lot of beautiful countryside to be explored. You can't just waste your day like that."

"Just watch us," Hopper smiled.

Max sat in his car and read *Ireland on Sunday*. He was supposed to be keeping an eye out for Daria but a piece in the social diary had caught his attention. *Leading sailor and Patagonia model, Mossy O'Keefe, has just been offered the deal of a lifetime – with Panther Sails. Mossy will be the new face of Panther Offshore Wear, and will feature in their famous nude sailing calendar which is published every Christmas. Mossy is delighted with the deal, which will make him a rich man. Asked what he was going to do with the money he said he was going to buy his girlfriend, Paula, a ring. Mossy O'Keefe settling down? Watch this space.*

There was a rap on his window and he looked up. It was Daria. Damn, he thought to himself. He'd meant to get out of the car and meet the train but he'd been too busy reading the paper to notice what time it was. He jumped out of the car.

"Hi," he kissed her on the cheek. "How was the trip?"

"Not too bad," she smiled.

"Here, let me take that." Max put her bag in the boot and opened the passenger door for her.

"What a gentleman," she said, stepping into the car. "How far is it to Baltimore?"

"About 60 miles or so," he said. "We should be down there by about three."

"What did you get up to yesterday?"

"Nothing much." He indicated left onto the West Cork road. "We had dinner out last night which got a bit rowdy."

"Rowdy?"

He smiled. "We were singing in the restaurant till all hours."

"Sounds like fun."

"And Lucy's cooking tonight."

Daria was silent.

"Or we could go out, just the two of us," he suggested.

"No, that's fine," she said. "Lucy's OK about me coming down, isn't she?"

"Of course. We've already been over this."

"I know, I just feel –"

"Honestly, it's not a problem. Just drop it."

Daria looked out the window. This wasn't exactly going as planned. And her guilty feelings weren't exactly helping either. Maybe she should just come clean. "You're right," she said trying to smile. "It's no big deal. So tell me about Baltimore. What's it like?"

"They're here," Lucy said jumping to her feet. Herself, Rowie and Hopper had been languishing on a double duvet in the garden of the cottage, enjoying the sun which had come out with a vengeance. Lucy's cheeks were looking decidedly pink and she'd pulled a flowery cotton sunhat over her head to stop them getting worse. Rowie's factor 8 sun cream didn't seem to be making any difference, but seeing that she was the only one who had remembered it at all Lucy could hardly complain.

"Calm down," Hopper sighed. "It's only Max and Daria."

Rowie shielded her eyes from the sun with her hand. "Pretty," she said decisively. "I remember her now." She looked over at Lucy.

"Yes," Lucy said. "If you like that sort of thing."

"Meow," Hopper said, scratching the air with her fingers. "Easy, girl."

"Sorry, it just slipped out."

"Hi, guys," Max said from the car as he pulled up beside them. He got out, followed by Daria.

Lucy immediately kissed her on both cheeks with loud lip-smacking sounds. "Lovely to see you."

Daria seemed a little overwhelmed. "Oh, yes, you too."

"This is Rowie, Eugene's girlfriend," Lucy said, nodding towards Rowie.

"I've met Rowie before – in the pub after *Strike a Match*, remember?"

"Yes," Lucy said, "sorry."

Rowie looked up at Daria and smiled. "Hello again."

"And you know Hopper," Lucy continued.

"Yes, of course. You look very relaxed, Hopper. Enjoying the sun?"

"Too right! Why don't you join us?"

Daria looked at Max. "I'm not sure –"

"That's fine," he assured her. "I'll go and find the lads. Where are they?" He looked around. "Are they in the house?"

"Where do you think?" Lucy laughed.

"The pub?"

"Bingo!"

"But it's lovely out," Max protested.

"I'm sure they're sitting outside, Max," Rowie said. "We'll look after Daria, don't you worry."

As Max walked down the road towards the pub he began to feel a little guilty. Maybe he should have stayed with Daria. But she seemed to be happy enough to stay with the girls. Anyway, he reasoned, I'll see her later.

Daria was fuming. How dare Max leave her on her own like that? They'd only just arrived and he was gallivanting off to meet 'the lads' in the pub. She was only in Baltimore for two days for heaven's sake, the least he could do was spend some time with her. She pulled her black trousers out of her bag, hung them up and sat down on the bed. What was she going to do? She sighed. She thought that now they were away from Dublin that they might have a chance to talk, really talk. But maybe Owen was right after all.

"Did you find your room?" Lucy asked as Daria come down the stairs. She was pouring herself a glass of water in the kitchen.

"Yes, thanks," said Daria.

"It's great you could make it down for a few days. I know you're really busy what with the play and everything."

"It's great that *Emma* is still running but it does mean that my days are not really my own. Still, I shouldn't complain."

"What happens tonight when you're not there?"

"Audrey's taking my place," Daria explained. "She's my understudy. I begged Owen for a day off and he gave it to me."

"And tomorrow?"

"Luckily we don't open on Mondays."

"So you're here till Tuesday then?"

"That's right."

"Isn't that great!" Lucy beamed a little too widely.

Daria looked at her. "Look, I've never had a proper chance to talk to you. I'm sorry about that whole business on the beach, I never meant to keep it –"

"It's fine, honestly," Lucy interrupted. "All forgotten. Would you like something to drink? Water or orange juice? Or I think there's Ribena somewhere."

"Water would be great, thanks," Daria said. "Can I ask you something?"

"Sure," Lucy said, pouring a second glass from the Evian bottle.

"It's about Max."

Lucy put the bottle back in the fridge and turned around. "Yes?"

"I'm finding it really difficult to talk to him at the moment. Is there anything bothering him?"

Lucy looked at her carefully. "I don't think so. Maybe you should try asking him."

"Of course. I'm sorry. It's just – forget it."

"No, go on."

"It's nothing. Forget it."

"Daria, Max keeps a lot of things to himself, that's all, I wouldn't worry too much about it. It's just his way. You'll get used to it. To be honest, I feel a little uncomfortable talking about him like this."

Daria's face coloured. "Sorry. You're right. I shouldn't have said anything."

"Let's go outside and join the others," Lucy said kindly.

Hopper was on the phone as they walked outside. "I'll just check with Lucy and Daria," she said as she saw them approach. "The guys want to know if we want to join them for a wee stroll."

"Good idea," said Lucy. "They're probably half-cut by now anyway. Hang on a sec," she looked at her watch. "You guys better go on without me. I have to go to Skibbereen and buy the food for tonight or no one will get any dinner."

"I'll come with you if you like," Hopper offered. "It'll get me out of mountain climbing."

"Great," Lucy smiled. "Do you think Alan would let you take his car? Max's is an embarrassment." She looked at Daria. "Sorry."

"Don't worry," said Daria. "I agree with you. It's a disgrace. There's so much junk in it that anyone would think he was running a permanent car-boot sale from it."

"I'm sure he won't mind," said Hopper. "We'll walk down to the pub and get the keys off him."

"Do I have to move?" Rowie groaned. She was lying on her back on the duvet. "I'm so comfortable."

"Stay here if you like, Rowie," said Lucy. "I'll send Eugene back up to keep you company. I doubt if he'll mind missing out on a walk."

"No, let him go with the others,' Rowie smiled without opening her eyes. "I'm going back to sleep now. I'd like some peace and quiet."

Hopper laughed. "A woman after my own heart."

"Would you look at my face!" Lucy exclaimed as they got back into the car in Skibbereen. "I look like a beetroot."

Hopper glanced over. "You look fine, very healthy. Anyway, I have some green cover-stick in my make-up bag back at the cottage – that'll do the trick."

Lucy sighed. "Me and my Irish skin. I always get burned."

"Is it sore?"

"Not really. It feels a little tight, that's all."

"Well then," Hopper reasoned, "stop complaining. We're lucky to have any sun at all. Have you got everything you need?"

"I think so. Hang on a second. I'd better check my list." She pulled out a scribbled-on envelope and scanned it. "Oops, I forgot the Parmesan and they won't have that in Baltimore. Give me one second." She opened the car door, ignoring Hopper's sighs. When she got back in, after finding and paying for the cheese, Hopper was singing along to an old Abba tape.

"Check your list again," Hopper commanded.

"But –"

Hopper glared at her.

"OK, OK." Lucy read it through one more time. "I have everything, I promise."

311

"If I get halfway to Baltimore and have to turn around I'll kill you, you know that?" Hopper threatened.

"Yes, yes." As they pulled out of the car park Lucy realised that she'd forgotten the olive oil. She prayed that there was some in the Baltimore shop or else she was in big trouble. She didn't have the guts to ask Hopper to go back. She text-messaged Max – *Get large bottle of olive oil urgently. Hope u r enjoying walk!*

"Max," said Daria, "is there anything wrong?"

"No, why would there be?"

"No reason, you've been very quiet the last few hours, that's all."

"Sorry, I've got a few things on my mind." Lucy and the situation with her dad was bothering him. He wanted to help her but she was so damn stubborn. She'd hate him to tell Daria anything about it.

"Like what?" she asked cautiously. Talking to him at the moment was like getting blood out of a stone.

"Work things. Nothing important." He looked out towards the sea. "There's a great view from up here, isn't there?"

"Yes," she agreed. There was an angry knot beginning to form in her stomach. Max was being infuriating.

"Have you been to West Cork before?" he said.

"Stop it, Max!" she said sharply.

"Stop what?"

"It's always the same, I try to talk to you and you change the subject."

"No, I don't."

"You do. You know you do."

"I'm not going to argue with you. So go on, talk to me. What do you want to say?"

"I'm not sure."

"Right," he said, standing up.

"Give me a minute. Don't be so bloody impatient."

"I'm not being impatient. I'm just trying to have a nice relaxed afternoon with my girlfriend. What's wrong with that? Excuse me if I don't want to get all heavy, OK. It's not my style."

Daria looked at him for a minute. "Maybe it's not." She sat down again. "Listen, I don't think this is working out. I'm not happy. You're not happy –"

"But I am happy," he said. "What makes you think I'm not?"

"I don't know. I just think that you're feeling –"

"Don't try to tell me how I'm feeling."

Daria sighed heavily. "I think I know what's going on here, and you don't have to do it."

"Do what? What am I doing?"

Daria shook her head. "Men! You're all the bloody same." She began to walk quickly away from him.

Max stared out at the sea for a second. What the hell was happening here? "Wait!" he shouted after her. "I'm sorry! Wait!"

"What's going on over there, do you think?" Eugene asked Alan. He'd decided to go on the walk after all as Rowie wanted to sleep. Although he'd never admit it to anyone, he was quite into walking in the countryside. They watched as Max ran after Daria and tried to give her a hug. She pushed him away at first, but then gave in and let him.

"Eugene," Alan said, "I thought you were looking for seals. Leave them alone."

"OK," Eugene said reluctantly, dragging his eyes away. "But will you ask Max later?"

"You're as bad as Hopper!" Alan smiled.

"I understand what you're saying but I'm not trying to push you away, honestly," said Max. "I'm mad about you. Can't you tell?" He tried to kiss Daria on the lips but she turned her head away from his.

"I want to go back," she said, "I could do with a drink."

"Don't leave it like this," Max pleaded. "Come here." He brushed her hair back from her face and smiled. "I'm sorry if I've been a bit

313

preoccupied. And it's nothing to do with you, honestly. Trust me. We're on our holidays. Let's enjoy ourselves."

"OK," Daria said. She kissed him on the cheek. "I'm sorry."

"I'm sorry too."

"We'd better find Alan and Eugene. They'll be wondering where we've got to."

"I'm really glad you're here," Max said. "Honestly."

Daria nodded. Why were things always so difficult?

"How was your walk?" Lucy asked as Alan and Eugene trooped into the cottage.

"Great," Eugene enthused. "We saw some seals just off Sherkin Island."

"I'm knackered," Alan said collapsing onto a kitchen chair.

"Where are the others?" asked Hopper.

"They stopped in the shop," said Alan. "Didn't you ask Max to get olive oil or something?"

Hopper looked over at Lucy who was chopping fresh herbs with vigour. "Lucy?"

Lucy looked up. "I was too scared to ask you to go back."

"Jeez," Hopper laughed, "am I that bad?"

Lucy didn't answer.

"So what are you making?" asked Eugene. The cooking smells were making him hungry.

"Mussels to start with," said Lucy, "then Ballymaloe hot buttered lobster."

"Not Jamie Oliver's lobster, then?" Hopper smiled.

"No," Lucy smiled, "I thought, seeing as we're in Cork, I'd use a Cork recipe. It's one of Darina Allen's."

"Sounds good to me," said Eugene. "Can I help?"

Lucy looked at him suspiciously. Rowie was certainly having a good influence on her baby brother. "No, thanks – but you can do the washing-up."

"*No problemo*," he said. He poked at a mussel with his index finger.

"How can you tell if they're fresh? I don't want to be barfing up all night."

"Eugene!" Lucy swatted his hand with a tea towel. "That's not nice. I don't want any of that kind of talk in my kitchen."

"I was only asking!"

"You only cook the ones that are closed, Eugene," said Rowie. "And if they open when they're cooked it means they're fresh. And I'm sure they're straight off the fishing boats so you don't need to worry."

Eugene grinned at Rowie. She was so intelligent.

"Take him away and keep him occupied, will you, Rowie?" said Lucy. "He'll get under my feet otherwise."

"I'm not a child or a dog," Eugene complained. "I don't get under people's feet."

Rowie smiled at Lucy knowingly. "Let's have a game of Twister, Eugene." Rowie spied the box on top of the mantelpiece. "I'm sure Max and Daria will join us when they get back. We'll bring it outside onto the grass."

"OK." He bounded out the door with the box. "I'll go and set it up."

"Thanks," Lucy mouthed to Rowie.

"*No problemo,*" Rowie laughed, imitating Eugene.

"I'll wash the mussels for you," said Alan. "Are you making a sauce for them?"

"No, I thought I'd just cook them in white wine with garlic, and throw in some cream and butter," said Lucy. "And serve them with garlic bread with melted Parmesan. Keep it simple."

"Sounds delicious," said Hopper. "Can I help with anything?"

Lucy nodded. "You could make the garlic bread. There's a bowl on the table and a wooden spoon in there." Lucy pointed at a drawer.

Hopper pulled out a wooden spoon. "What now, boss?"

"Throw the butter in the bowl and a couple of cloves of garlic."

Hopper peeled the wafer-thin purple skin off two garlic cloves and put them in the bowl on top of the butter. "What next?" she asked

Lucy who was extracting the meat from the lobster with a sharp knife and a teaspoon.

Lucy looked in the bowl and tried not to laugh. "You have to crush the garlic cloves, Hopper. And by a couple, I really meant three or four."

"Right," Hopper said unabashed. "Then what?"

Lucy put the knife and spoon down and wiped her hands on her apron. "Tell you what. I'll put the ingredients in the bowl and you can do the hard part."

"Which is?"

"The mixing and the bread-buttering."

"OK by me," said Hopper .

Alan smiled to himself as he pulled the hairy 'beards' off the mussels and scraped off the barnacles. Hopper was a disaster in the kitchen but he loved her anyway.

Lucy ground some black pepper into the bowl, added a large tablespoon of freshly chopped herbs, some lemon juice and a pinch of salt. "Now add the garlic and mix it all up," she told Hopper.

Hopper squeezed the garlic cloves through the garlic press and scraped the pulp into the bowl with a knife. Hey, she thought to herself, this is fun. I could do this. As she stirred the garlic-butter mixture, most of the lemon juice splashed onto the table. She looked up. Lucy wasn't watching. She grabbed the lemon half from beside her, and squirted some more into the bowl. This cooking lark wasn't as easy as it looked.

"How are my naked chefs?" Max asked as he came in the front door.

"Excuse me?" Alan asked. Hopper also looked confused.

Lucy smiled over at him. "I don't think they get it. Jamie Oliver is called 'The Naked Chef'. It was a joke."

"I see," Alan said. "Stick to the kites, mate."

Max laughed. "You're probably right. I just came in to see if I could help."

"No," said Lucy, "we're fine. Go back outside and help Rowie keep Eugene entertained."

"What are you cooking?" he asked. "Are those mussels in the sink?"

"They are," she said, "and I'm preparing the lobster."

"Lobster!" Max grinned. "My favourite. When will it be ready?" He walked towards Lucy, his mouth already watering.

"Outside!" Lucy laughed. "Don't be bothering the cooks."

"Tell you what. Give me a yell when you're finished with the table and I'll set it for you."

"Deal," said Lucy. "Now scat!"

28

"That was one of the best meals I've ever had," Eugene said, sitting back and rubbing his stomach. "I'm stuffed."

"It was delicious," Rowie agreed. "You're an amazing cook, Lucy."

"Thanks," said Lucy. "Does anyone want more chocolate mousse?"

"Yes, please," Hopper said holding out her bowl.

"I should have known," Lucy smiled. "Anyone else?"

"I couldn't eat another thing," Daria smiled.

Alan and Max shook their heads.

"Boys," Lucy laughed, "you disappoint me. And I even bought some West Cork cheese for you to try."

"Cheese?" asked Max. "What sort of cheese?"

"Smoked Gubbeen and Clonakilty Blue – can I tempt you?"

"Maybe just a taste," said Alan. "We wouldn't like to be rude."

Lucy laughed. "God forbid!"

"Where did you learn to cook, Lucy?" Rowie asked.

"Nowhere really. I pick it up as I go along. I love cookery programmes and cookery books."

"And cooks," Max added.

Lucy smiled. "Just Jamie Oliver. Not *all* cooks."

Alan squeezed Hopper's hand tightly under the table. "No," he mouthed.

Damn, Hopper thought to herself, he can read my mind. She was about to mention Dan but Alan had cut her off at the pass. "Rowie, why don't you get your guitar?" she said instead. "I'd love to hear you play again."

Rowie looked around the table. "If no one minds."

"'Course not," Lucy grinned. "We'd love you to."

"But Alan and Max are still eating," Rowie said.

"They'll be eating all night," said Lucy, looking at Max cramming as much cheese as he could onto a cracker. "They'll have the port out next."

"Great idea!" Eugene said. "I'll get it."

"Now we're in trouble," Hopper laughed.

"How about 'Brown-Eyed Girl'?" Max suggested when Rowie had settled herself back at the table. Alan and Lucy had cleared away most of the plates and Hopper was topping up wine glasses like it was going out of fashion.

Rowie began to play and Max glanced over at Daria. She seemed to be enjoying herself. She wasn't singing along like the others but she was watching Rowie and swaying to the music. Lucy, on the other hand, was singing her little heart out.

"Come on, Max," Lucy said, catching his eye. "Join in."

He smiled at her and launched into the chorus.

A little later Max realised that Daria had been missing for a while. He presumed she'd gone upstairs to the toilet but that was at least twenty minutes ago. He'd been so caught up in the music he hadn't noticed. Rowie was now making her way through all the U2 songs she knew, helped by Alan who was a huge U2 fan and knew all the lyrics backwards. Lucy and Hopper were humming along. Eugene, true to form, had fallen asleep on the sofa.

He went upstairs and knocked gently on the toilet door. "Daria? Are you in there?"

He jumped as a hand touched his back. He turned around quickly. It was Daria.

"Are you all right? I was worried about you."

"I'm fine. I just had to make a phone call."

"A phone call? It's nearly one in the morning! Who were you ringing?"

"My sister."

"Are you coming back downstairs?"

"I don't think so. I'm really tired. I might just go to bed."

"You'll never sleep with the noise downstairs." Max smiled suggestively. "Maybe I should join you."

"No," Daria said quickly, "you go downstairs. I'll be fine, honestly."

"If you're sure."

Daria nodded.

"I'll be up soon." He kissed her, his hands caressing her buttocks.

"Max!" she said pushing him away. "Go!"

Max stood in the hallway for several minutes after she had closed the bedroom door practically in his face. And she said there was something wrong with *him*. Women! He began to feel very alone. He opened the door and looked in at her. She was already in bed, her back turned towards him. Feck her, he thought. I'm going downstairs to enjoy myself.

"How was your quickie?" Hopper called to him as he walked down the stairs.

Max glared at her.

"Oops, sorry. Trouble in paradise, Max?"

"Hopper!" Alan said. "I'm sorry. She's had too much to drink."

"What's new?" said Max, walking towards the table and pouring himself a large glass of wine.

"Dat's unfair," said Hopper.

"You never know when to stop. That's your problem."

"And we all know your problem," she said. "You're with the wrong –"

"Hopper, I'm taking you to bed," Alan said sternly.

"Promises, promises," Hopper laughed, swinging her wine glass precariously in her hand. Luckily she had drained every last drop.

Alan put his arm around her and pulled her onto her feet. "Come on. If you're good I'll tell you a bedtime story."

"About Princess Hopper and Prince Alan and his truncheon of love?"

Alan blushed furiously. "Move!"

As soon as they had left, Rowie started playing some Tracy Chapman to calm the mood.

Lucy went over to Max. She was more than a little drunk herself but she wanted to help.

"Pay no attention to Hopper," she said, putting her hand on his shoulder. "You know what she's like."

"I know," he sighed. "I shouldn't have let her get to me like that. I'll go up and apologise."

"There's no need. She'll have forgotten all about it in the morning. Are you all right?"

Max shrugged. "Not really."

"What's up?"

"Nothing."

"This is me you're talking to," Lucy said gently.

"Can we go somewhere else?"

"Sure. Grab a bottle of wine and we'll go into my room. Rowie, we'll see you in a little while."

"No problem," Rowie said strumming her guitar gently. "I'm going to put Eugene to bed now anyway. I'll catch you in the morning."

"So, tell me," said Lucy. Max sat down beside her on the bed. She hadn't bothered with the lights as a full moon was shining through the window, illuminating the room with its waxy glow.

"It's Daria. I think it's over."

"Why do you say that?" Lucy asked gently.

"I just know."

"Have you talked to her about it?"

"No," he sighed, "that's just it. We don't seem to be able to talk to each other. We never have."

Lucy stayed quiet, allowing him to speak.

"It's not like you and me. I wish it was."

"I know. But I'm always here for you. OK?"

Max turned towards her and hugged her. "I love you. You know that, don't you?"

"Yes. Of course I do. You're my best friend."

He stroked the back of her head. "You're great. I love you."

"And you're drunk," she said, pulling back. "You should go to bed."

"I will," he smiled "in a minute." He leant forward and kissed her firmly on the lips.

"Max!" she said jumping back. "What are you doing?"

Max had had quite enough rejection for one day. He stood up. "Sorry," he murmured. "I'll go now."

"Wait!" She watched him walk out the door. "Wait," she whispered.

"About last night –" Daria said to Max the following morning as soon as he'd woken up.

"Yes?" Max sat up.

"I'm sorry, that's all."

"OK," Max reached over to the floor, grabbed a T-shirt and pulled it over his head.

"Where are you going?"

"Downstairs. I'll be back in a minute."

"Lucy?" Max said creeping into her room.

"Um?" she murmured opening her eyes and looking up. Max was looking dishevelled, his eyes were bloodshot and his face looked pale.

"About last night –" he said.

"It's forgotten," she said. "Don't worry about it. You were drunk. Now let me go back to sleep."

Max left the room and went straight to the bathroom. As warm needles of water struck his skin he tried to block everything out of his head. He tilted towards the showerhead and allowed the water to cascade down his face. He prayed for wind. He needed to blow away the cobwebs this morning, that was for sure.

Lucy tried to go back to sleep after Max had left but couldn't. She lay in her room, staring at the ceiling, thinking about the previous night. He'd been drunk many times before but he'd never kissed her – not like that.

"Here we are," Max smiled widely. "Inchydoney Beach. What do you think?"

"Wow!" said Lucy.

"Amazing!" Alan whistled.

"Beautiful," Daria smiled.

Hopper, for once, was speechless.

They all gazed at the beach in awe. The golden sand stretched out in front of them, the sea glimmering in the brilliant sunlight. A stiff sea breeze was lifting the coloured flags on the hillside and creating a choppy white surf on the water.

"Look!" Max pointed at the water. "Surfers."

And sure enough, wet-suit-clad surfers were negotiating the waves with practised ease.

"This is paradise," Lucy grinned. She couldn't wait to get down onto the sand. "Open the boot, Max and I'll grab the kites."

He unlocked the boot and handed her two large kite-bags. "You take the two tens for yourself and Alan and I'll take the two eights to stack together." He looked at Daria. "And a six for Daria."

Daria wasn't impressed. "I can handle a ten if Lucy can."

"Are you sure?" He looked up at the flags on the hillside. "It's pretty windy. I don't think –"

"Positive." She held out her hand.

He passed her a large kite-bag and she took it and began to walk down the steep steps towards the beach.

Lucy looked at Max. He raised his eyebrows at her. He still felt a little awkward with Lucy after the previous night's events. He'd studiously avoided mentioning it all morning and was trying to act as 'normal' as possible. But there was definitely a slight atmosphere. Max wondered if Daria suspected anything.

Lucy wondered if Max remembered kissing her. He was acting as if nothing had happened. Well, if that was how he wanted to play it, she'd play along too.

"She'll be fine," Lucy assured him. "She's had lots of practice on Sandymount Beach after all."

"Are you being smart?" he asked.

"No!"

"Actually, myself and Hopper were thinking of taking a dip," Alan said. "Can I do a bit of body dragging later with the kite? The six will do fine."

Max nodded. "Sure, but try not to dump it in the sea. They're a bitch to get back up when they're wet and sandy."

"I'll do my best," Alan smiled.

"You guys fire ahead," Hopper said to Max and Lucy. "I can see you're itching to get onto the beach and it'll take us a few minutes to get changed. Daria's almost ready to launch, I think."

Daria was laying out the kite lines on the sand and staring up at them from the beach, her hand shading her eyes from the strong sun.

"I think she's looking for you, Max," Lucy said.

"Lock the car up for me, Lucy," Max said handing her the keys. He headed down the steps to join Daria.

"Why don't you join us for a dip?" Hopper asked Lucy.

Lucy shivered involuntarily. "No, thanks. It may be sunny but it's still Ireland. The water will be bloody freezing. It's a pity Eugene's not here. He would have gone in."

"Maybe Rowie would have joined him," Alan grinned.

Hopper elbowed him in the ribs. "In that case, I'm glad she dragged Eugene off to Schull for the day. Saved herself from some pathetic male drooling."

Lucy waited as Alan and Hopper finished changing into their

trunks and tankini beside their own car. She lathered her arms, legs and face with factor 30 sun cream and plonked a white and green Quicksilver sunhat on her head. There was no way she was getting burnt today. The others were fine – they all had darker skin, but she'd been blessed with milk-bottle white and she wasn't taking any chances. Her nose had already started peeling from the previous day in the garden.

"No-Bo-Derek style beach antics, you two," Lucy said as they all walked together down the steps towards the beach.

"As if," Hopper laughed.

Lucy nodded at Max. He lifted the long, rectangular black and pink kite above his head and threw it into the air. The wind caught it and immediately Lucy felt a strong tug on her wrists as the lines went taut. She pulled on the right-hand line, sending the kite soaring to the right, then took her hands parallel, lifting the kite higher in the sky. She smiled to herself as she watched it ascend.

"Looking good," Max said, appearing beside her.

"How's Daria getting on?" she asked. She kept her eyes fixed on the kite.

"OK. She managed to fly the other ten for a few minutes but she pulled something in her left shoulder so she's having a break."

"Where is she?"

"She's gone up to the hotel to get a drink and to read the paper. She said she needs a rest."

"Should you not go up and keep her company?"

"I did offer," he said, "but she told me to stay down here."

Lucy's kite almost hit the sand but she managed to catch it in time and pulled it back up into the sky. "You're distracting me. Why don't you get your own kites in the air?"

"OK, OK. I know when I'm not wanted."

"Too right! Now scoot!"

Max attached the two blue eight-foot kites together with stacking lines. He then walked away from the kites, unravelling the lines as he went along. Standing facing them with his padded holders on, he pulled the lines taught and flicked his wrists expertly upwards and over his head. The kites rose into the air effortlessly.

"Yes!" he shouted as the wind caught the kites and lifted them higher and higher.

Lucy looked over. Max's body was straining to hold the double-load that the two kites produced. As she watched, he jumped in the air, using the power of the kites to lift him several feet off the ground. She was impressed. She'd forgotten just how good he was. She pulled her own arms parallel and let the kite hover in the air as she continued to watch him. He was being dragged along the sand by the kite, leaving deep heel-tracks gouged out behind him. From the huge grin plastered across his face, she could see that he was loving every minute of it.

Suddenly there was a sharp pull on her lines and her kite crashed to the ground. Max had wrapped his lines around hers and grounded her.

"Sorry!" he yelled over. "This baby has a mind of its own. I'll put it down and we can untangle the lines." He pulled his own lines in and brought the stacked kites onto the sand with a muffled 'whack'.

Lucy smiled over. "Don't worry. My arms are killing me. I'm going to take some time out." She massaged her upper arms through her T-shirt. After a few minutes of muscle-kneading, she gathered up the kite and lines and sat down on the sand. It felt warm against her skin, and she dug her toes under the grains, finding dark, damper sand underneath.

A few minutes later he joined her. He'd pulled off his T-shirt and beads of sweat were glistening on his forehead and his chest. "Hot work," he grinned. He balanced his sunglasses on top of his head and wiped his forehead and eye sockets with his T-shirt.

"Can you see Hopper and Alan?" he asked, putting his sunglasses back on and looking towards the sea.

"Over there," Lucy pointed. Hopper was sitting in the shallow water while Alan ran backwards and forwards in front of her waving his arms like a pantomime dame.

"What is Alan doing?"

Lucy laughed. "Who knows?"

"Who's Hopper talking to now?"

Lucy took her glasses off to get a better look. The tall man in the shortie wet suit looked very familiar.

Max jumped up. "It's Dan. And he has my kite with him – I can see it on the sand. Come on."

"Relax," she said to his disappearing back. She got up and brushed the sand from the seat of her shorts. Feck, she thought to herself. I'll have to go over or it will look really rude. Dan Rowan was the last person she wanted to see after the whole Sandymount Beach debacle.

"Lucy," Hopper said as she approached the group, "look who it is! Dan! Isn't that a coincidence?"

"Hi, Dan." Lucy was glad of her sunglasses and hat, which allowed her some degree of cover.

"Hello, stranger. I was just telling everyone about my cousin's wedding last night in Clonakilty – it was wild."

"Is that why you're down here?" Lucy asked.

He nodded. "I've surfed on this beach before a couple of times. Going surfing got me out of the family lunch today."

Max laughed. "Good man. And how's the kite? Have you used it yet?"

"Sure. I've been going to Skerries as much as I can. There are a couple of semi-pros based there who've been teaching me the ropes. I'm totally addicted now. And they're really impressed with your kite, Max. I think you may have one or two new customers next season."

"Excellent!" Max grinned, rubbing his hands together. "Bring them on."

"So when can we see you in action?" Hopper asked.

"Right now," said Dan. "I'm about to launch." He gestured towards the large white and yellow kite which was resting on the sand at the edge of water. Its leading edge was inflated and it reminded Lucy of Batman's wings with its scalloped edges and bat-like canopy. "But don't expect too much. I'm only a beginner." He walked over towards the kite and attached the short surfboard beside it to his leg with a Velcro strip. He then hooked the kite-line boom to the metal hook on his waist-harness.

"The lines are quite thick," Lucy said to Max.

"Have to be. The kite's so powerful they'd snap if they were any thinner. They're Dyneema."

Dan waded out into the water and faced towards the kite on the beach.

"Why is he facing that way?" Alan asked.

"The wind has to be behind him to fly the kite properly," Lucy explained.

"And it's safer," Max added. "The onshore breeze means he won't be pulled out to sea. He'll use the kite to pull him across the surf in zigzags."

They all watched as Dan sat in the water. He leant back, making the kite lines taut with the weight of his body and eased his feet into the foot straps on the surfboard. With both hands on the kite-line boom he launched the kite overhead and with a surge of power was pulled along on the surfboard.

"Wow!" Max whistled as he watched his kite soaring through the sky.

"That's amazing," Hopper said as she and the others watched Dan. "He looks great in the wetsuit, too. What'da think, Lucy?" She looked over at her friend. "Shouldn't have let him get away – he was nuts about you."

Max looked at Lucy with interest. She'd never said anything about herself and Dan. Why not? Was she blushing or was it the sun – he couldn't quite tell.

Lucy ignored Hopper. "How did you make the kite, Max? It looks pretty complicated."

"The material used is the same as for normal kites," he explained. "It just needs extra re-enforcement. It took me a while to work out how to put the latex tube in the leading edge but I rang an Irish guy who manufactures them in Southampton and he gave me some advice."

"It's very impressive, mate," Alan said. "Do you think you could make me one?"

"'Course."

Hopper began to laugh.

"What are you laughing at?" Alan said.

"Nothing."

"Go on. Tell me," Alan insisted.

"I just don't think it'd be your thing," said Hopper. "You're more of an armchair sports kind of guy."

Alan looked most perturbed. "I've surfed a few times. I lived in Australia for two years, remember?"

"I'm sure Dan would give you a go," said Max. "Ask him when he comes in."

"Not today, another time maybe. I'd need to go to the gym for a few weeks first."

Hopper began to make chicken noises. "Told you. He's all talk."

"Way to go, Alan!" Max yelled. Alan had pulled himself up on the surfboard for the second time and was managing to stay upright and fly the kite simultaneously. The last time he'd wiped out after a few seconds. "Hopper, he's great. You're in trouble now. Do you have any idea how much the kites and surfboards cost?"

"Break it to me," she said.

"You won't see much change out of three thousand euros. But I can make one for him at cost, seeing as he's a friend. So two thousand euros, I guess."

Hopper groaned. "There goes some of the house deposit. Me and my big mouth!"

"You and your big chicken noises, you mean," Lucy laughed.

"And you're sure he's never tried kite-surfing before?" Dan asked. He was sitting on the sand with them, watching Alan surf across the water in front of them.

329

"No," Max assured him. "But he's flown kites before and surfed before."

"That would help," Dan mused, "but I've never seen someone pick kite-surfing up so quickly. He's a natural."

"Don't tell *him* that," Hopper pleaded. "Please."

Dan laughed.

"Are there many people kite-surfing in Ireland?" Max asked Dan as Alan wiped out again.

"Not really. It's hard to tell, but from what the guys in Skerries tell me I'd say around four or five hundred."

"I think you're about to recruit one more," Max said as Alan took off across the surf again.

Hopper sighed.

"So that's what you're all up to," a voice came from behind them. It was Daria. "I was beginning to get worried. I couldn't see any kites on the beach except that giant one. I knew you hadn't gone without me as the cars are still here."

Max jumped up. "Sorry love. I'd forgotten all about you." As soon as the words came out of his mouth, he regretted them.

"Obviously. Listen, it looks like I'll have to go back to Dublin this evening," she said, looking at him carefully. "Something's come up."

"That's a shame," said Max. "Is everything all right?"

She nodded. "Yes, but I really need to get going. Can you drop me into Cork, Max? Do you mind?"

Max cursed inwardly. It was a beautiful day, the sun was miraculously still shining and he was itching to get back to his kites. And maybe try Dan's for himself. "Of course I don't mind. I guess I'll see you guys later in the cottage."

"I could come with you in the car if you like," Lucy said, surprising herself. Why would she want to do that? "It would give you some company on the way back."

"If you don't –" Max began.

"Thank you," Daria said, "but we have things to discuss. It was kind of you to offer."

"Fine," Lucy said, a little miffed at being so easily dismissed. "I'll just stay here and enjoy myself then. See you later, Max. Have a lovely trip, Daria. Myself and Dan have to catch up anyway. We haven't seen each other for ages, have we Dan?" She beamed at him.

"Um, no," Dan said, a little taken aback. Lucy had been practically ignoring him up until now.

"See you, Dan," said Max. "Glad the kite's going well. Maybe you'll give me a go at some stage."

"Sure," said Dan. "Anytime, give me a ring."

Daria and Max said the rest of their goodbyes and walked in silence towards the car.

"I'm sorry," Max said as he opened the car door. " I didn't mean to leave you –"

"It's fine," Daria sighed, "honestly."

"You don't sound very 'fine' about it to me."

"Leave it. We'll talk on the way to Cork."

That made Max very, very nervous.

29

On the way back from Cork Max replayed the conversation over and over in his head but he still couldn't quite make sense of it. He had understood what Daria was saying but somehow her words hadn't sunk in. It was over – he understood that much. Daria wanted to try and make a go of it with her director, Owen Hughes. Nothing had happened yet, she had assured Max, but Owen had made no secret of his feelings towards her. She was confused but the last few days had decided things for her.

"I need someone I can communicate with," she'd said, "and I just can't seem to talk to you. I'm sorry but I have tried, believe me."

"I can try harder," he'd said. "It doesn't have to be like this."

"Yes, it does," she'd said gently. "It's all for the best, honestly. It hasn't been right for a while. You're a very lovely man, Max, but you're not the right one for me. I'm so sorry."

"Is there someone else?"

That was when she'd come clean about Owen.

Max squeezed the steering-wheel hard. What an end to his holiday! The sun was still shining but he'd missed a large chunk of the day. He toyed with the idea of ringing Lucy and finding out whether they were all still on Inchydoney Beach. Lucy. That was who he needed to talk to right now. But she was probably still busy flirting with Dan Rowan.

"How was Schull?" Max asked Eugene. Eugene was lying on the sofa. The only part of him that was moving was his left foot which was stabbing the air to the dance music which was blaring from the loudspeakers. He pointed the remote controller towards the stereo and turned it down.

"Sorry?" he asked Max. "Couldn't hear you, man."

"Schull," Max repeated. "How was it?"

"Great! We walked to Mizen Head and checked out the lighthouse. And Rowie bought some books in one of the second-hand shops." He looked around. "Where are the others?"

"Still on the beach, I presume," Max said sitting down on the chair beside him. " I had to drop Daria to Cork. She had to go back early."

"Everything all right?"

Max looked at him for a second. He may as well tell him, everyone was going to know sooner or later anyway, and to be honest, he'd quite like to talk to someone about it – even if it was just Eugene. "Actually no. We broke up."

"I'm sorry. That was a bit out of the blue. You guys seemed fine."

"I know," Max sighed, "but I guess she hadn't been happy for a while. And there's another guy involved – Owen Hughes – her director."

Eugene's eyes widened.

"Nothing's happened between them. Or so she says. But I guess it will now. Maybe. I don't know." He stared into the fireplace. The fire wasn't lit but it gave him something to fix his eyes on.

"Might be for the best," Eugene said. "If she wasn't happy." He shrugged his shoulders. "Were you happy?"

Max looked at him. He hadn't really thought about it before. "I guess. Most of the time."

"Not all the time?"

"No," Max said reluctantly. "But no one's happy all the time."

Eugene shrugged his shoulders. "I am. With Rowie, I mean. She makes me happy all the time. She's a bossy old cow sometimes, but I kind of like that. It reminds me of Lucy."

Max smiled. "Lucy is bossy all right."

"No kidding." Eugene picked up the remote controller and pressed a few buttons. A more mellow, chilled-out track began to play. "If you don't mind me asking, man, how do yourself and Lucy get on? Do you fight?"

"Sometimes. We have our moments. But you know Lucy. If she's in a mood with you she tends to snap out of it pretty quickly."

Eugene nodded. "We took Jade and Aran to the zoo a while ago. She was missing you. You'd had some kind of fight, I think. She didn't say anything about it but there was an atmosphere when I mentioned your name."

"Did you enjoy the zoo?"

"Sure." Eugene leant over, picked a can off the floor and took a swig. "I'm probably way out of order here, but I know my sister. We don't always get on but I do love her. And I know she loves you. And I don't mean as a friend. You just have to give her some time."

Max looked at him in surprise. "Good one, Eugene. You nearly had me there."

"I'm serious, man. Honestly."

Max studied Eugene's face. He didn't seem to be smiling. "Really?"

"Really," Eugene nodded. "I just want to see her happy, man. And you make her happy, I know it."

Max sighed. "Eugene White, you certainly have a hidden side." He stood up. "I'm going for a walk. See you later."

"I'll come with you," Eugene said sitting up.

"Do you mind if I go on my own? I have some thinking to do."

"Where are you taking us, Dan?" Hopper complained. "I've already been stung by nettles – my leg has come up in red bumps. If I step in cow dung you're a dead man."

"Stop moaning, woman," Alan laughed.

"We're nearly there," Dan promised. "Just around the next corner and over the stream."

"I'm not getting my feet wet," Hopper said.

"You won't have to. There are lots of stepping stones. You'll be fine."

Dan was right – the wide, peat-brown stream was littered with large stones which had been smoothed and rounded by the fast-flowing water. Hopper nearly managed to land in the water regardless when she slipped on some moss, but luckily Alan was on hand to steady her.

"I can see a tower through the trees," Hopper pointed to the right. "Is that it?"

Dan nodded. "That's Castle Kane all right."

Hopper and Alan went on ahead. Dan waited for Lucy who was lagging behind. "Are you OK? You're being very quiet."

"I'm fine, thanks," she said. She was still smarting a little from Daria's rebuke on the beach. She was also a little embarrassed at her flirtatious behaviour towards Dan earlier. She hoped he hadn't taken it to heart.

He held out his hand. "I could pull you along," he offered, smiling.

Damn, Lucy thought to herself. He has.

"I'll manage." She picked up her pace.

As they walked to the right, the castle walls came into view.

"What do you think?" Dan asked.

"You weren't joking when you said it was impressive!"

The grey, ivy-clad walls were immense. The main body of the castle was still intact, but the towers and buildings surrounding it had fallen into ruin. At one end of the castle a tower soared into the sky. Lucy shaded her eyes from the sun and stared at the roof. Alan and Hopper were waving down at them.

"How did they get up there so quickly?" Lucy asked.

"I'll show you. Follow me."

He led her inside the castle. It was surprisingly light inside, the interior walls were punctuated by large, concrete-framed windows. The glass had long disappeared, leaving gaping rectangles, allowing the wind to blow straight through, from one side of the immense interior to the other. The floor was covered in concrete rubble, piled in staggered heaps against the walls and scattered in a fine dust over the entire area.

"How old is this building?" Lucy asked. "Surely they didn't have concrete until recently."

"This part was built over the original castle foundations. The rest of the buildings – the ones outside – are from the seventeenth century and earlier I think. But this bit was built in the nineteen sixties. It burnt down in the seventies and there was some problem with the insurance documents apparently. Anyway it was never rebuilt."

"What a shame. It's an amazing building."

Dan walked down the right-hand side of the huge main room. "Watch your step," he warned her. There was a gaping hole in the middle of the room. "There used to be a staircase there."

"What happened to it?"

"No idea. But the ceiling collapsed too. Look up."

There was a huge hole and Lucy could see the ceiling of the second floor though it. "Are you sure it's safe to be in here?"

Dan nodded. "I've been here several times over the years with my cousins. It's as safe as houses."

Lucy laughed.

In the far right-hand corner of the room there was a small doorway. "It's a little dark in here. It's the tower. Watch your step."

She followed him into the tower and up the surprisingly intact steps. They twisted their way upwards and soon Lucy could see daylight ahead. Dan stepped through another small doorway and she followed him.

"Hi, guys," Hopper looked up. "You found us." She and Alan were sitting on the edge of the roof, their feet dangling down over the edge. It made Lucy feel quite nervous just looking at them.

Lucy gazed in awe at the scenery from her standing position. Directly in front of them was the sea, sparkling and glistering in the early evening sun. To her left and right were undulating green and dark brown fields. She turned around. Behind her was a thick forest, pine and deciduous trees nestling against each other in a riot of greens.

"It's heavenly up here," she smiled. She sat down where she was, several yards away from the edge. Dan sat down beside her.

"Thanks for bullying us into coming here," Hopper said. "It was well worth it." She scooted herself back from the edge using her hands and stood up. "We're just going to check out the far side of the roof. Aren't we, Alan?"

"Um, yeah," Alan said uncertainly.

"Keep well away from the middle," Dan warned them. "It's weaker than the rest."

"Yes, boss," Hopper said, dragging Alan away by the hand.

"Just the two of us, then," Dan said after they'd left.

"Guess so."

Dan stared out at the sea. "It's nice to see you again."

"You too. And I'm sorry about everything."

"So am I."

There was silence for a few seconds.

"What are you doing later?" Dan asked.

"Nothing really," Lucy said. She began to pick at the skin around her thumb. "Just going to the pub or something."

"Right."

Lucy kicked herself for being so rude. "Would you like to join us?"

"Thanks, but I have to go back to Dublin this evening. I have a graduation lunch to cater for tomorrow. But thanks for asking. Maybe we could hook up when you're back?"

"Maybe. I'll give you a ring."

"I'd like that," Dan smiled. He put his hand on hers.

Lucy felt its warmth against her skin. She smiled back. Dan Rowan was a nice guy. She could do worse.

"So would I," she said.

* * *

When Lucy and the gang arrived in Read's two hours later Max was already drunk.

"How long have you been here, mate?" Alan asked.

"Couple of hours," said Max.

"On your own?" asked Lucy.

"'Sno law against it."

"Suppose not."

"Where's lover boy?" Max asked her.

"Who?"

"You know who."

"No, I don't."

"Daniel, darling."

Lucy stood up. "I'm going to the bar. Would anyone like a drink? Except Max, I think he's had enough."

"I'm going home," Max said, standing up.

"Sit down, man," said Eugene. "She's only winding you up."

"OK."

Lucy sighed. It was going to be a long evening.

"What's up with him?" Lucy asked Eugene later, nodding at Max who was now half asleep, his head lolling against the dark-red leather of the snug.

"Broke up with Daria."

"What? Poor Max. How do you know?"

"He told me earlier. He's a bit cut up about it."

Alan came over. "Myself and Hopper will take Max home. See you guys later."

"Are you sure?" Lucy asked. "I don't mind –"

"No," Hopper insisted. "You stay here with Eugene and Rowie. We'll put him to bed and come back down."

"Thanks."

"Have something to say," Max said, as Alan pulled him up and put his arm around him. "I tink Mossy and Paula's engaged."

"Really?" Lucy asked.

"'S true. Read it in the paper."

Hopper laughed. "Wonders will never cease." She glanced quickly at Alan who was grinning from ear to ear. Hopper was relieved. Maybe Paula could perform magic. She certainly seemed to have Mossy under her spell anyway.

"Good for them!" Alan exclaimed.

"Why didn't you tell us earlier, Max?" Lucy asked. "Why are you only telling us now?"

"Forgot," he said.

"The strange workings of the male mind," Hopper smiled at Lucy. "Who are we to question it? See you later."

"I hope Max is OK," Lucy said to Eugene. Rowie was standing at the bar, chatting to some local musicians.

"He'll be fine. He just needs some time to sort himself out. But what about you?"

"What about me?"

"How are you?"

"Fine," Lucy said firmly. "Just fine."

"Mum's worried about you."

"Why? She has no reason to be."

"She wants you to make your peace with D –"

"I told you, I don't want to talk about it," Lucy cut him off, "and that's final." She looked him in the eye. "Actually there is something I want to ask you. Why did you never tell me about keeping in touch with *him*?"

Eugene shrugged his shoulders. "I would have thought that was obvious. Because I didn't want to hurt you. You may be a pain in the butt, but I do love you all the same."

339

Lucy sighed. Like Max, Eugene made it absolutely impossible to hate him.

He put his arm around her. "Let go, Lucy. Let go of it all. I want you to be happy."

"I am happy," Lucy said stubbornly.

"But you have to let people love you. Don't push them away. You'll end up on your own."

Lucy could feel tears pricking the back of her eyes. "It's been a long day. Can we talk about something else?"

"OK. How about Max?"

She glared at him. "What do you mean?"

"Nothing that I have to say out loud." He picked up his pint and took a decent gulp.

Lucy stared at the table in front of her. Max. Plastered Max who was at this moment probably fast asleep and snoring loudly back at the cottage.

"No," she whispered. "I guess you don't."

* * *

"Are you sure the barman said two?" Lucy asked Alan.

Alan nodded. "Yes, positive."

"But there's no-one here," Lucy said, looking around. The pier was deserted, apart from a few sea gulls. The small ferry was tied to the stone bollard beside them.

"It's only just two," said Max. "Relax." His head was still throbbing a little and he hadn't been able to face any breakfast this morning.

Rowie and Eugene were leaning against the stone wall of the harbour gazing at Sherkin Island.

"There's a seal!" Rowie exclaimed, pointing excitedly at the water. "Look."

Lucy stopped sighing at the ferrymen's timekeeping and had a look.

340

"It's beautiful," she smiled. The seal's sleek blackness swam closer to them and stopped beside the wall. Its dark, hypnotic eyes stared up at them. "There's another one."

The second seal was larger, with greying whiskers and lighter brown eyes.

"So you've met our seals, then," a voice rang out behind them. A tall, stocky man in yellow oilskins was standing beside the ferry.

"Yes," Lucy smiled. "They're beautiful."

"There's a whole family of them," he said. "They come here to be fed. They eat the fishermen's leftovers. They say they bring good luck. Now, are you going to Sherkin at all?"

"Yes," said Alan. "When are you leaving?"

"Right now." A young boy appeared from the cabin of the boat, started the engine and began to untie the ropes.

They all clambered aboard with the rest of the passengers, paid the fare and took their seats.

"It's a good day to visit the island," the man said as they motored out of the harbour and towards the island. "You're lucky." It was warm and sunny, the clear blue sky interrupted by some white fluffy clouds.

After a while they pulled into the tiny Sherkin harbour and got off. "I'll be back at four and again at five," he said.

"Thanks," said Lucy. "See you later."

"Where to now?" asked Alan.

"The beach is that way," said Max, pointing up the hill.

"How do you know that?"

"The signpost," Max smiled, nodding at it.

They walked slowly, Max and Alan in front, Rowie and Eugene in the middle and Lucy and Hopper bringing up the rear.

"I haven't had a chance to talk to you on your own," Hopper said to Lucy as they passed a large field full of cows. "Are you OK?"

"Of course. Why wouldn't I be?"

"You seem a bit out of sorts. And Daria was a bit rude to you yesterday, I just thought –"

341

"Well, don't think," Lucy snapped. Trust Hopper to remember about Daria. "I'm fine. Everything's fine."

"What about Max?"

Lucy looked at her. "What about him?"

"Is he OK? He must be a bit upset about breaking up with her."

Lucy shrugged. "How would I know?" She had no idea how he felt. He'd been in no fit state to talk to anyone last night or this morning.

"I see," said Hopper. "You know you're both kidding yourselves, of course." She kicked a stone along the muddy road.

Lucy scowled at her. She was as bad as Eugene.

"Try to keep up, girls," Alan shouted after a while. He and Max were a good bit ahead by now.

"Control freak," Hopper shouted at him.

Alan laughed. "Who are you calling a freak? We're nearly there. I can see water over this hill."

"Good," said Rowie. "I need a rest."

Alan was right. As they came to the top of the hill the sea stretched out in front of them, shimmering in the sun. There was a sandy beach ahead, nestled in between two headlands, rivers of seawater dissecting it into groups of tiny islands.

Rowie ran towards it, pulled her runners off and rolled up her linen trousers. "I'm going paddling. Anyone coming?"

Lucy sat on the sand and watched Rowie, Eugene, Hopper and Alan paddling.

"We beat them to it," Max said, sitting down beside her.

"Sorry?" Lucy asked.

"Paddling. We did that the other day."

"Yes." She cupped her hand, scooped up some sand and let it trickle through her fingers. "We haven't been swimming though."

Max held his hand under hers and caught the falling grains. "What's wrong"

"I'm not sure." She stared out to sea.

They sat in silence for a few minutes.

"I'm sorry about Daria," Lucy said finally. "Eugene told me."

"He's a dark horse, that brother of yours. Wiser than his years sometimes."

"Are you OK? About Daria, I mean."

"I suppose I am. We weren't happy together, not really. It's for the best."

"She was nice," Lucy said a little reluctantly. "I wish I'd met her in different circumstances, I think we could have been good friends."

"Did Eugene tell you about Owen?"

Lucy looked at him. "No! Owen who?"

"Owen Hughes."

"Daria's director?"

Max filled her in on the details.

"I'm sorry, Max. But these things happen. Maybe it's fate. Maybe the right girl is waiting for you just around the corner."

"You always know how to make me feel better." He shook the sand out of his hand and held hers. She let him for a few seconds and then pulled it away.

"Stop," she whispered.

"Why?"

Lucy fell silent for a few minutes. "We're friends," she said finally. "Friends don't hold hands and they don't – you know."

"Kiss?" he asked.

"You remember the other night?"

"Of course I remember. I guess you're right. Then maybe we shouldn't be friends any more."

"Hey, you two," Alan yelled from the beach. "We're going to see what's over there." He pointed to a group of large rock pools.

"We'll follow you in a minute," Max shouted back.

Lucy put her hands out to push herself up.

"Stay," said Max. "Please. I want to talk to you."

"OK. You're saying that we shouldn't see each other any more. That's fine by me."

"That's not what I'm saying at all."

"No? It seems pretty clear to me."

"Stop being so contrary. You know what I mean."

"No, I don't."

Max started to laugh. "You know you're impossible."

"I am not!"

"Why are you making all this so damned hard then?"

"All what?"

"All *this*!" He waved his hands in the air. "You know what I'm trying to say. I should have said it a long time ago."

"I don't."

"Yes, you do."

She stood up. "I don't know what you're talking about. I'm going to find the others."

He watched her walk away. "I love you," he shouted at her back. "I want to be with you. You know that."

She spun around. Her eyes flashed. "How? By osmosis? I'm not bloody psychic."

He jumped up and grabbed her shoulders. "You've always known. You just never let yourself believe it."

"I can't. We'll fight and we'll break up and never speak to each other again." Tears began to form in her eyes. "I'll lose you."

"No, you won't. I'll never leave you. I promise." He kissed her forehead gently.

She began to cry. "I can't. I'm sorry –"

He kissed her wet face and then pulled her towards him. "Yes, you can. I'll help you." He placed his lips on hers and kissed her tenderly.

Lucy could feel her lips tingle. It didn't feel like any kiss she'd ever had before – it felt like magic – warm and gentle yet sensual. She felt like she'd come home.

Hopper looked over towards Max and Lucy and began to smile. "About bloody –"

Alan put his hand over her mouth. "No, you don't! You're such a troublemaker."

30

One month later

"So, have you found your own Jamie Oliver yet?"

Lucy turned around. Dan was standing in front of her, smiling gently. She blushed furiously. "Hi. I didn't expect to see you here." She put the cookery book she was thumbing through back on the shelf.

"I'm catering a lunch in the Mansion House. I'm just taking a break."

"I'm so sorry I never rang you after Cork."

"It's OK." Dan smiled. "Don't worry about it. You bruised my ego a bit, that's all."

"Still cooking?" she asked, then kicked herself. What a stupid thing to say. He'd just told her he was.

"Yes. And you? Still eyebrow plucking?"

Lucy winced. "Yes, unfortunately."

"I heard about yourself and Max. Mum told me."

Lucy blushed again. "Ah." She glanced out the window. The cookery department in Hanna's was elevated above street level, ideal for watching the world go by. She dragged her attention back. Dan was staring at her. "Sorry. Yes, we're together now. I'm still getting used to the idea though."

"He's a lucky guy. I'm happy for you both, really." He leant over and kissed her on the cheek. "Be good to each other. Oh, and Lucy, Cafe Sola on Wicklow Street are looking for a cook, if you're interested. You should call in. Barney, the manager, is a friend of mine. Tell him you know me."

"Thanks. That's really kind of you."

"It's nothing. Take care of yourself."

"You too."

She watched his back as he walked away. Then she sat down on the window seat and gazed at the pedestrians walking past. A few minutes later she was crossing Dawson Street, dodging the late afternoon traffic.

"Max, I'm going to be a little late getting to your place," she said into her mobile. "There's something I have to do." She hummed to herself as she walked up Wicklow Street, holding her head up high and swinging her arms.

* * *

"Hi, is Bob there?" Lucy said. Her hand was shaking so much she could barely hold the receiver.

"I'll just get him," a woman Lucy assumed was Stella said. "Who will I say is calling?"

Lucy took a deep breath. "Lucy."

"Oh, right," the woman said nervously. "Hang on a second."

Lucy heard mumbled conversation and finally her dad came to the phone.

"Lucy? It is really you?"

"Yes."

"You don't know how happy this makes me. Let me just sit down. There we go. I can't tell you how happy . . . I'm sorry."

Lucy could hear him breathing but he wasn't saying anything. "Hello?" she said.

"I'm sorry, love. I'll be all right in a minute."

He's crying, Lucy thought. A lump began to form in her own throat. "Take your time. I'm not going anywhere."

"I'm very glad to hear that," he said. "I don't know where to start. How are you?"

"Good. I'm good. And you?"

"Getting there. Are you still working in the beautician's?"

"No," she said proudly, "I have a new job now – as a cook."

"That's great. You always did like helping your mum in the kitchen when you were little."

Lucy smiled to herself. She'd forgotten that.

"Your mum told you about the bypass operation?"

"Yes. That's why I'm ringing, I suppose. To see how you are."

"In that case I'm glad. I'm glad I was sick if it means I get to talk to you again. I've missed you that much. I'm so sorry about everything."

"It doesn't matter," she said levelly. "It's in the past now."

"Your mum was right. You've turned out lovely. She's right proud of you."

"I'm proud of her too. She's told you about the fostering?"

"Yes. And it's funny really, because I'm going to be a grandad soon."

"Really?"

"Yes, Amanda's having a baby in April. She's been with her boyfriend for three years now and they've decided to get married next summer."

"That's great. A grandad, imagine that."

"Do you have someone, Lucy? If you don't mind me asking. Someone special?"

"There is someone, I guess. You remember Max?"

"I don't think so."

"Sitric Maxwell?"

"Sitric? The little blond fellow you used to play with?"

"The very same."

"How extraordinary."

"Yes," said Lucy. "It is. Quite extraordinary!"

THE END